Seared

Bethany Adams

Seared

Return of the Elves

by Bethany Adams

ISBN: 978-0-9975320-7-4

First Edition

Edited by Jody Wallace at www.jodywallace.com
Cover art by Eve Milady at http://venetian-eve.tumblr.com
Interior design by Gaynor Smith of Indie Books Gone Wild
www.ibgw.net

Published in the United States of America

Acknowledgements

As always, I would first like to thank my husband and children for all of their patience and support. I couldn't do any of this without you!

Thank you to all of my readers for staying with me this long. Your love and support has been phenomenal, and I hope this book doesn't disappoint.

To Jody and Shiloh—From Jody's awesome editing to Shiloh's quick critique, this book never would have been done in time without you. Seriously. Thank you for answering all my panicked Facebook messages. I count both of you as dear friends, and I'm so very lucky to know you. Don't blame them for any mistakes. They probably tried to warn me.

To Eve Milady—I don't know how you do your cover magic, but I am beyond grateful. You always manage to create the exact thing I didn't know how to ask for. Thank you!

To Gaynor Smith—Your formatting work is amazing. Thank you for making my books as beautiful on the inside as they are on the outside!

To Jessica and Natasha—thank you for always being amazing friends and critique partners. I love you guys!

To Nick C—Thanks for helping when my anxiety was at its worst. Yes, I took the fucking advice.

To Roxana—Thank you for messaging me about that mistake in Exiled. Thanks to you, it wasn't there for long. Your love for my books means the world.

Books by Bethany Adams:

Soulbound

Return of the Elves Book 1

Sundered

Return of the Elves Book 2

Exiled

A Return of the Elves Novella

To my fellow
anxiety sufferers.
We've got this, friends.

1

The pain of impact seared through Ralan's side, forcing him awake. His muscles convulsed with the remnants of the fire that had licked through his body, followed by the cold of death. Shuddering, he blinked his eyes open and searched the dimness for the source of the threat. But he saw nothing except the usual shadows of his bedroom.

His heart gave a leap as realization settled in.

The same vision again.

His eyes adjusted to the light, and the chair beside his bed took shape—but higher than it should have been. Had he actually fallen out of bed? Dreams of future strands were often tumultuous, but they hadn't caused him such physical turmoil in centuries. He'd been trained to remain motionless during visions even while sleeping.

Groggy and sore, Ralan shoved himself to a sitting position. He rubbed his hand along his arm, still hurting from the impact. Didn't seem broken. At least he wouldn't have to share this embarrassment

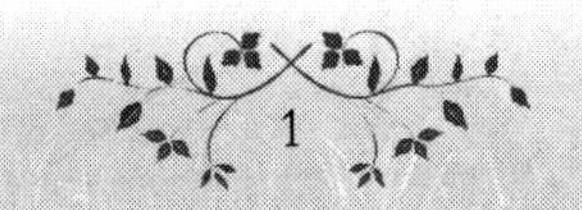

with Lial. The healer was biting in his sarcasm at the best of times.

Ralan sent out a tendril of magic, lighting the spell globe beside his bed, and propped his elbows against his knees while his body adjusted to the present. As a seer, he often woke at odd times from some vision or another. But it wasn't usually of his own death. How many times was he going to have to experience it?

Was it even real?

Gods knew his gift hadn't been reliable lately, and it was complicated even at the best of times. Nearly every choice sparked a new possible future, a strand to follow. Not even a seer of his power could track them all, and most of the time, he didn't even try—not unless it was for something serious. Through training, he'd grown adept at recognizing and tracing the important strands. Only the visions were beyond his control.

Despite his skill, he'd failed to See so much—the attacks on Lyr, Kai and Arlyn's capture, Kien's interference on the rescue mission. After three centuries of refusing to look into the future, at least voluntarily, Ralan's power had grown erratic. Or perhaps it was punishment. Megelien, Goddess of Time, had not been pleased by his decision to forego his Sight.

The door clicked open, and his daughter, Eri, padded in, her long white nightgown swishing around her bare feet. Despite his worry, Ralan couldn't help but smile at the sight of her as she rubbed her tired eyes and squinted through the dim light toward the bed. His love. Hard to believe she was already six.

"*Laial?*" she asked, frowning at the empty bed.

"Down here."

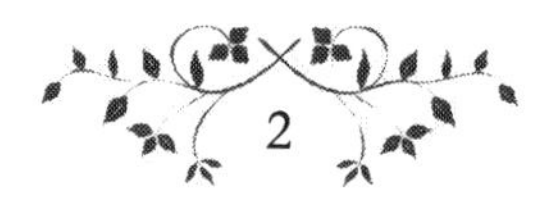

Eri paused in the middle of the room. "On the *floor?*"

Wincing, Ralan pushed his shaky hand through his hair. "I took a tumble. Did I wake you?"

"Yeah." Suddenly, she giggled. "I didn't know grownups fell out of bed."

He huffed. "The vision was a bad one."

"Oh. One of those." Just like that, her humor fled, a spark of power taking its place in her eyes. "Want me to search the strands? My Sight is clear, and—"

"No!" Ralan said. As her lower lip poked out at his harsh tone, he pushed himself to his feet. His stomach roiled at the movement, but he ignored it as he strode to his daughter. Sighing, he pulled her into his arms. "Forgive me, love. This one…I hope you don't find it. You're too young for this."

Eri snuggled her head against his shoulder, and her soft arms squeezed him close. "Tomorrow might change stuff."

Ralan pressed a kiss against her hair and headed toward the door. "Perhaps."

But he knew it wouldn't. After the first time he'd had the dream, Ralan had searched the strands carefully. All of the favorable ones required one thing—his death. Nothing would change that. But if his daughter hadn't realized that yet, he didn't want to tell her. Chances were good that she'd See for herself soon enough.

A lump caught in his throat as he pushed into her room and strode over to her bed. He'd have to find someone to raise her. Gods.

"*Laial?*" Eri whispered, her hand pressed against his cheek.

"You need to sleep," Ralan answered. He knew she'd been asking what was wrong, but the explanation tangled in his mind,

unable to work free. Not yet. Dammit, she was only a child. "I won't have you overtired."

He settled her on top of the mattress, tucked her blanket around her, and dropped a kiss on her forehead. She smiled blearily up at him. "Night, *Laial*. Don't fall out of bed again."

Ralan chuckled. "I won't."

It was one promise he could keep. After a dream like that, he wouldn't even try to sleep.

Cora stared into the shimmering blue portal, brighter than the moonlight spilling through the trees. She lifted her hand and skimmed her fingers close. So close. A tremble shook her as power flooded in, though her skin didn't make contact. By the Divine, but it was glorious to be so close to her home.

And agony knowing she could never return.

As energy flowed through her, restoring her reserves, a moan slipped free. Nothing could compare to the power of her homeland. Her fingers flinched against the urge to touch the shining blue. If only things were different. If only.

"Come back, Cora."

The words whispered through her mind, and Cora flinched. *"I can't."*

"Orn is betrothed now. He'll not bother you."

Her brow furrowed. Betrothed? Orn had tried to capture Cora for three centuries, though his efforts had lessened over the last fifty years. Had he given up? Would it change anything if he had? Her family had lost a great deal of status at her escape, and Orn's marriage to another wouldn't alter that.

"My failure will never be forgotten," she whispered.

"You failed nothing."

"Tell that to Father."

Pain squeezed her chest, and she stepped back, cutting herself off from the magic—and the voice. Without her connection, the blue faded, leaving nothing but a shallow depression in the side of the hill. She blinked her eyes against the sudden dark and the tears that had gathered despite her resolve to avoid them.

Every time she visited, it was the same. The power. The entreaties to return. Cora spun away and forced her feet down the path to her house. It *was* news that Orn had decided to marry. He must have found another way to solidify his hold on the crown. Regardless, returning wasn't something she was willing to risk.

Maybe she should bond to Earth's magic and be done with it.

Each world had its own flavor of energy, some more similar than others, and her people could only gather power if they bonded with that place. But it was permanent and intimate. She would have to touch that world's energy from time to time or it would become painful. A link also made her vulnerable to any changes in that world's magic, like the poison that had recently crept into Earth's energy. Even after three centuries, she hadn't decided if she wanted to bond to this realm. It would be the ultimate acknowledgement that she would have to stay.

A concession of her weakness and defeat.

Forcing her mind away from that line of thought, she headed for the soft glow of her porch light beyond the small grove of trees. Despite her years in the human world, she wasn't rich. But when the eight-acre plot containing the portal had come up for sale, she'd

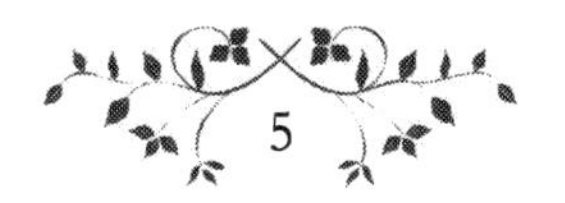

been able to afford it. Only a Galaren would have known about the gateway the land held, since other fae races used a different portal and humans were generally clueless.

The wooden deck creaked as Cora climbed the steps of her back porch. The house was old and needed work, but she'd had the structural problems fixed and the wiring replaced already. Over the last 342 years, she'd lived in way worse—tents, shacks, tenements. There was a charm and strength to this little craftsman, and someday it would be gorgeous again.

If her shop kept doing well.

Cora opened the back door and strode through the kitchen. Her body hummed with energy—no way she could sleep now. She headed straight to the small spare bedroom to the right of the kitchen and flipped on the lights. Her magic might lend itself to earth and fire, not cloth, but she didn't need magic to create. A few hours of design work would calm her down.

Her fingers gripped a pencil as she sat in front of her desk and reached for her notebook. A dress that wavered like the portal's blue light? Or ready-to-wear in tones of red and brown? Cora set to sketching, letting the ideas flow free.

And shoving the pleading voice of her mother to the back of her mind.

Ralan tapped his fingers on the arm of the chair and considered how to broach what was on his mind. Lyr sat behind his desk, pouring over an alliance contract with Kai's newfound father, Naomh of the Sidhe. He'd looked askance at Ralan but hadn't said anything when

Ralan had plopped down in one of the reading chairs beneath the skylights in the long, oval room.

How could he ask his friend to watch after Eri without telling him the full truth? It wasn't the time for Ralan to reveal the vision of his impending death, but he had to make sure his daughter would be cared for by someone outside of court. He could think of few more suited than Lyr and his bonded, Meli.

Arlyn, Lyr's daughter, would also be an excellent choice, as both she and Eri were part human. But Arlyn was young, not even thirty, and new to Moranaian ways. She had enough to worry about without taking responsibility for a precocious six-year-old. And as Lyr's heir, she would be around to help guide Eri, too. There would be no prejudice against his daughter's human blood here.

Well, nothing for it. The longer he delayed, the tougher it would be. Ralan cleared his throat, catching Lyr's attention. "I am relieved that the meeting with my father went well."

Lyr's eyebrow rose, and Ralan held back a grimace. An awkward beginning, indeed—especially since the meeting had happened days ago. But his friend merely tapped a finger against a nearby stack of papers. "Easy for you to say. You don't have to provide frequent reports to the king. As if I needed more paperwork."

Ralan smiled. As Myern of this estate, Lyr was at the top of the third branch down the Callian line. The third duke, as he'd explained to Eri. Every branch beneath reported to him, so his friend had much to sort through at the best of times. "Sorry. At least he wasn't angry that I had you deploy part of the army. Or that we risked war with the Sidhe."

"Sure." Lyr waved a hand. "Now are you going to tell me what this is really about?"

Mouth going dry, Ralan nodded. "It won't be long until I have to go after Kien. My brother's madness must soon come to an end."

"We all know that," Lyr said wryly.

"I'm not taking Eri." Ralan leveled his gaze on Lyr. "But I don't want her at my father's court. It isn't her place."

The corners of Lyr's lips turned down. "What do you mean? She's next in line for the throne after you."

"Eri will never be queen of Moranaia."

His friend tensed, then leaned forward as the silence stretched. "I can't imagine you would speak casually of her death. So what—"

"As I said, it isn't her place. She is not best suited and will not be chosen." Ralan's fingers tightened around the arm of his chair until the wood bit into his palm. He wanted to tell Lyr all of it, but he couldn't. Revealing the truth now would ruin everything. "She will grow into another task."

Though annoyance lined Lyr's face, he didn't press for answers. He knew better than to demand too much of a seer. "What are you asking, then?"

"Will you care for Eri while I'm gone?"

"How long will you be away?" Lyr asked.

Ralan swallowed hard at the suspicion lurking in his friend's eyes. How much had he guessed? "I have not Seen a precise time, but I don't believe it will be much more than a month. Possibly much less. I will return from time to time, as well."

Eyes narrowing, Lyr leaned back in his seat. "I have a feeling that isn't all."

"The future strands are perilous. I should return from Earth without incident, but I would like to know Eri will be cared for if

something goes wrong." Dammit, Lyr deserved to know the certainty of Ralan's death. But he hadn't lied. He should return from Earth at least once. The problem was what happened after. "I realize I ask much."

"You want me to raise Eri if you don't return?" Lyr rubbed his fingers against his temples. "Me? I know nothing about her gift. You think I'm the best choice to guide her?"

"In all my visions, you and Meli are the best," Ralan said. "And you should have time to find her the right teacher. Though her Sight developed early, her other magical gifts have not."

Lyr went silent, his expression unreadable as he considered the issue. Finally, he shook his head. "I'll obviously have to speak with Meli about this. Unlikely or not, I will not agree to raise a child without her consent."

Ralan's mouth twitched, but he didn't let his relief show. There had been one possible future where Lyr refused outright. "Of course."

"Have you pinpointed the time you'll need to leave?"

"Not yet." Ralan ran his hand through his hair as the frustration of that failure bit at him. No matter how often he searched the strands, he couldn't find it. "Something hasn't happened yet, I suppose."

Lyr frowned. "Don't you see all the possibilities?"

"I used to," Ralan muttered. "Unless Megelien wished otherwise. But She has said nothing to me of late."

"That sounds ominous."

Ralan's gaze landed on the view of the valley beyond the estate. "Let's hope it is not."

The bell above the door gave a jaunty jingle as it opened. Cora glanced up from the purse display she'd been organizing and caught sight of the newcomer as he entered. Her brows pinched. She sold men's clothing at The Magic Touch, so it wasn't unusual to have male customers. It was the strange aura surrounding him that grabbed her immediate attention.

Cora forced a smile to her face anyway. "Welcome. Is there anything I can help you with?"

The man's skin was the palest she'd ever seen, as was everything else about him. His short hair was stark white, his lips a faint pink slash. Even the brown eyes he focused on her were unusually light, almost taupe. Combined with the way his energy raised the hair on her arms, the effect was uncanny. She didn't detect evil, but this guy was far from innocent.

"I've heard there are…many ways you grant aid."

"Really?" Cora straightened at the mocking lilt to his voice. Was that a code or a threat? She let a hint of magic pool in her palms in case it was the latter. "How so?"

He smiled. "Clothing is magic. As am I."

"Of course." He *did* know the code. Some of her tension eased, but she found she couldn't relax. Danger surrounded him too closely for that. "If you'll follow me?"

She strode past him, flipping the door sign to *Closed*, and then on to the opposite side of the room. She opened a small door marked *Staff Only* that was tucked behind a display of shoes. It was, of course, not the staff room, though it did have a small table, water

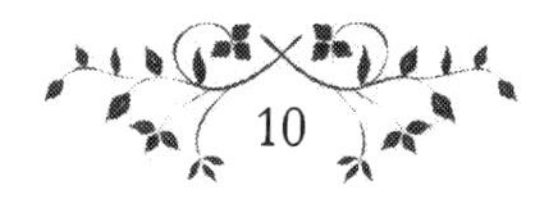

cooler, and coffee stand. As the customer entered behind her, she gestured him toward a chair and closed the door.

"What kind of clothes do you need, and what do you have to trade?" Cora asked, not bothering to attempt pleasantries as she sat across from him. Most of the fae who came here had no interest in idle chit-chat.

"So direct," he answered softly.

Of course Sir Creepy would be the rare exception.

"Forgive me," Cora said with a smile. "Most prefer to stick to business."

"Ah, yes." The man leaned forward, and she fought to shove aside her nervousness as his odd, not-quite-dark energy wafted around her. "Business. Very well. I need a full wardrobe."

Cora eyed him, taking in his form, and then nodded. "I believe I have your size in stock, but it depends on a few things. First, is there a specific style? Climate?"

He waved a hand. "Human style."

"But for what region?" she asked, biting back impatience. So many of the fae were clueless when it came to Earth. "Are you staying in this area or traveling somewhere else?"

"You do not need to know my location," he snapped.

Cora almost rolled her eyes. "Not specifically. Humans dress differently in different areas. Surely it's the same where you're from?"

His lips pursed. "I'll grant you that is true. I'll be staying in this portion of the land called United States. How far could I travel with such a wardrobe?"

"You could get by anywhere in this country and most nearby, as well as much of Europe for certain." Cora paused, chewing at

her index finger as she thought. "Really, any major city with enough access to Western culture. You'll be an obvious foreigner, but not like you would be in whatever you have on under that glamour."

The man shook his head. "Then why did you ask?"

"Well, if you're wanting to truly blend in, you'll want clothes more traditional to the region you're traveling to," she answered, shrugging. "Not so much if you don't mind looking like a tourist."

"I see."

He stared at her, and Cora wondered if he was about to simply get up and leave. It had happened before, though usually during the trade portion of the discussion. She'd gained a reputation for fairness amongst the supernatural creatures in the area, and newcomers to the human world were often sent her way. Without human money, they couldn't just walk into any store. The local fae had come to trust her not only for clothing but for transferring their riches to useable cash. Only a few decided a human wardrobe wasn't worth the effort and chose to use their energy maintaining glamours instead.

He seemed likely to be one of them.

But the strange man surprised her by giving a sharp nod and pulling a small velvet pouch from his shirt pocket. He spilled the contents on the table, and Cora couldn't help but gasp. Diamonds. The guy had a pouch full of nothing but diamonds.

"Umm," she managed to get out.

His laughter filled the room. "I was told you'll help convert this to human money in addition to trading for a wardrobe?"

She'd had gold and various gems, even a diamond here or there, offered before. But this? "I have to be honest," Cora began,

swallowing against the dryness scratching her throat. "I'm not sure I can handle this much."

"Really?" His voice lowered. "I would imagine a woman like you handles many things."

Her body froze at the innuendo. "If you can't be professional—"

He chuckled again. "Forgive my lapse." He draped himself against the back of the chair like a prince, his eyes dancing. "I'm given to understand that humans find such transactions suspicious. I wouldn't need it all at once."

Cora eyed the glimmering pile. There probably wasn't a single one of them under three carats, and even without testing them, she'd bet all of her savings that they were flawless. Maddy's father usually set the stones into jewelry to offer in his shop or sold the gems to some of his contacts. There was no way he'd be able to do that so easily with all of these.

"I'll have to check with my associate on how long this might take." She met his eyes. "If you want clothes quickly, I'll need something closer to an even trade."

The man straightened, gave a nod, and then pulled out another pouch. But from this one, he only took a single gold coin. "Will this do for the wardrobe?"

Cora took the coin in hand and let her magic surround it. Pure gold. "Depends on how fancy you want. Designer stuff will be more."

He lifted a shoulder. "Casual for now. I can buy more with human money later."

"If you're sure." Cora hesitated before asking her next question, always a risky one with the fae. "How will I contact you when I

have more information about the diamonds? You haven't given me a name."

"Nor will I. Yet." The man gathered all but one diamond back into the pouch. "I'll leave you one for now. If you prove worthy, perhaps I'll gift you with my name. I'll return periodically to check for news."

He stood to leave, and Cora held out a hand. "Wait. Do you have any particular preferences when it comes to clothes? Colors or fabrics you hate?"

The man shrugged again. "You're the designer. I'll wear what you choose."

Cora watched, dumbfounded, as he strode from the room like he owned the place. She'd been around enough nobles to know one when she saw one. Hell, she'd been one. Whoever the man was, he was high ranking. Shaking her head, she drew the diamond into her palm with the gold coin and headed toward her office as the bell jingled his exit.

2

Ralan crossed his arms and leaned against the cool stone of the practice tower. A welcome relief, that hint of chill amidst the stifling heat of early autumn. Though the leaves overhead had begun to flush into bright shades of red, yellow, and orange, only the nighttime hours benefitted from a decrease in temperature. Not even the crisp, rain-scented breeze playing havoc with his hair provided much respite.

Naturally, his new apprentice was late.

When Delbin had arrived on Moranaia a few days ago, he hadn't been able to control his gift with the greater magical energy of Moranaia. His power had already been strained from a confrontation with Ralan's wicked brother, and the influx of magic hadn't helped. Thankfully, Delbin had learned enough over the last few days that Ralan no longer needed to place an energy shield around him.

That had been beyond awkward. That kind of shield required a link, and Delbin was alarmingly good at sending not only thoughts but emotions. Ralan had received more than enough of both. He

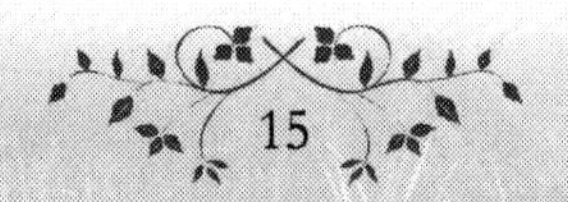

was entirely too celibate right now to be privy to all the things Delbin was doing with his new girlfriend.

Ralan let his head settle against the stone. Why bother forming attachments with death looming close? Then again, he didn't need a relationship to satisfy his desires. He'd never had a qualm about sleeping with any woman who'd been equally interested. Why abstain so long as he was up front? At least then he wouldn't die *completely* miserable.

He was still grinning at that thought when Delbin stepped into the clearing. His apprentice halted, brows rising in surprise. "You look happier than I expected. Sorry I'm late."

"Making out with Inona again?" Ralan asked as he straightened.

Delbin laughed. "Nope. Lynia sat me down in the library with a history book. She insists that being on Earth for a hundred years isn't an excuse to shirk my Moranaian education. Gotta admit, I'm a little afraid of her."

"Good instincts," Ralan said. "Lyr's mother is a scholar, and few things rankle her more than ignorance."

"So I gathered," Delbin answered, though his voice sounded more amused than bothered. "Meli was there, too, but she didn't say much. She spent most of the time darting up and down the stairs bringing books to Lynia."

With a quick gesture, Ralan led the way into the sparsely furnished practice tower, stifling a sigh of relief as the spell-cooled air circulated around him. It was good that Lynia had taken it upon herself to educate Delbin, though Ralan would still need to speak to her formally. Delbin might have been exiled to Earth at a young age to keep him out of their enemy's hands, but he was no less Moranaian. He deserved to be taught properly, and Lyr's mother was the ideal person to do it.

Ralan bypassed the small table with its single chair and stopped by one of the cushions in the center. "Did Meli search with runes or without?"

Confusion wrinkled Delbin's face. "Huh?"

"I'm guessing without." Ralan chuckled as he lowered himself onto a cushion. He waited until Delbin took his own place to explain. "Meli is a Diviner, but she's just beginning to learn how to use her power. Sometimes she practices with her runes to help Lynia find the answer to a tricky bit of research."

Delbin's expression cleared. "No runes today. Just a great deal of climbing."

"I'm glad she found Lyr and decided to bond with him. That one strand where—" Ralan snapped his mouth shut. Dammit, Delbin's friendly personality often drew out more than Ralan really needed to share. "Never mind. Let's get to work."

"Sure." Delbin grinned. "We can gossip more later, Your Highness."

Ralan couldn't help but roll his eyes. "Oh, shove it."

Despite Delbin's joking, he settled into work without complaint. Ralan had him start with lowering and raising his mental shield, the invisible bubble of energy that kept others' thoughts from invading. A delicate process to adjust a magical shield without being overcome by the force of all the thoughts crushing in from the people around them—and the skill Delbin most needed to master before he could return to Earth.

After half a mark of *that* riveting entertainment, Ralan called a halt. "You're getting better. Now practice connecting mind-to-mind without losing control."

Delbin rubbed his hand across his face and groaned. "Yay."

"You have to learn to control what you let through the way I can," Ralan said. On their last attempt, Delbin had sent a jumbled mess of thoughts that had been almost painful. "Just try not to blast me."

Ralan closed his eyes and waited for the mental nudge that would signal Delbin's attempt to connect. For several moments, all Ralan could detect was the steady drip of the water clock on the wall. What was taking so long? With his student's power, the connection should have been almost instantaneous. He scowled and began to consider establishing contact himself. But before he could act, Delbin's energy brushed against his shield.

"Sorry," Delbin sent. *"Had to deal with another energy surge. Didn't mean to show up late to the training party."*

Late.

The vision slammed into Ralan, stealing his breath.

"Forgive me for being later than my missive had indicated," the Sidhe lord Naomh said, inclining his head toward the three on the small dais.

Lyr, Arlyn, and Kai stood in front of Lyr's desk in the study. Afternoon sunlight streamed around them through the abundant windows. Behind Naomh stood his brother, Caolte, expression serious as he scanned the room.

Kai let out a sharp laugh. "You imprisoned me and tried to kill me. Your tardiness is the least I have to forgive."

"You must—"

"This meeting is pointless," Kai interrupted. "We both know I'm not going to…"

Flicker.

The island began to rise, the tip breaking free of the waves. Grinding. Floundering. Implosion. A piercing scream. Eri.

Ralan sucked air into his burning lungs. He gasped for breath, his chest heaving. Then he shoved himself to standing, wavering on his feet for a moment before he strode toward the door. He was almost there before he realized he was still connected to Delbin.

Fuck. So much for being able to control what he sent.

As he jerked the door open, Ralan closed the connection. He glanced over his shoulder at Delbin. "Don't even say it."

But instead of the humor he expected after his flub, Delbin stared at him with a considering frown. "I've got to say, your gift blows."

An unexpected laugh slipped free. "That it does."

Cora secured the lock on the shop door before turning back to the counter. Her friend and shop assistant Maddy sat on a stool behind the cash register and sorted through receipts. Red-gold hair spilled over her pale shoulder as she tilted her head and leaned closer to one of the small scraps of paper. Cora smiled. From her coloring to her tall, thin frame, Maddy bore the clear marks of her Irish Sidhe heritage. A stark contrast to Cora's black hair and tanned skin.

"You're quiet," Maddy observed as Cora neared. "Something happen?"

She'd waited until closing to tell her friend about their unusual new customer. No use risking someone overhearing or interrupting. With the strange power that had swirled around the man, it seemed best to be secretive. Fae like him invariably had an odd array of both enemies and friends.

"Nothing bad. I think," Cora answered, even as she gestured toward the stock room.

Maddy's green eyes narrowed, but she nodded at the silent signal. In the empty store, the extra caution was a bit much, but some instinct screamed at Cora not to take chances. The storeroom was shielded—and not just by the expensive security system that lowered her insurance rates.

Once they were inside the shield with the door firmly closed, Cora knelt beside her safe and entered the combination. She lifted out the small pouch with the diamond and faced Maddy. "Wait until you see this."

Her friend's brows drew together. "The way you're acting, I'm not sure I want to know."

"Sorry." Cora opened the drawstring and shook the diamond into her palm. "A new customer came in while you were at lunch. Some kind of fae, but I couldn't tell you what. Noble, arrogant, and a little creepy."

Maddy snorted. "Well, that narrows it down."

"True enough." Cora grinned and lifted her hand closer to Maddy's face. "But he also had an entire bag full of these."

"Holy shit," Maddy whispered, her wide eyes focused on the stone.

Exactly Cora's thought. "I've never seen a round-cut diamond this nice. I'd say it's about a carat, and this was one of the smaller ones in the bag."

"I'd bet a week's salary this is a grade D colorless with flawless clarity," Maddy said. She took the diamond from Cora and held the glittering stone to the light. "Damn."

"Yeah, and he wants to trade the whole bag for cash."

Maddy's brows rose. "I'm not sure how quickly Dad could sell even one ring with a diamond like this. It's going to be insanely expensive, and it's not like the mega-rich are frequent customers. I'll have to ask him what he thinks."

"Maybe he can sell a few through some of his Sidhe connections?" At her friend's frown, Cora nibbled on her lip. Would that draw attention? Maddy's father was Sidhe, but he'd chosen to live among humans. If this customer was from the Sidhe court, the diamonds might somehow be recognized. "But that might be a bad idea."

Maddy shrugged and pulled a silver locket from beneath her shirt. She mumbled a few words, and the locket clicked open. After placing the diamond inside, she whispered another spell to seal it closed and slipped it beneath her clothes. Even the chain faded from sight once it settled against Maddy's skin.

"Dad is going to have to make me something bigger if he thinks he can sell the other diamonds," Maddy said with a chuckle. "Or I'll be a walking target."

"I can always call in Jase."

Her friend winced. "Yeah, no. If my mom finds out, she'll get her hopes up again. If I even look at a guy, she starts planning the wedding. She still refuses to acknowledge Anna's existence."

Cora's heart ached at the pain beneath the lightly spoken words. Maddy's mother might accept that her husband was Sidhe, but she couldn't stand the thought of her daughter being bisexual. "I'm sorry."

Maddy waved a hand. "It is what it is. Anyway, I'll go talk to Dad now. Here's the bank deposit."

Cora took the bag from Maddy and shook her head as her friend darted through the stockroom and out the back door, opening and closing the magical shield behind her.

Why did Maddy's mother have to be so strange?

Ralan shoved open the door to Lyr's study, once again interrupting a meeting in order to alter the course of events. He might as well start marking it on his calendar: *Break in on Lyr. Issue imperious order.* Of course, if people would just choose the right path the first time, he wouldn't have to bother. Didn't anyone, elven or human, bother to think about the repercussions of their decisions?

Kai was glaring at Naomh. "This meeting is pointl—"

"Shut up, Kai," Ralan interrupted, though his voice sounded more tired than authoritative even to his own ears. "You're going."

Five pairs of eyes turned his way, but Ralan was too accustomed to being stared at in varying degrees of consternation to care. When the future strands were this chaotic, there was more to worry about than mere offense. Considering the last part of his vision, *more* could end up being an apocalypse.

Lyr initiated mental contact without preamble. *"Honest to all the gods, Ralan, if you keep doing this—"*

"I won't," Ralan answered. A promise he could honor, considering he'd be dead soon. *"And I'm sorry for it. I had a rather unexpected vision."*

"Don't you always?" Lyr grumbled. But he inclined his head in formal greeting and continued aloud. "My lords, allow me to present Moranai Elaiteriorn i Ralantayan Moreln nai Moranaia. Prince Ralan, this is Lord Naomh a Nuall and Lord Caolte a Nuall."

Both Sidhe gave a slight bow before Naomh spoke. "It is a pleasure to have a name to put to your face. I will be sure to pass your name along to my guard."

"He is certainly welcome to call upon me here if he misses my presence," Ralan answered.

Naomh's eyes narrowed, but Ralan thought he caught a hint of a smirk on Caolte's face for the briefest moment. Ralan had to stifle his own grin. When he'd gone with Lyr to save Kai and Arlyn from Naomh's estate, he'd taken control of one of the guard's minds. A necessity, but clearly one not forgiven. If he visited that place again, he would have to be alert.

As Naomh lifted his chin, his long pale hair rippled around him. "Beware you do not cause offense to my House."

"I only sought to return the sentiment I was given," Ralan retorted smoothly. A more subtle form of *you started it*. "If it would please you to return to business, I am more than willing."

At Naomh's grudging assent, Ralan strode to the dais. Arlyn gave him an amused, questioning look as he neared, and he winked in reply. After living on Earth for more than three hundred of his 833 years, Ralan preferred to shirk formality. As Arlyn had only been on Moranaia for a couple of months, she hadn't seen him exhibit a great deal of elven etiquette, so of course she would be bemused by it now.

Polite diplomacy wasted so much time. And his father thought to make him king.

Stifling a sigh, Ralan settled to Lyr's left and plastered a neutral expression on his face. He'd interrupted at the crucial time, and now he'd have to pay the price by suffering through an hour of that polite diplomacy. Maybe he could order Kai around again, if stubbornness

took him down the path of refusal once more. Not the most likely strand, but possible.

Naomh's gaze pinned Kai. "You are heir to my domain. That alone should prompt you to return with me." At Kai's sound of protest, Naomh lifted a hand. "Beyond our differences, you must have felt the shift in your magic after you attuned yourself to my spells."

"I can seek my training here," Kai answered in a hard voice.

Ah, damn. Ralan stifled a sigh as tension hummed through the room like a coming storm. It was going to be the difficult path. He leaned forward to glance around Lyr. "No, you can't."

Kai's jaw clenched. "Stay out of it, Ralan."

"On this, we agree," Naomh snarled. "Prince or no, this is a family matter. Honor demands—"

"You may keep your Sidhe honor if it leads to destruction." Ralan took a deep breath. He had to calm himself before he revealed the full truth of his visions. "I speak as more than a prince in this matter."

Fists clenched, Kai took a step forward and spun to face Ralan. "The future can take care of itself. My place is here, and I don't care what the strands say. I have my own family to think of, and I will not force Arlyn to choose between her new home and the place where she was bound into a fucking wall and almost died."

Ralan's nostrils flared. "No one said—"

"Enough!" Lyr raised both hands, palms out. "No matter your rank, Ralan, I am in charge of this meeting. Unless you wish to formally remove me from negotiating this matter?"

Ralan glared at his friend at the reminder. As a prince, he outranked Lyr and could issue commands. But Ralan was completely

breaking protocol to disrupt this meeting. Negotiating alliances between Houses was standard and didn't typically need input from the royal family. If he took complete control, he would indirectly imply that Lyr wasn't capable of doing his job.

And almost as bad as slighting his friend? Ralan would become responsible for all of the decisions. With everything that loomed, he didn't have time to be responsible for anything else.

"Of course not," Ralan answered. "But you are well aware that I possess information that others do not."

"True." Lyr studied Ralan for a moment, considering, and then glanced at Kai. "And if *you* cannot yet discuss this calmly, I invite you to excuse yourself until you can."

Kai's lips pinched into a thin line. "You know he wants us to remain in his domain. You can't possibly be fine with your own heir moving to another realm."

"I am not." Lyr's piercing stare spared no one. "It is time to stop arguing and find a solution. There must be some compromise that will allow you to receive the needed training."

Ralan settled back into place, resigned. Damned diplomacy.

3

Shivering, Kien winced as the hammering started again. He shifted, and mud squished beneath him with a sucking pop. At least he'd grown accustomed to the dank, earthy smell that surrounded him. Still, he had to find the energy to escape before he died beneath this ramshackle house. It was taking far too long to build up his power.

Fucking Delbin. Fucking Moranaian scouts. Their fault. And the fucking half-human scum he'd thought loyal. Not a damn one of them had come searching for him. How many days had he lain beneath this house, asleep or unconscious? He'd woken to the sound of the human working overhead at least three times.

Or was it four? Five?

With a heave, Kien rolled himself to his stomach. He bit his lip as pain seared his side, for once dulling the burn of hunger eating at his gut. Like most elves, he could go a fair amount of time without food, so long as he could pull in energy. Too bad he could barely manage that. It had taken this long to gather enough to remain awake more than a minute or two.

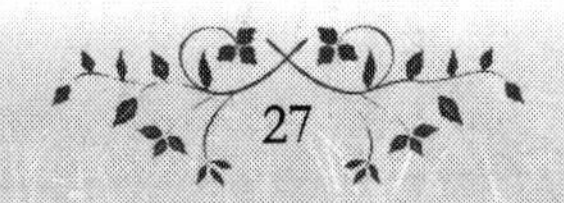

He stretched out his right hand, fingers digging into the mud as he prepared to slide toward the pale square exit of the crawlspace. With all his might, he tugged. A hiss of pain slipped from his lips, but his body barely budged. Could he do this? He had to do this.

A shadow blocked the light, and Kien froze. Had the human heard something? But no, the hammering hadn't stopped.

Arf! A single bark echoed through the crawlspace, and Kien almost smiled. A dog. It must have heard. But an animal was a small problem. Just had to remain motionless until it was gone. Kien closed his eyes against a wave of dizziness and waited for the dog to leave.

Then the barking began in earnest.

A thud as the human dropped something. The hammer? The flooring shook dust over Kien's body as the human stalked across the house.

"Ginger! You're not coming with me next time if you don't stop."

The barking cut off, and the shadow disappeared from the exit. Kien didn't move, letting the mud cool the side of his face. Maybe he should wait a little longer. The human would eventually go away, wouldn't he? At least for a while.

A bit of a rest wouldn't go amiss.

"You'd better not be wrong about this," Lyr said wearily as he slumped into his seat.

Ralan ran his hand across his hair and turned to the window. The negotiation hadn't been an easy one, but it was settled. "There are many possible futures, but Kai mastering his Sidhe powers is crucial to all of them."

"Tell him that," Lyr said. "When he'll speak to you again."

"Yeah."

After the Sidhe lords had gone, Kai had stormed out, Arlyn following quickly behind him. They had decided that Kai would travel to Naomh's home for training as often as possible, but he had flat-out refused a position as the Sidhe's heir. Still, he was furious that he would be away from Arlyn during the times she couldn't accompany him due to her own training. Furious that he would be forced to spend time with yet another father who'd tried to kill him.

Ralan spun to face his friend. "I'm doing my best, you know."

Though Lyr blew out a frustrated breath, he nodded. "There are times I want to ask for details, but… All things considered, I believe I'm happier not knowing the possibilities. How do you bear it?"

"As I must." He shrugged. "I suppose you grow accustomed to the gift or go insane in its thrall."

"Fairly certain I'd do the latter."

Ralan smiled at his friend's grumbled words. Lyr was one of the steadiest people he knew, current events notwithstanding. Lyr had been confronted by a daughter he hadn't known about, had been captured and almost killed a couple of times, and had found a new soulbonded—all within a couple of months. Yet here he was, carrying on with his duties.

Lyr leaned his elbows on his desk and peered at Ralan. "When do you leave?"

"I don't know." Ralan's shoulders drooped. "Even though Lord Naomh was able to provide Kien's location, I feel like there's some information missing. Except for today's lovely vision in the middle of Delbin's training session, my Sight has been unclear."

"Wait." A slow grin spread across Lyr's face. "In the middle of a training session? Literally?"

Heat crept up Ralan's neck. "Quite literally. After I chided Delbin for errant thoughts, no less."

"That's perfect," Lyr said with a low laugh.

Ralan ground his teeth and fought to control his embarrassment. Gods knew he deserved a bit of ribbing after all the interruptions his gift had brought. "And to think I'd felt a bit guilty after breaking in on another meeting."

Lyr snorted. "Right."

"Well, only a little."

The door clicked open, and Meli, Lyr's bonded, entered. She looked different with her long blond hair contained in braids and a gauzy, Moranaian-style gown floating around her. More relaxed and at home. She nodded at Ralan as she crossed the room, but her gaze barely brushed him before returning to Lyr.

Some of the strain that had remained after the meeting eased from Lyr's expression. "Meli."

There was a wealth of sentiment in his friend's tone, and suddenly, Ralan felt out of place. Perhaps it was time to attend to his own errant gift. "Looks like I should find somewhere to be."

Meli's lips twitched. "I was just going to share the outcome of today's research."

"Right," Ralan replied, echoing Lyr's earlier skepticism. "Well, unless it concerns the royal family, I believe I can miss that riveting discussion."

Meli grimaced. "Nothing to help with Kien, I'm afraid."

"An iron knife to the heart is the only thing that will help with Kien," Lyr muttered.

"Sounds about right," Ralan said.

And so would Ralan's death.

Swallowing a lump of foreboding, he smiled at Meli and gave Lyr a quick, mocking salute. "I'll let you know when I have a better idea of when I'm leaving. And please don't forget to speak with Meli about the other issue we discussed."

Lyr frowned for a moment before his expression cleared. "I will do so now."

Ralan nodded as he headed for the door. A quick scan of the futures revealed the possible outcomes of the discussion. There were so many potential choices from this one moment that it was difficult to trace, but the odds were good that Meli would agree to help raise Eri if Ralan didn't make it. And if not… he sighed. Well, he'd have to find another way.

Cora punched the security code into the alarm system and darted out the door before it set. Though the light had softened as afternoon shifted to evening, echoes of sound from a nearby bar floated down the alley to the back door. It was the height of tourist season, but foot traffic in her part of town invariably slowed as families sought dinner and the rowdier crowds searched for fun. Still, she scanned the empty side street as she locked the door.

Even with her fire magic for protection, it didn't pay to be reckless.

Squeezing her purse beneath her arm, Cora headed down the alley leading to the main road. Her car was parked in a lot near the back entrance, but the bank was only a block away. A pleasant walk,

especially with the excited energy of tourists that invariably swirled through the air.

She'd lived in many places since escaping to Earth, but tourist cities were her favorite. Sure, there was some stress involved in a vacation—tight schedules, lines, crowds—but that sense of adventure, fun, and newness was what remained. It drew people back year after year, layering those feelings until the energy was almost palpable even to the non-magical.

Cora would have to move on from her shop in Chattanooga soon if she didn't use magic to make herself look older. Maintaining a constant glamour exhausted her, but in this case, it might be worth it. At least for a little longer. The energy here was sublime, and having a home near the Galaren portal was perfect.

She smiled wistfully at a passing family as their toddler tugged his hand from his mother's and stomped a foot, one finger jabbing toward Two Scoops. A teen girl lifted the boy to her hip and did a quick dance, making the child laugh. Then the three moved on, more relaxed as they made it past the ice cream shop without a tantrum.

A sweet family. Too bad Cora would never be able to risk having one of her own, not while she was hunted.

She shoved that thought down until it knotted in her chest. She needed to remain vigilant. Aside from thieves and other criminals, Orn's spies were always a threat. She'd avoided detection for a solid decade, having transformed her concealment shield into an art form. But although she didn't live in fear, part of her always scanned the area she was in. Just in case.

Cora kept her magic at the ready as she strode past a bar and neared the bank. She'd worked a little later than usual organizing her

books and inputting new inventory, so the bank was deserted. No sign of trouble, human or otherwise, but anything was possible.

If she were strong enough to face Orn once and for all, she wouldn't have to worry so much.

She shrugged her purse strap down to the crook of her elbow and dug the money pouch from the main compartment. Her other palm cooled against the smooth brass handle of the night deposit drawer as she pulled it open and shoved the bank bag inside. She closed the box and opened it again to make sure the pouch had fallen through. Then she stood there, biting her lip at the thought of yet another night alone.

Maddy had invited her over for a girls' night, but she'd declined. Although Cora counted her a friend, she couldn't become a close one. It was too dangerous despite how long Cora had evaded Orn. That could change at any time. Besides, watching Maddy and Anna snuggling on the couch inevitably brought a twinge of envy.

Forcing her loneliness aside like always, Cora headed back into the humid evening air. Dwelling on her problems never helped. Instead, she would grab takeout from the Chinese place near her house. After dinner, she could start sketching designs and picking fabric for the new wardrobe for her mystery client.

If she worked late enough, she might exhaust herself enough to sleep.

Ralan shifted against the base of the tree, the rough bark a comfort rather than an annoyance. Then he closed his eyes and let his weight settle against the trunk. For a moment, he concentrated

on his breathing, each exhale slower than the one before. Then a hint of the world seeped into his senses as he relaxed.

The heat. The scent of rain on the wind. The trickle of the nearby stream. Birdsong.

Time suspended as his mind cleared of all else.

Finally, Ralan reached out, hoping to connect with the only one who'd been consistently ignoring him—Megelien, Goddess of Time and Seers. She Who Hid and Revealed. She who was blocking the fuck out of the things he needed to See. There was a time he hadn't had to search so hard for the answers he needed.

Hadn't he atoned enough?

"NO."

Her voice dropped into his mind with sudden force, and the air rushed from Ralan's lips. He paused to gasp in a breath before he dared try to answer. *"My lady."*

"YOU THINK I'LL SOON FORGET BEING ABANDONED FOR ALMOST FOUR HUNDRED YEARS? NOT LIKELY."

Ralan grimaced at that. He hadn't been thinking about the offense he might cause Megelien when he had fled home and abandoned his talents so long ago. Still, She hadn't seemed this angry when he'd returned from Earth a couple of months before. Had he done something else?

"YOU HAVE DONE NOTHING," she replied, each word reverberating through his mind. *"YOU HAVE NOT VISITED MY TEMPLE, NOR HAVE YOU STOPPED AT MY SHRINE IN THE PALACE. YOU OFFER NOTHING AND ASK FOR ALL."*

Hadn't he…? Ralan thunked his head against the tree trunk at the realization that he had, in fact, not. Had Earth made him so

thoughtless, then? *"Forgive me, my lady. My time on Earth has stolen my good manners."*

When Her answer came, the tone was softer. *"THE OUTCOME OF YOUR VISIT TO EARTH WAS BETTER THAN I HAD HOPED. PERHAPS I CAN FORGIVE THIS LAPSE."*

Better than She'd hoped? Ralan frowned over that, but he shoved his curiosity aside. Had She wanted him to know, She would not have been vague. Besides, he had other things to consider. *"My lady, may I ask a question?"*

"ONLY ONE."

He let out a sharp snort of laughter. As the goddess of seers, She no doubt knew what to expect from him, yet still She made him ask. "What am I missing in my search for Kien?"

Silence.

Had his humor offended Her? It hadn't in the past, but that was before—

Blackness. Silence. Then a voice that shook his very soul.

"I'm sorry, but the shop is closed."

The world took form—a street on Earth. Pavement, brick sidewalks, cars. Humans. Then it faded as a woman filled his mental frame, almost shocking him from the vision. Long hair, black as night. Kind brown eyes. Gods, her eyes. His thoughts blurred, save one. Her soul was the match to—

"PAY ATTENTION," Megelien chided.

Ralan jolted and scrambled to obey before he lost control of the vision. Hoping distance would help, he shifted his focus outward until more of the scene took shape. Oh, he'd return to the woman. First, he needed to discover who she was. And where.

"But I hear this place is magic." A male voice this time. "Or something."

Scowling, Ralan steadied the vision until the entire scene became clear. Both the woman and the man stood in front of a storefront. THE MAGIC TOUCH *was painted in letters across the broad window, and he caught a hint of a mannequin in a summer dress before the woman's voice caught his attention.*

"Yeah." Amusement danced in the woman's dark eyes. "Magic is *in the name, after all."*

The male stared at her, his expression showing no sign that he'd registered the wry humor. "You look like a special kind of lady. Surely you can open up for a special kind of guy?"

"Excuse me?" The woman straightened, her posture going rigid. Even through the vision, Ralan could feel power building around her. "You can take your stupid innuendo and shove it."

Crimson flushed the male's cheeks, matching his red hair. "No! I didn't mean… Look, I'm just trying to find a missing friend."

"Well, the police station isn't on this end of town."

"I can't ask them about this."

The man reached out and almost managed to catch hold of her arm before she took a step back. A hint of flame flickered in her palm for the briefest moment. "Leave. I have nothing to do with troublemakers, and next time I won't be so polite."

Sudden darkness as the scene cut off.

Ralan's eyes shot open, and he found his fingernails digging into his palms. *"Who is she? Did he hurt her?"*

"I SAID ONE QUESTION, DID I NOT?" Megelien asked, Her tone almost bored. *"YOU HAVE YOUR ANSWER."*

He sensed Her presence depart as quickly as it had arrived. But he waited a few moments more before he bit out a curse. Just in case.

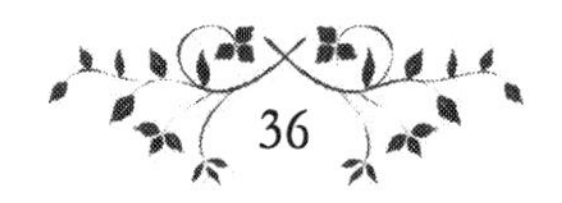

4

Cora's heart pounded as she stared after the strange man who'd been gazing into the window of her shop. On the surface, he'd appeared innocent—young, concerned for his friend, and embarrassed by his unintentional innuendo. He had turned so red at his last blunder that he'd looked like a sunburned tourist after a day boating on the river.

But a hint of dark Sidhe energy had stood out as clearly as his crimson hair. Cora swallowed against the bitter taste it had left, though the sensation was magical rather than physical. Death and blood magic. The boy might look young, but he'd been into some seriously bad stuff. She shivered, grateful to see his retreating back almost a block away already.

A woman's voice broke into her thoughts. "Excuse me."

Cora tensed, prepared for more strangeness, but when she spun around, the person she saw was human. "Yes?"

"I…" The woman bit her lip. "Sorry to bother you. I just wondered if there's a bike rental spot nearby. The condo listing mentioned it, but my host didn't leave directions."

The woman's nervous expression finally registered, and Cora forced herself to relax. "You're not a bother. This weird man was trying to get me to open my shop." Cora gestured toward her display window. "Some guys just can't take no for an answer."

"Ugh," the human answered with an eye roll. "You've got that right. Do you need someone to walk with you?"

Cora glanced over her shoulder and caught a hint of the guy as he took the crosswalk to the other side of the street. She gave the woman a smile. "No, I'm pretty sure he's gone. You're looking for the bike rental? Go back down the sidewalk behind you and turn left. It's about halfway down the block."

The human smiled back. "Thanks! I'll have to give your shop a try. When it's open."

Cora waved as the woman headed down the sidewalk. Despite the normalcy of the interaction with the tourist, Cora couldn't shake the unease twisting inside. She examined the area and found no sign of further danger. But she wouldn't let down her guard. Something was coming.

If only she knew what.

As soon as Ralan reached the broader main path through the garden, he broke into a sprint. He knew from long experience that Megelien wouldn't speak on the matter again, no matter how much he pleaded. Not anytime soon. But he couldn't stand not knowing the fate of the woman in his vision.

She was his soulbonded.

Ralan hadn't even considered the possibility of a soulbond for years, not after his first love's betrayal. He'd been willing to defy his father for Kenaren, but she obviously hadn't felt the same. She'd slept with his brother and plotted to kill him instead. Since that day over three hundred years before, he'd kept his relationships light. But a soulbond was something else entirely.

Dammit, why did he have to find a potential mate when his life was so close to an end? He was going to die in flames—he'd never had such a clear, repeating vision not come true. Had he angered the gods so terribly that they'd torture him with a soulbonded now? Megelien Herself had shown the woman to him. Was it a cruel trick, or was he missing something important?

The estate came into view, and Ralan slowed to accommodate the other people on the path. Then he spotted Arlyn and Eri in the middle, clearly waiting for him, and frustration climbed like bile up his throat. His daughter, at least, should know that he didn't have time to converse. She had a better understanding of the futures than he did these days.

He came to a grudging halt. "Arlyn. Eri."

Arlyn's brows rose at his brusque tone. "What's happened now?"

"Nothing. Everything." Ralan shook his head. "I don't have time to explain. But there's no immediate danger here."

"You're not going to defeat him this visit," Eri said softly. She wrapped her hand around two of his fingers and squeezed. "But you're right to go. You and Cora will need each other."

Cora. His bonded's name was Cora. "You *do* see more than I can."

"Yes."

Eri's sad gaze met his, and his heart lurched. She knew. "Eri—"

"You need to go, *Onaial.* You should take Delbin and Inona." She let go of his hand and stepped back. "I promise I won't get into trouble."

Ralan snorted at that. "You're under Lyr and Meli's charge, but I expect you to obey any of the adults of the House. No wandering off, and no using your talents carelessly. If I come back to find—"

"I promise," she interrupted, her small voice full of resolve. "Go."

He didn't hesitate again. Cora. She must be in danger if Eri, the imp, was willing to obey the rules. But when she truly promised, she meant it. A bit of his worry easing, he rushed down the path, angling for the guest tower where he and Delbin each had their rooms.

Arlyn's voice echoed from behind him. "*Onaial?* What does that mean?"

"Dad," Eri answered. "That's what Iren calls his father."

Despite his tension, Ralan smiled. A new bit of slang since he'd been a child—but a welcome one. *Onai* meant heart. Then his smile faded. He was all Eri had, but soon, he'd be gone. His friends didn't mind watching his daughter for brief trips, but had Meli agreed to raise Eri with Lyr if something happened? A quick check of the future strands showed Eri with them, but Ralan had no talent for viewing the past.

He'd have to ask to be certain.

Ralan changed directions, heading through the back door and straight for Lyr's study. He forced himself to stop and knock this time, and a seeming eternity passed before Lyr called for him to enter. Automatically, he scanned the area as he opened the door. His friend was alone. Perfect.

As Ralan crossed the room, Lyr set aside the stack of papers he was studying. "Should I be worried or relieved that you didn't rush in?"

Despite the situation, Ralan chuckled. "I'm not sure."

"Another Sidhe colony in need of saving? Kien bringing an army of his minions through the portal? King of the Unseelie demanding a duel?" Lyr rubbed his hand across his face, and though his words were light, his eyes were weary. "I'm not certain I could be surprised at this point."

"Lady Megelien showed me a vision of my soulbonded."

"Your…" Lyr blinked. "I stand corrected."

Ralan shoved down the sudden impatience churning his stomach. "I need to get to Earth. She might be in danger. Is Inona free to take me and Delbin through the Veil?"

"You have a human soulbonded you've never managed to foresee who's in sudden danger on Earth?" Lyr snorted. "Of course you do. And yes, Inona is available. She just finished another assignment."

A scene from his vision popped into Ralan's mind—Cora holding fire. "I'm not sure she's human. And I haven't searched the strands for my bonded since I was a teenager. Much can change."

"Obviously," Lyr said.

"One more thing before I go." Ralan hesitated, though everything within him wanted to hurry out the door. This was too important. "Did you and Meli come to a decision about Eri?"

Lyr sighed, but he nodded. "Yes. We will care for her if something happens to you."

"Thank you." Ralan let out a huge breath. "She has promised to be good while I'm gone. I am fairly certain I'll return without too much trouble this time."

"But not the next?" Lyr asked, his eyes narrowing.

"Not even I can predict all that will happen. Megelien…" Ralan clamped his lips shut. He did *not* want to confess to angering the Goddess of Seers. "Much is shifting."

Lyr leaned his elbows against his desk. "So it seems. Well, go. Perhaps finding your soulbonded will make the strands clearer."

Ralan didn't bother to correct his friend before he hurried from the room, although Lyr out of everyone would understand. Lyr hadn't been able to claim his first soulbonded, Arlyn's mother, and Ralan wouldn't be able to bond with his. He couldn't be so cruel with death looming, considering the pain a broken bond would bring.

Only if the vision of his demise proved wrong could he—

No. Ralan cut that thought off before it fully formed. No use considering the impossible.

Meli heaved out a sigh and shut the book she'd opened just a few moments before. For the third time. How was she supposed to concentrate on Moranaian history now? She'd just agreed to become the parent of a seer when a few months before she'd believed she would never have a child.

Lynia approached, her steps slow without the walking stick leaning against the table. That the lady could carry a book and walk unassisted was a sign of improvement after she'd shattered her spine in a fall from the top of the library tower. It was a true miracle that the healer had saved her at all.

"Is something wrong?" Lynia asked as she placed her book on the table across from Meli.

"I…" Meli took a bracing breath. "Lyr thinks we'll find ourselves parents soon. Well, again. For him. Not that he feels poorly about Arlyn, just—"

"What?" Eyes going wide, Lynia dropped into her seat. "You're having a baby?"

Meli choked on a cough, and it was a moment before she could speak. "No! Not as far as I know. It's Ralan's daughter, Eri. He asked us to adopt her if something happens."

Lynia waved a hand. "Ralan's young. Not even a thousand years old."

"True. But Lyr is certain that Ralan has foreseen something dire," Meli said. "By Freyr, I hope he's wrong. I'm not ready to raise any child, much less one with such power."

"Wait a moment." Lips pinching, Lynia leaned forward. "Please tell me my son did not agree to this without consulting you."

Meli gaped at her. "Of course not."

"Good. I'm too tired to give him a piece of my mind right now," Lynia said.

Another type of concern squeezed Meli's chest. She'd come to think of Lyr's mother as a friend during their work together. "Perhaps you should rest."

"Oh, no," Lynia answered. "I want to know why you agreed to this if you're so doubtful."

"My parents love me dearly, but if something had happened to them, no one would have taken me in. I can't imagine leaving a helpless child an orphan." Her lips twitched. "Even if Eri doesn't seem particularly helpless."

Lynia settled back against her seat, and the strained quality of her smile had Meli's heart squeezing with worry. "Indeed. Well, you and Lyr will always have my support."

"Thank you. Now maybe you should—"

A sharp knock interrupted her words, and Lial poked his head in the door. "Go rest."

Meli concealed a laugh as Lynia flushed and scowled at the healer. Lyr might not want to think about it, but his mother and the healer definitely had something building between them. And if they didn't work it out, it was going to explode. She caught a hint of affection in Lial's eyes as Lynia told him to get out, and suddenly, Meli hoped they found their way together.

Lyr would just have to adapt.

Ralan halted outside Delbin's door and then scowled. The shielding on the room was strong, which meant that Delbin and Inona were likely in there together. Probably having sex, but Ralan didn't care, not right now. With an impatient huff, he knocked on the door and tried not to fidget as he waited.

When Delbin sent a polite mental inquiry, Ralan greeted it with the image of a raised middle finger, a favorite human gesture he didn't get to use here. He caught a hint of Delbin's humor before the shield weakened and the door opened.

Delbin ran his hand through his short blond hair and raised a brow. "I don't want to call you an asshole, but—"

"Not now," Ralan interrupted. His gaze flicked to Inona, who was smoothing her hair. "We need to go to Earth. Immediately."

"What?" Delbin's brow furrowed. "Weren't you off bossing Kai around just a few hours ago? That vision was intense, but it didn't have anything to do with Earth. Did it?"

Ralan made a sharp, impatient gesture. "No. I'll tell you on the way."

"Prince Ralan," Inona began. "If I might say so, I recommend you find a guide. The Veil has grown turbulent and difficult to cross. Kai or Lyr could help find someone."

"When I said 'we,' I meant all three of us."

Inona's eyes widened. "I'm not on assignment, but I'll have to check—"

"I've cleared it all with Lyr. You're coming with us."

"But where are we going, *Elaiteriorn*?" Inona asked.

"You needn't use the title with me," Ralan answered absently. *Third son and heir.* And a foolish one he'd turned out to be. "Unfortunately, I'm not sure where on Earth the vision will happen. Give me a moment."

Ralan took a bracing breath and searched for the strands connected to the event. Nothing. His shoulder muscles tightened. There couldn't be *nothing*. His Sight had been unpredictable since he'd resumed using his talents, but visions didn't typically disappear. How could he have let himself panic so thoroughly that he lost the very strand he needed?

Then realization hit. Megelien. *Clechtan.* She truly was furious with him. No telling how many offerings he'd have to leave Her before She forgave him.

In this, he might be on his own.

"Prince Ralan?" Inona asked, her tone hesitant.

"I lost the strand leading to the future in my vision," Ralan confessed.

The other two stared at him for one long moment.

Then Delbin's snort of laughter filled the silence. "This isn't your day, is it?"

"Shut up." Ralan's fists clenched. "If you could try to be useful? The shop was called The Magic Touch. Chances might be slim that you've heard—"

"Oh, Cora's shop," Delbin interrupted. "What exile hasn't heard of it?"

"She's an exile?" he asked.

Delbin shook his head. "No. The Magic Touch is a clothing shop, but Cora also runs a side business. If you know the password, she'll outfit you in current human clothes for barter. Exiles and travelers from many of the fae realms visit her for help. Gotta say, if someone is planning to give her grief, they'll pay in blood. She's well-liked."

Ralan replayed the vision in his head. "I don't think the stranger knew that. I think he was Sidhe, a young one. Maybe a half-blood."

"Wait." Delbin's face went pale. "A young half-Sidhe? What did he look like?"

Without a word, Ralan sent the image of the red-haired stranger along a mental link.

Delbin bit out a harsh curse. "Patrick. He was in Kien's little cave."

"Then we need to move. You can direct Inona to the right place?" After Delbin's nod, Ralan tried one last time to find the strands surrounding the vision. And came up blank. "I don't know

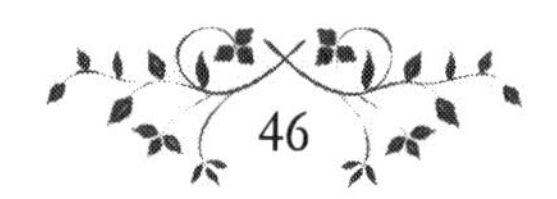

what might happen, but we're going to find out. Meet me downstairs in a quarter of a mark with anything you think we'll need."

After darting up the stairs to his own guest suite, Ralan rushed through the living quarters and into his bedroom. He hadn't carried much from Earth when he'd brought Eri home to Moranaia, but he'd thankfully included a few things at the last minute. Like his cell phone and the wallet containing cash and his debit and credit cards.

He shrugged out of his tunic and pants and flung them toward the bed on his way to the closet. In less than a mark, Ralan had pulled on the designer button-down shirt and casual slacks he'd kept in case he needed to go back. Then he grabbed a backpack and shoved the wallet, his keys, and his other set of Earth clothes inside.

As Ralan turned back to the door, he noticed the altar set under the window. He let out a soft curse—but not a blasphemous one, at least. He hadn't lit the incense this morning or made any observance. Though there were many degrees of piety on Moranaia, he was a seer and the crown prince. It was part of his duty.

How had he lost his faith so thoroughly during his time away from home?

He checked the water clock dripping away by the door. In a few marks, they'd expect him below, but they'd have to wait. Ralan strode to the altar and sank to his knees. With a quick spell, he lit the incense. And for the first time in centuries, he truly began to pray.

5

It was just after midnight by the time Ralan reached Chattanooga, but the streets still echoed with music and the hum of voices from nearby bars and restaurants. At least none of the bar hoppers noticed them. Inona had cast a light cloaking spell over them in a tingle of power, but it didn't block them from the world, only diverted human attention. With the Sidhe possibly nearby, it was best to avoid drawing notice by using too much power.

Ralan peered into the glass window of The Magic Touch. Streetlights lent a yellow-gray tone to the simple floral wrap dress draped over a mannequin and cast the clothing racks beyond into shadow. Even with his keen eyesight, he couldn't make out much. Maybe a shelf of purses on one wall. He found himself eager to see inside during the day.

His last career on Earth had been a fashion designer, and his potential bonded owned a clothing shop. The universe had its own kind of humor.

"I've done a mental scan of the area and found no sign of Patrick," Delbin sent. *"I'd recognize his energy anywhere."*

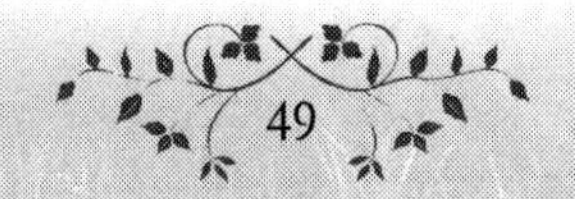

"Gone already?" Ralan huffed out a breath. *"Figures."*

"I take it you were eager for a confrontation."

"Cora is my soulbonded," Ralan said, his mental tone calmer than he felt. *"He threatened her. Even if I never join with her, I'll see her safe."*

"Your…" All hint of sarcasm faded from Delbin's voice. *"We'll find him."*

With a quick stretch of his power, Ralan connected Inona to their mental conversation. *"Since there's no sign of him, I suggest we look for somewhere close to stay. There are several hotels nearby."*

Delbin's brows lifted. *"It's summer. Tourist season. You want a room in one of these hotels, you'll have to pay a fortune."*

"Good thing I have one," Ralan answered with a grin.

"Lucky you," Delbin said. *"Hope you didn't use your talen—"*

"A room would be nice," Inona interrupted. She gave Delbin a light shove and a sizeable glare. *"If Delbin can stop being rude."*

But Ralan found himself chuckling. *"He's just mad that he was living in a tent."*

"Nothing wrong with that."

"Of course not," Ralan answered. *"I did my fair share of that when it was needed."*

Delbin turned toward the nearest hotel, its bright sign beckoning against the dark skyline. *"Then why'd you give me a hard time?"*

"Eh, it's the best part of having a student."

The music and voices faded as they headed down a darkened street. Ralan sent his senses out around them, seeking any minds full of ill intent, but the sidewalk remained empty for a solid two blocks. With one block to go, a small group of drunk men stumbled out of a dive bar, but none looked their way.

As Ralan paused beyond the lights spilling from the hotel entrance, he reminded Inona to remove the spell cloaking them. It might have been amusing to watch the desk clerk struggle to notice their presence, but he hadn't fallen to that level of jerk.

Since there weren't any two room suites available—he was *not* sharing with a new couple—Ralan booked the hotel's best two connecting rooms. He listened to the spiel about the rooms' features before he slipped into the clerk's mind. Ah, good. Not many complaints of cleanliness issues, and the housekeeping staff did a fair job. That was more important than the whirlpool tub.

He handed Delbin and Inona their key cards as they headed for the elevator. Delbin smirked. "What, no top-level penthouse?"

Ralan made a rude gesture. "There wasn't one available, so you'll have to be content with the fancy bathroom."

"Joking," Delbin muttered.

Ralan smirked as he pushed the button to the elevator. "I know."

The doors opened, and Inona's sharp laugh startled the young man about to exit into the lobby. Ralan shook his head in mock dismay as the man sidled around them. "Really, Delbin. See what you've done?"

"What I've—"

"Are you two going to do this the entire trip?" Inona asked, her voice full of amusement.

Grin widening, Ralan pressed the button for their floor. "Maybe."

They parted at their respective doors, and as Ralan dropped his backpack on the king-sized bed, his good humor began to fade. Sighing, he ambled to the window and pulled back the curtain. In the

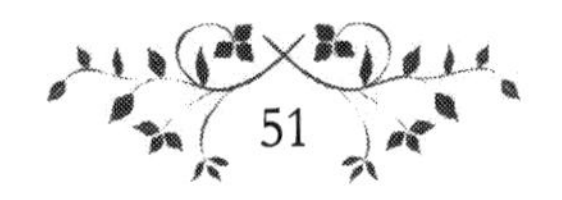

distance, he could make out the silver gleam of the nearby river, and more of the buildings in the city had gone dark.

Closing time.

Lyr stared at the carved arch and tried not to shudder. The last time he'd passed through the portal linking all Moranaian estates, he'd been captured by Allafon and almost killed. Worse, his mother had nearly been murdered in his absence. And although Allafon had been dead for a couple of months, the thought of traveling to Oria still had his stomach wanting to consume itself. Every time he thought he was past the ordeal, another reminder hit. Dealing with the trauma was the main reason he'd decided to go instead of calling Moren to Braelyn.

It was time.

"Myern?" Kera asked.

Swallowing hard, he glanced at his guard and assistant. "Forgive me for delaying us. I was considering…"

"Lord Lyr," she said softly, "you do not have to pretend. I've never been in battle, but we were both trained about the burdens warriors must bear."

He let out a breath. "Shouldn't it have been long enough?"

"The mind takes as long to heal as it wants, I've found."

"For certain," he responded.

Lyr straightened, bolstered by Kera's quiet reassurance. He could do this. Kai and Arlyn weren't coming with him this time, so there would be no repeat of their capture. Meli and his mother were in the library with Lial. Elite guards had been stationed everywhere, and five of his own bodyguards stood behind him and Kera.

And this time, he had not dressed for diplomacy, even if that was his mission. He would not be caught unarmed again.

With a nod, he stepped forward and activated the spell that linked Braelyn with Oria. He hadn't warned Moren that he was coming, so when the image of the great hall coalesced, it revealed the stunned faces of several guards. They unsheathed their swords before they caught sight of Lyr on the other side.

Lyr's chest squeezed, and he took another deep breath before gesturing Kera and the others forward. Kera smiled as she moved past, but her hand settled on the hilt of her sword as she walked through the portal first. Lyr's heart pounded, and he forced his feet to move. He could do this. He *would*.

His head spun slightly and a tingle passed over his skin as he stepped through to Oria. Lyr blinked against the shift in light, then blinked again. Moren had certainly changed things. Before, elaborate red tapestries had lined the walls, but no other decorations had cheered the room. Anything else might have distracted from the huge dais, complete with massive stone throne, at the far end, and Allafon wouldn't have allowed that.

Not so anymore.

Most of the tapestries had been removed, replaced here and there with soothing paintings of nature scenes. Comfortable seats had been situated all about, and ample mage lights dangled from delicate chains. And while a colorful carpet still led to a small dais, the throne in the center was now more of an elaborate chair in warm-toned wood. This place had never been such a...well, a home.

Had Kai returned to Oria? If so, he hadn't bothered to mention the changes.

"Myern Lyrnis," one of the guards said. Rehn, if he recalled correctly. "Please forgive us. We were unaware of your imminent arrival. I have sent for Lord Moren."

"Rehn?" Lyr asked. At the guard's nod, he continued. "It is I who must ask forgiveness, Rehn, as we have traveled here without any warning. You have my thanks for notifying Moren of our presence."

Moren's voice sounded from the other side of the room. "I detected the portal's activation and was already on the way."

Besides having blond hair instead of black, Moren looked remarkably like Kai even though they were only half-brothers. *Their mother's bone structure,* Lyr thought as he studied the approaching elf, although Moren had inherited Allafon's pale hair and skin tone.

Now that he'd met Naomh, Lyr could see the source of Kai's differences.

The elf in question stopped in front of Lyr and saluted. "Lord Lyr, you honor us with your presence."

"You will not find it an honor by the time I leave," Lyr replied. "Do you have…another place we might discuss this in private?"

Moren's expression blanked. "Milord?"

"Do you have a separate study from the one your father used?"

"Of course," the other elf answered, his mouth tightening at the mention of Allafon. "I do no business from that space."

Lyr inclined his head. "Then let us adjourn to yours."

Though Moren's face had gone tight and his eyes had grown shadowed with worry, he made no further comment as he led Lyr and Kera, the bodyguards trailing, from the great hall. When they reached the door to Moren's study, Lyr ordered his guards to remain

outside, brining only Kera with him. The other elf entered alone, a clear sign of trust and loyalty. But when the door had closed behind him, Moren let his confusion—and a hint of annoyance—show.

"I have given my loyalty in the ancient way, Myern," Moren began. "A blood oath. I have reported faithfully on each of my father's nefarious dealings as I have discovered them. I must confess I am not certain what I could have done to earn your ire."

Lyr's brows rose. "Careful of your tone, Morenial. I've discovered one issue you were less than forthcoming about. Care to explain Delbin Rayac?"

"*Clechtan*," Moren breathed. "I forgot to get Delbin. He'll be elated that—"

"I'm more interested in why you exiled a sixteen-year-old child to another world," Lyr snapped. "Without a word to my father or myself."

Moren's throat bobbed. "I didn't have enough evidence. I told you before that I had found no sign of any plots against your House, and that was the truth. Yet I knew that leaving a telepath of Delbin's power in my father's sphere of influence would be a terrible mistake. It was to everyone's benefit that Delbin be nowhere near my father, but I didn't have the evidence I needed to bring you. How could I explain that with nothing to go on?"

"Sixteen. Years. Old," Lyr ground out. "How many others have you sent to Earth under false pretenses?"

"Only three," Moren answered at once.

As though such a small number wasn't just as terrible.

"You will have a list containing all details at once, and you will bring all three home as soon as possible." Lyr turned for the door,

then glanced back. "And Moren? If there's anything else you've forgotten, I suggest you send a report with the list. My patience is beyond thin."

Cora closed the cash register with a click and boosted herself onto her wooden stool. "I need more coffee."

Beside her, Maddy laughed as she arranged new stock on the countertop jewelry stand. "I bet you can fit in your fourth cup before we open. If you hurry. You've got ten minutes."

"Too much effort. I'll live," Cora mumbled as she straightened the decorative flowers in their vase.

Her tolerance for caffeine was higher than her half-human friend, so she often didn't bother. But when she'd hit a solid spurt of inspiration the previous night, she hadn't been able to stop herself from sketching until the wee hours. It had been just what she needed to shake her glum mood. And yesterday's mystery visitor would be well-outfitted. She'd lose a great deal more sleep in the sewing since she only worked on her side business at home, but she didn't mind.

Maddy made an odd noise, and Cora looked over to see her friend staring at the window with wide eyes. "What…?"

Then Cora looked for herself, and she couldn't help but agree with Maddy's whispered *holy shit*.

Long black hair, model-worthy cheekbones, kissable lips, leanly muscled body? Yum. But… Her brow furrowed. Did she know him? He seemed oddly familiar, though she was certain he'd never visited her shop before. Aside from Maddy, Jase, and a handful of clients, Cora didn't socialize much. Where could she have seen him?

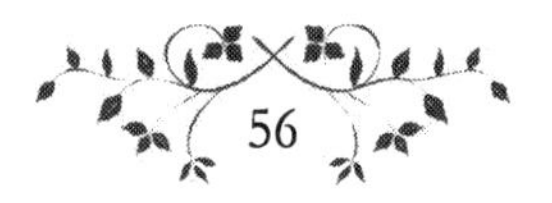

"Anna's lucky that I'm a faithful woman," Maddy said, her tone somehow full of both cheer and regret.

Cora gave an absent nod to her friend, her focus on the stranger peering at her window display. Surely she would remember if she'd ever encountered him. Her heart thumped, and her body heated at the thought. Yeah, she wouldn't be able to forget exchanging words with this particular man. A local celebrity? Chattanooga didn't have many. It was hardly New York, where many of her fashion idols lived.

When realization hit, Cora almost smacked her palm against her forehead.

"Roland Morne," she whispered.

Maddy's eyebrow lifted. "You want to talk fashion *now?*"

"That's him," Cora said. Her throat went dry, her voice scratchy. "Roland Morne is standing outside of my shop."

What was a famous designer doing in Chattanooga checking out a small local store? Oh, Great Divine. He couldn't have heard of her. She'd never dressed anyone famous. Well, except for a couple of fae nobles and one princess over a century ago, but he obviously wouldn't know about them. Unless…

Cora let her senses sweep out, subtle as a soft breeze, until they brushed against his energy. Only to pull back at once as his gaze connected with hers through the glass. He'd noticed—and no wonder. Fashion designer or no, Roland Morne wasn't human.

His energy was pure elf.

"One of his friends looks like Delbin, but I haven't heard about him being in town," Maddy said. "He's already noticed us, so I might as well let them in. Only five minutes until we open, anyway."

Cora's mouth opened, but she couldn't form either an assent or a denial. She'd barely even registered the man and woman beside the elf. Her gaze was captured by his. Brown. Were his eyes brown? At this distance, it was difficult to tell, but for some reason, the answer became vitally important. She wanted to know everything about him.

He was hers.

Stifling a gasp, Cora looked away. *Hers?* What was wrong with her? Laying claim to strange men—or familiar ones—wasn't her style. She hadn't had a serious date in…five years? A decade? Relationships were not a priority, not when Orn might try to cause her grief.

The click of opening locks hit Cora's heart like gunfire, and the jingling bell over the door made her flinch. How was she supposed to carry on a normal conversation with a hot, famous elf she'd placed mental dibs on? As Maddy's welcome rang out, Cora sat up straighter on the stool and lifted her chin. She glanced up as Roland Morne answered, his voice warm and deep. Cora gave an involuntary shiver at the rich sound.

Of course he noticed. He smiled, a wicked, knowing curve. "Forgive me if my staring worried you."

"Staring?" she asked, all attention on his eyes.

Gold. In the light, they were gold. Like rich amber.

"In your shop window. I didn't mean to arrive before you opened."

"Oh." Swallowing hard, Cora tried to look away but ended up studying his mouth. Which wasn't particularly better for her state of mind. "It happens sometimes. I'm sure people line up outside your store every day."

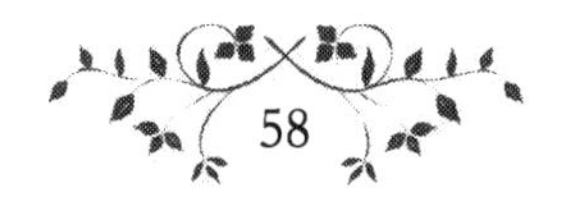

"You recognize me."

She frowned at the odd, disappointed tone to his voice. "I make clothes. You're a famous designer. Why wouldn't I have?"

"I thought…" His lips firmed into a line. "Never mind. You seemed jumpy when I entered, so I feared that I disturbed you. My friend here tells me you get a wide variety of clientele."

He gestured at the man beside him, and for the first time, Cora truly noticed him. Short blond hair. Rakish smile. "Delbin!"

"Hey, beautiful." His grin widened. "You look great."

Maddy leaned against the counter. "It *is* you. I shouldn't have doubted my instincts."

"When did you get in town?" Cora asked.

Wincing, Delbin ran his hand across his hair. "That's a long story."

"One we're not telling out here." Her brows rose at the sour expression that crossed Roland Morne's face as he glanced at Delbin. "You didn't mention that you knew her personally."

The woman beside Delbin wrapped her hand around his wrist and tugged. "You didn't mention that to me, either."

Delbin's grin slipped at the woman's rebuke, and Cora chuckled low. She doubted the striking blond who'd captured his attention had anything to worry about, but a pal in need…

"We're just friends," Cora announced. She tensed as Roland's gaze returned to her face. "Although why Mr. Morne cares, I couldn't say."

"I—" His mouth snapped shut. But after a moment, he let out a sigh. "Please, call me Ralan. If you have someplace private, I'll explain."

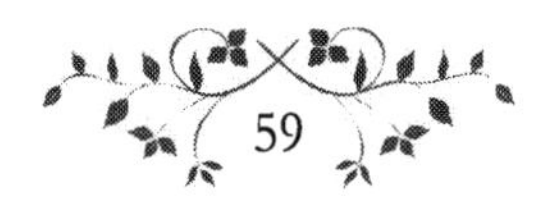

Cora peered at him for a moment, considering. Finally, she nodded. "Fine. Since you're with Delbin, I'll even waive the password."

She caught Maddy's eye and gave the signal for her to take over the shop. Then Cora led the others toward the back room. *So Roland Morne's real name is Ralan,* she pondered as the group followed her in. Interesting. But she had a feeling that was the least of what she would learn this day.

6

Ralan's gaze followed Cora much more intimately than his body did. He was making a mess of their first meeting, but not even his vision had prepared him for seeing her in person. Could she feel the connection between them? The potential? He'd flustered her and possibly upset her, but he had no idea if he attracted her.

She more than attracted him.

As his feet propelled him along with the group, his eyes lingered on her delectable ass, highlighted by the long black hair tangling around her waist. She appeared to be a size eight or ten. And all curves. His body came to life at the thought of touching her, and he had to force his attention to the clothing racks to avoid embarrassing them both. Good grief, he was 833. Where was his control?

Cora led them into a side room and closed the door behind them. As soon as she did, he detected a shield forming around them like a blanket. A quick probe revealed its simple purpose—keeping their words secure from mundane or magical listening. Smart move for someone who often worked with the fae.

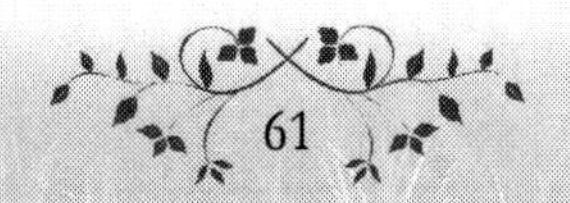

She gestured at the table in the center. "I suppose we should sit for whatever you're about to tell me. I suspect it'll be a doozy, especially if Delbin's involved."

"Hey!" Delbin protested, though a laugh slipped free.

She really did know him, then.

Ralan waited until Delbin plopped into a seat and Inona sat more sedately next to him, leaving the chair beside Cora. As he settled in, he almost grinned. A move worthy of a teenager, but it had gotten him as close to her as possible. A gentle blend of vanilla and flowers wafted over to him as she shoved her hair out of her face.

Her brown eyes pinned him. "You're quite good at casting a glamour, you know. I've seen recordings of you on the runway at the end of a show, and I've never caught a hint that you aren't human. I've seen others slip under the pressure and attention. Why choose such a high-profile career?"

His earlier disappointment came storming back, twisting his insides. His fame was what interested her, not him as a person. "Most people only see what they expect."

Could *she* see beyond his fame? Her next words gave no answer.

"I suppose." Her gaze flicked to Delbin and back. "So what are you doing here? Chattanooga isn't exactly a fashion capital, and I doubt our friend has been raving about my designs."

"Not fair," Delbin retorted. "I've sent you three clients."

Cora's lips twisted. "And you forgot to mention Roland Morne was your friend, so…"

"He wasn't." Delbin leaned back in his chair, one arm draped casually over the back. "I've only known him a few days."

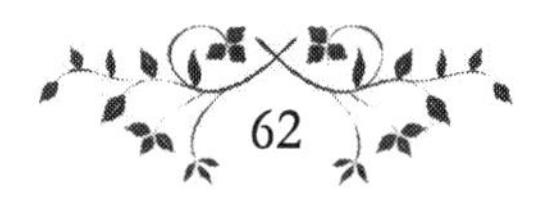

She paused, a frown wrinkling her brow. "And you brought him here? You know—"

"I'm not trying to break your trust," Delbin said. "Things have happened you need to know about. For one, there's a guy who's going to confront you outside your shop. He's bad news."

"Another one?" She huffed out a breath. "Some creep pestered me last night when I was leaving."

Ralan's heart skipped a beat. Had Megelien shown him something as it occurred, or was there more than one of Kien's minions lingering in the area? "Surely you can open up for a special kind of guy," he murmured.

Cora stiffened, her eyes going wide. "You'd better explain before I show you the door."

"That's what he said." Ralan leaned forward. The spark of helpless anger he'd felt the night before flared again, and he did his best to keep it from showing. "I had a vision of you standing in front of your shop. Has it already happened?"

Her breath hissed in. "A vision. Sure."

"He's from my home world, Cora," Delbin interjected. "My prince and a powerful seer. He showed me his memory of the vision, and I recognized the jerk. We want to help."

"If it would help, I could send the memory to your mind, as well," Ralan said.

She shook her head, and that odd sense of disappointment filled him once more. "I'll keep my thoughts mine, thank you," she said. "I can take Delbin's word. He might be a rogue, but he's the best kind."

Delbin chuckled. "Thanks."

Cora relaxed against the back of her seat. "What is going on? The guy said he was searching for someone. One of you?"

"My brother, I'd wager." Ralan's nostrils flared at the thought of Kien. "He's an enemy to our people, and he has several half-blood fae working with him. They are certain to cause trouble wherever they go."

Her lips pursed. "I know a huge chunk of the Other community, and I haven't heard of anything like this. Maybe a bit of sickness here and there, but that's it."

"That's Kien's doing." Ralan held her gaze, though he wanted to look away. "He's been poisoning the Earth just to get to me. Two of our people disrupted the spell, but one of them was injured. My brother got away during the confrontation. Then a few days ago, Delbin and Inona almost captured him in a cave not too far from here, but he escaped again. I'm not sure what he'll try next."

Her frown returned. "Poisoning the Earth? You mean the entire planet, not just sickness in one area? Sounds farfetched."

"Nevertheless, it's true," Ralan said. "My brother would do anything to kill me."

"What, did you mess up the clothes you'd designed for him?" Cora scoffed.

Ralan let out a surprised laugh. "No. It's a longstanding feud, but he didn't find me again until recently. His hatred runs far deeper than my latest career."

His jaw clenched around the rest of the explanation. He wanted to tell her about Kien's betrayal, the event that had driven him from Moranaia, but that involved Kenaren. The woman he'd loved. How could he explain that to his soulbonded? He'd tell her eventually, if he had the chance to spend time with her before his death.

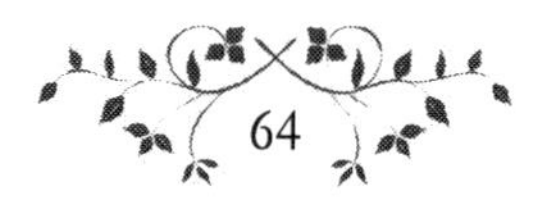

But he couldn't bring himself to talk about it today.

Cora peered at him. "And?"

"I recently returned to my home world." There was one fact he could offer. "My daughter was ill. It was in the press, but she didn't have cancer as stated. The energy poisoning affected her. I had to take her home for healing."

"Oh, yeah, I remember reading that. Is she okay?"

Ralan nodded. "She's doing well, but I didn't dare bring her back. Not until I stop Kien."

Cora's brows rose. "You'd better keep a low profile if you don't want to answer questions about her absence."

"I'll handle it if I have to."

She stared at him again, and in the silence, he finally thought he caught a hint of interest in her eyes. What would it take to bring it out? Ralan wasn't certain if he should mention their potential bond. Were soulbonds recognized where she had been born? Not all realms had learned how to bring like souls together even if their spirits resonated correctly. Her energy wasn't human, but there was nothing in her appearance to tell him where she might be from. Her hair was midnight black like a Dökkálfar, but her tawny beige skin could come from many types of fae. With hundreds of other dimensions to consider, it would take time to puzzle out.

"So, uhh…" She pulled her gaze from his. "How am I supposed to help with this? I have no idea who the guy is. I can feel around for information, I guess, but I don't have much to go on."

He made her nervous. A good sign if it was caused by attraction. Satisfaction had Ralan sitting taller. "I came to ensure your safety. There is no need for you to get involved."

Three knocks sounded on the door. A pause. Then two more.

Cora shot to her feet. "Maddy needs me. That's the sign for a potential problem customer."

Delbin lifted a brow at Ralan. "Patrick?"

He didn't answer. His concentration shifted to the future strands. A bleary image took shape of Patrick arguing with a young, red-headed woman out in the storeroom. What was the best path forward? If Ralan stood now, his chair would scrape loudly, and the noise stood a fair chance of startling Patrick into leaving. But sitting wouldn't help. If—

A poke on his arm broke his concentration.

"What's your problem?" Cora asked.

Ralan grimaced. "I'm a seer. I was trying to help."

"You can help by not stalling. My friend is out there with that weirdo."

Quiet Inona finally spoke up. "Is there a back way out of this room? Delbin and I can go make sure he doesn't get away."

Cora paused to gesture at another door beyond a small counter. "Go through there, then cut right. The back entrance is that way."

Then she opened the other door and walked through without looking back.

As a half-Sidhe, Maddy wasn't helpless, but they'd created the panic code for good reason. Plenty of humans patronized Cora's shop, it was true, but any number of Other creatures, some of them dangerous, did, too. And the code was never used casually.

Sure enough, her friend was lingering close to the door when Cora emerged. Maddy's fair skin was ghost-pale, and a glimmer of light shimmered around her hands from power barely constrained. Beside her, the red-haired man who'd stopped her outside her shop stood scowling.

"May I help you?" Cora asked, her tone cool but professional.

Some of the frustration eased from his face, but she wasn't reassured. "I decided to return when you were open. Please forgive my rudeness yesterday. My friend is missing, you see, and—"

"I believe I advised you to go to the police."

His jaw firmed. "We both know there are things the police can't help with."

"What I *know* is that you've been bothering my employee while I was with a client." Cora's palm heated, though the flame she gathered was not yet visible. "I will not be bullied. See yourself out and do not return."

"We seem to have started off on the wrong foot," he persisted. "I mean no harm, and I don't want to make any trouble."

Cora's nose tipped up. "You reek of death magic. Go. This is your last warning."

The Sidhe studied her and then Maddy, no doubt considering his next move. But whatever it might have been, Ralan's sudden presence wiped it away. When the prince followed her into main shop, Patrick's mouth gaped, and he took a step forward.

"Lord Kien!" Then he froze, his brow scrunching with concern. "Or not. Gotta go."

Before Cora could blink, he fled. She stared after him for a moment before turning a questioning look on Ralan. The prince

shrugged as the bell signaled Patrick's departure. "Aren't you going to stop him?" she asked.

"Inona is a scout," Ralan answered. "She'll track him, and she and Delbin can capture him. It might be a few minutes here in the middle of the city."

"Well." She swallowed down a sudden lump at the glint in his eyes. "I suppose you don't need to stay, then. Mission accomplished."

His lips curved up as he ambled her way. "Oh, no, Cora. My mission is definitely not accomplished."

Beside her, Maddy choked on a laugh, but Cora didn't glance her way. She was too busy trying to calm her raging heart as the prince halted within touching distance. Suddenly, her palm wasn't the only thing heating up.

She almost groaned at the breathy note she couldn't keep out of her voice. "What's left?"

His smirk widened. "You."

"I can't believe you just said that." Somehow, her tone sounded amused. She hoped. Inside, she was melting like a candle in her fire's grip. "I think you've watched too many movies."

Ralan's low chuckle filled the space between them. "Probably."

"Are you seriously going to flirt with me while the bad guy you're supposed to catch is on the loose?" She tucked her hair behind her ear, unable to resist teasing him. "Because it works for me, but I don't think your friends would agree."

His gaze grew distant. "He'll make it another block before Inona and Delbin trap him in an alley. I might as well spend the wait doing something pleasant."

Maddy shifted, and Cora almost laughed at the sight of her friend trying to sidle around them. "I'll just…go to the back or something."

"No need," Cora said.

But Ralan's eyes focused on her again, and she lost the words to keep her friend near. Suddenly, she had an intense urge to touch him, and not a quick poke to snap him out of a trance. She'd love to run her thumbs across his gorgeous cheekbones and tug him close for a kiss. Fire was her power, and there was enough simmering between them to sear them both.

Great Divine, how glorious that inferno would be.

She heard his breath catch, and he took a step closer. "Cora. If you keep staring at me that way…"

"What?" Her mouth watered even as her throat squeezed tight. "You'll do what?"

Ralan's hand lifted toward her face, but before his fingers made contact, he flinched. "Dammit."

Confusion flared quickly into anger. "If you aren't interested after all, it's fine."

"No, I—" Then he bent over, bracing his hands on his knees. "Delbin. Dammit."

Cora's mouth fell open. What did Delbin have to do with this? "I don't understand."

"He's hurt." Ralan shoved himself to his feet, his expression now filled with fury and pain. "I was wrong again. Dammit. That mental blast… I have to go."

Before she could offer to help, he hurried out the door.

The sound of the bell echoed through the room and then fell into silence.

"What just happened?" Maddy finally asked.

Cora shook her head to clear it, but the motion didn't help. "I have no idea."

But she was certain of one thing—she had to have Ralan as her own.

Daylight brought a glorious kind of pain as it heated Vek's pale skin and sliced into his eyes in a constant stream. Like a well-placed whip to flesh, the sensation made him shiver. His home was dim, the false sun lighting his underhill a weak one. Every time he walked the surface of true Earth, he became more convinced that there was no substitute for the real thing.

After all the time he'd spent outdoors today, he was certain to have a sunburn. Even traveling to that shop in search of human clothes and money had exposed him to more natural light than he'd seen in years.

Vek strode down the forest path, giving a pair of hikers an absent wave as they halted to stare. At his smile, one of the females blanched. The other simpered. Ah, the life of the Unseelie. Humans were either drawn or repulsed by the dark energy his kind wielded like breath. They never figured out that the beguiling Seelie were the true danger.

Too bad he didn't have time to explore either woman's reaction. Without pause, he wiped the memory of his presence from their minds and kept going. Fun and games would have to wait until he'd seen to Fen, his nephew. The idiot would be killed by the king, his own grandfather, if he couldn't make up for what he'd done.

Following the tug of their blood connection, a link no shield could ever hide, Vek slipped off the trail and into the forest. The hills and mountains in this area held more than a few caves, some of them huge. If Fen wanted to hide, he'd choose one of those, although the proximity to the source of sick energy that still lingered like a bad smell was a surprise.

It made his nephew all too easy for anyone to find.

Scowling, Vek shoved a low branch out of the way and cursed his sister. Why had Ara been so foolish as to leave her half-blood son unattended? Their line was ancient and powerful, their magic dangerous. Intimate. Now the boy was barely into his twenties and full of justified resentment for being abandoned on Earth while the rest of his family lived in luxury.

Ara was a cold bitch.

When he reached the entrance to the cave, he paused to strengthen his magical shields. Fen would sense his identity as surely as Vek could do the same, but that didn't mean the whelp wouldn't be prepared to attack. Whether the kid greeted him or lobbed a ball of death magic depended entirely on his current mood.

The air chilled around Vek as he started down the tunnel, and he took a deep breath, filling his lungs with the comforting cool. The sun might be a welcome novelty, but it was not home. Not like the dark and shadowed places. But the shadows ended abruptly as the tunnel opened into a small but brightly lit chamber, mage lights dancing between the stalagmites and stalactites spearing the air at random.

Between two stalagmites on the far wall, his nephew huddled. Vek tensed at the boy's pallor, and a quick probe revealed the youth's low energy. "What have you done?"

"Fucked up," Fen answered succinctly.

"You have no idea how true that is." After a quick scan to ensure they were alone, Vek stalked across the cavern floor. "I told you to leave off with that group of renegade half-bloods when last we met."

"Yeah, five years ago."

Vek didn't miss the bitter tone of his nephew's voice. Anger deserved. "Why the hell would you poison the energy fields? Affecting the Seelie is one thing, but it's started to sicken our people, too. The king has commanded your presence."

Fen's lips twisted. "You mean I finally get to see my mother's home? How nice."

"You won't see it for long." Vek paused, and his fists tightened with grief barely repressed. "Our cousin died from the poison, Fen. He was only forty-seven."

"No way," Fen said, though he'd gone paler than Vek would've thought possible. "Kien shielded the Unseelie. He swore it would only enter the Seelie realms."

Vek's hand darted out to grab Fen's shirt. "If you believe that, you're a fool."

The fight fled from his nephew's eyes, and the kid slumped in Vek's hold. "I was a fool. But I'm not with them anymore."

"You think that matters?" Vek let his nephew drop against the stone wall. "If I take you home now, I'll be taking you to your death."

Fen peered at him, eyes narrowing. "If?"

"You're rejoining the group. You'll undo—"

"Kien will kill me on sight."

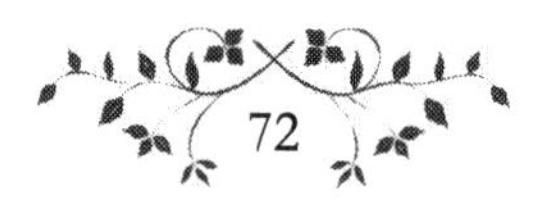

"Then I suggest you find a way to ingratiate yourself. Because if he doesn't kill you, the king certainly will." Vek scowled down at Fen. "Now, come on. I'll help you until you can feed enough to restore your energy. Then you will fix what you have wrought."

7

When Ralan darted past Inona's shield and into the alley, he found Delbin slumped against the wall. He'd taken off his shirt and shoved it against his side, but his abdomen was streaked with blood. Inona knelt beside him, digging through her backpack. Aside from the three of them, a dumpster, and the occasional skittering mouse, the alley was empty. The shield Inona had cast diverted the passing humans' attention.

"It's just a graze," Delbin said in greeting.

Ralan cursed as he saw the blood seeping through the shirt. "Like hell it is."

None of the possible futures he'd checked had led to this. Maybe if he hadn't been distracted with Cora, he would have seen the shift. Or his gift was still blocked by Megelien.

Hardly better.

"Take me to the carnival," Delbin said. During his exile, Delbin had spent a great deal of time traveling with fairs. "Grunge can stitch it up."

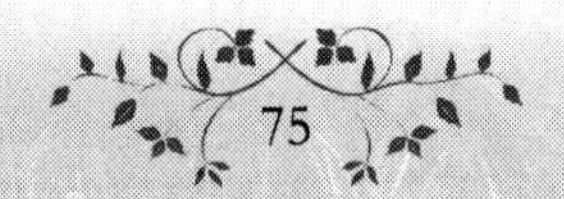

Inona stood, a length of bandage in her hands. "This is spelled to stop the bleeding temporarily, but you'll have to see an actual healer. Lial can restore you to full health."

"But—"

"You have to be at your best, Delbin," Ralan interjected. He rubbed his hand across the back of his neck. "What happened? I felt your pain through our link, but I had no vision of this. It wasn't one of the strands."

Inona's jaw clenched as she bent close to Delbin with the bandage. "I managed to lead Patrick into the alley, and Delbin was about to take control of him with telepathy. Then someone else showed up."

"Victor." Wincing, Delbin lifted the T-shirt from his wound. "He's been working on his mental abilities."

Blood gushed from the slash across his student's side, and Ralan's stomach roiled. But Inona appeared unaffected, wrapping the bandage around her lover's waist without comment. He hadn't considered himself squeamish, but he had to avert his eyes before he lost his free hotel breakfast.

"Did he hit you with a mental blast?" he asked.

Though pale and tense, Delbin nodded. "I wiped Victor's memory when we carried Kien from the cave, but it must not have worked. He *was* tough to control. Or somebody warned him."

Ralan's teeth ground together at the reminder of Kien's near-capture. Delbin and Inona had found his brother's cavern hideout and disrupted his poisoning spell. They'd incapacitated the guards and forced Kien to leave with them. But his brother had found a way

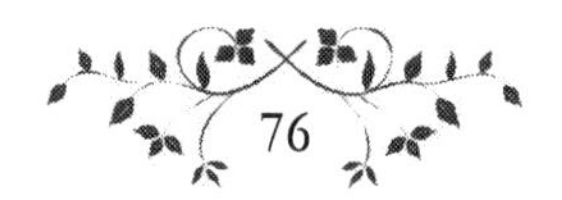

to escape. Of course, if Ralan's Sight had been working properly, he'd have killed Kien a month ago.

"How were you injured?"

"Victor attacked Inona, and I interceded." Delbin's expression turned sheepish. "Unfortunately, I'm not much of a fighter."

Inona turned a scowl on Delbin. "I could've taken them both if I hadn't had to worry about you. I *am* a warrior."

His student winced again. "Yeah, I know. Sorry."

"It's my fault," Ralan said. "I should've monitored the strands better."

"Does it matter?" Delbin held his gaze. "You see the future, but you don't make it. Give yourself a break. It was my choice to be an idiot."

Ralan grimaced at the reminder. Lyr had once told him something similar, but it didn't make failure any easier. What good was being able to see the future if he couldn't change it for the better? But he hadn't been able to stop Kien from stealing Kenaren. He hadn't been able to stop his father's rejection. And he couldn't keep his friends safe.

"Let's head back to Cora's shop," he decided. "If you have enough energy to glamour yourself a shirt so we don't startle the humans."

"I can manage."

Inona frowned. "Milord, shouldn't we return to Moranaia?"

Ralan shook his head. "If there's a local healer, that would be faster. With Patrick on the loose, I'd rather not leave Cora unguarded."

"She's tough," Delbin said. "But I'm sure she'll help us."

Once Delbin had made himself presentable, they shuffled down the alley and into the street. Though the bandage had stopped the

bleeding, his student still moved slowly. Ralan tried not to worry as Delbin grew increasingly pale, but there wasn't much he could do. Nothing but hope his instinct to return to Cora was a good one.

Cora struggled not to fidget with impatience as her customer twisted the purse around in her hands and frowned at it. It was the fourth one the woman had examined, but none of them had been right. The first two had been the wrong color. This one didn't have a cell phone pocket, and the zipper wasn't easy to open.

The zipper wasn't easy to open?

Cora almost groaned when the lady placed the purse back on the shelf. Curse it all, she wanted to know what had happened to Delbin. Would they even come back here? If they'd captured the guy they'd been looking for, they might not. But Ralan had caught her interest. She should've gone with them. Then she wouldn't be stuck wondering while her customer examined every purse in the shop.

"Is there a certain color you're trying to match?" she asked, careful to keep the impatience out of her tone.

The woman's shoulders slumped. "The dress is a summer floral. I knew I should have worn it, but it's hideous against this." She held up her brightly patterned bag. "Maybe I should go with something neutral."

Cora sorted through her stock. She thought she had… *Yes, here.* She held up a cream and brown purse from the bottom shelf. "How about this? It's not as cheerful as the one you have, but it's a great neutral. Plenty of pockets, and there's an inside phone sleeve."

"Let me see."

As the customer inspected the compartments, Cora ducked back behind the counter. She could tell from her expression that the woman would go with her choice, but she was the type who'd have to examine others first. Sure enough, the lady set the bag beside her and took a brown purse down to look inside.

Cora fought the urge to tap her fingers against the counter. Where were they? Maybe she should call Maddy from the back and go looking for Ralan and the others. What if they needed help? She was about to push away from the counter when the customer started toward the counter, brown and beige purse in tow.

Yep. Called it.

She'd just handed the lady her receipt when the front door opened. Delbin stumbled in, his face pale and haggard, followed by Inona and then Ralan. The customer's steps hitched as she passed them, then sped up markedly. By the time Cora had rushed around the counter, the lady was gone.

"You look like hell," Cora said when she reached Delbin. She stretched out her hand to steady him when he wavered, only to shiver at the cool feel of magic surrounding him. "And that's with a glamour. Why don't you go ahead to the stock room?"

Inona slipped her shoulder under Delbin's arm. Abruptly, he released the glamour, and Cora gasped at the sight of his bloody, bandaged chest. She gestured toward the back room and slipped the lock closed on the shop door. Then she stuck a *Be Back Soon* sign on the glass so she could follow.

They'd barely made it to the counter, so she hurried ahead and opened the stock room door. "Maddy! Counting shoes can wait. We have a problem."

Her friend stuck her head around the edge of a shelf. "What's wrong?"

"Delbin's hurt." She hesitated. They couldn't take him to a human hospital without risking his elven blood being discovered, and there weren't any other healers around. Still, she braced herself to seek another solution. "Do you think you can help?"

Maddy's mouth thinned into a line, but she nodded. Cora hadn't been certain she would. Ever since she'd almost killed someone with a healing spell gone awry, Maddy had avoided much beyond basic training. She'd tried taking nursing classes so she would understand physiology better, but she'd ended up dropping out. Nothing had overcome the memory of the experience.

"He might just need stitches," Cora offered.

"We'll see," Maddy answered, then ducked back behind the shelf.

Cora waved Delbin over to the small desk that held her computer. As Inona helped him into a seat, Ralan met Cora's eyes. "Is your friend a healer?"

"Of a sort," she answered. "How bad is it?"

Ralan shoved his fingers through his hair. "A gash, but it looks like nothing major was hit."

"Easy for you to say," Delbin quipped. "I'm rather fond of my skin."

He was joking at a time like this? Cora's brows quirked, and he winked at her. But she could see the strain beneath the forced humor. "Sounds like you'll live."

Inona shot her an annoyed glance and bent to examine the bandage. Cora grimaced. If she'd hoped to be friends with Delbin's new love, she was rapidly blowing all chances. Little did Inona know

that he'd become too much of a brother-figure for Cora to want to date.

She opened her mouth to explain but closed it at the sight of Maddy rounding the shelf. Her friend was so pale her freckles stood out like embers against her ivory skin, but her chin lifted with resolve as she took in the scene. Though her steps faltered when she saw Delbin's blood-smeared chest, she reached his side in short order.

"I could cauterize the wound if you don't think you—" Cora began.

Maddy interrupted with a frown. "I will handle this. On my honor."

Cora sighed. Honor was well and good, but the Sidhe transformed it into an art. "The offer stands if you change your mind."

"I really hope you don't change your mind," Delbin said.

Unexpectedly, Maddy chuckled. "I won't. Let me grab a chair while your girlfriend removes the bandage."

Inona looked taken aback by the accurate guess, but Cora didn't even blink. Maddy had an uncanny ability to pick up on such nuances.

"Let me get it," Cora said.

Cora slid a chair from the other side of the desk and settled it beside Delbin. Maddy mumbled a "thanks" before turning her attention to her patient. No one spoke, all focus on the bandage Inona slowly unwound. When the deep gash was finally revealed, Cora couldn't hold back a gasp.

She glanced away before her stomach revolted. Why had she been dumb enough to look? She closed her eyes and took a few deep breaths. Good thing Maddy hadn't backed out. Cora would've had to view the wound to cauterize it.

A warm hand gripped her shoulder, and she shivered. Knowing without words who it would be, she opened her eyes to meet Ralan's. "I'm okay."

"You don't seem the squeamish type," he said softly.

"I'm not." At his raised brow, she gave a low chuckle. "At least I didn't think I was."

He scanned her body so intensely she wondered if he had the power to see through clothing. Not a skill she'd ever heard of, but the world was full of variety. Maybe he was secretly Superman. "What?"

"I could find a way to distract you."

Cora snorted. "You really have watched too many movies."

"Oh, hell, would you two stop it?" Maddy grumbled. "This is hard enough as it is."

Her face growing hot, Cora spun away from Ralan. "Sorry."

The prince chuckled, but he backed off, leaning a shoulder against a shelf and crossing his arms with a smirk. Cora sighed and focused on Delbin and Maddy. But not the wound. She didn't need to see the flesh knit back together to know her friend was at work. A low hum filled the room, and then pale green light surrounded Maddy's hand and Delbin's side.

After a moment, her friend jerked away, her chest heaving with each breath. Only then did Cora rush forward to wrap her arm around Maddy's shoulders. Cora risked a glance at Delbin and relaxed to see the wound gone, not even a scar left behind.

"You did it," Cora said, squeezing her friend's shoulder. "See?"

Maddy's breath hissed out. "The spell almost reversed again. What is wrong with me?"

"Hey—"

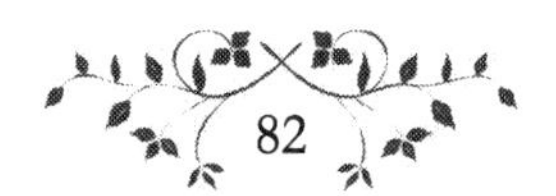

"Don't," her friend snapped. Then she paused to take a deep breath. "Sorry. I'll talk to Dad about it later. Just… I'm going to go count shoe inventory again, okay?"

Cora studied her friend for a moment before nodding. "Fine. But if you need to talk, I'm here."

Maddy nodded. "I know."

Regret stabbed at Cora's heart as she watched her friend dart away. But what choice had she had? No other healers were close enough to help on such short notice, and traveling to another dimension with an injury would have been time-consuming if not dangerous. Poor Maddy. Hopefully, Cora wouldn't have to ask for her help again.

Delbin frowned in the direction Maddy had fled. "She didn't give me the chance to thank her."

"I'll tell her," Cora said. "She's a bit sensitive."

He didn't ask what Maddy had meant about the spell almost reversing. Had he sensed that the magic had almost gone wrong? If he had, he was kind enough not to say so in her friend's hearing. Cora gave him a grateful smile and gestured toward the door to the shop.

"It seems you need a shirt."

Delbin glanced down at his chest and chuckled. "Looks like it."

"Come on, then. You're definitely in the right place.

Ralan stared after Cora as she followed the others out of the room. Damn, he wanted to get to know her better. But should he? All paths led to a painful death for him, so nothing good could come

of a relationship between them. Then she tossed a teasing glance over her shoulder, and all bets were off.

He'd tell her. If she could accept their short time together, maybe—

"Dude," Maddy said as she peeked around the shelf at him. "If you hesitate, you're an idiot."

His brows rose, and he did a quick check of his shields. But she hadn't invaded his mind. "Perceptive."

She snorted. "It's not like you're subtle."

With a laugh, he shoved himself away from the shelf and started after the others. Maddy was right. Couldn't the futures shift? Then Ralan halted in the doorway as a new thought hit. Was the vision of his death any more accurate than anything else these days? Reoccurring dreams like the vision of his death always came true. Always. But the strands had never led him astray before, either, not the way they had been since he'd returned to Moranaia.

Cora looked up from a T-shirt display and caught his gaze. "Everything okay?"

Was it? He smiled slowly. Maybe it would be. Maybe it was time to stop waiting for the future—and create it.

Ralan nodded. "It will be."

8

Ralan dropped into the overstuffed chair beside his bed and let his head fall back. They'd spent hours searching downtown Chattanooga for any sign of Patrick and his friend, but the two had disappeared in the time it had taken to heal Delbin. What a waste of effort. Ralan's feet ached, and he was exhausted from trying to use his talents for so long.

They'd followed at least ten strands that could've led to Kien's servants, but the futures had always deviated just enough. In the end, the only image that had filled Ralan's Sight was the inside of a cavern. And when he'd sent the picture to Delbin, he'd found out that it wasn't even the same damn cave that Delbin and Inona had found Kien in before.

Too bad he couldn't See the strand where all three of them traveled to the cavern. That would've been an easy trail to follow, but no. Either the possibilities were too infinite for a clear picture or they wouldn't find this particular place. Ralan let out a sigh and acknowledged one more possibility—his Sight could still be messed up.

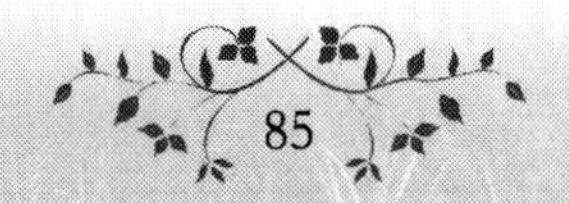

So much for creating the future.

Well, he'd lived without his talent as a seer before. Except for the dreams he'd been unable to stop, Ralan had forgone his Sight for more than three hundred years. At least consciously. He'd slipped back into relying upon it more quickly than he would have expected, so perhaps part of him had never stopped tapping into his gift. Could he ever truly function without it?

There was only one way to find out.

Ralan pushed himself to his feet and strode to the bed to find his backpack. His jaw clenched as he dug inside until he found the small vial hidden in a side pocket. Kien's blood, provided by Delbin and Inona after their failed capture attempt. Blood magic always held risk, so he'd been loath to use it.

Now it might be the only way—but not yet.

He placed the vial back in its slot and pulled out a small mirror instead. After he checked with Lyr to see how Eri was behaving, he would talk to Delbin about another idea he'd had. If Delbin could reestablish himself with the carnival, he might be able to trace information through the groups of fae who hid on Earth. No risky magic involved.

Ralan settled in the chair again and bent over the mirror in his lap. With a surge of magic, he activated the link to the other mirror on Moranaia. If his calculations were correct, it would be rather late there, but Lyr often stayed up working. Then again, now that he was bonded to Meli, he might not be at his desk. A frown creased Ralan's brow, but the mirror flared to life before he could worry about it.

As the image stabilized, Lyr turned in his chair to face the mirror. "Ralan. I was about to seek my bed."

"Sorry," Ralan said automatically, though he was too tired to feel much remorse. "I've just now had a break to check on Eri."

"She has been suspiciously well-behaved. I haven't had word of a single prophecy."

Ralan chuckled. "I'm glad she's keeping her promise."

"You look terrible," Lyr said without hesitation. "Has something happened?"

Ralan provided Lyr a quick rundown of all that had occurred. Well, except that he'd invited Cora to dinner. Some things he preferred to keep to himself. "So far, that's it. I'm going to see about getting Delbin rehired at the carnival. Maybe Kien will try to approach him again."

Lyr's brows rose. "Or kill him."

"I'll make sure he's prepared. Can you spare Inona for longer? She could stay with him."

"I'll find a way," Lyr answered. "She's of better use there. Now go get some sleep."

"I'd say the same to you, but…"

Lyr merely grinned before he cut off the link.

With his own smile, Ralan set the mirror aside. It was good to see his friend happy. After he'd been captured by Allafon and almost killed, Lyr had been a shadow of himself for some time. Meli was good for him.

Ralan tucked the mirror back in his bag. After a glance at the clock, he realized he still had an hour before he needed to get ready for dinner. He dropped face-first onto the bed without bothering to change clothes.

He wouldn't see Cora again until tomorrow, but he'd given her his room number. If something happened, she'd know how to get in

touch with him. *Maybe I should dig out my cell phone,* he thought as his mind began to drift toward sleep. If he was going to be here for a while, he'd like to be able to call her.

If…

Kai stared out the window, barely noting the dim, silver-glazed garden below the observation tower. Arlyn had started calling it the brooding tower, since Lyr often came here to think, and it was apt enough that Kai thought he'd give it a try. A little distance from the world was great for introspection.

Fuck it all, how was he supposed to leave for Lord Naomh's estate tomorrow morning? Kai hated—*hated*—the thought of dragging Arlyn back there, and the place wasn't exactly full of fond memories for him, either. His own father had bound them into a stone wall and almost killed him in a duel. Fun times.

Kai spun from the window and began to pace. Was it really so important for him to learn about any Sidhe powers he might have? He might have felt more connected to earth magic since he'd visited his father's home, but it wasn't something that popped up unexpectedly to cause him trouble. He was fine being a guide and diplomat for Lyr. So why had Ralan insisted? The bastard had refused to give any details.

"He's too cautious."

Kai jumped at the sound of Eri's voice. "Gods! I didn't even sense you."

"You're busy brooding." The little girl grinned. "Great name for this place."

He let out a laugh. "Maybe we should ask Lyr to make it official."

Eri's head tilted, and her expression grew serious. For a long, uncomfortable moment, she studied him. "Do you really want to know why you must go?"

"I don't know," Kai admitted, his shoulders tensing. "Is it worse if I do? And aren't you supposed to be behaving yourself?"

"I promised to keep out of trouble, obey adults, and not use my powers carelessly." Her chin lifted, and he could almost see the woman she would grow to be. "This isn't careless, and no one told me I had to stay in my room."

Kai added *be very specific* to his mental list of parenting rules. "Fair enough. So what do you want to tell me?"

"There's a lot you don't know." A hint of worry and maybe fear entered her eyes. "A lot no one knows. I wish…I wish I didn't know."

Her whispered words hung between them. "Eri—"

"I'm fine," she interrupted. "The Goddess guides and comforts me. That's not why I'm here. See, you have two choices right now. Go as planned or stay here. Don't stay. Arlyn and I will need your mastery of earth magic, and it doesn't matter why right now. Suck it up and do what needs to be done."

Kai blinked, taken aback by the stern tone of her young voice. "You can't be only six."

A grin broke across her face. "Megelien says I'm feisty."

"You seem…close to her."

"My daddy is a good father, but I've never had a mother." Eri shrugged. "Lady Megelien is the closest I've come."

He frowned. "But you were born on Earth. Raised there until a couple of months ago. You couldn't have known Her for long."

"Couldn't I? The Lady goes where she wants." Kai wanted to ask more, but Eri shook her head before he could form the words. "You don't need to know. Just stop brooding and go to bed. That's where I'm heading."

She spun away and started down the stairs without another word. Kai stared after her. Had he just been bossed around by a child? He let out a laugh. Yeah. Yeah, he had. Thank all the gods Ralan had put Lyr in charge of her instead of him and Arlyn.

Cora flipped the sign to closed and locked the door. Then she turned to face her friend at the counter. "Are you sure you're okay?"

Maddy let out a long sigh. "It sucks, but I'll be fine. Just…try not to ask me to heal anyone again anytime soon."

"Here's hoping," Cora said as she approached. "Though I'm kind of worried that creep will come back. Did he threaten you? You looked really upset."

Maddy's lips firmed into a line. "He said he could tell I'm just a wimpy healer."

"What?"

"There's something wrong with that guy," her friend answered. "I could sense that he's part-Sidhe, and he could tell the same about me. But there's a darkness within him that reminds me of an Unseelie."

Cora thought the prejudice held by the Seelie for the so-called dark fae went a bit too far, but it wasn't a debate she wanted to have right now. "We'll just have to stay cautious. Jase will be here tomorrow for the weekend rush, so we'll have an extra pair of eyes. In fact, why don't we make sure we leave together today?"

"Good plan."

By the time they headed down the side street toward the parking lot, Cora had begun to wonder if she was being paranoid. More than usual, anyway. The guy seemed to want her help finding Ralan's brother, but there was no reason to hurt her. He had to know she wouldn't help him then. And although he'd seen her with Ralan, he might not assume they were together.

Or the guy would conclude the worst and come after her. It had happened before when she'd refused to take sides between factions. If he did, it wouldn't be in view of any human. She'd shield her house extra strongly and sleep with an iron knife next to her bed. The metal didn't give *her* any trouble, but it was hell on the Sidhe.

The parking lot came into view. "There. Tomorrow—"

"Hey, stop," a voice called from an alley to her left.

Cora slipped her arm through Maddy's and picked up the pace. A man stepped from the alley, but she didn't relax when she saw that it wasn't Patrick. "I'm armed," she warned him.

Of course, she was armed with fire, not a gun, but he didn't have to know that.

"Just looking for directions, ladies."

The man tried for a non-threatening smile. Honestly, there was nothing about him that was strictly menacing. He had soft brown hair and an easy expression, and he wore a tourist T-shirt from the aquarium. His body language was relaxed, his hands shoved in his pockets. But none of that mattered when his energy washed over them like fetid water.

"Yeah, right," Cora answered.

Maddy jerked against her hold. But when Cora looked to see what was wrong, her chest squeezed tight. Patrick had slipped up behind them and tugged Maddy against him. Sure enough, he held a blade against her stomach.

Not obvious to anyone who happened to pass by.

As a car turned down the side street, Patrick leaned down to kiss Maddy's cheek, like a lover sneaking up as a surprise. But if the driver noticed the distress on Maddy's face, he didn't stop to find out what was wrong. Cora cursed under her breath and glanced at the other guy.

His affable smile had turned to a smirk, and as he ambled over to Cora, he leered. "Good instincts. Well, except for detecting Patrick."

Cora's teeth ground together, and her palms began to heat. "Let her go. We don't know anything about your friend."

"Oh, we don't care about that. We'll figure out another way to find him," the guy said in a mocking tone. "Patrick found us a little healer. A pretty one, too. If Kien's hurt, he'll thank us for bringing him this piece. Then maybe he'll forgive Patrick for being an idiot."

Cora eased closer to her friend. If she could touch Patrick, he'd pay in fire. "An idiot?"

Instead of answering, his hand darted out, and she reacted without thinking. Her own hand shot up to meet his, her power sparking into him the second they made contact. He squealed, a high-pitched cry, as she scorched his palm. The awful smell of burned skin wafted around them, mixing with the musty smell of the nearby river.

The man dropped to his knees and jerked his arm from her hold. As he gathered his palm close and wailed, Cora whirled back to help Maddy. But now the knife was at her friend's neck.

"Come closer and she dies," Patrick said, the blade wavering in his shaking hand.

Cora was almost afraid to breathe. "Don't do this."

"I don't care if we need a healer. I'll slice her throat if you take a step my way." Patrick's throat bobbed with nerves. "Get off the ground, Victor. We'll make this one fix it."

Eyes filled with hate, Victor shoved himself to his feet and sidled around Cora.

What could she do? Everything within Cora wanted to blast them with a fireball and damn any humans who might see. But even without any passerby, she couldn't do it. Not with Maddy solidly between her and Patrick.

Her friend met Cora's gaze. "Don't."

"Better listen," Patrick said. "We won't hurt her. Not if she's… cooperative."

Cora wanted to vomit at the insinuating lilt to his tone. "If you dare—"

"Shut up, bitch," Victor snarled.

The two backed away a few more paces, then turned and jogged to a nearby car. Cora almost cried out at the sight of Maddy bouncing in Patrick's hold, and she could only hope he'd shifted the knife from her friend's throat. Helplessness boiled within her until she wanted to scream. But as Patrick rammed Maddy into the back seat, Cora shoved down her anger and examined her options.

First things first? Find Ralan.

With a groan, Ralan rolled onto his back. What the hell was that sound? *Crack, crack, crack*. Construction? He opened one bleary eye and tried to shake off sleep. The table next to his bed came into focus. Then the rest of his hotel room. Couldn't be construction here, could it?

Crack, crack, crack.

The door! Ralan shot out of bed, running his hand through his hair as he headed toward the sound. He peeked through the peep hole even as he tried to pull a snarl from his long hair. But when he saw Cora's face on the other side, all other thoughts fled.

He turned the locks and jerked the door open. She froze, gaping at him with her hand still lifted to knock, and he considered that he had to be an amusing sight. He only hoped he didn't have drool anywhere.

"Cora." He blinked against the sleep in his eyes and glanced along the hall. Empty. "What's going on?"

Her hand lowered. "Can I come in?"

"Of course."

Ralan stepped back and gestured for her to enter. Then he looked out again and frowned. If she'd been pounding on his door for a while, why hadn't Delbin and Inona come out to see what was wrong? He checked the clock as he followed Cora in. Well, that explained it. He'd slept for over two hours. They must have gone for dinner without him.

A vague memory filtered through. His bedside phone ringing. A mumbled conversation. Maybe he'd told them to bring something back? He tended to sleep deeply when he'd used his talents so much.

He rubbed at his face and focused on Cora. "Our date is tomorrow, isn't it? Not that I mind you coming to my room."

Her gaze took in the rumpled bed before returning to him. "Sorry to wake you, but this is important. Patrick and some guy named Victor… They took Maddy."

"Took Maddy?" His exhaustion fled at her words, and he pulled her into a hug as her composure crumpled and tears began to roll down her face. "Tell me."

Cora rested her forehead in the V between his neck and shoulder. Her tears wet his shirt, but he didn't mind. "We were leaving the shop. They cornered us. I tried to use my fire on the one called Victor, but Patrick had Maddy at knife-point. I couldn't…"

"It's okay," Ralan soothed. His sigh ruffled her hair. "Well, not okay. But we'll find her. I'll search the futures and see if I can find a trail."

She leaned back to frown at him. "Isn't there only one future?"

His smile was gentle. "No. Each choice makes a new strand of possibilities. Some are more likely. Sometimes they merge with different choices. The first thing you learn as a seer is that nothing is set."

Cora took a deep breath and stepped out of his arms. "If you can find her…"

"I'll try." Ralan pulled an elastic band from his pocket and tied his hair back. Then he dropped onto the overstuffed chair. "Everything about this situation is causing me trouble. I'm missing things I should have Seen. Letting people down. But I'll do what I can."

Expression inscrutable, she studied him for a moment. "I'm surprised you admitted it. You're always so arrogant on the runway, and rumor has it you're a hard-ass in the workroom."

"Mostly part of the persona. And in this case, I can't afford pride." He thought back to Arlyn's and Kai's capture. He'd insisted the mission would be safe, never Seeing the danger. Just today, he'd missed the threat to Delbin. Now this. "I refuse to offer false hope."

Cora gave a sharp nod. "Just do your best."

Ralan settled back in the seat and let his eyes slip closed. For a long moment, he concentrated on his breathing, blocking out all else. Then he slipped into the maelstrom of the strands. His head throbbed at the breathless number of them, but he steadied himself out of long practice.

Only then did he begin his search.

9

Maddy winced against the pain in her head and struggled to open her eyes. Finally, she managed it, but she immediately wished she hadn't. The grinning face of her captor was the first thing she saw. Then her hazy memory crystalized. The bastard had actually hit her.

She shifted, and relief filled her when she realized nothing else hurt. Well, except for a spot on her hip where a rock stabbed her. Maddy gathered her strength and pushed herself to sitting. All around her, stalagmites rose, and when she glanced up, she saw stalactites spearing down, mage lights hovering between them. They'd brought her to a cave? A small one, but definitely a cave.

"Thanks for joining us," Patrick said.

Maddy's lips twisted. "Like I had a choice."

"Look, just cooperate. I meant what I told your friend."

"That you need a healer to help you?" A helpless chuckle slipped free. "Boy, did you kidnap the wrong chick."

Patrick scowled. "I can sense your power. Don't bother lying."

"You're the one who said I'm wimpy."

"Healers are weak. Easy to kidnap, for sure," Patrick said with a smirk. "They only want to help people, not hurt them, and they have no idea how to fight."

Oh, he had no idea. Maddy almost laughed again. She was more likely to do damage than help. "Just know this. Try to rape me, and I'll make sure you never have sex again."

His eyes widened, and a choked sound slipped from his lips. "You can't."

"There are two sides to healing magic, you know," Maddy told him.

But she left it at that.

"I'm not…" Patrick swallowed hard. "I wouldn't do that. But try not to rile up Victor until Kien's here to keep him in line."

"How can you bear it?" she asked. "Betraying your own kind?"

His cheeks flushed red, and his nostrils flared. "I was abandoned by my kind."

Comprehension flooded her. He might be another half-blood, but his life had been in no way similar. "I'm sorry."

"Save it." Patrick glared at her. "Just behave, and you'll get out of this alive. Probably."

He jerked to his feet and strode to the cave's entrance, leaving her alone. But she had no illusions of escape, not at this point. Maddy pulled her legs up and settled her head on her knees. A shiver went through her as the coolness of the cave seeped through her thin dress.

What had happened to Cora? Would she find help? Maddy fought back a sudden surge of tears. Would she ever see Anna again?

Thank goodness she'd told her she loved her before leaving the house this morning. If she made it out of here, she would be sure to say the words a million times a day.

For Anna, she would fight to survive.

Gods, Ralan wished he could see the past. He'd found an image of Maddy inside a cave, but her journey there was a blank. Now even the futures were murky. Sometimes, she fought. In a few, she was badly hurt. Tortured once. Killed. In many, she escaped. She managed to injure Kien in one. But no matter how many strands he searched, he couldn't find her location.

"Dammit," he cursed, finally opening his eyes.

"That bad?" a pale Cora asked.

Ralan's breath hissed out. "She's in a cave, but I couldn't find where. There are many things that could happen, and I won't lie. Some of them are bad. Most aren't."

"Did you foresee us saving her?"

"No." Ralan's hands clenched into fists. Another failure. "I didn't See anything about us at all. Those strands are just…missing."

"Missing?" she demanded.

His insides twisted at the anger and fear he saw in her eyes. "The goddess blocks me. If it involves me and Kien, the strands remain out of reach."

"What am I going to do?" Cora dropped onto the side of the bed. "Her mother's human. Her father is Sidhe, but he's a jeweler not a warrior. Maybe he can track her. I don't know. And Maddy's girlfriend. I need to tell her, too."

Ralan wanted to slam his fist into the wall. He wanted to bellow in rage. But how could he add to the fear that flowed from Cora in a steady stream? He speared his fingers into his hair and tugged, the bite of pain grounding him. He couldn't. There had to be some solution.

He'd already decided to send Delbin to the carnival to gather information. Would that be quick enough to help with the search for Maddy? Ralan closed his eyes and scanned the strands leading from the decision. Delbin working a ride. A man approaching. Then the vision blurred before cutting off in yet another dead end.

"What is it?" Cora asked.

Ralan's eyes snapped open. "I had a plan, but I can't see the outcome."

Frowning, Cora nibbled on her lower lip. After a moment, she shrugged. "Maybe that's a good thing. If you can't see futures involving you and your brother, then you should follow the blank spots."

The idea was so obvious Ralan almost groaned, but such a plan would still be dangerous. He wouldn't be able to avert danger once his Sight became too obscured. He'd be going in blind in a way he never had, not when he needed to do something that truly mattered. In his time on Earth, he had relied on telepathy and the contacts he'd made among humans and fae, and that had been enough. It wouldn't be now.

Wait. Contacts.

Ralan rounded the bed and lifted his bag from the floor. As Cora stared, eyebrow raised, he dug inside until his fingers connected with smooth glass. His phone. But once he pulled it out, he discovered a new problem. He might have decided to include it in his packing at the last minute, but he hadn't remembered the charger.

"I need to find a store."

She jerked to her feet, anger darkening her expression. "Now? You're kidding me."

"Hold on." Ralan held up the phone. "I know people, Cora. They may not be able to help, but it's worth checking. Unfortunately, my phone is dead."

Cora frowned. "And?"

"I can't remember their phone numbers." He shrugged sheepishly. "I need to find a store or go back to my estate in New York for the charger. A shopping trip seems more efficient."

"Let me see it," she huffed.

Wordlessly, Ralan handed her the phone and waited while she examined it. "I've got one like this at home. But I guess a store would be just as fast."

He had the urge to argue that point. He'd love to see her home, to learn more about her in such an intimate space. But speed was important, and he would not delay the search for Maddy to satisfy his own curiosity. He'd like to have plenty of time with Cora if they were ever alone in her home. His body heated, and he forced his mind to other things before she realized the direction his thoughts had taken.

"Let me check and see if Delbin's back from dinner," Ralan said.

Ralan sent his senses out, nudging against the shield Delbin had wrapped around his room. He gave a mental pluck, a twinge that would alert Delbin to his presence, and waited. A moment later, a knock sounded on the door joining their rooms. Sensing his student, Ralan hurried to open the door.

Delbin rubbed his fingers against his temples and glared. "You could've used the room phone, you know."

"This was faster." Ralan grinned. "Besides, you should've embedded a communication line in the shield."

"Guess so," Delbin grumbled.

Ralan's humor faded as he prepared to discuss the latest events. "Where's Inona?"

"Here," she called as she stepped out of the bathroom.

"Something has happened," Ralan said. "I need you both in here."

"What's wrong?" Delbin asked as he followed Ralan across the threshold.

But Ralan waited until Inona had joined them before he gestured at Cora. "Maddy, her shop assistant, was kidnapped by Patrick and his friend."

"Fuck," Delbin spat.

Ralan nodded. "Basically. I've tried to search the strands without luck. We're going to have to find her the standard way."

Frowning, Inona slipped her arm through Delbin's. "Why did they take her? I thought Patrick was trying to get Cora's help to find Kien. What does your friend have to do with it?"

"Because she's a healer," Cora answered. "They said they'd figure out another way to find Kien. They want Maddy in case he's hurt."

Delbin glanced between them. "So what's the plan?"

"You rejoin the carnival," Ralan said. "Inona can work with you. In one strand, you are approached there. I'm not sure why or who, but it wasn't Patrick or Victor. I believe that strand will lead us closer to Kien."

"You believe?" Delbin asked, eyebrows raised.

Ralan's jaw clenched. "We can't rely on my Sight. It is at best a suggestion these days."

Thankfully, Delbin didn't give him a hard time. "I know Grunge held a spot for me. I'm sure he'll let Inona help out, too. What else?"

"I have to get a charger for my phone. Then I'll call some of my contacts." A new thought occurred to him. "Cora, what about you? Delbin said you're well-liked among the local fae. Don't you have contacts?"

Her face flushed. "Yes. I should've thought, but I…the only thing I could think about was getting to you. Crazy since we just met."

Despite the situation, Ralan's heart warmed. She must feel the potential bond between them, though she might not know what it meant. "Not crazy, but I hope the effort wasn't wasted. Know that I'll do what I can to help your friend. Anything for you."

Ralan held Cora's gaze as heat flashed between them. If they were alone…

Delbin cleared his throat. "So. Hand me your phone."

"My phone?" Ralan blinked at his student, but he passed it over. "Why?"

"Watch and learn, Master," Delbin answered with a grin.

Phone in his left hand, Delbin closed his eyes and lifted his right. Energy trickled into his palm, heating the air around them. Then he lowered his hand to the phone and pushed the energy slowly through. Ralan's mouth fell open as Delbin held down the power button and the phone's screen flared to life.

"How in the hell?"

Delbin's grin widened. "You should've hung out with more misfits. We know lots of tricks like that."

Beside him, Cora muttered, "I didn't know that one."

"Magic is just another form of energy." Delbin shrugged. "Find the right frequency and you can power things that require electricity. Don't practice on your phone, though. It's easy to fry stuff."

Ralan shook his head in disbelief. His student had lived on Earth a quarter of the time Ralan had, yet he seemed to know a great many more tricks. "I suppose it pays to arrive here near the technological age."

"Don't feel bad," Delbin said, humor lacing his tone. "I bet you could beat me at a horse and carriage race."

For once, Ralan didn't have a ready rejoinder.

Inona tugged at Delbin's arm. "Pester each other later. We have work to do."

"I agree." Cora shoved her hand into her purse and pulled out her own phone. "Starting now. I'll begin by contacting Maddy's father."

"I'll call us a ride to the carnival," Delbin said as his smirk faded.

Ralan rubbed his hand across the back of his neck. "Fine. Good. Think your telepathy can reach me across the city?"

Delbin shrugged again. "It should. I'll give you my phone number just in case."

In a matter of moments, Delbin and Inona had departed, and Cora stood over to the side speaking softly into her phone. Ralan forced down a surge of frustration as he searched through his contact list. Dammit, he should've been able to solve this years ago. Kien should already be captured or dead.

Now, Ralan could barely even See him.

Kien slumped against a tree trunk and stared at the gap in the ridge that held the portal. Only a few more steps and he could regain his energy at the gate. Once he'd worked his way free from beneath the house, he'd discovered the reason for his slow recovery. When the Moranaian couple had captured him, they'd thrown him into the truck bed without thought. The impact had cracked the crystal that kept the energy poisoning from affecting him.

Sickened by his own damned spell.

He'd come too far, too close to stopping Ralan, to quit now. He'd worked with the half-bloods and that fool Sidhe Naomh, trying to poison the energy fields on Earth. Not only would the poison have killed Ralan's daughter, but the half-bloods had been willing to help Kien break the enchantment keeping him from returning to Moranaia.

Now his initial spell lay in tatters—but it could be rebuilt.

Scowling, Kien shoved away from the tree. It would all be worth it. As soon as he regained his energy, he'd put his newest plan in place. This time, he wouldn't use a subtle poison that took years. But he would need Fen.

No matter how much he longed to torture the little half-Unseelie traitor until the whelp burned himself into dust.

10

Ralan dropped onto the side of the bed and held back a groan of frustration. His contact, Thom, had been unable to help. The older elf had lived on Earth for several hundred years, but his base of operations was firmly in the northeast. He'd said he would see what he could do, but Ralan didn't hold out much hope.

"How can two fae just…disappear?" Cora asked as she sank down beside him.

Ralan's brows lowered. "Assassins were causing trouble for a friend not long ago. They had cloaks that hid them. But Patrick was dressed in human clothes."

"Maybe they found another way."

"How long has this been going on, Cora?" Ralan shifted to face her. "As soon as the energy poisoning began, I spent most of my time trying to keep my daughter alive. I've since learned that many of the Sidhe realms have been affected. With such an underground of fae, why hasn't anything been done?"

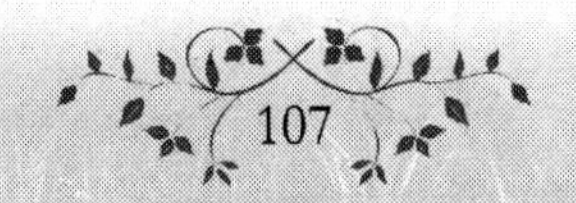

She let out a long sigh. "I don't know. It hasn't been that bad here until a couple of months ago. I've heard whispers, but no one has been able to track down the source. Then several days ago, something happened. The bad energy fractured and started to heal. Everyone I've spoken to is confused. Frightened."

Ralan settled his hand over hers. She froze, but she didn't pull away. "Did it cause you trouble?"

"No." Cora hesitated, then turned her hand over and laced her fingers with his. "I don't draw in energy the same way. Maybe someday I'll tell you the difference. *If* I get to know you better."

"I certainly hope I get to know you better." His lips curved slowly upward. "Very well, in fact."

He heard her breath hitch. "How can I feel so close to you in a day?"

Ralan ran his fingertips down her cheek. "Perhaps we're meant for each other."

"Hah," Cora said, though she smiled softly. "A romantic thought, but I don't think I'm meant for anyone. Trust me."

His fingers stilled, and a frown creased his brow at the sadness that entered her eyes. What had put that belief into her head? Some past rejection? Cora was kind, talented, and beautiful. It would take a special kind of fool to reject her. Well, it could be his gain.

Ralan leaned closer. Their breaths mingled, lips so close he could almost taste her, and she didn't push him away. "May I?"

"I—"

Ping.

They both jumped at the sharp noise from Cora's phone. She let out a breathless laugh and looked down. Then her amusement cut off. "Anna."

Ralan shoved down his disappointment and forced himself to lean back. "One of your contacts?"

"Maddy's girlfriend," Cora whispered. She stared at the phone for a moment, her expression pained. "She texted me to see if Maddy had worked late because she isn't home yet. I don't know what to tell her."

"Go ahead and call," Ralan said gently.

"I…" Cora stared at him for a moment. Then she shook her head. "Never mind. I'll do that now."

As Ralan headed into the bathroom, he considered Cora's conflicted expression. Had she been upset that he'd almost kissed her? Gods, he hoped not. The timing might be awful, but he had every intention of trying again. Maybe more than kissing, though he'd have to confess to his impending death first.

He wouldn't add to the pain he'd seen in her eyes if he could help it.

By the time Ralan brushed the snarls from his hair and returned to the bedroom, Cora had finished. She huddled in the overstuffed chair, looking bleak. He longed to gather her close, to offer comfort. But most of all, he longed to fix the problem.

"Let's head into town," he said.

Her gaze flicked to his. "Did you have a vision?"

"No, but I have other talents." He stepped closer. "If I have to scan every mind in Chattanooga for a clue, I will."

Her small smile was tinged with sadness. "Her father is scanning for her energy signature through their blood connection. Maybe between all of us, we'll find her soon."

Blood. He could use the vial of his brother's, but if Patrick and Victor hadn't yet tracked down Kien, the blood wouldn't lead to

Maddy. Though it would take time to use telepathy on so many, it was the surer bet right now.

And it was one thing he knew he could do.

"Yo, Delbin, been on vacation?" Rick called from his tent near Grunge's trailer.

"Nope," Delbin answered. "Family emergency."

Rick winced, and regret pinched his face. "Damn, I'm sorry. I hope everything's okay. I wouldn't have given you grief if I'd known."

"It's fine. Everything is better at home now." True enough, except that Delbin had no real home. But the other man was human. No way Delbin could explain the complexity of his situation. "Don't worry about it."

"If you say so." Rick eyed Inona. "Hey, that your sister?"

Delbin settled his hand against Inona's lower back. "Nope."

Though he let out a dramatic groan, Rick's smile seemed genuine. "Can't blame a guy for hoping."

"If he messes things up, I'll let you know," Inona said, poking Delbin in the side.

Rick's laughter followed them to the door of the trailer. Delbin paused, eyebrow raised, and caught Inona's eye. "Getting tired of me already?"

"No." But she grinned. "Maybe your humor is wearing off on me."

"That's not the only thing I'd like to—"

The door creaked open, and Grunge poked his head out. "Get in here and stop flirting on my doorstep, would you?"

Delbin chuckled and motioned for Inona to precede him. Once he'd followed, Grunge shut the door behind them. Delbin joined Inona beside the small bench seat across from the tiny kitchen counter. The travel trailer was old school, the amount of standing room almost non-existent, but he didn't sit down. No way he would offend the Sidhe if he could help it.

Not that Grunge looked like one of the Sidhe. His glamour was a strong one, and until recently, Delbin had never seen him as anything but an older human male with scraggly, gray hair. Only after Inona's arrival had Grunge let him glimpse the elegant male beneath the lie.

"Guessing you didn't catch the elf responsible for that bad energy," the fae said without preamble. "Unless you're here to say your goodbyes."

Delbin winced. "You got it the first time. Are you still holding a job for me?"

"Reckon so." Grunge leaned his shoulder against the doorframe. "I could find some work for your girlfriend if need be."

"Yes, please," Inona said.

"There's only one condition," the Sidhe said. "You tell me what the hell is going on."

Night was falling and most of the shops had closed by the time Cora and Ralan made their way down the street. Cora's hands curled into fists as they passed one more Closed sign a block away from her store. How were they supposed to gather clues when everyone was gone? But Ralan looked as calm as ever. Was he even scanning minds?

His fingers, warm and firm, wrapped around her wrist as he halted. His eyes found hers as he uncurled her hand and lifted it to his lips. "The server in the restaurant just ahead saw Patrick. We're going the right way."

Cora frowned over at the restaurant two stores away. "You can read people at such a distance?"

"If they're human," he answered with a shrug. "It's a rare human who knows how to shield themselves from such things."

She grimaced at that. Though telepathy wasn't her strongest talent, even she had been bombarded by the humans' thoughts when she'd first arrived. "It must drive you insane at your strength."

"I was well-trained in my gift," he answered. "I imagine Delbin had it far worse when he was sent here."

"The prince and the exile," Cora said with a shake of her head. "How did that come about?"

"That's a long story. Perhaps I'll tell you when we get to know each other better."

She laughed at the echo of her earlier words and returned his sly grin. "Touché."

Cora didn't protest when he took her hand in his and resumed their walk down the street. Now that they were touching, she could feel the energy humming through him, making her fingers tingle with the force of it. But she didn't let go. She couldn't say why, but just touching Ralan brought her a sense of comfort she'd never quite experienced before.

Still, nothing could ease the sick feeling slithering through her, filling her with anxious tension tinged with guilt. How could she

smile and flirt when her friend was in such danger? Cora pulled her hand from Ralan's. She needed to keep their task in mind.

Ralan gave her a questioning look. "Cora?"

She blew out a breath. "My mind keeps circling back to what Maddy must be going through."

"She's a healer," he said. "I wouldn't want to mess with her."

Cora knew he meant to reassure her, but his words did nothing to lessen her anxiety. "She barely has any control over her gift."

"That makes her even more dangerous."

"It does," Cora agreed. "But it's so hard on her when she messes up. I'm afraid of the harm this could cause her. Mentally. She's so young, Ralan. Only twenty-three."

Now Ralan's hands clenched. "We'll do our best to save her."

Though she could hear the resolve in his voice, her stomach churned with dread. He might want to help. But could he?

Hours later, they stood beside her car, no closer to finding Maddy than when they'd set out. Ralan had found two more memories of Patrick, but neither had been helpful. No images of his car or where he might have ultimately gone. Cora twisted her keys in her hand and tried to push down her anger and her fear.

It wasn't Ralan's fault.

His fingers traced her cheek, and she shivered. "I don't know what to do," she said.

"Get some rest." Ralan took a step closer. "We'll set out early. How's your knowledge of local caves?"

"There could be thousands of them," she answered wryly.

He leaned closer, staring at her mouth as though he wanted to kiss her. But he looked away instead. "We'll look for a map."

"I'll search the internet when I get home." Great Divine, but she wanted to shift nearer. Let her lips connect with his. Then her thoughts turned to Maddy, and she grasped for the door handle behind her. "You should rest, too. You used a lot of energy tonight."

Ralan shrugged. "Not as much as you might think, but I will do so."

It took all of her willpower to tell him goodnight and climb into her car. As she backed out and started out of the hotel parking lot, she caught sight of him in the rearview mirror. Watching her as she watched him. Whatever the draw between them, it was a powerful one. If not for Maddy's kidnapping, Cora had little doubt she would've been spending the night in Ralan's bed.

Her body heated, and her hands tightened on the steering wheel. She had no problem with sex—passion was a blessing, and she had been lucky enough to have some amazing lovers over the last eight hundred years. But she had a feeling that sex with Ralan would eclipse anything she'd ever known. *Hah.* Cora shook her head at herself. Their chemistry was intense, but *eclipse*?

A tall order, that.

Maddy shivered against the cold floor and considered for the millionth time how she could escape. Night had long ago fallen, but the cave was at least bright. The one called Patrick had suspended a few more mage lights from several of the stalactites before taking his turn at the door. Now she was stuck in here with Victor, who eyed her with suspicion.

"I know you're lying when you say you can use your power to hurt," he finally said.

She tipped her chin up. "Then why haven't you asked me to heal your hand?"

Victor shifted his hand closer to his chest at the reminder. "You need to save your energy for Kien."

"Sure," she said with a snort.

The murmur of voices sounded from the cave entrance, then a muffled shout. Maddy tensed. Was it the person they'd been waiting for? After a moment, Patrick darted inside. Another man trailed him, and at first sight, her body stiffened with fear. Not because of his startling paleness or his scowl. It was the energy that hovered around him like a cloud, that tinge of predatory darkness that made her skin prickle.

Unseelie.

Victor jerked to his feet. "Fen! What in the hell are you doing here? Kien will flay you alive as soon as he sees you."

Maddy sank in on herself, trying to avoid attention. His kind hated hers. *Hated.* He could suck her energy dry without a thought. Gods. Her head spun, but she didn't dare take her eyes off the newcomer to reorient herself.

"Then I'll just have to convince him he needs me," Fen said in a low voice.

A deceptively beautiful voice, Maddy thought at she shuddered.

His pale blue eyes turned her way. "My, my. What did you two find?"

"A healer," Victor said. "A useless one, too."

Fen ambled closer, not seeming to notice when she scooted herself back. What little good that did. His fingers gripped her chin, and her whole body trembled. But she met his gaze with a glare. A Seelie Sidhe wouldn't yield to the likes of him.

"How old are you?" he asked.

"None of your business," Maddy spat.

Fen's laugh rang out, rich and dangerous. "Young, then."

Shock coursed through her as the Unseelie released her and spun to face the others. He hadn't made any attempt to drain her energy, though he could have. He hadn't insulted her, either. But she'd hardly become complacent. If there was one thing his kind enjoyed, it was tormenting hers.

"You can't just come back here and expect to be welcomed," Patrick said.

Fen chuckled again. "It's not up to you, is it? It's up to Kien."

"He's still missing," Victor said. "Thanks to you."

"Yes, well," Fen drawled. "Lucky for you I know how to track him."

Maddy drew her knees to her chest and struggled to get air into her lungs. Of course the dark fae knew how to track the bad guy. Of course. Lucky was far from the word she'd use right now.

Very far.

11

Ralan held his daughter's gaze through the mirror. "You're certain you're behaving yourself?"

Her grin lit up his world. "I've listened to all the adults like you told me to."

"And?" he asked, not fooled by her evasion.

"I only gave Lord Kai one little nudge," Eri admitted. She didn't bother looking contrite, but he wouldn't have believed her if she had. "I didn't want your work to go to waste."

Ralan's brow creased. "He considered disobeying my order?"

"You didn't know there was a chance he would?" she countered.

"I was distracted by my vision of Cora," Ralan said with a wince.

Eri only laughed. "Don't stress it, *Onaial.* You're doing what you're supposed to do."

Her words chilled him despite her easy tone, and power glinted in her golden eyes for the briefest flash. Ralan leaned closer to the mirror. "Please give my regards to Megelien."

Eri blinked, and the hint of power was gone. "Okay."

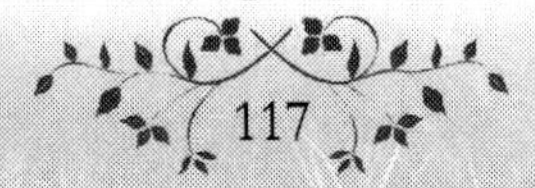

Ralan stared at his daughter, almost overcome with the desire to ask her what she knew. Then shame coursed through him. Eri was only six and already burdened with the Sight. How could he ask that of her? He knew well enough what it was like to have those around him demanding answers about the future. Answers he dared not give for fear of ruining it all. But Eri's Sight wasn't blocked—she might be able to tell him much.

"Stop getting upset," she said. "I will freely tell you all I can. But if I don't offer…"

"Then you can't," he finished. "I recommend you not disobey Lady Megelien. Trust me."

Eri's lips turned down. "This isn't only anger, *Onaial.* These paths…a seer could ruin the future. Your very Sight could ruin everything. Someday, you'll see."

"Maybe," Ralan said. If she hadn't foreseen his death, he wasn't going to enlighten her. "Ah, Eri. You should not be weighed down with this."

A hint of a smile crossed her face. "It's fun if you let it be."

Fun. Never in his life had he thought of the futures in quite that way. But he'd made certain Eri didn't grow up with the same expectations he'd had. She would be no one's pet seer, not even the king's.

Certainly not Ralan's when *he* finally became king.

A knock sounded at the door, and Ralan sent out a quick tendril of energy. Cora. "I need to go now, love. Remember your promise to behave."

"I'll do my best," Eri answered, his own wicked smirk crossing her lips. "I love you. Tell Cora I said hi."

"I will. I love you, too," he said. "Always."

Though his heart pinched as he closed the connection, Ralan didn't have time to dwell on missing his daughter. As Cora knocked again, he set the mirror down and hurried toward the door. He tugged it open, and happiness curled through him at the sight of his bonded. This morning, she wore jeans and a snug T-shirt, and her hair was pulled back in a braid. Gorgeous.

She eyed him curiously. "Were you talking to yourself?"

Ralan chuckled. "No. Come in and I'll explain."

She still looked dubious, but she strode past him and waited for him to close the door before speaking again. "Did you hear from Delbin?"

"No." Ralan walked to the bed and lifted the mirror, holding it up so she could see. "I called home to speak with my daughter. Eri sends her regards."

Cora frowned. "You've spoken to her about me?"

"I didn't have to," he answered as his shoulders slumped. "She's a seer, too."

Cora stared at him for a moment. "I take it that's not a good thing."

"It's a difficult thing."

Ralan tucked the mirror into his backpack and slung it over his shoulders. Most housekeepers were honest, but he wasn't going to leave a bag containing magical implements and his brother's blood behind during cleaning hours. Aside from theft, he'd rather the human police not get involved. It would take hours to wipe that many memories.

"Did you find anything useful on the internet?" he asked.

She tucked a strand of hair behind her ear. "Not much. There's plenty of information on the touristy caves like Ruby Falls or Raccoon Mountain. I might be able to find a book or map at one of those places. Gift shops almost always have that kind of stuff."

"Think they'll be open?" He glanced at the clock. Just after eight. "A lot of the stores downtown probably won't be. Speaking of which, what about yours?"

Cora grimaced. "Poor Jase is by himself for most of the day. My part-timer can't be there until the afternoon. He can handle it, though."

"Any word from Maddy's father?"

"He can tell she's alive." Cora's expression hardened. "But her energy signature is muffled."

Ralan cursed. "Let's go, then. We aren't going to find her here."

By the time Cora settled across from Ralan in the diner's booth, she was ready to scream. She jerked the lunch menu from the metal holder to the side, but she didn't bother to look at it. Useless. All of their searching had been useless. She hadn't been able to find a book on local caves, and Ralan's mental scans around town had yielded nothing but a couple of quick sightings.

She met Ralan's gaze. "What are we going to do?"

"Think of something else." He placed his hand over hers and squeezed softly. But his eyes held none of the patience of his touch. "Scour the area. There are thousands of strands from this point."

"Any of them muddled?" she asked, leaning forward.

His jaw clenched. "All of them past a few branchings."

Before she could comment, their server appeared, a cheerful young man who looked college aged. Probably a student. Cora forced a smile to her face as he asked for their order. She glanced down at the menu and picked the first thing that caught her eye, a cheeseburger. Good enough. Shrugging, she ordered it with fries and a soda.

"I'll have the same," Ralan said, then tucked the menu back into the holder without even looking.

Once their server headed toward the kitchen, Cora's thoughts returned to Maddy. Her father said she was still alive. But well? Cora's stomach clenched and her mouth went dry. How could she sit and eat when her friend was trapped and terrified? Would they ever find her? She only had Ralan's word that Maddy was in a cave at all, and his Sight seemed far from reliable.

If he was wrong, well…the kidnappers could have taken her anywhere.

"I should have gotten their license plate," Cora said. "Chased the car down. Something."

Ralan took her hand in his. "You know, there are only so many caves they could easily drive to. Correct?"

"Maybe." Cora considered the question. Quite a few took hours to hike to, but how many would be accessible, and inconspicuous, for two guys with a captive woman? "Let's skip more walking downtown. We can check out trailheads and parking lots for the car."

"Sounds like a good plan."

Ralan toyed with her fingers, and heat flared low in her belly. *Not now,* she warned her libido. Thankfully, their server arrived with their drinks, and Cora used the distraction to free her hand

from his beguiling touch. Regret rippled through her at the loss of connection, but she hid her reaction behind her glass as she took a sip of her cool, fizzy soda.

The glint in his eyes told her he wasn't fooled, but he didn't call her on it. "Tell me about yourself."

It seemed like such a pointless question in light of Maddy's kidnapping, but she answered anyway. "What do you want to know?"

"How long have you lived here?" Ralan leaned closer and lowered his voice. "On Earth."

Cora bit her lip. "That's not something I typically share."

Ralan nodded, not looking offended in the least. "Then I will. Before my recent return to my home world, I lived here for three hundred and forty-two years."

"About the same for me," she found herself admitting after his candor. "It was beyond difficult at first. There are few natural portals to my original home, and it wasn't easy for a woman to establish herself alone. But I managed."

Expression curious, Ralan propped his elbows on the table. "How many jobs have you had?"

Cora laughed. "I have no idea. Who could even keep track?"

"I did," he said, a sheepish smile crossing his lips. "Thirty-three in total, although several were similar enough to be repeats."

She blinked at him, and for a moment, some of her worry faded. "You're serious?" At his nod, she chuckled again. "Fine. Then what was your favorite?"

"This latest," Ralan answered at once. "It's fun to play with expectations."

Cora considered his words for a moment. "Do you mean others' expectations for a male fashion designer? Or the image portrayed by those wearing your designs?"

"Both." A wicked grin tugged at his mouth. "Not to mention the many beautiful women I got to dress. Human men are beyond foolish for neglecting this career path, I assure you."

Anger surged through her at his offhand comment. "You're telling me you became a designer to ogle women?"

"What?" Red rushed up his throat, and his eyes flashed. "I don't sneak into dressing rooms to stare at the models, if that's what you think. Gods. But I'm not blind, and I can't help but notice the lovely women who grace the runway. I don't date those who work for me. Ever. I'm sorry if I gave you any other impression."

He didn't sound at all sorry, and she didn't blame him. Perhaps she shouldn't have assumed the worst. "I didn't mean to insinuate that you took advantage, but you sounded…"

A small smile formed. "Bad. I get it. Look, if there's one thing I've learned as a designer, it's that beauty is relative. Some models are outwardly gorgeous, but they're so messed up inside I can't believe the world doesn't see it. My favorites are the ones who are truly nice people. No makeup or design can emulate that kind of glow."

His words left her humbled. He was known to include a diverse range of models in his design work, much more diverse than many other big-names, but she'd never considered that he would look beyond their surfaces. What could she say to that after she'd practically accused him of being a perv?

"Sorry," she murmured.

The server provided a distraction again, this time bringing their food. As the kid placed her plate on the table, Cora sought another topic. Any other topic. But it had been a fair question, dammit. She had no interest in going out with a creeper, famous or no. Scowling, she picked up a French fry and bit into it with more force than strictly necessary.

"Cora?"

She refused to answer him until she'd chewed the fry to nothing. What could she say to get out of this awkward discussion? "I considered pursuing design on a bigger scale," she blurted.

Surprise crossed his face, but she couldn't tell if it was because of her words or the change in topic. "Recently?" he asked.

"Yes," Cora said. "I've worked as a seamstress or assistant many times over the centuries. Sometimes, I included my own creations rather than just reproduce others' designs. I sell some of my own label at The Magic Touch, but it isn't a focus."

"If that dress in the window is one of yours, then it should be," Ralan said firmly.

Pleasure warmed her cheeks in a blush. "Thank you. But I'm not sure I want that much attention, provided my fashion line even took off. I know you said people tend to see what they expect, but it's amazing that you've managed to keep the truth about yourself a secret when you're in the spotlight."

Ralan lifted his shoulders. "I'm far from the only famous person with fae blood. Hard for humans to notice what they don't believe in."

As Ralan paid for their food, she thought about his words. It was standard practice for their kind on Earth to relocate fairly often and

to keep friendships light. But was it necessary to stay as hidden as possible? Oh, even humans would note the lack of aging after a time, especially with modern technology. But perhaps people had moved so beyond belief in their kind that they no longer needed to live with such careful paranoia.

Who would believe that there were elves living in the modern world?

It was Fen who finally offered Maddy food. She stared up at him in disbelief as he held the bread out to her, and wry humor lit his eyes as he jiggled the loaf in front of her face. Hesitantly, she reached out and took it, her attention darting between the food and his mocking expression even after the bread was safely in her hand.

"Why?" she whispered.

His brows lifted. "Can't have a weak healer when Prince Kien shows up."

"Aren't you supposed to be out tracking the guy?"

"No need," Fen answered with a shrug.

Maddy waited until he moved away to study the small loaf. Should she eat it? It could be poisoned or enchanted. After making sure no one was watching, she did a quick magical scan. Nope, just regular bread. She tore off a small piece and popped it into her mouth, almost moaning at the simple joy of food after a day of nothing. It even tasted good.

Why would one of the Unseelie be nice to her?

She didn't have much time to contemplate the question. Halfway through the loaf, there was a commotion at the entrance to the cave.

A call of greeting, a few muffled words. Across the small cavern, Fen stiffened, his attention fixing on the entrance. Maddy found herself staring as well.

When the elf walked in, she almost called out a greeting. But though the newcomer had the same black hair and golden eyes as Ralan, the malevolent energy around him bore no resemblance. Maddy shuddered, and the bread in her stomach turned to stone. This was the guy they'd been waiting for? The one they expected her to heal?

But he didn't notice her. His eyes focused on Fen at once, and fury darkened his face. "Just the mage I hoped to find."

"Prince Kien," Fen said calmly. "Please allow me to apologize. I fear I was out of my head after that blast. My energy dropped low enough to render me insensible."

The prince's eyes narrowed. "That's your excuse for letting them capture me?"

"I could barely move after being so thoroughly drained."

Silence descended, and tension built until Maddy's eardrums throbbed with it. Were they going to start blasting one another? Then a smile crossed the prince's lips. She tried not to breathe, not wanting to be involved in whatever evil he clearly had planned.

"Perhaps I will accept your excuses," Kien drawled. "But you will have to prove yourself before I allow you to rejoin."

"I've been taking care of the healer the other two found." Maddy stiffened as Fen gestured at her. So much for being nice. "The fools have been starving her. She hardly has the energy to mend any wounds."

Her whole body began to shake as the prince's dark gaze scanned her. Then he turned a scowl on Patrick and Victor where they hovered by the entrance. "A hungry, dehydrated healer is worthless. Do you know nothing?"

Patrick's throat bobbed as he swallowed. He left it to Victor to speak up. "We thought weakness might keep her from escaping."

"You can't force a healer, fools," Kien snarled. "They'd kill you before you knew what was happening. Honestly, I don't know why I don't string you up and flay you here and now. At least Fen and I could make use of your energy."

Maddy couldn't stop the whimper from escaping at that mental image, and she clapped a hand over her mouth. But only Fen looked her way. And…had he winked at her? The motion was so quick, she wasn't sure if she'd imagined it. What was his game? The loaf of bread grew mangled in her grip as she agonized over the issue.

"I'll go find her a feast," Patrick blurted.

Kien waved a hand. "The healer is the least of my worries. See to her health, but leave her alone. I'm more concerned with proving Fen's loyalty."

Fen stood taller. "I take it you have something in mind?"

"Find me Delbin and that scout who was with him." Dark energy pulsed around the prince, turning her stomach once more. "Bring them here so I can have my revenge."

Oh no. Maddy shoved her hand harder against her mouth. Considering what Prince Kien had casually contemplated doing to his allies, she didn't want to imagine what he'd do to Delbin and Inona. She had to get out of here. Warn them. But how was she going to do it without getting herself killed?

Maddy forced another bite of the mangled bread into her mouth and began to chew. First thing? Make sure she was at full strength.

Cora slammed the car into park at yet another small trailhead. "This is useless."

"How many trails are there?" Ralan asked.

"A million, for all I know," Cora answered with a sharp, impatient gesture.

They sat in silence, both peering out the windshield at the nearly empty parking lot. The light was going soft with the coming evening, but they'd only had time to check a handful of possible places. Dammit, how could she leave Maddy out there another night? Anything could have happened by now.

With every breath, Cora failed her friend.

She glanced at Ralan. "Any idea if we're even on the right track?"

"I haven't—" His voice cut off, and his eyes went blank. But it only took a few heartbeats for him to focus on her again. "We need to head back to your shop."

Everything within Cora went still. "Is there… Is she…"

"She won't be there," Ralan said softly. "But I believe we'll find a lead."

"You believe?" Her chin jutted out. "If you don't know, then you're wasting my time. How can I trust any vision of yours?"

Ralan shoved his hand through his hair. "You can't."

Cora's shoulders slumped at the lost, frustrated expression on his face. He didn't deserve her rancor, not when he was trying so hard to help despite his own troubles. "That wasn't a fair question."

He let out a long sigh. "No, it was."

"Yeah, but—"

The cheerful ring of her phone interrupted Cora's words, filling her car with a jaunty Celtic tune. The ringtone for the shop. She tugged her cell phone from the front pocket of her purse and swiped the answer button.

"Jase?"

"Are you near the shop?" Jase asked without bothering with a greeting.

Her heart lurched. "I can be. What's wrong?"

"It's not an emergency," he answered quickly. "It's just there's this guy here. Pale as fuck, unusual energy. He says he talked to you a couple of days ago?"

Cora frowned. "Already? I thought I'd have a few days more."

"Guess he didn't feel like waiting." Jase hesitated. "I can get rid of him if I have to. But if you're close enough to deal with this…"

"I'm checking the Lookout Mountain trails, so it'll be a while before I can get back. If he's fine with the wait, show him to the private room," Cora said, resigned. "I'll head back."

Cora blew out a breath as she slid the phone back in her purse. "Looks like you were right about returning to my shop. Here's hoping the guy who wants to see me is the lead you're expecting."

"He will be," Ralan said.

She didn't bother to answer as she eased the car out of the parking spot.

They would just have to see.

12

The artificial sun shone from the top of the massive cavern, but Kai didn't feel cheered. Not when his father and uncle waited with stoic expressions a few steps from the portal. Arlyn's hand tightened on his arm as they stepped into the small courtyard and stopped in front of the two Sidhe.

"I see that you decided to keep to our agreement."

"Yes, Lord Naomh," Kai answered. He would not call the Sidhe father. "I may have no interest in what you have to teach, but I'm capable enough of following orders."

Though his uncle Caolte's lips twitched, Naomh's expression didn't shift. "You have a great deal of your mother in you. She, too, was hasty. But dutiful. We shall see if you possess any of my qualities."

"I wouldn't know," Kai muttered around a sudden surge of pain.

He'd been an infant when his mother had been murdered by the man who'd claimed to be his father. Allafon. He had gone more than five hundred years without knowing the truth. His limited of

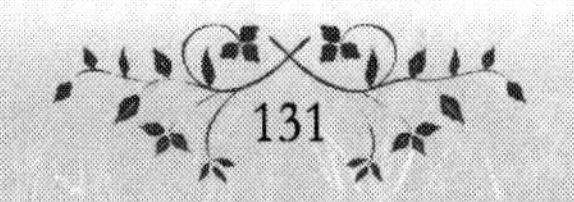

experience with Naomh had taught him little about his true father. Cold. Fierce. Aloof. And not much better than Allafon.

"Forgive my careless words," Naomh said smoothly, though his face remained stoic. "Perhaps we should adjourn to my home."

Arlyn squeezed Kai's arm in reassurance and answered for him. "That would be lovely."

They followed Naomh and Caolte down the path, and this time, Kai was able to marvel at the forest growing around them. It didn't matter how often he traveled to underhill caverns—forests thriving by the light of a spell-created sun always amazed him. In this realm, trees, flowers, bushes, and greenery burst into carefully cultivated life, richer than he'd seen in other underhill homes. A benefit of Naomh's earth magic?

Eventually, they passed through the clearing where Kien had confronted them. Kai's shoulders knotted with tension, and Arlyn's fingers tightened on his arm. At least she didn't remember the confrontation, since she'd been unconscious. He wasn't so fortunate. Kai found his gaze darting around warily although logic told him it was safe.

"I trust that you've warded against Kien," Kai said. "Unless you still work with him? If that is the case, then our deal is at an end."

Naomh spun on his heel, and his nostrils flared with fury. "I would kill that liar where he stood should he dare appear before me again. Our very world is threatened because of him."

Kai lifted a brow. "You are hardly innocent."

"I did it for her," Naomh bit out. "How could I ride the night for your mother if the humans knew we existed? They would hunt us. There would be no peace. The poison was only supposed to

make the surface unappealing for the Sidhe, not sicken the underhill realms."

Pain darkened Naomh's eyes, but Kai had seen too much to let it soften him. "Have *you* ventured into one of the affected areas? *I* have. Did you know I found the Neorans your brother ordered slaughtered in the name of your queen? I still see their sightless eyes in my dreams."

Naomh paled but didn't look away. "Learn from me, and we will fix what we can. Meren will face justice for his actions, I assure you."

Kai's teeth ground together. "That will not return the lost to life."

"No," Naomh agreed. "But it can prevent more death."

Kai considered his father's words for the rest of the walk to the house. Was that what this was about? Atonement? It made more sense than a sudden affection for a son he'd just met. But Naomh was correct. If they could prevent more deaths, then Kai needed to suck it up and learn about his Sidhe powers. Even if he had to work with the *second* father who'd tried to kill him.

Cora rushed in the back entrance and through the stockroom, almost plowing into Jase as he opened the door. Ralan tugged her back just in time to avoid running into her friend, who balanced several boxes of shoes against his chest. Jase's tense expression eased a bit at the sight of her.

"Hey, you're here. The guy's still waiting."

She let out a resigned sigh. "And he's sure to be ticked. There was a wreck on the interstate. Took forever to get through."

Jase grimaced. "He seemed okay when I last checked, but that was twenty minutes ago."

"I'll take care of it."

Cora spun away and headed toward the stockroom. She paused when she reached the door tucked between two shelves of shoes. Was she about to have to deal with a furious, insulted fae on top of everything else? As she pulled in a bracing breath, Ralan's hand settled, warm and solid, against the small of her back. Just that simple touch eased her nerves.

She tossed a grateful smile over her shoulder and entered.

The door clicked shut behind them, and Cora froze. The fae man was the same, yet he wasn't. And not just because of the sunburn that reddened his skin. His energy had been eerie and dark, a cold shiver beneath the skin, but now the chill of it danced along her flesh and through her body in a deluge. Had he grown stronger, or had he decided not to hide as much of his true nature?

Ralan's fingers tensed against her back. "Vek."

"Why, Prince Ralan," the fae drawled. "I wouldn't have expected to see you here."

"Nor I you. If you have come to bother my bon—" His words cut off abruptly, drawing Cora's attention. But he didn't explain. "I suggest you take trouble elsewhere."

The fae's eyes narrowed. "My business is not with you."

"It will be if—"

"Stop!" Cora stepped away from Ralan so she could glare at them both. "Please do not discuss me as though I'm not here. If you have bad blood between you, you can argue about it somewhere else."

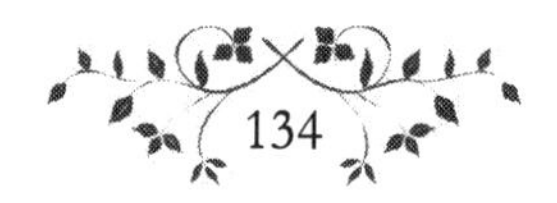

"I have nothing against him," Ralan surprised her by answering. "But I've known Vek long enough to have concerns about his presence."

Vek draped his arm over the back of his chair and smirked. "Don't let him scare you."

"I'm not that easily startled," she said.

Cora shot Ralan a warning look before she strode to the table and took a seat. Instead of joining her, he crossed his arms and leaned against the wall. His face had smoothed, his expression impassive, but she'd been around Ralan long enough to notice his tension in the set of his shoulders.

She directed her attention to Vek. "Please forgive me for your wait, especially as I fear it's in vain. My contact hasn't had time to sell your diamond, and I have not finished your clothing."

"I thought as much." The fae waved a hand. "That is no matter. I now have need of real estate. This world has drawn my interest, and I've decided to buy a home as soon as my money is ready."

Cora shrugged. "I can connect you with someone who handles that kind of stuff for our kind. That's not something I deal with."

"Any aid would be appreciated."

She stared at him, her brow lowering. There was something he wasn't sharing. "Why did you really come here?"

"Family," Vek answered instantly.

Cora hid her shock. He wasn't talking about his visit to her shop, and the intimate detail caught her off guard after his reticence during their first meeting. His grin widened. She did gasp, then, as the light caught the tips of two perfect fangs. A blood elf. An Unseelie prince.

Oh, hell.

Her fingers gripped the edge of the table until her fingertips stung. "There's enough royalty in this room to host a ball."

Vek chuckled. "If you desire."

Abruptly, Ralan straightened, his arms dropping to his sides. "What do you know about the energy poisoning and my brother?"

"To think a seer is asking me a question." The fae prince leaned forward. "I suppose that means you're still neglecting your Sight. I hope she was worth the centuries of trouble."

She? Cora's attention swiveled to Ralan, whose expression had grown shadowed. Had he given up his talent at one point for a woman? They'd started getting to know one another, but neither of them had shared much about their past. For all she knew, he was married.

"You'd better be single after all of that flirting," Cora whispered.

Ralan met her eyes without hesitation. "I am. Kenaren…that was a long time ago."

It might have been centuries ago, but his pallor told her the pain wasn't forgotten. When the hint of jealousy surged, she forced it down. She had a past, too, one that inhibited her future. If she ever fell in love and Orn found out, he would do his best to kill the unfortunate man and force her to return home.

She had no right to judge.

"I understand," she answered.

"You'd better catch up, Ralan," Vek said, interrupting without qualm. "Your brother has fucked a lot of things up. If my nephew can't… Let's just say my father is furious."

Ralan latched on to the fae prince's slip. "Your nephew?"

"A misguided boy." Vek's lips thinned. "And the reason for my presence."

"If you know where I can find Kien, then tell me."

"No."

Ralan strode to the table and slammed his hands down, leaning close to Vek. "They took Cora's friend. You'll tell me where, or there will be trouble between our people."

Vek merely laughed. "No need to bring our fathers into this. My nephew has rejoined your brother's group. If I out him now, Kien will kill him before he can fix the mess he's caused in the underhill realms."

"She's an innocent healer, Vek. A youngling."

The fae prince stilled. "A child?"

"No," Ralan admitted. "But barely into her twenties. She doesn't deserve the kind of hell Kien will put her through."

"Then use your Sight."

Ralan jerked back, fury and frustration lining his face. "It's not that simple, as you well know. Right now, you're our only lead."

The two men stared at each other, and Cora's heart pounded with hope and fear as Vek's eyes took on a considering gleam. Surely he wouldn't put his own family at risk. But after a moment, he gave a sharp nod.

"I won't out him, but I can give you a direction," Vek said. "Too bad your kind can't follow blood connections as easily as mine can. But I doubt you carry around each other's blood."

"Such magic is dangerous," Ralan murmured, a strange expression crossing his face.

"As you say." Vek's fangs flashed as he grinned. "I sense my nephew to the west. I'd recommend a hike in the Raccoon Mountain area. For my aid, I trust you will not allow harm to come to Fen."

Ralan inclined his head. "So long as he doesn't try to kill me."

"Always a given." Vek stood and then glanced down at Cora. "How might I get in touch with your real estate contact?"

"I'll give you his address."

Cora hurried over to the small table holding the microwave and pulled out a drawer. After a quick search, she grabbed the card she needed and handed it over. Vek bowed, low and formal, before turning for the door. As he neared Ralan, he paused.

"I am trusting you to keep your word." Cora shivered as the Unseelie prince's magic pulsed. "Don't make me regret it."

The closing door thundered through the room, and silence descended in Vek's wake. Cora stared at the door for a moment, the remnants of his energy still shuddering through her. Blood elves were rare despite the Unseelie king's many relationships. Only a few of his children carried the ability. No wonder Vek had seemed odd. Instead of pulling energy in from the natural world, Vek replenished his magic like a vampire.

With blood.

She ran her hand reflexively over her neck. It didn't matter that she'd never heard of the royal family killing anyone in this manner. The idea still creeped her out. Predator. It must be the energy of the hunt that brought those around him to uneasy awareness.

"Are you okay?" Ralan asked.

"I think so. I guess you were right about finding a lead."

"At least my gift was useful for something," Ralan grumbled, though a slight smile curved his lips.

"Well, let's go." She rubbed her suddenly damp palms along her pants. "By the time we get to Raccoon Mountain, it'll be dark."

His brows lifted. "Won't they close the trail access at night?"

"Maybe." Cora shrugged. "Guess we'll find out."

Ralan studied her for a moment and then shook his head. "We can't go hiking at night into certain danger. We aren't scouts or warriors. Inona is, but by the time we meet up with her and Delbin, they'll certainly have closed the trails. We'll have to wait until morning."

Her stomach pitched with dread. How could she leave Maddy out there another night? But he was right. They wouldn't be able to save her friend if they got lost or killed muddling their way into unknown conditions. Dammit. Too bad she wasn't better at this sort of thing, but she'd never been the outdoorsy type.

"There has to be something we can do."

Ralan placed his hand on her shoulder. "We'll get with Inona on what we'll need and gather supplies. We have a direction. Now we need a plan."

Cora nodded. The warmth of his touch settled her, easing the unconscious anxiety evoked by the blood elf. Ralan's arms wrapped around her and drew her close, and her heartbeat drummed in her ears. Gathering her courage, she stared into his eyes for a moment before she brushed her lips across his.

His surprised exhale mingled with her sigh. Then Ralan slid his fingers into her hair and tipped her head back as his mouth claimed hers. Cora groaned. His kiss was heaven. Home. She twined her arms around his neck and let herself feel.

At a knock on the door, Cora jerked back. Color singed her cheeks, though she couldn't say why. "Let's go."

"I suppose we must." He ran his thumb across her bottom lip. "But rest assured we'll revisit this later."

Her knees weakened at his soft words. "I certainly hope so."

Dammit, it would be so easy to fall in love with him.

The one thing she couldn't do.

But I doubt you carry around each other's blood.

Ralan gazed out the passenger side window as Vek's words floated through his mind. The run-down buildings on the outskirts of downtown flashed past as Cora drove, and the bleakness was fine match for his mood. Although Vek's comment had been said in passing, it still felt like an admonishment.

Should he have used Kien's blood already? Ralan's brother might not have rejoined his group yet, but he would. He and Cora could have spent the day scouting out the proper trail instead of floundering around town looking for clues. Maddy might be safe at home with her love.

Kien and Kenaren had thought to use Ralan's blood against him. Wouldn't it be justified retribution for Ralan to do the same?

"So how'd you get to know a blood elf?"

He glanced back at Cora. Though she stared at the road ahead, her curiosity buzzed through the air like an electric current. "My father invited his father for a State visit when I was young. Maybe in my sixties? Vek was part of their entourage."

"He is…" Cora's nose wrinkled. "Uncanny."

Ralan chuckled. "I suppose I find myself lucky that you weren't drawn to him. Some people are."

Cora shot him a dubious look. "Seriously?"

"They fly straight into the bug zapper."

She laughed, and some of the tension eased from her shoulders. As he'd intended. "Great mental image, there. I thought their kind didn't actually kill."

"Oh, they don't. Outside of battle." Ralan grinned. "But I imagine there's quite the sting."

Her lips pursed, but the glow of the carnival lights caught her attention. Ralan pulled up the text program on his phone and read Delbin's directions again. "Cut down that street to get to the back entrance."

"Got it." Cora navigated her way around a crowd of teenagers spilling across the street.

Eventually, they reached the turn-off into the employee lot. The car bumped over the ruts in a bare, dirt path that ended at a chain-link fence with a gate. Cora pulled the car to a halt as a muscular man made his scowling way to her window. After a brief hesitation, she pushed the button to roll the glass down.

"Employees only," the man barked.

"We're here to see Delbin," Cora answered calmly.

The man's scowl deepened. "Don't care. Come back when the fair's not open."

Ralan settled his hand on Cora's thigh and gave a gentle squeeze. Even as lust speared through him and Cora turned a shocked look his way, he leaned over and focused on the carnival worker's face. No shielding. Human. A slow smile stretched his lips as he took control of the man without resistance.

In moments, they were through, complete with directions to Delbin's tent.

Cora squirmed in her seat, reminding Ralan of his hand's blessed location. He longed to slide his fingers higher until they met

her heat. Until he gave her a better reason to squirm. Her breathing hitched, and his body went hard. Gods, what he wouldn't give to be alone with her at this moment.

She stopped the car beside Delbin's tent, and Cora's wide eyes met his. "Ralan."

"I hadn't intended to grope you," he said quietly. "But I admit the idea has merit."

She let out a choked laugh. "Agreed. But maybe not here?"

Had he been hard before? Ralan forced his hand from her thigh before he embarrassed them both. "Stay with me tonight."

"I don't know." Tension pooled around them like the lights spilling from the fairway. "I can't…I can't offer a relationship right now."

His heart thudded at the pain in her voice. "Nor can I." He paused, and the silence stretched between them. "There's a good chance I won't survive the confrontation with my brother, Cora. This I have Seen."

She took in a sharp breath. "Well."

"I'll fight it." She made him want to fight it. "But I thought you should know before you decide."

Cora's expression turned thoughtful, and her gaze dropped to his hand where it rested on his leg. Then she reached out and slowly wrapped her fingers around his. "Sounds like we need to make the most of our time."

He turned his palm to hers. "Is that a yes?"

Though she smiled, her eyes were solemn when they met his. "It is. Yes."

13

Ralan took a moment to get himself under control before he followed Cora out of the car and joined her beside the tent. Lingering on the night to come wouldn't help. If their earlier kiss was any preview… Cursing to himself, Ralan shoved those thoughts aside again and tried to focus. There weren't many people near, but a few paces away, a woman leaned against a travel trailer. She frowned warily at them, but she didn't speak. Instead of calling out, Ralan let his mind sweep out in a tentative scan.

The woman was human, and within the trailer, he sensed a sleeping child. A protective mother, then. He scanned farther, finding few back here at during the carnival's peak hours. A couple of minds were shielded, but he didn't attempt to breach their protections to find out who they might be. Their energy didn't match Delbin's or Inona's.

"What do we do now?" Cora asked.

"Wait a moment," Ralan answered as he sensed the approach of one of the shielded people.

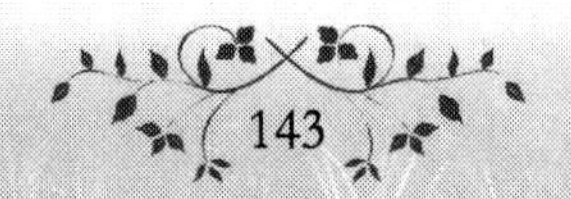

It only took a few heartbeats for the old man to appear. His scraggly, gray hair and grease-smeared overalls were a stark contrast to the intense energy coalescing around him. Ralan might have been able to break through, but he had a feeling he would regret it.

"You'd better have a damn good reason to be here," the old man grumbled. His shrewd gaze swept over Ralan and Cora. "Delbin didn't warn me you were stopping by."

Ralan returned the man's stare. "I texted him about it."

"Eh, he's been fixin' the dunk tank. I haven't been his way in a while." The old man pointed his thumb over his shoulder. "Follow me, and I'll take you to him. Name's Grunge."

Ralan exchanged a bemused glance with Cora and trailed Grunge across the field. Ralan settled his hand low on Cora's waist. The feel of her body shifting beneath his palm, even innocently, brought other thoughts to mind, and he nearly groaned. Later. They would have time alone later.

He concentrated on the lights that flashed ever brighter from the fairway and the sweet scent of funnel cake that drifted on the breeze. The hum of conversations grew louder, punctuated here and there by shouts and squeals of excitement, but he detected no sense of danger.

They rounded a small tent and wove their way along a line of food stands and games of chance, dodging the crowds as they went. Ralan's stomach rumbled at the jumble of scents wafting from the vendors, although he knew he'd regret such rich fare. He'd grown accustomed to human food during his centuries on Earth, but some choices were wiser than others.

Finally, they reached the dunk tank. Ralan spotted Inona leaning against a nearby stall. He followed her gaze to a soaked, shirtless

Delbin perched above the water, his feet wedged between the tank wall and the cage that protected the worker. One hand wrapped around a cage bar as he leaned over the small seat with a wrench.

"Damn latch," Delbin cursed.

Ralan stopped beside Inona. "How many times has he fallen in?"

Inona chuckled. "Three."

At a soft sound from Cora, Ralan glanced her way. Her lips twitched as she stared at Delbin. "Think he'll fall in again? Maybe I should start recording just in case."

Frowning, Inona straightened. "Recording?"

"I bet the video would go viral." At the scout's blank stare, Cora smiled. "Sorry. You must be new here. A picture of him falling in would be quite amusing."

After a moment, Inona returned her smile. "Yes, I imagine it would."

Grunge halted beside the tank and rapped hard against the side. Delbin jumped, teetering for a moment before managing to catch himself. He scowled over his shoulder at Grunge. "Not cool."

The old man laughed. "Almost got you. You gonna have this thing up and running soon?"

"Who knows?"

"Well, your friends are here." Grunge slapped the side of the tank. "Come on out. I'll see what I can do."

Delbin let himself fall into the dunk tank, making Grunge curse as water sprayed over him. Then the old man chuckled again. "Guess I deserved that."

Grinning, Delbin swiped water off his face. "Yep."

Ralan's jaw clenched as Delbin made a show of hefting himself out, pausing to let water dribble down his back. He might be well-muscled, but did he have to make a point of highlighting that fact in front of Ralan's bonded? Inona drew in a sharp breath, and even Cora appeared to be riveted to the sight. Damned showoff. Ralan sent a mental nudge Delbin's way and smiled as his student almost fell in the water again. Then he fumbled out and grabbed a towel from a hook on the back.

When he finally joined them, Delbin gave an unrepentant smirk. "Let's head back to the tent."

This time, they followed Delbin behind the booths. The sights and sounds of the carnival faded somewhat, and the shadows beneath the gleam became more obvious. The edge of a banner held up by tape. The dent in the side of the food cart. The exhausted worker slumped in a chair behind one of the games. All of the little details that went unnoticed by the fair-goers.

Delbin rubbed the towel over his hair and glanced back at Ralan. "I hope you didn't have any trouble. I gave my phone to Inona while I was in the tank, so if you texted, I didn't get it."

"We managed," Ralan answered.

What Delbin didn't know, the man at the employee entrance couldn't get mad at him about. Not that the human would ever realize that he'd been controlled, but still. Caution was as integral to living on Earth as knowing the right shady contacts.

When they reached the employee area, Delbin wasted little time changing into dry clothes. Then they sat in a circle of camp chairs outside of the tent. Ralan scanned the area again and discovered that the human woman from earlier was tending her child in the travel trailer. No others were close enough to hear.

Ralan leaned forward, elbows resting on his knees. "Cora and I need to check the Raccoon Mountain area."

"How difficult will the wildlife be?" Inona asked.

Ralan looked to Cora, who shrugged. "There's the rare bear sighting, but I've never heard of anyone being bothered."

A line formed between Inona's brows. "What about the raccoons? There must be many to inspire the name."

"I…" Cora rubbed her hand across the back of her neck. "Honestly, I don't know how to answer that. I've never heard anyone talk about the actual raccoons. They aren't known to be dangerous animals, anyway. Pesky scavengers that like to climb into tents but not predators."

"There could be other hazards," Inona said. "I should go with you."

"That was my thought," Ralan said. "If you can get away. Weekends are busy, I know, and I'd rather not ruin your positioning here."

Inona winced. "I fear I am not as useful as I could be. I give too many pointers at the games, and I—"

The world faded into a haze and then refocused. Ralan's head spun as he struggled to adapt to the switch. Faces swirled past, unremarkable. Then Delbin and Inona stood together outside a vending booth.

"How could you burn corn dogs?" Delbin asked, humor lacing his tone.

"I was arranging the others most carefully." Inona tipped her chin up even as she dumped the ruined food into the trash can behind the stall. "Meg said I should include around twenty fries. After I finished counting and placing the cooked corn dogs with the proper amount, I'd forgotten about the ones cooking. At least those baskets have been completed properly."

"Yeah, but—" Delbin's breath huffed out on a laugh. "Never mind. We'll straighten it out."

A smooth voice broke through. "Just the two people I was looking for. Kien said I'd…"

A whirl of color. Blackness. Ralan tried to grip at the strands, but they evaded him.

The bite of his elbows digging into his knees brought him back to the present. Ralan blinked, taking in the world around him. The other three stared at him in varying degrees of surprise. With a sigh, he dragged his hand across his hair.

"Sorry. You're staying at the carnival."

Inona's brows rose, and Cora gaped at him. But Delbin only grinned. "This is a real habit for you, isn't it? Glad we weren't connected this time."

Ralan's lips thinned at the reminder. "As am I."

"I thought your Sight wasn't working," Cora said.

"It isn't. Wasn't." Ralan met her questioning gaze. "I caught only a snippet. I'm not sure when, but Delbin and Inona will be contacted here by someone connected to Kien. The vision faded before I could See more."

"Seems convenient," Cora whispered.

"Convenient would be clear strands to follow." His hands clenched into fists. "If I could See effectively, Maddy would be home."

She looked down and sighed. "I'm sorry. I'm just worried."

"You have every right to doubt." Ralan forced his fingers to go lax. "I can't even tell how long it'll be until the person shows up. I didn't See them at all."

Delbin's seat let out a soft squeak as he leaned forward. "So we'll stay. Inona can tell you what you'll want to pack. I hope you'll come get us before you charge into danger, though. Find the cave. Then we'll make a plan."

Maddy huddled in her spot, shivering as night set in once again. The bread had long ago worn off, and her stomach rumbled in supplication. Weakness weighted her limbs. If she didn't get more food soon, she would be sick. What a lovely contradiction. She swallowed, but her mouth had gone dry from lack of water. Too bad the cave water wasn't drinkable. If she hadn't picked up that tidbit on a cave tour, she would've already braved a sip from the pool a few paces away.

At least she didn't have to go to the bathroom as often. Having Patrick stand guard in the woods outside had been humiliation at its finest. Still, it would be the best chance to escape. If there was a weak link in this group, it was him. She could wait until the others were occupied and get him to take her outside. Her stomach turned at the thought of using her healing gift for ill—on purpose this time—but she didn't have much choice. Even getting lost in the woods would be better than this slow death at the hands of evil bastards.

It was too quiet in the cave. Patrick and Fen had both left a while back. Victor dozed against a stalagmite, his legs across the only trail out. But the true danger, the one called Kien, paced the small open space to her left. Maddy tried not to look at him, lest she catch his attention, but sometimes his maddened gaze would meet hers.

A shudder traced through her at the memory, and she made sure her face remained averted. His shuffling steps echoed through the

small space well enough that she didn't need to look. That and his energy. It sputtered and leapt, tendrils sometimes seeming to reach for the cave around her. Was he trying to connect? His power had the smoky flavor of enchantment and illusion, not earth. But she wasn't going to ask.

His steps sounded closer, and she froze. Warily, she looked up just enough to see his legs drawing nearer. Bile rose in her throat as he paused and knelt beside her. Oh, no. He'd said it was foolish to force a healer. Had he changed his mind?

"Look at me," he said, his smooth voice ringing with command.

Maddy swallowed and focused on his mouth. Anything but his eyes. "Yes?"

"Perhaps it would help you to know what I fight for."

The blood magic that swirled around him told her well enough what he fought for, but she wasn't going to argue with the crazy person. "Maybe."

Kien's lips pinched. "You met my brother, Ralan?"

"Yes," Maddy answered slowly.

"He's a seer," Kien said with a snarl. "And my father seeks to make him king. Can you imagine a Seer King, able to bring his every vision to reality? He could solidify his power so thoroughly none could ever contest it. My people would be unable to fight."

Maddy dug her trembling fingers into her legs. An evil seer could do much damage in a place of power, it was true. But Ralan hadn't seemed particularly bad. His energy had been clean and his demeanor kind. Plus, he was friends with Delbin. She couldn't imagine Delbin hanging out with someone who'd bring a country to ruin.

But she couldn't say any of that to Kien. "I can see how that might be a problem."

"Can you?" Kien took a deep breath, and his voice pitched low. "Work with me. We could use a healer, and I'll make sure you are well taken care of. I could give you wealth, property, servants. Anything you desire."

Oh, jeez, the *wealth beyond your imagining* promise. If the guy hadn't been so terrifying, Maddy might have laughed. Instead, she tried to keep her face blank as his maddened eyes caught at her. He was serious. He really believed she'd see his way as right and follow along. Shit. She wasn't a good enough actress to pretend, and there was no way she was joining this crazy train.

"I…I need to think about this," she finally answered.

"You would be wise to do so quickly." His expression turned dark before he forced it smooth once more. "Might I do something to help you consider the matter?"

Oh, yeah. She was totally going to take advantage of this. "I could use some water and good food. I was forced here, after all, and for potential allies, you've treated me like shit. It's hard to believe you want me to join you. I'm worn out and starving."

"Patrick should return with a meal for you soon," Kien surprised her by saying. "And I will personally ensure that no one disturbs you during your rest."

Maddy stifled a nervous laugh. Like she'd be able to sleep with this weirdo watching her. But she only gave a mumbled "thanks."

Kien jerked to his feet and resumed his pacing. With a sigh of relief, Maddy slumped against the stalagmite behind her. She really did need to sleep, but how could she risk it? Between her rumbling

stomach and unrelenting fear, she'd only managed to doze since she'd been kidnapped. But maybe a full stomach would help, provided Patrick really did show up with food.

She needed to be stronger before she made a run for it.

14

Cora dropped the plastic bags on Ralan's bed and rubbed her damp palms along her pants. She wanted to be with him, but she hadn't been able to stop her nerves from ramping up as the evening had gone on. All through their shopping trip for supplies, he'd kept touching her in small ways. A hand on her elbow or waist. A quick brush of his fingers across her cheek.

As he bent to sort through the supplies, Cora stared at his face. She'd lusted over his pictures in magazines for years. He carried himself with an innate confidence, and his smile always hinted at a knowledge he never shared—and mischief barely repressed. She'd enjoyed his designs, but not nearly as much as she'd liked looking at the man himself.

What would it be like to have that intensity focused only on her?

His golden eyes met hers, and he frowned. "Are you okay?"

"Yes.".

Ralan straightened, his full attention now on her. "If you've changed your mind, I understand."

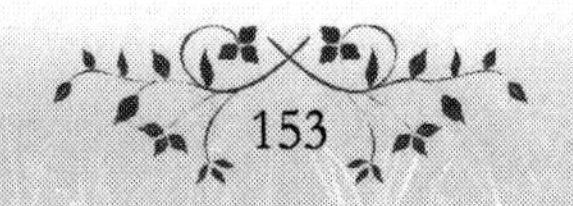

"No!" Cora bit her lip. "No, I haven't. It's just surreal. I've followed your career for years."

"If I get a chance, I'll design something for you." His narrowed eyes scanned her body. "A bold color, I think. Something that caresses your curves. A light fabric that will slide across your breasts and flow around your thighs."

Her body went hot at his words, burning away her nerves. "We'd better shift this stuff off the bed."

Ralan's brows shot up, and a smirk played around his lips. "There's time, love."

"Is there?" Cora shoved the nearest bags to the floor with a thud. "We have no idea what's going to happen tomorrow. For just this night, I want you. I want to not think."

He studied her for a moment, passion flaring in his eyes. One corner of his mouth tipped up as he reached out and grabbed the rest of the bags. He held her gaze as he lowered them to the floor. Then he gave her a challenging look.

Her move.

Cora took a deep breath and gripped the bottom of her T-shirt. She'd expected him to take the lead at her words, but she didn't mind. As her magic sang with the heat of her desire, she tugged the shirt over her head and dropped it. His attention moved instantly to her breasts, covered in a thin, lacy bra. She wiggled, then grinned as his mouth fell open.

"Your move now," she teased.

Whatever control he'd held snapped. In a couple of strides, he rounded the bed, and his hands dropped to her waist. He tugged her against him as his mouth descended. Plundered. She wrapped

her arms around his neck, and a moan slipped free at the feel of her breasts rubbing against his chest. Her hips tilted to meet him, his own desire hotly evident, and she suddenly wanted to climb him. Be one with him. She'd never needed to be so close to another person in her life.

Cora pulled her lips free. "Naked. Now."

With a groan, Ralan set her away from him. A flare of magic surged through the room, startling a gasp from her, before settling into the walls. "For privacy," he said. He yanked his own shirt off and tossed it away. "I plan to spend a great deal of time making you scream. I thought you'd rather the rest of the hotel not hear."

Good. Gods. Her breath came in soft gasps, and her clothes seemed to weigh a million pounds. She had to get out of these pants, but she couldn't stop staring at Ralan's leanly muscled chest and his fingers as they fell to the snap of his jeans. He paused, and a teasing glint entered his eyes when she glared at him.

"Who goes first?" he asked softly. "Though you're a bit more dressed than I am."

A pendant dangled between his pecs, a silver disk that might have been carved with symbols. Cora smirked. "We both have something up top."

Ralan let out a slight growl and tugged her close again. His fingers found the clasp of her bra, and he wasted no time jerking it free and sending it flying. Cora's eyes slid closed as her breasts met flesh, his necklace warming slightly between them. He kissed her again, and she barely noticed when the backs of her knees hit the edge of the bed.

Cora pulled him with her when she toppled back. They rolled together, hands tugging at their remaining clothes. She gasped out a

moan when they finally drew together without barriers. She ran her fingers into his long hair and guided his mouth back to hers.

Heat flared between them, her magic calling to him as it never had with another before. Why? It seemed important, but she couldn't think. Not with his fingers at her core, bringing her to life. Maddening. Cora cried out, though in fear or passion, she couldn't say. She had to have him within her or she would burst into flames.

She tore her mouth away. "Now."

"Are you sure?" He muttered a curse as her fingers wrapped around him. "I haven't made you—"

"Of course I'm sure. Now."

His lips took hers as he entered her, and her vision hazed with the passion and magic between them. They began to move together, frenzied, and she had a moment's gratitude for the shield he'd cast as her voice grew hoarse from her cries. So much. Almost too much.

Her world flared into light and heat as she shattered with him. Her chest stung, but she hardly noticed as they crashed together. Merged. Gods, what…? He poured into her—mind, body, soul.

And as the glow settled, his spirit remained joined to hers.

Ralan's breath heaved in and out as he struggled to right his world. Cora's hands went lax against his back, and he dropped a kiss to her sweat-slicked shoulder. What had just happened? Thoughts muddled, he rolled to his side, tucking her against him.

His fingers tangled in her hair when he ran his hand down her back to gather her closer. Her arm slipped around his waist, and her sigh cooled his heated flesh. He felt her everywhere. Within.

Around. The potential bond that had hovered between them was somehow complete.

It defied all that he knew.

"What was that?" Cora whispered.

Ralan shook his head. "It shouldn't have happened."

An *oomph* slipped out as she shoved against his chest, pushing herself to a sitting position. "Thanks."

"No, Cora." Her distress rolled through him as he sat up, and feeling sick inside, he turned her face to his. "I didn't mean our lovemaking. I was talking about the soulbond. We spoke no words, but we bonded. That shouldn't happen."

The color drained from her face. "Bonded?"

Her fear settled in his own gut like a weight. "Do you not have soulmates among your people? Linked souls?"

"Rarely." Her fingers wrapped around his wrist as her pupils dilated in panic. "Undo it. I can't be bound to anyone. *I can't.*"

"Cora?" His heart began to pound with hers, and he forced his breathing to slow in the hope it would help calm her. "We'll work it out. I'll check with our priests at the palace. There should have been steps to this."

"What steps?"

Ralan gathered his medallion in his palm. "First, I'd speak the words of bonding to activate the necklace. The other person usually has a necklace to exchange in return. Only after that exchange does consummation complete the bond in full."

Her wide eyes landed on his pendant. "I felt it heat against my chest."

"As did I." Ralan stifled a curse at her clear distress. "I'm sorry. I never would have started our bond. Not with my death so near."

Cora dropped her forehead to her knees. Then her head jerked back up. "You knew?"

"As soon as I Saw you in my vision, I recognized you as my soulbonded," he admitted.

"And you didn't think it important to tell me?" Anger began to edge out her distress. "I might not have taken this risk."

Ralan lifted his hands, palms out. "I've never heard of anyone bonding without completing all three steps. I swear to you I would not have done this on purpose."

Her eyes slipped closed, and she tugged her hands through her tangled hair. Finally, she sighed. "I can feel the truth of that like my own breath. But this is impossible. If Orn finds out about—"

"Who is Orn?" he demanded, brows lowering.

"I'm not married, if that's what you're thinking." Cora settled her crossed arms on her knees. "Among my people… Well, kings are elected by the council. Not on a schedule, like here. Usually they're replaced due to death or incompetence, and firstborn sons are typically favored."

"But what does this—"

"Just listen," she said. "My father was widely considered next in line. Orn was his rival. But my father is much older, and I'm his only child. That meant he had no son to pass his power to, much like the dying king. My father had been working to see me betrothed to a prince of another realm, an alliance that would have offset his lack of male heir."

Her gaze lowered. "That prince rejected me. Not long after, the old king died. Orn was elected despite his lack of heirs, since he was still young enough to provide them. And he'd passed around the

rumor that we would wed." Her fear surged through him. "So I ran. He'd managed to hide his cruelty from the council but not from me."

Ralan rested his hand against her shoulder. "What does that have to do with our bond?"

"Orn didn't give up on the alliance. Over the centuries, he's sent more than one person to bring me home." Cora nibbled at her lower lip. "I heard that he finally chose another, but I don't dare believe it. I'm certain he'd try to kill any man I grew close to."

Ralan's teeth ground together at all she'd been through. Some idiot *had* rejected her, leaving her to contend with this mess. "You need not fear in that regard. When I die, it will be at my brother's hand."

"Your vision." She let out a choked laugh. "Doesn't this bother you?"

He ran his palm up and down her bare back, and she shivered, though the touch had been meant for comfort. "If the past months have shown me anything, it's that control is an illusion. But beyond that, the future is never set. Small changes matter."

"Orn might cause more trouble," she said. "I've learned to cloak myself magically from his detection, but his spies sometimes find me. I wouldn't want to bring that to your door."

Ralan's lips twisted. "Tomorrow, we're hiking into the mountains in search of my insane brother and your kidnapped friend. I don't think we started from a baseline of normal."

Her shoulder muscles loosened, and a more natural laugh slipped free. "You do have a point."

"Cora, if we decide to break the bond, it can be done." He swallowed against a sudden lump. "But that break would be final. Let's deal with this crisis before we decide."

She stared into his eyes for several breaths. Then she nodded. "Okay."

Hours later, Cora lay curled around Ralan, his breathing measured and steady beneath her ear. They'd made love again, slowly this time, and her body was pleasantly tired. But her mind couldn't relax. How could she be so caught up in him in a matter of days? She snorted. More than caught up, considering the bond that had formed. Soulbonds were so rare among her people that she'd never thought one might happen to her, and she had no idea what to do about it.

She should have been angry, not twining herself around him like a vine, yet being with him brought a simple happiness she'd never experienced. Maybe she was too damned tired from looking for Maddy to feel upset, and it would all come rushing in once the crisis was through. Or maybe there was a reason she'd been drawn to him from the first time she'd seen his picture.

Ralan twitched. Then the muscles beneath her cheek went taut. Cora heard a hum against her ear like a groan suppressed, and she shifted back slowly until she could see his face. His closed eyelids twitched, and another low moan slipped from his lips. He had to be dreaming, and she had a feeling it wasn't pleasant. Cora grimaced. Should she wake him?

A sick sense of dread slithered into her stomach, and her fire magic leaped in response. She gasped as her skin heated and her vision to blurred. As Ralan started to thrash, Cora struggled to get her power under control. But it only continued to build. Worse, her muscles began to ache.

At first, it was a dull bearable pain. Then her entire body exploded with it. Cora cried out and jerked herself upright, wrapping her arms around her knees in a futile attempt to ease the agony. With her eyes squeezed tightly shut, she beat her magic back until her skin returned to its normal warmth. But the pain didn't stop.

Ralan cried out. Through the agony, she forced her head to turn so that she could see him. She lifted heavy eyelids in time to see his body spasm, almost lifting from the bed. Cora reached out a trembling hand and wrapped her fingers around his hot, sweat-slicked arm. He jerked against her hold, breaking her weak grip, and groaned once more.

Then his body went rigid, and just like that, the pain cut off.

Breath heaving in and out, Cora stared at him. Her magic might have responded to the event, but the source hadn't been her. He'd drawn her into his dream world somehow. The bond? She rubbed her hands up and down her shivering arms as her skin began to cool. It made no sense.

Ralan's eyes popped open, and he shoved himself upright. His wide-eyed gaze darted around the room before landing on Cora. "I'm alive."

She blinked. "Shouldn't you be?"

He stared at her, his expression blank. Then he gave his head a shake and ran his hand through his hair. "Forgive me. I had a dream vision."

"It must have been a bad one."

"Why?" His eyes skimmed her huddled form, and a frown creased his brow. "Did I do something? I usually stay still, but lately…"

Cora pulled her knees closer to her chest. "I felt it, I think. At first, I thought it was my own magic, but no. What the hell did you dream?"

"My death," Ralan said softly. "Consuming fire and then death."

Her breath caught. He'd told her he'd foreseen it, but it was another thing entirely to feel it. She couldn't think of a single thing to say. Instead, she twined her fingers with his.

After a while, his tension eased, and he stretched back out, tugging her hand until she curled around him once more. "I'm sorry you were drawn in."

Cora fought back the moisture gathering in her eyes. He was worried about *her* after such a horrific vision? "We have to find a way around it."

"I've never had a dream vision not come true." He let out a huff. "But then, I've never had my Sight fail so spectacularly before."

Her arm tightened around his waist. "Let's hope it's wrong."

If Cora had any say, it would be wrong.

Kien eyed the girl's still form where she huddled in the sleeping bag Patrick had brought. Her breathing was slow and steady, and a quick mental scan showed her thoughts to be drifting in slumber. But he didn't trust her. He'd seen her quickly stifled horror when he'd spoken to her. A test was in order.

"Perhaps I'll torture the healer, after all," he said, watching her closely. No movement. "We can use her body if I can find a way to stifle her powers."

Her breathing and her thoughts remained steady. No jump in energy. He glanced at the other two and forced back a sigh. Victor

leaned forward eagerly, and Patrick frowned. Typical. If Patrick hadn't been skilled at imbuing spells into objects, Kien would have killed him long ago. He was too soft. Of course, the latest plan didn't require such services…

"Do you really think we can get around her magic?" Victor asked. "There's a great deal I'd like to do to that bitch."

Kien waved his hand. "Forget it. I was testing to see if she slept. There are greater goals than sex. Besides, once you have Earth, you'll have your choice of women."

Patrick caught on first. "The poison spell was destroyed. How are we going to take over?"

"There's another version, but it requires a more…personal touch." Kien peered at Maddy and found her unchanged. "If Fen connects me into Earth's energy, I can channel the poison myself. It's riskier and more potent, so I will expect your rapid cooperation in breaking through the spell barring me from Moranaia."

"You were supposed to help us gain control of Earth before you leave," Victor grumbled. "You help subdue the full-blooded fae so that we can rule with our magic, and then we help you claim your throne. That was the deal."

"You'll not need me here for that." Warmth streamed through Kien's blood at the satisfying thought. "Once I'm king, I'll release the spell. After the destruction that the rebound will cause, they'll be begging for your help."

"Destruction?" Patrick asked.

"The humans will be fine, but the fae races?" Kien chuckled. "Not so much."

It took all of Maddy's willpower not to move. The charm her father had taught her held, a simple enchantment that shielded her thoughts. But only force of will kept her body motionless at Kien's foul words. Poisoning the energy and destroying the fae? She had to warn her family.

She had to escape.

15

Once again, Ralan stared out the passenger window at the passing landscape. This time, at least, they had a clear destination. But that didn't ease the knot that had been in his stomach since the night before. Why had their bond formed on its own? He tried to think back to the moment it had happened, but all he could recall was his pendant heating as it settled between them.

Perhaps their souls had known something their minds hadn't.

He tugged his necklace from beneath his shirt and ran his thumb over the medallion at the end. Like most of his people, he'd worn it all of his life, even during the long centuries he'd spent on Earth, though he'd been careful to keep it glamoured to hide the engravings. No human could've read the Moranaian writing, but the strange characters would have raised questions—dangerous ones during some time periods. Now? Now, it was his no longer.

As soon as he had the chance, he would give the necklace to Cora. It was usually part of the first step, but though they'd bypassed that, it should still be hers. Just as *he* was hers. He couldn't say he

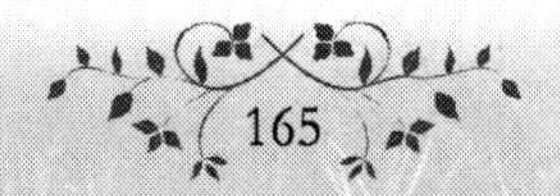

loved her, not this early, but he felt whole in her presence. Unlike with other women, he had no need to hide his true nature.

In a lot of ways, that was better than love—an emotion he had cause to dread.

"You're quiet," Cora said.

Ralan glanced at her, taking in the serious lines of her profile. "I was thinking about our bond."

Her mouth turned down. "Me, too."

"Oh?" The knot in his stomach tightened. "You've been surprisingly calm about it after your initial reaction."

Cora shot him a wry look. "Initial reaction? A nice way to put the threats I face from Orn."

"We," he said at once. "We face. I'll not leave you to deal with it alone."

"Thank you." Her fingers tapped the steering wheel. "But that isn't the part I was thinking about. I just…I should be angry, but I'm not. I don't understand why."

Ralan smiled. "And I was thinking about how I am comfortable with you. We don't feel like strangers."

"You're right." Cora hit the turn signal, her full concentration on the road as she exited the interstate. When she stopped at the end of the ramp, she gave him a quick smile in return. "I don't understand it, but it's true."

Once they left the interstate behind, the city faded away. There were a few businesses and houses, but this stretch of road looked like a different world than downtown Chattanooga. A mix of rural development and forest. Ralan found himself relaxing as the area grew heavier with trees. It wasn't Moranaia, but it certainly looked

more like it than the city. Though he'd grown accustomed to urban life, nothing touched his soul like the natural spaces.

Near a small neighborhood, he saw a sign for Racoon Mountain Caverns, but Cora didn't slow. "Isn't that it?"

She shook her head. "It's a great cave, but humans have tours all through the caverns daily. It would be a terrible place to hide out. I'm thinking we should head up to the Raccoon Mountain Reservoir area."

"Okay," Ralan said. "Why?"

"I'm not sure about caves, but there are trails all over the top of the mountain." She turned down a heavily treed road and pointed at a sign. "There's a Visitor Center. Let's see if we can find a map."

Ralan took in the forest surrounding the road to the reservoir. No development here. The trees were far smaller than those on Moranaia, but this was a true forest. He smiled at the memory of Inona, worry creasing her brow as she asked about raccoons. Wildlife would flourish here despite the park's proximity to the city, but the humans wouldn't let anything too dangerous live near their settlements.

For a time, the road veered near a river, another mountain rising on the other side. Ralan peered thoughtfully across the water. There could be any number of caves there, too, but he had no idea how tough they would be to access. Vek had said his nephew was near this spot, so that mountain might be close enough to warrant a check.

"Do you know what's on the other side of the river?" Ralan asked.

Cora shrugged. "No clue. Signal Mountain? I think there's a state forest somewhere over there, too. I've become a city girl over the centuries. I spent more than enough time in the woods when I first arrived on Earth."

"Really?" Ralan studied her for a moment. "You said you've been here around the same amount of time as me. There were plenty of cities in the seventeenth century."

She stared out the windshield for so long he feared she wouldn't answer. "There are few portals to my homeland, and they're all in North America. My people rarely use them. First, we had difficulty in establishing relationships with the many tribes living across the continent, each with their own customs and rules. Then came the Europeans with another set of customs."

The road curved up the side of the mountain, circling toward the summit, but Ralan lost all interest in the view. "Had the European settlements reached this far inland at the time? I didn't travel to the Americas until after the revolution."

"I don't think so, but I emerged in the Appalachians to the northeast," Cora said. "That's where I spent my time in the woods. I was half-starved when a couple of native hunters found me."

"What happened then?"

A fond smile crossed her lips. "They were from the Aniyunwiya, now called the Cherokee. They named me a *Nunnehi,* a magical traveler, though that wasn't quite accurate. They were thinking of another type of fae who lived in the area, but I'm close enough that I rolled with it. I was able to be myself for the most part, not having to bother with glamour. But as time passed and I didn't age, some became uneasy."

"Did they force you to leave?" Ralan asked.

Cora shook her head. "Of course not. They had a great deal of respect for the *Nunnehi* and would not have caused me offense. Beyond that, they were kind. The women taught me traditional weaving and farming. But the wary gazes and the deference wore on me. I moved to a European city on the coast and pretended to be human after that."

"Wait," Ralan said, brows lowering in thought. "If you lived that long among the Native Americans, how can you be so uncomfortable in the woods?"

She tossed him an annoyed look. "The Aniyunwiya lived in villages, Ralan. Houses, community buildings, even a wooden palisade. I never had to stray farther than the fields. Honestly, don't you know anything about the different native cultures?"

Heat crept up his neck. "I knew that much, at least. But the woods were all around you. You never explored?"

"After almost starving in the forest?" Cora chuckled. "No."

He studied her profile. With her long black hair, tan skin, and brown eyes, Cora would fit in with the Cherokee. Only the soft point of her ears set her apart. "I'm surprised you weren't swept up by some noble warrior."

"Who's to say I wasn't?" Cora asked with a quick grin.

His eyebrows rose. "You were married?"

She laughed. "No. But I wasn't always lonely, either."

Perhaps Ralan should have been jealous, but he couldn't find it in himself to be. The thought of her spending centuries feeling unloved was much worse than any blow to his own ego. He'd been lonely often enough in his own life to never wish it on another. Besides, he wouldn't expect celibacy from anyone.

"Good," he simply said.

The road passed beside the massive reservoir, a giant lake in the middle of the mountain. When had they curled their way up to the top? The slope of the road and the surrounding forest had largely hidden the climb. Ralan still didn't see anything except trees, water, and power lines. They could've been on flat ground.

"With this bond, I expected you to be more possessive," Cora said softly.

He smiled. "Our souls may be linked, but we are each our own person. The thought of you with another makes me ill, it is true, but I don't own you. I would never seek to."

With sudden clarity, Ralan knew he would let her go if it made her happier. Even though it would hurt like hell. Even though the thought of severing their bond sliced into his heart. And that wasn't even considering the social consequences. If she requested a priest break their soulbond, it would be assumed that Ralan had done something terrible. Prince or not, he would be shunned. But despite all of that, he would do it for her happiness.

He stifled a groan. Dammit, he was beginning to love her.

Cora leaned against the overlook rail and studied the trail map they'd been given in the visitor's center. She was no seer, but none of it seemed right. "I don't think they're here."

"Hmm?" Ralan asked, his attention on the valley below.

"There are lots of trails, but this place isn't private." She caught sight of a group of bicyclists parking next to the visitor's center. The concrete building wasn't huge, mostly housing a small exhibit about the reservoir, but it appeared to be a popular starting point for hikers and cyclists. "And I'm not sure there would be any caves that aren't flooded. Not with a giant reservoir in the middle of the mountain. I didn't realize it was this big."

Ralan propped his elbows on the rail. "We need to cross the water."

Cora frowned. "The reservoir?"

"No." He inclined his head toward the view. "The river."

"The…" Cora focused on his face. His eyes weren't as blank as when he'd had the vision at the carnival, but they weren't quite normal either. "Ralan?"

He continued to stare into the distance for several heartbeats. Then he blinked and shook his head. "Sorry. It's all muddled. But the hardest strands to follow lead across that river."

"I don't know how to get there from here." With a sigh, Cora tugged her phone from her pocket and pulled up her map. "It's Prentice Cooper State Forest. Do you have any idea how many miles of hiking that could be? And it'll take a while to get there. You'd better be certain."

"As much as I can be of anything." He straightened, his expression softening as he faced her. "I think she'll be okay, Cora. The strands where she isn't are the clearest."

Cora looked out over the railing at the river in the valley below, another mountain spearing up beyond. Such a beautiful view to hold so much future aggravation. But she would do anything to save Maddy, even hike the untamed. "Let's go. We've wasted enough time, and it'll take a while to drive over. We'll have to go all the way back to downtown Chattanooga to get to the bridge over the river."

"I'll have words with Vek over this," Ralan said with a scowl.

She thought back to their encounter with the Unseelie prince. "He's even less familiar with this area than I am, I think. If the cave is across the river, it *is* near Raccoon Mountain."

"Still—"

"Come on." Cora grabbed his wrist and tugged. "You can grumble about Vek in the car. I want to scope out a good starting point and see how much day we have left."

Ralan pulled his arm free and laced his fingers with hers. Warmth curled through her, a lightness she hadn't felt since her youth. They'd joined together in passion, yet somehow their linked hands felt almost as intimate. Bodies blending in daylight with joint purpose.

A declaration of togetherness.

At his desk, Lyr struggled to focus on the paper he held as Meli wrapped her arms around his neck and leaned against his back. They'd worked on their separate tasks in the quiet study until she'd abandoned her book on Moranaian history to torment him. And it was working. The first few crops had already been harvested, hadn't they? He could read about it tomorrow.

"It's getting late," she said. "Are you almost done?"

He tapped his finger on the stack of papers. "I'm never done."

But Lyr shifted, turning his head so he could give her a quick kiss. Then another. Perhaps it *was* time for bed. Sensing his change in intent, Meli let go and stepped back. He stood, his hands going to her waist. Her arms looped around his neck again, and she grinned.

"I suppose I should be grateful that you fight more paperwork than people." Some of the humor faded from her expression. "Usually."

Lyr lowered his forehead to hers. "Let's hope things will remain peaceful for a while."

As if on cue, a knock sounded on the door. Lyr let out a wry laugh and let go of Meli. He sensed his mother's energy on the other side, and there was a bite to it that said she brought news. "Come in."

Lynia strode through, her steps slowing only a little at the sight of Meli. "Headed to bed?"

"Soon enough," Lyr answered. "Is something wrong?"

"Not precisely, but I thought you should know what I found." His mother halted on the other side of his desk and lowered a book to the surface. "Remember that I found reference to the energy poisoning spell?"

He frowned. "Yes."

"I tracked down another source." She placed her finger over a line of text. "If Ralan hasn't found Kien, he needs to do it soon. From what Arlyn and Selia said, Kien used a spell imbued in crystals for the original. But there's a riskier form. He could also hook it into himself."

"*Clechtan*," Lyr cursed. Just what they needed. "What is the risk?"

Lynia's lips thinned. "One wrong move, and he could damage Earth's energy. Permanently. Kien is able to transmute objects and alter energy fields. All he needs is to be connected directly."

"I'll contact Ralan."

His mother nodded and bent to gather the large tome. She winced as she straightened, and Lyr had to grit his teeth to stop himself from offering help. Even Lial admitted that her spine was healing well, and the healer was more protective than Lyr. Still, he struggled to see his mother hurting, even if it was a simple twinge.

She smiled, a knowing glint in her eyes. "Thank you for not fussing over me. Now, try to speak to Ralan."

As his mother hurried out, Lyr gave Meli a resigned look. "It looks like bed will have to wait."

Had he ever felt bored with life? He would never take peace for granted again.

16

Cora turned off the ignition and dropped her forehead against the steering wheel. They'd made it to the other side of the river, but this parking area was empty. "I am so sick of driving."

"I could take a turn when we start out again," Ralan said.

She couldn't help it—she laughed. "And have you blank out in some vision while driving and get us into a fiery crash? No."

He grimaced. "You do have a point. I managed to mostly block my talents when I lived on Earth before, so it wasn't an issue. I'm sorry, Cora."

"It's okay." She rubbed her weary eyes and peered around the abandoned lot. "There's not much on this side of the river. Where could they have gone? Do you think they ditched the car? Or concealed it with magic?"

"Could be." Ralan rubbed his hand down her back. "Maybe we should get out and look for a—"

He cut off so abruptly that Cora straightened in concern. But he hadn't been gripped by another vision as far as she could tell. Instead,

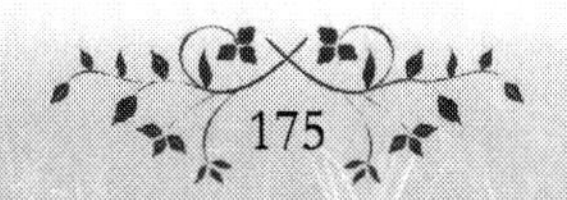

he'd bent down to dig in his bag. Her brow furrowed. What in the hell was he doing? When he sat up holding a tablet-sized pouch, her confusion was in no way cleared.

"What's that?"

Ralan glanced warily out the windows before reaching into the small bag. He pulled out the mirror from before, and she couldn't help but stare. She hadn't gotten a good look at it when he'd shown it to her at the hotel. The delicate silver frame formed in the shape of vines and leaves. Light pulsed softly across its surface, and a hum of magic brushed her skin. Stunning.

"It's the communication mirror, remember?" He held it low, out of sight of any passing cars. "I used it to speak to my daughter. Someone is calling."

His daughter. Oh, man. Cora had been so caught up in events that she hadn't had time to contemplate that aspect of her new relationship. If they stayed bonded, she would be a stepmother. What if the girl hated her? What if she turned out to be terrible at parenting? She hadn't thought about having children in so long it was almost a foreign concept.

Her skin tingled as Ralan, oblivious to her distress, channeled more magic into the mirror. The light flared, then settled to reveal two elves standing in a beautiful study. Cora leaned closer, not sure what to look at first. There was a handsome male with long brown hair and a delicate blond woman beside him. Light streamed all around them from myriad windows, ancient trees visible beyond the panes.

Cora bit back a grin. It looked like a scene from a fantasy movie.

"Is Eri okay?" Ralan asked as soon as the magic settled.

The man nodded. "She is well. Behaving perfectly, in fact."

Ralan's brows drew together. "Has something else happened? I was supposed to contact you later."

"My mother found another source on the energy poisoning." A worried frown crossed the elf's face. "Have you found Kien? If not, put a rush on it."

"Why?" Ralan asked.

"According to Mother, he might be planning to connect himself to Earth's energy despite the danger. I recommend you kill him first."

Ralan went silent, and Cora glanced over to see his nostrils flaring. Finally, he spoke. "My Sight has completely failed. And Cora's friend was kidnapped by Kien's minions. We're making progress, Lyr, but I'm going into this blind."

"You've had three centuries of life without your Sight," the elf said. "Think of something else."

Cora's attention returned to the mirror as the female took a step closer. "What about my runes?"

Beside Cora, Ralan let out a curse. "No. You would be beyond lost in the human world, Meli. If you think Lyr's home is different from Alfheim, imagine a place with speeding vehicles and skyscrapers," Ralan said. "Beyond that, it would take too long to get you here."

Meli's chin tipped up. "I have a few memories from my past life."

"What about Kien's blood?" Lyr asked in a rush, his face a shade paler in the glass. "Didn't you take it with you for that purpose?"

Cora jerked back, and if the others continued to speak, she didn't notice it. A memory popped into her mind, and suddenly all she could hear were Vek's casual words. *Too bad your kind can't follow*

blood connections as easily as mine can. But I doubt you carry around each other's blood.

Her heartbeat roared into her ears as realization hit. All this time, Ralan had possessed the very thing they needed. Almost two days of fruitless searching. Of leads that never worked out. Her palms heated until she forced her magic down.

Barely.

"Cora?" Ralan asked, concern in his tone.

"You asshole," Cora said softly.

His hand lowered to her shoulder, but she shrugged it away. "What's wrong?"

Cora took a deep breath, struggling for control, and spun to face him. He stared at her with mouth agape. Didn't he realize she'd heard? "You lied to me. You've been lying to me all this time."

Confusion lined his brow. "What are you talking about?"

"Your friend just said you have Kien's blood." She poked a finger against Ralan's chest, not caring if she singed his shirt. "All this time, you could have found him and thus Maddy. All this fucking time. Did you want to sleep with me that badly, or were you trying to capture me in this damn bond first?"

She felt the punch of emotion in her own soul as pain washed away his confusion. "That was low, Cora."

The air heated as her fury spiked, and Cora scrambled for the door handle. Without a word, she shoved her way free of the car. She heard his door slam as he followed, but she didn't look. Instead, she paced as she fought to control her fire. Only when she knew she could speak without blasting him did she spin to face him.

"That's all you have to say?"

"No," Ralan answered. Regret tinged with fear flowed from him, souring her stomach. "Vek said Kien had found his group, but that could have been a lie."

"Bullshit," she snapped. "You gave no indication that you doubted him. So *why?*"

Ralan shoved his hand through his hair. "There's risk."

Her fists clenched, and she had to stifle to urge to punch him. "Vek didn't think so."

"He's a blood elf."

"Your friend in the mirror seemed to have no qualms," Cora retorted.

"Dammit, I don't want to end up like Kien," Ralan shouted, his voice raw with pain. "He's a butcher. Some of the things I Saw when I still could… Gods, Cora, he absorbs power from the lifeforce of others. What if his blood is as vile as his soul?"

The sound of chirping birds and burbling water filled the silence. Cora's anger dampened at the tortured look on Ralan's face, but it didn't go away. "You aren't like him."

"He's my brother." Ralan's shoulders slumped, and he rubbed his hand across his face. "I can't help but wonder if I hold something like that inside of me."

"Oh, for—" She cut off the expletive she wanted to utter and strode over to Ralan. When his gaze dropped, she put both hands on his cheeks and forced him to look at her. "Why would you even think that?"

His sigh brushed her lips. "I share other traits with him. A certain arrogance to be certain. And I've bent rules to get my own way."

"Everyone has," she said. "Humans. Fae. Everyone."

Though he smiled, it held little humor. "Cora—"

"Shut up, Ralan." She tugged him closer as her anger faded to embers, simmering but banked. "I'm connected to your soul, so if anyone in the world could answer this, it would be me. You. Are. Not. Evil. Stop wasting time over something that isn't real."

His hands framed her face. Then he lowered his mouth to hers, pouring his worry and his pain into their kiss. Cora let her arms drop to his shoulders and shifted closer. For a moment, they devoured, his agony feeding the remnants of her fury. But then the tone shifted.

For the first time ever, he brushed his mind against hers. She hesitated only a heartbeat before allowing his thoughts in. *"I'm sorry,"* he whispered.

He had so much worry suffused in his thoughts. A burden, a weight, so great she wanted to cry for him. Cora shifted back until their lips parted and she could look into his eyes. *"Thank you."*

His eyebrow arched. *"For?"*

"Apologizing." She let her lips curl upward. *"I like people who can admit a fault."*

"I've had plenty of fault to admit to lately," he answered wryly. *"Trust me."*

Cora found herself laughing. With a shake of her head, she ended their mental connection. Aloud, she said, "What do you need to do the spell with Kien's blood?"

"A shielded space free of possible disruption." Ralan examined the clearing with a frown. "This is a serious spell, one I haven't fully performed before. A parking lot beside a public road would not be a safe spot."

She bit her lip. There was one place she could take him. Her haven—home. Only her closest friends had ever been, and they but rarely. But she could hardly chide him for holding back if she did, too.

"Let's go to my house."

They didn't speak a great deal on the way to Cora's house, but that was fine with Ralan. Their argument had given him more than enough to process. Why hadn't he realized the true source of his hesitation about using Kien's blood? He hadn't known himself until Cora's goading had brought it forth.

He and Kien had always been in competition, at least as long as Ralan could clearly remember. Both of them were confident and hated to lose. But Kien's games had always been tinged with a hint of cruelty. Sometimes, it was a joke that held more than a little mocking. Others, an accident that ended in injury. Like the time Kien's sword had slipped during practice, cracking the bone in Ralan's arm.

Cora was right—Ralan didn't have that cruelty inside him. But fear and logic were far from friends.

They turned down a quiet street of well-kept older homes set around a broad hill. The lots here were generous, more so than near the city proper, but they were far from private. Ralan peered curiously at the neighborhood and wondered which belonged to Cora. Did she like living so close to humans?

But as they continued around the hill, the yards grew larger and the homes older. Finally, Cora pulled into a driveway at the end of the road. Trees lined the drive and partly obscured one corner of

the house, a craftsman style in decent repair. A quick glance around revealed the yard to be fairly private.

"How much land do you have?"

Cora smiled as she parked the car. "Eight acres."

"It's beautiful," he said, unbuckling his seatbelt.

"I'm sure you have penthouses that are bigger." Cora chuckled. "But it's my favorite home so far."

"A penthouse that large in a city? Not even I can do something that impossible."

They shared a grin before climbing out of the car. Ralan did have a five-hundred-acre estate in New York, but he didn't mention it. The place had never felt like home, and its size was no substitute for the peaceful energy that caressed him as soon as he stepped onto Cora's land.

Ralan hefted his backpack to his shoulders and followed Cora up the sidewalk. Her fingers shook as she unlocked the door, and she dropped the keys with a clatter. Shoulders going stiff, she bent to retrieve them. Then she took a deep breath and pushed open the door.

Why was she so nervous? He hesitated a moment before following her again. Ralan found nothing embarrassing in the living room. The furniture was in good repair, and the room was fairly free of clutter. To the left, a television hung above the fireplace. To the right, a cozy chair had been placed beside a set of bookcases.

"I was beginning to worry I'd find something terrible," he said.

Cora blushed as she placed her purse on a side table. "Oh?"

"You looked like you'd rather run than open the door." He scanned the room before returning his attention to her. "It's obviously nothing here. What's wrong?"

"I..." She swallowed hard. "I don't let many people in. To my life, I mean. Even Maddy and Jase have only been here a few times."

"Because of the jerk on your home world?"

Cora nodded. "And because I move so often. I'll have to close this place up and leave before long."

Ralan knew that annoyance all too well. It was the main reason he'd bought the five-hundred acres. His neighbors were too far away to see him, so he didn't have to hide his lack of aging. He only needed to sell the place to himself every few decades. But eight acres wouldn't be enough to ensure that Cora wasn't watched too closely by her neighbors.

"So," she said, interrupting his thoughts. "My back workroom is magically shielded. I have my drawings there, though, so just..."

Some of the reason for her nerves became clear. "Your fashion designs? I won't say a word about them."

Cora waved a hand, her expression wry. "I'm not sure that's better. I'll be wondering if you hate them either way."

He chuckled. "Then what do you prefer?"

"Honesty," she answered. Then she nibbled at her lower lip. "So long as it isn't brutal."

"My ego is healthy enough that I don't need to bruise another person to augment it."

Cora grinned at him. "That's a fancy way of saying you aren't a jerk."

Ralan gave a flourishing bow. "As it pleases you, milady."

"Ha ha," she answered. She gestured toward the archway behind her. "Come on."

Despite the difficult task ahead, Ralan found his mood lighter as he followed Cora into a small kitchen. She opened a door on the left and motioned for him to enter. He paused in the doorway, a little nervous himself. It would be awkward indeed if he hated his soulbonded's work.

A few framed pictures of her designs hung from the walls, and many more were pinned over a drafting table cluttered with work. A table occupied the center of the room, fabrics piled on one end. She also had a sewing table against the wall and a rack of clothing in various stages of construction.

Ralan circled the room, examining the drawings first. Then he stopped next to the rack and pulled out a fun, floral dress with a scooped neckline. "Custom order?"

Nibbling at her lip again, Cora nodded. "I've been trying to work on winter designs, but I keep getting requests for other things. At this rate, I might as well start on spring stuff."

Ralan shrugged. "You aren't as constrained as I am. Make what you want."

"Constrained?"

"The bigger you get, the more you have to stick to a schedule." Ralan placed the dress back on the rack. "Fashion weeks, big shows, magazines, store ordering times. It makes it harder to follow your inspiration."

Cora studied him. "Are you going back to design once this is through?"

"I doubt it." Ralan smiled against a wave of sadness. Another chapter of his life ended, one more to add to thousands of others. "I'll formally hand it over to my assistant. She has already been

running things in my absence and is more than skilled enough. If she wants to start her own business, I'll end the line. Eri will not be ready to return to Earth for some time."

"Your daughter," she said, a strange expression crossing her face.

Ralan's brows drew together. "What is it?"

"Our bond." Cora squared her shoulders. "If we keep it, it's a form of marriage, right? She would be my stepdaughter. That's something we'll have to consider. She might not be receptive."

That was what was bothering her? Ralan smiled. "She's the one who told me your name and urged me to find you. Remember that she sent her regards when last we spoke. She likes you."

Cora's lips pursed. "She hasn't met me."

"She's a seer of great power," Ralan said. "She has probably foreseen every interaction you'll have for the next thousand years."

"Thousand years?"

Ralan strode to the table and set his backpack on the clear side. "Maybe not literally. There are many strands of possibility. But she has Seen enough to know if she likes you."

He hid a grin at the stunned expression on Cora's face as he dug in his backpack for the vial of Kien's blood. When his fingers connected with the cool glass, Ralan's humor cut off like the end of an unexpected vision. It was time. As much as he hated the thought, it was time to track his brother.

Cora paled when he pulled the vial free. "Do I want to know how you got that?"

"He left behind a pool of blood when he escaped from Inona and Delbin. Thankfully, Inona brought some back with her."

"How much time are you going to need for…whatever you're doing?" she asked.

Ralan grimaced. "An hour or more. Probably. I learned this spell hundreds of years ago, so I'm rusty." He met her gaze. "I'll need privacy."

"I'm fine with that," Cora said with a shudder. "I'll take a walk and start on dinner."

"You cook?"

A quick grin flitted across her lips. "Passably."

Though he wanted to return the smile, Ralan couldn't quite manage it. Not with his brother's foul blood in his hand. As Cora slipped out of the room, he sighed. Whatever effect this might have, he would have to deal with it.

No more delaying.

17

Ralan shoved his hand back in his bag and pulled out a small metal bowl, a cloth, and a knife. He set them on the table and dropped down into the chair he'd grabbed. For a moment, he rolled the smooth vial of blood between his fingers. All that he'd dreaded was contained in this small tube of glass.

I hope this doesn't destroy me.

He took a deep, bracing breath and placed the vial next to the bowl. With a tendril of energy, he tested the room's shielding. Strong. Then he glanced around her room and frowned. He didn't want any hint of this to touch upon her work, but he wouldn't have to add much with her protections already in place. Closing his eyes, he lifted a hand and cast a thin but solid shield around himself and the objects on the table.

Ralan eyed the knife, then sighed and picked it up. No time like the present. Quickly, he slid the blade along the top of his forearm. With a wince, he held his arm over the bowl and let a few drops of his blood plop in. Then he wiped the knife clean on a corner of the cloth and pressed the fabric to the cut to stop the bleeding.

His stomach turned as he set the knife on the table and stared at the red splattering the middle of the bowl. His arm burned, but elves healed fast. Already, he could sense his energy pooling around the wound, aiding his body's natural response. In only moments, he was able to pull the cloth away to reveal a scab across the cut.

Now for the truly unpleasant part.

Bile scalded the back of Ralan's throat as he let energy pool in his palm. He sought inside himself for the spell he'd learned as an apprentice, one based on similarity. It would form a link between him and Kien, and it would only be stronger and easier since they were brothers. Fortunately, it also blocked the other party from recognizing the link.

With a sharp exhale, Ralan connected the spell to his own blood.

Only then did he lift the vial again. Deep breath in. Out. With numb fingers, he pulled the seal free. Then he tipped the tube over the bowl, letting a few drops of blood land and mingle with his own. He corked the rest inside and set the vial next to the bowl.

His vision went black.

"Come on, Ral, I'll go with you."

Ralan scoffed. "Aren't you too old to be sliding down the banister?"

"You're ten," Kien answered, laughing. "You're probably too old, too. Let's do it anyway. I dare you."

Wary, Ralan peered at his older brother. Kien was a couple hundred years older, way beyond this kind of stuff. Besides, he left Ralan to take the blame as often as not. He'd dared Ralan to hide their other brother's practice sword last week, and Teyark had lectured him for hours. Kien had laughed about it for days.

"Look, I'll go first," his brother said.

Sure enough, Kien plopped down on the rail, grinned, and slid all the way down. Ralan sighed. If he didn't follow, Kien would give him endless grief about it, and that would be worse than any scolding.

Ralan sat on the smooth banister, closed his eyes, and shoved off. Despite his annoyance, the rush brought a smile to his face.

A smile that ended as the vision slammed into him. Kien darting from the room. His mother storming across the entry a heartbeat later.

Ralan's hip connected painfully with the end of the bannister, startling a cry from his lips as his eyes popped open on the present. And the sight of his mother opening the door to the entry.

A dull pain entered Ralan's awareness as his vision hazed and cleared again. Gasping for air, he forced his fingers to uncurl. He glanced down to see the half-moon indentions of his fingernails reddening his palm. Then he looked at the bowl of mingled blood. He'd heard the spell sometimes caused random images—but not full visions.

His mouth went dry at the reminder of that day. Even then, Kien had played unpleasant games. But they had been brothers. After the betrayal, Ralan had forced aside such painful memories. That vision on the banister had been the first time Ralan had Seen the future. When his mother had stormed over and started to berate him, not noticing his shock, Kien had come back to charm away her anger as he sometimes did. Of course, Kien had left him hanging just as often. Ralan had never known what to expect from his brother.

But when had Kien started to hate him?

With trembling hands, Ralan lifted the bowl and swirled the blood to better blend it. Gods, what a fucked-up mess. To have to hunt his own brother… Even when he'd first discovered Kien plotting with Kenaren, he'd taken the matter to his father. He hadn't dreamed of handling it himself. Now, Ralan had no choice.

He would have to kill his own brother.

He muttered the words to the seeking spell, and his heart gave a thud as it snapped into place. Suddenly, he could feel the pull, an inner compass that would lead to Kien. But that was all—no dark and twisted thoughts or demented fragments of his brother. Ralan heaved a sigh of relief as he tucked the vial of blood into the compartment in his pack.

All he had left was clean-up.

After a stroll through her backyard, Cora scanned the area around her with her magic. Satisfied that no one was watching, she ducked into the small grove of trees at the back of her property. She usually visited the portal at night, but she needed the soothing touch of her homeland's energy after so much stress.

When she reached the small depression in the side of the hill, Cora lifted her hand. The portal flared to life, the light duller in the light of day, and she stretched her fingers as close as she dared. Energy poured into her until she moaned. Ah, how she missed the power of her home!

"Cora."

Her hand jerked as her father's voice streamed into her mind for the first time in decades. *"Papa?"*

"Come home."

"I can't," she said. *"You know I can't."*

"I would have never sought the crown had I known it would lead to your loss." Sadness beyond words tinged his tone. *"I do not care that Orn is king, Cora."*

"He's cruel. He has sent many after me, and they have not all been kind. You know this."

Surely her mother had told him.

"Orn wed yesterday eve. Our families are at peace."

Cora frowned at that news. Time passed differently in the two realms, and she'd never devised a reliable way to calculate it. Had it really been that long for them, or had the wedding taken place unusually quickly? The sick feeling in her gut told her that Orn wasn't finished bothering her regardless.

"We'll see," she merely answered. *"There are other things that hold me here right now."*

"You have bonded to that place."

"No."

"Your energy is different," her father said. *"As though you've merged with another source."*

Her breath caught. Could he sense her bond with Ralan so readily? The soulbond *was* similar to the connection her people made to the energy fields of other lands. Her power twined with the magic of a location in just such an unbreakable way. Cora lifted her free hand to her lips as a new thought struck her.

It was her fault.

Her magic must have reached for Ralan and created the bond he'd assumed would only form with a spell. The process was all too similar.

"Cora?"

"I have to go," she sent in a rush. *"I'm well. Just…I need to go. I love you."*

"I love you always," her father answered.

Cora tugged her hand away and stumbled back. The portal quieted, but her pulse raced at her revelation. Would Ralan be angry? He'd made it more than clear that he'd had no intention of bonding with his life so uncertain. And it was all her fault. To think *she* had been upset at *him.*

Her stomach clenched as she rushed from the grove and across the yard to the porch. When she entered the kitchen, the door to her workroom was still closed. Groaning at the wait, Cora opened the refrigerator and stared blankly inside. What would Ralan even want to eat? They'd shared a few meals during the search, but not enough to give her a clear idea.

She was bonded to him, and she didn't even know his favorite foods. She didn't know his favorite *anything.* What a mess. Cora leaned her forehead against the cool edge of the refrigerator door. With all of the danger surrounding him, there was no guarantee she would be able to find out. Sighing, she shoved back and peered at the food once more. Worrying wouldn't help. She needed to do something.

Finally, she settled on a chicken and vegetable stir fry—in no small part because it gave her an excuse to chop things. She busied herself with cleaning the vegetables and then arranging the spices and supplies on her small counter. If she didn't do something with this nervous energy, she would be cooking the food with her bare hands instead of a pan. Her magic already wanted to surge out of her control.

When Ralan emerged, Cora was almost done. The spatula scraped against the pan from her frantic movements, and she fought to control the panic that leapt within her as she sensed his presence. When his hand settled on the small of her back, she jumped.

"I thought you weren't worried about the spell's effect on me," he said.

Cora moved the pan off the stove and spun to face him. His hand shifted to her waist, low and intimate, and she swallowed. "I wasn't. I'm not."

"You're acting like I'm going to devour you." His lips twisted. "And not in a good way."

"It's my fault," she blurted.

Both of his brows rose at that. "What's your fault?"

"The bond."

His other hand cupped her face. "It was an accident. No one is to blame."

"I don't think that's true." She settled her own hand alongside his. "I didn't think about this, but…my people bond to places. To different kinds of energy. When your medallion pressed between us, my magic must have triggered the spell. I'm sorry, Ralan."

Her heart thundered at his frown. But after a moment he relaxed, and a smile crossed his lips. "I'm not."

Cora blinked. "What?"

"From the moment I saw your face in my vision, I wanted you." One corner of his mouth tipped higher. "The goddess chided me for my lack of attention, in fact. I might not have chosen this time to begin our bond, but I don't regret it."

Suddenly, she knew what it meant for her heart to melt. To turn over. Cora stepped closer, her arms going around his waist, and lowered her head to his chest. He settled her snugly against him, their hearts and spirits for once in accord. Neither of them knew what was going to happen in the future.

But she would always have this moment.

Inona stomped over to the trash can, a tray of charred food balanced in her hands.

"How could you burn corn dogs?" Delbin asked, and she wanted to smack him at the humor in his tone.

"I was arranging the others most carefully." Inona tipped her chin up and tried not to blush as she dumped the ruined food into the garbage. "Meg said I should include around twenty fries. After I finished counting and placing the cooked corn dogs with the proper amount, I'd forgotten about the ones cooking. At least those baskets have been completed properly."

"Yeah, but—" Delbin's breath huffed out on a laugh. "Never mind. We'll straighten it out."

Inona stiffened as smooth voice broke through. "Just the two people I was looking for. Kien said I'd find you here."

She pivoted, her hand darting into her pocket for the knife concealed within. A pale, familiar-looking man leaned against the back corner of the food stall. Though his gaze flicked to her pocket, he didn't bother to uncross his arms as he smirked at them. Inona sent out a tendril of energy in a quick scan, but she recoiled at his dark magic.

A blood elf.

"Who are you?" she demanded.

The man's smirk widened, and she caught a hint of fang. "A friend, if you'll let me be. I'm surprised you don't remember me."

A memory flashed into her mind. The cave. He'd been slumped against a stalagmite, drained after Delbin had shattered the energy poisoning spell. This was the mage who'd been working with Kien. But he'd claimed to be finished with the prince and hadn't done anything to stop them. Whose side was he on now?

"I remember," Delbin said from beside her. "And if you've aligned with Kien once more, then we've no interest in your friendship."

"He believes me to be an ally." The elf straightened. "The truth is more complex."

Inona's hand tightened around the hilt of her knife. "What do you want?"

"Your help."

At a mental nudge from Delbin, she opened her thoughts to him. *"What?"*

"Ralan said this would happen, didn't he? There's something important about this guy."

"Yeah," Inona grumbled. *"I imagine getting us alone is really important to Kien's people. I don't trust him. Ralan did not indicate that we should."*

Delbin's lips quirked. *"Well, I don't think Ralan left us behind just to tell the guy to go to hell."*

"Have you reached a consensus yet?" the elf asked, obviously not missing their mental conversation. "I need to return to Kien if my plan is to work."

Inona glanced around. "This is not a good place to talk."

The door on the back of the food stall opened, and Meg poked her head out. "We're getting a line. Are you two done goofing off?"

"Sorry. We'll be right there," Delbin said. As soon as Meg ducked back inside, he pinned the stranger with a look. "We have an hour left in this shift. Look for the striped tent at the end of the fairway. That's the staff tent, and it'll be marked. Meet us there when we're done. If you can't wait that long, then forget it."

"I'll be there," the elf said.

Inona scowled at him as she followed Delbin back to the stall. From what she knew, blood elves weren't necessarily evil, but they were dangerous. He smirked again and gave a quick, mocking salute as she passed. No way she was going to trust him.

18

Cora smiled as Ralan set a plate of stir fry in front of her. Odd to be served by a prince. But he'd insisted on doing so since she'd cooked, and she was still shaky. *Why argue?* she thought as he sat across from her at her small kitchen table with his own plate. Then her smile faded. Her own worry might have distracted him, but she could tell by his pallor that the blood spell had taken its toll.

"Are you okay? Did it work?"

"It did." A hint of grief reached her through their bond as Ralan picked up his fork. But he didn't attempt to take a bite. "I feel fully myself. It's just that the spell brought a vision. Of the past, that is. A memory from my youth."

Cora winced at that. She might be an only child, but she could imagine the turmoil of having to hunt down a family member. "I'm sorry."

"I could have done without the reminder." Sighing, Ralan stabbed a piece of chicken with his fork. "It's easier to think of him

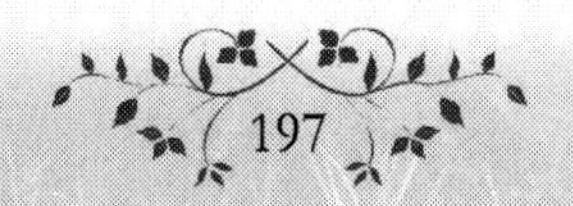

as another enemy, a madman who needs to be stopped. Much harder to think of him as normal, if a bit mischievous."

"I'm assuming he was a troublemaker."

"Unrepentant," Ralan answered. "I guess that says it all, doesn't it?"

They ate a few bites in silence. What could she possibly say to comfort him? She had no idea, but she had to try something. "Do you want to talk about it?"

Ralan canted his head, considering. Finally, he shook his head. "Not while the blood spell is so fresh. Though I'm unharmed, it was an uneasy process."

"Will you be able to track him?" Her hand tightened around her fork. "I'm worried about Maddy. Her dad called earlier and said her energy is still strong, but there's no telling what she's going through physically."

"I know, and I'm sorry." Ralan's lips turned down, and his shoulders drooped. "We need a plan to go after him."

Cora popped another bite of food in her mouth and forced herself to eat it before she spoke again. "It feels strange to be sharing a meal right now. Like we should be moving instead of just sitting here. I wish I'd made something portable so we could be on the road."

Ralan stretched his free hand across the table and tangled his fingers with hers. "The journey ahead will be difficult, love. Gaining strength is not a waste of time."

Though warmth trickled through her at the endearment, she didn't let herself dwell on it. "I know."

Abruptly, his hand jerked against hers, and his eyes went wide and a little glazed. Cora stilled, afraid to disturb him in case he was

having another vision. But after a moment, he let out a soft curse and focused on her once more. She lifted a brow in question.

"Delbin just contacted me." Ralan pulled his hand free and pushed his chair back with a scrape. "I hope you're almost full. One of Kien's lackeys approached them, as I'd seen in my vision. They're supposed to meet soon, and Delbin isn't inclined to wait for us."

Cora shot to her feet. "Are they in danger?"

"I don't know." Ralan huffed out a breath. "It didn't seem so in my vision, but we both know how reliable that is. I'd prefer to be near them during the meeting just in case."

As Ralan ducked into her workroom for his backpack, Cora grabbed their plates and carried them to the sink. She eyed the pan on the stove. She hated to leave a mess, but it couldn't be avoided. After a quick check to make sure she'd turned off the burner, Cora tossed one last frown at the dishes and headed from the room.

Ralan followed close on her heels as she snatched her purse from the living room table. She ushered him out the front door before locking it behind them. Then once again, they rushed to her car. With luck, traffic wouldn't be too bad. She looked at her watch and winced.

Lots and lots of luck.

Delbin ambled along the fairway, Inona's hand in his, and forced a slight smile to his lips. People surged around them, quite a few for a Sunday evening. He tried not to look too closely at any of them, hoping to appear casual. It wouldn't matter if *he* missed anything.

Inona was the expert, and he trusted her to catch sight of anyone giving them undue attention.

Tomorrow was the last day of the carnival. Then Tuesday, they'd pack it all up and move to a new location an hour on the other side of town, toward Knoxville. Delbin had begun to worry about that, so for him, it was a relief that Kien's contact had found them today. But Inona's reserve told him she did not agree.

"You know we need to do this," he said into her mind.

Her hand tightened on his. *"I know. But you have already been injured once. If this is a trap, they might attack you again."*

"I'll try not to do something stupid this time."

"Please," Inona grumbled.

A quick grin crossed his lips and then faded. He wouldn't attempt to be a hero, but he was more than ready to send a mental blast into the mind of any who tried to hurt them. They'd caught him unawares last time, and he'd strengthened his mind magic while working with Ralan. Delbin had spent a great deal of time since considering what he could have done differently.

The staff tent came into sight. Sure enough, the blood elf waited over to the side, focusing on them as they neared. An insolent smile lit his face, and Delbin lifted his chin in return, refusing to be cowed. He'd seen this mage crumpled in the cave, energy drained, and though he'd clearly regained his strength, Delbin wasn't intimidated.

"Hey!" Delbin said, filling his voice with false cheer for any who might be listening. "How about we take a walk away from all this noise? I want to hear what you've been up to all this time."

Expression inscrutable, the elf nodded. "Sure."

They circled the tent and headed toward a small stand of trees near the edge of the property. As they passed the area where Kien had once confronted Delbin, he couldn't help but look around warily. But this time, there was no sign of the dark prince. Delbin's attention shifted to the mage, who walked quietly beside him.

"What have you been up to lately?" Delbin asked, mindful of their proximity to the tent.

The elf's brow quirked, but he answered. "Looking for a new place to stay. Until recently."

"Sounds exciting."

"I'm sure you can guess."

Delbin grinned at that. "Considering when I last saw you, yeah."

Silence fell between them until they reached the small grove. Delbin let go of Inona's hand and leaned casually against one of the trees, his arms crossed. The mage echoed the gesture, but Inona stood at the ready. Delbin had no doubt her hand was wrapped around the hilt of her knife in its resting place within her pocket.

"What was that all about?" the elf asked.

Delbin shrugged. "I didn't want to look suspicious. Most of my co-workers are humans and wouldn't understand. They'll probably think I'm buying drugs or something anyway."

The stranger laughed. "Alas, nothing that simple. But probably more legal."

"True. There aren't laws against magic." Delbin's gaze sharpened. "Now. Who are you, really, and what do you want?"

"To the point. I like that." The mage peered at him for a moment. "I'm Fen. You know I worked with Kien. Gotta say, that was one of my dumber decisions. But as I was about to strike out on my own, I

was…made aware of a good reason to return to Kien's employ. This time in order to stop him."

Inona's eyes narrowed. "Just like that?"

"He swore to spare my mother's people," Fen said, expression going hard. "The poison was only supposed to harm the half-bloods on the surface and weaken the full-bloods who tried to interfere."

Delbin's nose wrinkled. "Just a little casual genocide?"

"We didn't intend to kill them." Fen shrugged. "Just rule them. Anyone with magic who might have thought to protect the humans would have been incapacitated, leaving the humans defenseless against our powers. We have crystals that block us from the spell's effects. And once we got Kien back to Moranaia, he would have taken over the throne and used his army to help us."

"Now you've decided world domination isn't for you?" Inona asked, her tone furious.

Though Fen winced, he made a sharp gesture with his hands. "It was a stupid idea, okay? I thought the fae deserved what they got for abandoning me here. My own mother dumped me on Earth the very day I was born. And I'm not the only one this kind of thing has happened to. I've run across many half-bloods, some of them lost and confused with no clue about their heritage. But Kien is no better than the heartless fae who left their offspring behind. By the time I realized how demented he is, I was stuck."

Inona's face reflected Delbin's own disbelief. "Right," she said.

"Look, it doesn't matter at this point," Fen said. "If I don't fix this, my uncle will have to kill me. As he's the only one who has ever been decent to me, I'd like to avoid that. And, you know, survive."

Delbin considered the mage's words. After his own exile to Earth, he'd run across half-bloods himself. It was true that more children had been left behind by careless or neglectful fae than many full-bloods realized. Still, poisoning the energy to take control of the world? A mad scheme indeed.

"Why are you approaching us if you're trying to return to Kien's group?" Delbin asked.

"I'm done hurting others for his pleasure." Fen's jaw clenched. "He ordered me to bring you both back to prove my loyalty. But if we work together, maybe we can defeat him."

Inona strode up to Fen, stopping an arm's length away. "I don't trust you."

"Probably wise," the elf answered. "Still, if you're hunting Kien, I can lead you right to him. Got a better offer?"

Damn. It would speed things up if Fen took them straight to Kien. Wasn't that why they'd returned to the carnival? For information? Delbin exchanged a glance with Inona, who gave a slight shake of her head.

"I don't like this," she sent.

"We'd be idiots to like this," Delbin answered. *"But he has a good point. I can relay the cave's location to Ralan along the way. We both know Kien has to be stopped."*

Inona sighed and spoke aloud, gaze fastened on Fen. "What's your plan?"

"I pretend to take you in. They already have a healer captured. If you can get her on your side, you three could take out Victor and Patrick without much trouble." Fen's eyes flashed red, and his fangs glinted with his smirk. "During that bit of distraction, I can slip up

on Kien. If I can break through his shields quickly enough to get my fangs in him, I can drain him."

Delbin laughed. "Your plan is to eat Kien?"

Fen shook his head. "You know nothing about blood elves, do you? The blood is just a conduit. What I'll drain is his energy. All of it."

"And then?" Inona asked.

"Then I'll use it to kill him."

Ralan tapped his fingers along the edge of the door and glared at the bumper in front of them. Every few minutes, they crept forward, but progress was slow. "I can't believe this."

"I was hoping it wouldn't be too bad on a Sunday," Cora said. "But six o'clock is always a bit crazy."

"It's not your fault," he said.

Traffic shifted, and she inched the car forward again. Only to stop once more. "How long until they meet with Kien's friend?"

"Any time now." Ralan shoved down a surge of dread. He hadn't sensed anything amiss with Delbin, but he couldn't help but worry about his apprentice. "He didn't answer my latest attempt at contact, but his energy was calm."

"We can take the next exit and cut along the side roads," Cora said.

Ralan looked up at the sky. The sun was lowering, but they had two or three hours of light. Unerringly, his head turned in Kien's direction. The connection to his brother unsettled him, like an itch under the skin or clothes too tight. It only added to his aggravation.

When Delbin's energy tapped against his, Ralan opened his mind at once. *"You'd better not be in trouble."*

"The contact's name is Fen," Delbin said in response. *"A young blood elf. He's going to lead me and Inona to Kien in exchange for our help."*

Ralan frowned. A blood elf. Could he be Vek's nephew? *"Why?"*

"He said his uncle would kill him if he didn't fix the trouble he caused."

Ralan nodded, though Delbin couldn't see. *"I've found my own trail, but a clear path would be nice. Ask him his uncle's name."*

There was a brief pause before Delbin answered. *"Vek."*

"Good."

Even with the blood link, Ralan and Cora would have fumbled through the woods in search of the exact cave. A shortcut would save hours. Aligning with Fen was a risk, but Ralan had known Vek long enough to trust his nephew's words. If Fen had caused damage to the Unseelie, Vek wouldn't hesitate to kill family to resolve it.

"What will you be doing?" Delbin asked.

Ralan tried to scan for the strands, but the futures muddled together into a murky mass. Impenetrable. He bit back a groan of frustration and went with his gut. "We'll follow."

"Ah, good. Fen's on his way back."

Maddy glanced at Kien out of the corner of her eye, careful not to draw his attention. Her heart squeezed oddly at the thought of the dark Sidhe's return. Though Patrick had eventually brought her food and bottled water, Fen had been the only one to show her any sort of kindness. She suppressed a snort. A sign of her crappy situation that his meager actions were the nicest things to happen at her.

She couldn't decide if his return was a good thing or a prelude to something worse.

"Think he managed to capture those two you wanted?" Victor asked.

A wicked smile lit Kien's face. "He sent me a mental image of them trussed and bloodied in the back of his car. He said it was easy once he'd taken out the woman."

Patrick shifted against the stalagmite across from her. "Against a telepath?"

"Fen isn't as weak as you," Kien snapped. "Watch the girl. I found a larger chamber through a fissure in the rock, and I'd like to prepare it for a bit of…fun. I have great plans for Delbin and Inona."

The others fell silent as Kien crossed to the back of the narrow cave. Even after he disappeared behind a column, no one spoke. Maddy stared at the dirt crusted on her toes. She'd never get the muck off of her favorite sandals, but she couldn't summon the energy to care. All of her focus was on her plan to escape.

Maddy had waited all day for Kien to leave. Of all of them, he was the one she truly feared. He knew about healers, for one thing, and might have a shield that would slow her powers. Or nullify them. The most vulnerable was Patrick. She suspected he was even younger than she was, and though he tried to appear tough, he wasn't as hardened as the others.

Once she had him alone, she could use her magic to render him unconscious, one of the few healing spells she had almost mastered. It was supposed to be for treating patients who couldn't be awake for a procedure. In this case, she figured it was forgivable to turn it on Patrick. It wouldn't kill him.

Probably.

Maddy shuddered, the motion drawing the others' attention. Victor scowled at her. "What's your problem?"

"I need to pee," she said softly, lying without compunction.

"Ugh," he grumbled. "Take her out again, Patrick."

Patrick's nose curled, but he didn't argue. Instead, he watched Maddy as she shoved herself to her feet, wavering for a moment on legs gone numb from the cold. She jogged her legs back and forth to restore feeling and prayed they'd hold out when she made a run for it. Still shaky, she followed the young Sidhe from the cave.

The light was growing dim as the late afternoon sun slid behind the trees. It couldn't be too far from twilight. Maybe an hour? Nighttime would have been better for her escape, but Maddy couldn't delay any longer. Not if she hoped to help Delbin, Inona, and the rest of the fae races.

Maddy studied the slope that fell away from the landing in front of the cave. The trees were thinner there, letting more light through. When she'd gone out to take care of business before, she'd headed to the right. But the area to the left held the densest forest, probably because the slope was gentler and less rocky. Perfect.

When Patrick gestured to the right, Maddy shook her head. "I don't want to go in the same spot," she said, letting a whine slip into her voice.

"Whatever," he grumbled. "Just move it. This is disgusting enough as it is."

"You're the one who did the kidnapping," she couldn't resist saying.

"Shut up."

Maddy hid a grin as he led her into the trees. Finally, he stopped beside a bush. Arms crossed, he tapped his foot and stared at her. She lifted her chin and stalked past him, squatting an arm's length away. She waited until he turned his head and then flung her arms out as though she were losing her balance.

She'd done that earlier, when he'd escorted her out here before. But this time, Maddy let her magic loose, so quickly he didn't have time to react. His body teetered for a moment before he collapsed in a heap beside her.

Swallowing against the lump in her throat, Maddy leaned over to examine him. She let out her own breath in a rush when she saw his chest rising and falling, if slowly. She hadn't killed him. No matter what, she didn't think she could bear to kill someone. Her whole body shook as she jerked to her feet and peered around the clearing.

Silence. No shouts or footsteps.

Maddy braced herself, seeking courage, and darted away. Well, as close as she could come to darting in her impractical sandals. The damp, muddy leather dug into her feet, making her want to cry out with every hurried step. After a few days in the chilly cave, the humid summer heat pressed down on her like a weight.

Should've gotten into Hot Yoga, Maddy muttered to herself. *Or at least done more cardio.*

Her breath heaved in and out. Her footsteps sounded like explosions, destroying the quiet of the forest as she rushed through the trees. Then her toe caught something sticking up beneath the grass, and she went down hard.

Pain shot through her hands and knees. Maddy shifted, and warm blood trailed down the front of her leg. Shit. She glared at the patch of rock she could now see between the blades of grass. Then

she forced herself upright and scrambled forward once more. If she failed, it wouldn't be because she gave up.

A rush of air was her only warning—and it didn't come in time. The side of her head exploded with agony, and the world cut sharply to black.

19

This time when Cora pulled into the small parking lot they'd stopped at before, another car was already there. Empty. She exchanged a glance with Ralan. Then they both slid out of her car. In silence, they took the two packs full of trail food and other supplies out of the trunk. Ralan shifted a few things, including the mirror, from his other bag before slipping a backpack over his shoulders.

Delbin had been sending images of the path up the side of the mountain, so they shouldn't be wandering for days. But anything could go wrong, and Cora and Ralan had agreed that it was better to be prepared.

Cora stared across the road at the mountain. If she hadn't insisted on going back to her place for Ralan to perform the blood-tracking spell, they would have already been climbing through the forest. She snorted. His visions might not be reliable, but he'd been correct about Maddy's location.

Too bad neither of them had trusted it.

"Going in circles," Cora said.

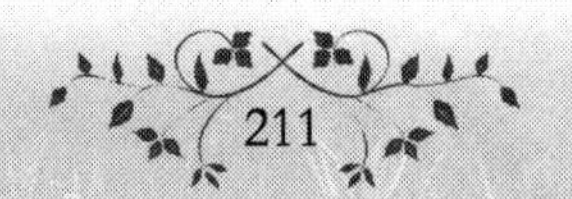

"What?"

She met Ralan's confused gaze. "That's all we've done. It's like the universe itself is standing in our way."

He took her hand as they looked both ways, then darted across the street. On the other side, he gave her a pensive frown. "Maybe it is. But what got you thinking so?"

"We were here. Right here." Cora's hand tightened on his. "You saw this area and knew, even from the other side of the river. Then I led us away to cast a spell we didn't even need. What else is going to go wrong? Ugh. Don't bother trying to Look. I don't think I want to know."

"I could follow the possible strands for the cashier at the gas station we just stopped at," Ralan said softly. "She'll likely get a better job next week and meet her future husband at the office across the street. But everything around us and those close to us is a blur. I'd say your idea about the universe is accurate."

They headed into the trees. Frowning, Ralan paused, scanning the area before settling on a tree to their left. Cora studied it for a second. There. A thin strip of white cloth fluttered from one of the lower branches. The sign Delbin had left to mark the way. This path wasn't part of the official trail system, so they would have struggled to find it otherwise.

As they headed up the slope, silence descended. The forest darkened into a twilight gloom as the sun neared the horizon, but they could both see well enough in the dark to risk it. Still, Cora's heart pounded with each step. She had lived a long time, but she'd never done anything this risky. Leaving her homeland had been difficult, it was true. Just not *head into the lair of an insane elf bent on world domination* sort of difficult.

Ralan curved to the right, angling up the slope at a gentle incline. *"What's your favorite thing in the world?"* he whispered into her mind.

Cora found herself smiling. *"Creating. My magic doesn't actually tend toward such things, but I don't care. I love to design and to make."*

"What do you create besides clothing?"

"Artwork, mostly. I've always loved to draw and paint." The fading light cast his face in a dull glow as she glanced at him. *"What's your favorite thing in the world?"*

"Being a father," Ralan answered at once. A slight, fond smile tipped his lips. *"I was a drifter before Eri, never taking anything too seriously. At least nothing after I moved to Earth. But from the moment I first knew of her, everything changed."*

Cora rubbed her hand against the sweet ache his words brought to her chest. All of the sudden, the image of holding a baby—his baby—popped into her mind. Black hair, golden eyes, a winsome smile. Her body heated at the thought of Ralan's child, and a blush burned her cheeks as she tried to force it away.

"Cora?"

She could only imagine what her face looked like. Had he detected her arousal along their bond? *"How much farther, do you think?"*

Ralan smirked, and she wanted to groan. Yep, he knew. But thankfully, he didn't comment. *"I'm not sure. Delbin's a fair bit ahead of us, and he still hasn't reached the cave."*

Cora nodded. Her feet ached from the pinch and scrape of her rarely used hiking boots, and the climb had her winded. She gritted her teeth and carried on. Ah, but if only she had the moccasins she'd worn when she'd lived with the Aniyunwiya. She hadn't left the

village often, but she'd found the shoes perfect on her journey east when it was time to find a new home. She'd kept those moccasins until they crumbled. Too bad she'd been terrible at leather work.

If she ever found another pair like that, she would treat them like gold.

"Getting tired?" Ralan asked.

Cora let out a soft huff of laughter. *"Dreaming of better shoes."*

He grimaced. *"I wish I had something better myself."*

As the last of the light gave way to dark, Ralan came to a sudden halt. His brow pinched. *"Delbin said they're close. He scanned the cave telepathically. Maddy's there, but she's unconscious."*

Her body went cold. *"Let's go."*

Tension hummed through Ralan like electricity, heightening his senses and stinging through his blood. He hadn't yet told Cora the worst of what Delbin had seen. They'd found Patrick dead, a knife wound in his chest, not far from the entrance to the cave. Delbin hadn't been able to glean much while scanning the cave, but he'd caught a gleeful memory from Victor of the murder.

The trees started to thin, and Cora shifted forward until they walked side-by-side once more. Ralan took her hand. *"There are signs that Maddy fought."*

She shuddered. *"What kind of signs?"*

"Patrick was dead outside the cave. Killed by Victor." He tightened his fingers on hers. *"The memory Delbin discovered... Victor found Patrick unconscious and Maddy gone. She must have used her magic against him."*

"She's going to take that hard."

Ralan frowned at Cora's words. *"She didn't kill him."*

"But he would be alive if she hadn't used her power." Cora's sigh filled the night. *"Maddy has a soft heart, even for a healer."*

He would have to introduce her to Lial. His cousin was a good healer, but he'd never be accused of having a soft heart.

When Ralan sensed Delbin's energy nearby, he sent his mind out in a quick sweep. Inona and Fen waited beside his student. Ralan gave Delbin a mental nudge to warn them of his presence before he and Cora stepped into view. He'd rather not be gutted by Inona or have his throat ripped out by Fen.

Delbin lifted a hand in acknowledgement. His pinched expression gave Ralan pause, since his student tended toward humor during times of stress. *"That bad?"*

"I can't take control of Victor," Delbin answered. *"He's stronger. Maybe once I see him, I'll be able to. But Fen was going to handle Kien while we deal with the others. We're trying to decide if the plan is still worth the risk now that Maddy's unconscious."*

Ralan stared at the cave opening, the small gap illuminated by light from within. Kien hadn't bothered to conceal it, and that seemed…wrong. All of this was wrong. He glanced to the right at the stranger among them. Fen. He'd led them here as promised. But was this part of a greater trap?

Ruthlessly, Ralan shoved his mind into the half-blood's. Fen flinched, but he didn't resist. Ralan scanned the other's thoughts, especially his recent memories. Some of Ralan's tension eased when he confirmed there was no trap, though the kid had seen more fucked up stuff than he wanted to contemplate.

Had Kien really—

Ralan jerked his mind free as the image of a severed head clarified in Fen's memories. That had been the boy's turning point, but it had taken him a while to work his way free. Now he was determined to regain his uncle's trust. Fen would make a good ally in this.

"Send Fen in first."

A frown pinched Delbin's brow. *"He's supposed to be bringing us back as captives."*

With a deft twist of power, Ralan brought the others into the mental conversation. Cora winced and Fen scowled—but no one argued. *"How were you going to bring them in by yourself? You couldn't have carried them."*

Fen's expression turned sheepish. *"I hadn't considered it. I suppose I could tie them together and march them through."*

Inona stiffened. *"You will not—"*

"Only the appearance of being bound, not the reality," Fen said quickly. *"But with these two here, I'm not sure what we should do."*

Ralan considered the matter for a moment. *"Carry on with that plan until you've secured Maddy. I'll take care of my brother."*

Quietly, they crept away from the cave until the entrance was no longer in sight. Trees thickened overhead, blocking much of the moonlight that had begun to trickle through. It took a moment for Ralan's eyes to adjust, but when they did, he found Fen already digging through the backpack he'd dropped on the ground.

Most fae races had excellent eyesight even at night, but none could match the Unseelie or the Dökkálfar.

Fen stood, a length of rope and a knife in his hands. In short order, he had Delbin's and Inona's hands tied behind their backs with loose knots. Another rope linked their hands, a tail dangling

free for Fen to hold. But before he grabbed it, he pulled a pouch from his bag and shook it.

"Fake blood. I sent Kien the image of them bloodied."

A few dark smears and they were ready to go. Ralan shifted closer to Cora as Fen waved his knife and grabbed the end of the rope. He marched Delbin and Inona through the trees, this time not bothering with stealth. Small branches and leaves crunched underfoot as the group walked.

Ralan straightened his shoulders. It was almost time. Live or die, he would face his brother. He'd believed he would return to Moranaia at least once more. Even Eri had told him he wouldn't defeat Kien this trip. But there was nothing consistent or reliable about the strands, and he could count on nothing. If only he hadn't brought his bonded into danger.

Once Fen and the others were out of sight, Ralan turned to Cora. *"I hate the thought of taking you in there."*

"I can defend myself."

Cora lifted a finger, and his brows rose as a tiny flame sparked to life at the tip. *"Well, then."*

The fire winked out. Her expression turned grave as she lifted her hand to his cheek. *"I'm not too fond of you going in there, either. Let's both live through this."*

Ralan leaned down and brushed his lips over hers. Once. Twice. *"I'm good with that plan."*

He pulled away with a regretful glance as Delbin signaled that they'd entered the cave. The plan was for Ralan and Cora to wait, but there was no way he'd leave his apprentice on his own in a situation like this. Delbin might not be able to gain control of Victor.

But Ralan could.

"I'm going to stick your blood-sucking head up your ass," Delbin snarled with relish as Fen shoved them through the cave entrance.

Delbin noticed Victor leaning against a stalagmite only a body-length away. The fae man scowled. "You."

As Victor strode forward, Delbin gathered his energy and reached for the other's mind. Only to thud with mind-ringing force against an impenetrable shield. He cried out as pain bloomed in his head. Then Victor jabbed a fist into his gut, and Delbin doubled over with a new kind of agony.

"You'd better not damage them before Kien gets the chance," Fen said in a casual tone.

But even that soft reminder must have alarmed Victor, who stumbled back at once. Scowling, he spun and marched down the long, narrow cave. Delbin bit back a groan as he straightened. If he found a way to take control of that bastard…

Victor froze a few paces away from Maddy's prone form. For a moment, Delbin ignored him, focusing instead on the Sidhe woman. Her skin was pale, but her chest rose and fell. As he stared, she shivered in her sleep. Relief poured through him, dulling the ache in his head. She was alive. If they could get her out, it would all be worth it.

Then Victor stooped down beside Maddy, a knife in hand, and Delbin's heart jumped. He jerked forward, forgetting for a moment that his bonds were false. But Inona hadn't. The rope that had kept their hands connected went lax as she burst into action. She rushed

across the cave at full speed as Victor slipped his knife close to Maddy.

Only to cut the bonds trapping her hands behind her back.

Inona drew to a startled halt as Victor stood and lifted his hands. His blank, unseeing gaze passed through them as though he was being controlled. Delbin frowned. What the hell? Then he sensed Ralan's energy behind him, and the odd behavior became clear. He should've known the prince wouldn't be able to resist stepping in.

"Well, well," a smooth voice called from the darkness at the end of the cave. "It seems Fen caught more than I could have anticipated."

The room seemed to still as Kien strolled into the light. He halted beside Victor and lowered his hand to the man's shoulder as though offering comfort. "Release my friend, brother, won't you?"

Ralan gave a low laugh. "I think not."

"Foolish as always," Kien said.

Before Delbin could blink, Kien whipped a knife from his belt and plunged it into Victor's eye. The man made a sound, a scream barely formed, before his body slackened. As Ralan cried out, Kien tugged the blade free with a sick, sucking pop. Grinning, he licked both sides of the knife clean.

"I might not be a blood elf, but I admit I love the taste."

Delbin couldn't help it. He retched.

20

Ralan gagged at the surge of agony that cleaved his head. He'd barely managed to disconnect from Victor quickly enough to avoid death, but he hadn't been fast enough to avoid the echo of pain. Kien laughed, a wicked sound that pounded against Ralan's aching head. Damn, that had been close.

Cora reached for him, and her soothing touch snarled with the worry that streamed from her along their bond. Even as he fought back the pain, he sent her a wave of reassurance. His brother wouldn't fell him so easily.

And besides, he already knew he'd die by fire.

Ralan's eyes refocused on Kien. Sneering, his brother glided closer to Maddy. Then Kien's attention shifted to Inona where she stood in the middle of the cave. "I'm glad to see you've returned. I look forward to killing you."

"Not likely," she answered.

Kien shrugged and toed Maddy with his boot. "Fen. You'll do as I say, or I'll kill the little healer."

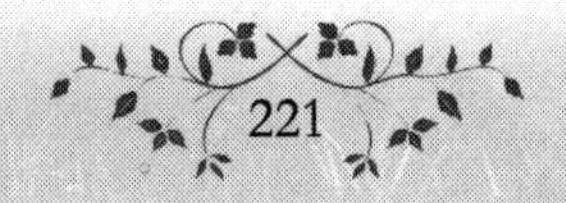

"You probably will anyway," Fen called.

"Astute." Kien bent down and ran the flat of his blade along Maddy's cheek. "But in this case wrong. Your cooperation means more to me than the joy of her death."

Inona shifted slightly, preparing to spring, but Kien's gaze darted to her face. Even Ralan's breath stilled for a moment as his brother and Inona stared at one another. Then Kien smiled and stood. He took a step closer, his body between Maddy and the others. A sick and twisted parody of a guardian.

"I suppose you believe you have me outnumbered."

Ralan chuckled. "You killed your only ally, so I'd say yes."

Kien's eyes flashed with power a heartbeat before his magic pulsed through the air. Ralan cast a shield around himself and his allies, but the spell did not wing their way. Instead, the mage lights hovering above them throbbed like his pulse. Then the light surged, filling the space with nothing but bright, painful blue.

As Ralan covered his eyes against the visual blow, he cast his mind around him. He'd expected Kien to attempt escape. Instead, Ralan found pain and panic emanating from Inona in waves. The flare of light began to fade, and he squinted against the remaining glow. When it settled back to normal, he cursed.

Kien had her.

He'd wrapped his left arm around her body, trapping her arms, and his knife was shoved against her throat. Inona froze, and her panic disappeared, replaced by the resolved calculation of the warrior. Her own weapon rested a few feet away, too far for her to reach. They'd have to distract Kien long enough for her to fight free of his hold.

"This looks familiar," Ralan drawled. "You certainly do like to grab women from behind. But since young Meli was able to defeat you, I imagine a trained warrior can fell you easily."

"Not a warrior disarmed," Kien answered.

Out of the corner of his eye, Ralan caught sight of Inona's left hand creeping slowly toward her pocket. She must have another knife. Ah, his brother always underestimated women. Maybe someday it would be his downfall.

Ralan focused on Kien. "Stop this madness."

"I said I'd kill her, and I meant it." Inona's hand stopped as Kien's arm tightened. "I almost bled out in the fucking mud beneath that old house. Me, a future king."

Delbin's anger vibrated the air around them. "You deserve worse."

"This from an elf who was banished here, abandoned by our people." Kien's eyes glinted. "Sure you don't want to join me? Perhaps I could let your woman live for the promise of a strong telepath on my side."

Delbin gestured at Victor's body. "Your allies don't exactly fare well."

"They've all turned out to be traitors and fools."

Ralan took a step forward, pushing away from Delbin and Cora. "What have I ever done to you, brother? What is the point of all of this?"

Kien laughed, a wicked chuckle that speared the ears like needles. "You've never done anything to me. Isn't that the funny part? You were a good brother, gullible and easy to push around. But our aunt? *There's no future in which you will be king,* she told me. Then she gave

that prophecy to our father saying the first son to have a child with an outworlder would be the next to rule."

"Teyark was still the heir," Ralan said, his frustrations rising. "I was in love with Kenaren, not an outworlder."

Kien's eyes narrowed. "Father was determined to see you married to that Galaren princess. I couldn't risk him talking you into it."

A gasp sounded behind Ralan, and he glanced back at Cora. He frowned to see her skin so pale, but he couldn't allow himself to ask her why. Not with Kien so close to snapping. Unease slithered through Ralan as he turned back to his brother.

"Perhaps you were correct, since Kenaren proved untrue."

"Actually, she loved you dearly," Kien said, his tone calm and almost friendly. Ralan knew better. "Do you know how many months it took me to wear her down? Each time you reassured her that you wanted no other, I found a way to undercut your words. I even promised her she would be my queen. Finally, I seduced her. She cried when we were done, you know. But it didn't take long to break her after that."

Ralan's heart twisted, and bile scalded his throat. "I will kill you for that alone."

"Did they tell you what got me banished?" Kien's grip tightened, and Inona let out a soft sound as his blade cut into her skin. But the thin line of red wasn't what had Ralan's attention. "I doubt they'd want to upset the precious prince. See, Teyark caught me torturing the lovely Kenaren after she threatened to confess."

"That's a lie," Ralan said. "They would've killed you, not sent you into exile."

Kien smiled, an odd hint of pity coloring the curve. "If our father wasn't weak, perhaps. I kept her chained in my workroom for days. Her pleading screams were so beautiful. She even called for you. Ah, the sweet slice of knife through flesh. It's not as easy as it might seem, you know. Even the soft parts of the body provide resistance. But I do have to wonder if the tiny life I cut from her womb was yours or mine."

Ralan's vision blurred, and he swayed on his feet as the shock of his brother's words hit. Kenaren had been pregnant? Oh, Gods. If she'd been very far along, it would've likely been his, not Kien's. Why hadn't he Seen it? Had Megelien hidden this, too, or had he been too deluded to Look?

"She never said a word," Ralan choked out.

Kien shrugged, jostling Inona. "I had her convinced you'd ditch her for the Galaren and ruin Moranaia. The last was certainly true. We both know a seer shouldn't be king."

"You!" Cora gasped out.

A new surge of agonizing fury ripped into Ralan along their bond, blending with his own rage until he almost vomited. Cora surged forward, half-turning Ralan to face her. He'd thought her pale before, but now her tan skin was drained of all color. Her wide, wild eyes found his.

"You're from Moranaia? A prince?" she demanded.

Ralan blinked at her vehemence. "Yes. Same place Delbin is from."

"He never told me that. Great Divine." Cora shoved a hand against Delbin. "Why didn't you tell me that?"

"Exiles rarely talk about such things," Delbin answered in confusion.

As Kien's laugh filled the cave, Ralan reached out and gripped her arms. "What is it?"

"When your name sounded familiar, I thought it was because of your career. Roland Morne," she whispered. "What's your real name? The full one?"

He wanted to crumple. To be ill. To blast his brother into oblivion. And she was worried about his name? "Moranai Elaiteriorn i Ralantayan Moreln nai Moranaia."

"Ralantayan Moreln." Her eyes slipped closed, and she swallowed hard. "I'm the Galaren. The one you rejected, sight unseen. The one who apparently ruined your life." Her broken gaze met his. "Just as you ruined mine."

Even Kien fell silent for several long breaths. Cora was from Galare? Ralan shook his head, refusing to believe. The coincidence was too great. His father couldn't have possibly found his soulbonded, and if he had, he would have used that to convince Ralan. Surely he hadn't rejected his own bonded without knowing.

Cora wrapped her arms around her waist as if she needed to protect herself. From him. Ralan's body shook from the force of her pain joining with his own. He wanted to sweep her into his arms, tell her it wasn't true. But as memories seeped through, so did doubts.

There's enough royalty in this room to host a ball.

She'd said that with a mocking tone Ralan had found strange at the time. Now, he realized that she hadn't been talking only about him and Vek. She'd also told him that there were few portals to her land, and only a handful of places didn't connect directly through the Veil. He'd just been too preoccupied to consider it.

A princess. A Galaren princess.

That made Ralan the fucking idiot who had rejected her.

"This may just be the best day of my life," Kien quipped.

Fury surging like fire, Ralan took a step toward his brother. "Your games ruined everything."

"Ah, but the best part? You can't blame me for this." Kien smirked. "Just think. I saved you from having to choose between the mother of your child and your soulbonded. Well, probably your child. Who knows, really?"

As Ralan's body vibrated with rage and Kien's laugh rang out, Inona's hand reached her pocket. She gave a slight squirm as though she'd lost balance. But if Kien's sudden scowl was any indication, he wasn't fooled. Ralan drew energy into himself, ready to blast his brother. From the other side, he sensed Delbin do the same.

Even the water dripping from the stalactites seemed to freeze in that moment. Then everything happened at once.

Inona pretended to stumble again, tugging her knife free with the movement. As Kien's left arm tightened, a calm, sickly smile twisted his lips. Ralan sent a mental blast toward his brother. A killing blow. But it bounced off Kien's shield at the same time his brother dug the knife into Inona's neck.

Her eyes widened, and a moan slipped from her lips as her blade clattered from her fingers. Still smiling, Kien tossed her to the ground. Delbin cried out, and Ralan had only a moment to shield himself and Cora before the force of his apprentice's magic shook the cavern.

Stalactites and stalagmites shattered, pieces blowing away from the force of it. Kien and Fen were flung away, and Ralan struggled to keep his own feet as the wave hit his shield. Cora landed against

him. His arms went around her in reflex, but she shoved away almost at once.

In a heartbeat, Cora darted across the cavern, skipping over fallen bits of rock. Ralan called after her, but if she heard, she didn't care. Heedless of anyone else, she knelt beside Inona. Her hands pressed to Inona's neck. Then a new kind of power pulsed through the room.

Ralan didn't stop to examine it. As Delbin dropped to his knees, stunned senseless by his own spell, Ralan rushed after Cora. He pulled a knife from his belt, ready to defend his bonded, but Kien was nowhere in sight. Yet. The air around Ralan began to heat, but he didn't look down at Cora. Instead, he scanned the area.

Scanned and waited.

Thank the Divine Source she'd recharged herself at the portal.

Cora's fingers slipped in the blood pouring from Inona's throat, but she caught the hint of a pulse. Inona must have shifted her body enough to keep the blade from severing her carotid. But a nick was bad enough. Cora pushed down hard to stop the flow as her magic began to build.

Then she let her flame pour free.

Her fingers began to sting, but her slight cry was drowned out by Inona's sudden scream. Cora closed her eyes and struggled to focus as the air began to steam. The wound. She had to cauterize the wound.

She wasn't a healer, but she had trained for this. Her breath heaving in and out, Cora sealed the gaping flesh in the unrelenting

heat of her fire. First the artery. Then damaged muscle and flesh. Inona jerked beneath her, a keening moan sounding endlessly from her lips, but still Cora kept on.

Then it was finished.

She'd done it. She hadn't let fear stop her. And her magic had worked.

Her fire winked out, her energy drained. Cora wavered, leaning her weight on her shaky arm as she fought for breath. If she'd bonded to Earth, she would have had enough energy to stand. As it was, she didn't even have the strength to check Inona again. At least the injury had been a small one.

"Cora?" she heard Ralan ask.

As shudders overtook her body, the strength in her arm gave out, and she dropped hard onto the cold cave floor.

21

Ralan fell to his knees beside the two women, not certain who to tend to first. He lowered his hand to Cora's back as he peered between them. Cora's chest rose and fell steadily, and her eyes were open, if a bit glazed. But Inona. His stomach lurched at the sight of her neck.

Where the slash had been stood a charred, livid scar, like a brand. The skin surrounding that was red and welting before his eyes. Inona lifted her hand to touch and let out a startled scream of pain. Her breath heaved in and out like a runner's after a marathon, and her body convulsed with the strength of her trembling.

"Inona," Ralan said softly. "I'm here. You're not alone."

If she heard him, it gave her no relief.

Across the cavern, Fen sat up, rubbing his head. A few paces away, Delbin groaned and shoved his palms against his temples. Then he stumbled to his feet, wavering for a second before weaving his way closer to Inona.

Delbin knelt beside her and took her hand in his. "Love, be calm."

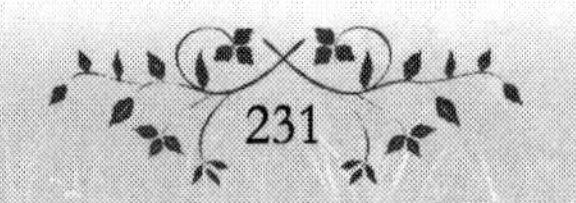

Inona settled somewhat, but Ralan could tell from her frantic breathing and dilated pupils that panic held her in its grip. He could hardly blame her. Had Cora not acted, Inona would already be dead. As it was, they needed to get her to a healer right away. She had lost a lot of blood, and Ralan had no clue how effective Cora's magic had been.

His bonded shifted restlessly. *"How is Inona?"* she sent.

"Alive, but I don't know if there was any greater damage." The sound of tumbling rocks clattered through the cavern, and Ralan jerked to his feet, his hand tightening on his knife hilt. *"Don't move. The danger isn't over."*

Kien stood at the other end with Maddy in his arms. Oh, hell. Ralan had forgotten about the healer entirely between Inona's near-fatal wound and Cora's collapse. Now Kien carried Maddy as a lover would, his arms beneath her knees and shoulders. Her head was tucked gently against his chest. But his eyes were full of nothing but hatred.

"I believe I have captured your prize," Kien said.

Ralan wished to all the gods that he could punch the smug grin from his brother's face. "Let her go. You want me, not some healer from Earth."

"Your death would be a bonus, but it is no longer my main goal." Kien began to edge around the cavern toward the entrance. "I have greater things to do."

Ralan lifted a brow. "Translation? You don't think you can defeat me."

This time, Kien's laughter sounded forced. "You'll die soon enough. I'm more concerned with making it out of here with my little hostage."

"Take me instead."

Kien snorted. "*You* won't help me return to Moranaia no matter how I torture you."

Ralan tracked his brother's movements as he passed by, only a couple of arm-lengths away. It was tempting to spring forward and grab Maddy, but the risk was too great. Kien was a talented mage, and he held the knife in his hand besides. Inona's blood still covered the blade, staining the fabric of Maddy's dress where it brushed.

"A half-Sidhe healer can't get you there, either," Ralan said.

"Not directly." Kien smiled. "But she'll help."

"You've lost your—"

"Fen!" Kien shouted, his attention shifting to the dazed blood elf. "Come with me and give aid, or the healer dies."

Fen shoved to his feet. "Why do you think I care?"

"I've seen the way you look at her. You're never nice to anyone, but you were kind to her."

"I thought we could get her on our side," Fen said.

Kien's forehead furrowed. "That might have been convincing if you hadn't betrayed me with this group. Now move it, or I'll slit her throat, too. Think anyone else can save her?"

As Kien neared, Fen wavered on his feet, and Ralan shoved his mind ruthlessly into Fen's. *"Do it. Save Maddy, and I will plead your case with Vek myself."*

Fen gave a slight nod. *"If I live, I will hold you to that."*

Kien reached the blood elf and kept walking, already certain of his victory. Fen squeezed his eyes closed for a second and then straightened. Without a word, he followed Kien from the cavern.

The sound of Inona's ragged breathing and the plop of dripping water filled the space they'd left behind.

"Fuck it all," Ralan said with a snarl.

Delbin's worried gaze met his. "We have to get Inona back to Moranaia."

"I know," Ralan said. "But we're at risk of running into my brother."

"Do we have a choice?"

Ralan shoved his hand through his hair and tugged. "No."

"Need to save Maddy," Cora whispered.

As his bonded shoved herself to a sitting position, Ralan knelt at her side. He'd never seen her so wan, and he could feel through their link that she was barely functional. But still she fought for her friend. He brushed a strand of hair out of Cora's face and helped her to her feet.

"Fen's going to save her," Ralan said, though he was by no means certain that it could be done. "Perhaps we'll catch them on the way to the portal."

Cora nodded and leaned against Ralan as he wrapped his arm around her waist. "Let's go."

Delbin gathered Inona into his arms. At first, she thrashed, and her hand connected with Delbin's cheek with a sharp slap. He bent to whisper in her ear, but she was too caught in the grip of her fighting instincts to hear. Ralan placed his fingers on her forehead and sent her to sleep.

"Thanks," Delbin said. "My head hurts too much."

"Normally, I would chide you for losing control, even in the grip of strong emotion, but it created a needed diversion," Ralan

said. "We need to work on harnessing that ability so you don't hurt yourself doing it by accident."

"Ralan—"

"Let's just go. I'm too tired for banter."

Lyr's study was dim, but Eri didn't bother to brighten the muted mage lights. There would be enough to see by, and she didn't want to draw attention. Moonlight streamed through the windows and across the wooden floor as she padded across the room on bare feet. She wasn't precisely being sneaky.

No one had told her not to do this, after all.

Eri rolled her eyes at herself. Right. Her father would surely care about that difference once he found out. Then she grinned. Good thing he would forgive her once he fussed at her for a while. Maybe they could even skip that part if she told him she'd already Seen the whole strand where he lectured her. It would save them both time.

She stepped up on the small dais and circled Lyr's big desk. The moonlight bounced her silvered reflection back at her in the tall mirror near the windows, and she gave herself a laughing curtsey. Then she sobered as Lady Megelien's instructions drifted through her mind. This wouldn't be as easy as sharing a prophecy.

Eri sucked on her lower lip. She'd never done magic like this before. The Lady had told her she'd have some talent for it when she got older, but Eri had only just learned to activate mage lights. Could she do it? Could she help her father get back home?

There were a few strands where she failed or was too scared to try. But no. She shoved her shoulders back. She would do this

because she had to. No way Eri was going to let one of those other futures happen.

"I am with you," Lady Megelien whispered into her mind.

Without hesitation, Eri stretched out her hand and touched the edge of the silver frame.

"Kai," Naomh said, a hint of impatience threading his tone. "Feel the rock beneath your hand with your magic. Let it resonate."

So far, all Kai had felt was the rough texture of the stone. And frustration. Boundless frustration. "I've been trying for a solid mark."

Or however they measured time here. The artificial sun that lit the massive cavern had begun to slip toward the tree line. But no matter how long Kai tried to sync his power with the rock the way his father directed, it remained stubbornly out of reach. He'd begun to sense the steady hum of earth energy, at least, but that wasn't enough progress toward the mastery he needed.

"Are you distracted?" Naomh asked.

"Perhaps." Kai stared into his father's eyes. "I may have been ordered here, but I don't trust you."

The heavy weight of grief flickered in Naomh's gaze for a moment. Then it was gone. "Fair enough. But the longer this takes, the longer you'll have to stay."

"The more we'll be required to visit, you mean." Kai's fingers dug into the rock at the reminder. "Arlyn has her own lessons. You know we have to return to Moranaia from time to time for our other duties."

Naomh glanced away. "I know."

Kai sighed and forced his tingling fingers to relax. He frowned. Tingling? His breath caught as he realized that the stone had been reacting to his emotions. Suddenly eager, he sent his power back into the rock to solidify the connection. Only to curse as the sensation slipped away entirely.

"This is not like finding a path through the Veil," Kai grumbled.

His father surprised him by laughing. "It is not. That is the realm of air and spirit. Earth is deeper and slower. It is the heartbeat unending."

The affection in Naomh's voice had Kai peering at him. That hadn't been an idle comment. Would he, too, feel such love for the earth if he unlocked the power within? Or was emotion the key to learning this in the first place?

When Arlyn's mind brushed against Kai's, he opened to her at once. *"I thought you were resting, my love."*

"I was." Arlyn hesitated, and a hint of consternation trickled along their bond. *"Until the mirror chimed. Eri insists that you're needed."*

"Eri?" he asked aloud and then shook his head at Naomh's questioning look. *"Ralan's daughter, a little girl, called for me through Lyr's mirror? She can't use magic yet. You're joking with me."*

Arlyn sent a wave of frustration his way. *"Do I feel like I'm joking?"*

"Okay, fine." He couldn't help but grin. *"What did she say?"*

"We need to go to the Earth portal near Chattanooga to guide Ralan and the others through."

Kai's brows lowered in thought. *"They had a guide with them."*

"Inona was or will be injured." Arlyn's worry curled through his gut. *"Eri said there were quite a few strands but that they all need us."*

"I'll be right there."

"Head to the portal," Arlyn said. *"I'm gathering our things."*

Kai smiled as Arlyn ended the link. She'd known without benefit of a seer's gift what he would say. But his humor faded at the sight of Naomh's worried face. "We have to go."

Concern fell quickly to anger. "You agreed to stay for five days on this first visit. You would break your word already?"

"I promised to stay provided there were no pressing duties or emergencies to deal with," Kai clarified. "Arlyn received word that I am needed."

Naomh's nostrils flared. "There are others in your homeland who could—"

"No." Kai shoved to his feet. "When a six-year-old seer with the touch of the goddess tells you to go save someone, you do it."

"Six?" Naomh asked as he stood.

"And a princess of Moranaia, too." Kai started down the path, not surprised when Naomh kept pace beside him. "I give my word this was an unplanned event. I will return as soon as the crisis has passed."

"Fine," Naomh answered sharply. Then he sighed. "Allow me to show you the fastest trail."

Fen pulled his car to the shoulder of the road near the ridge that held the portal to the Veil. He met Kien's furious gaze in the rearview mirror and then looked away. If he survived this, he'd have this whole car trashed. Sell it for scrap. Push it off a cliff. He didn't want to see it again after hauling this sick bastard around town.

With a shove, he opened the car door and stepped out. On the other side of the street, the lights were on in most of the houses in the neighborhood. Fen no longer cared enough about stealth to park somewhere subtle, and he doubted Kien did either. No matter what Ralan said, Vek would probably kill Fen as soon as this was over.

If he couldn't stop Kien from perpetuating this fucked-up mess, Vek wouldn't have a choice.

Fen tugged open Kien's door and waited for the prince to slide out with Maddy in his arms. God knew what the humans would think if they happened to look out their windows. Probably close to the truth, minus the magic. Unfortunately, the police would only cause more trouble in a situation like this. Not intentionally, but they weren't exactly trained to deal with mages.

As soon as Kien steadied himself, he strode toward the ridgeline. Fen shut the door softly behind him—no use drawing attention—and followed. He hurried until he could walk alongside Kien.

"I want you to leave the girl a good distance from the portal," Fen said.

Kien shot him a mocking look. "You think I'll abandon my hostage before I've gained your aid?"

Fen's shoulders stiffened. "I won't help if there's the chance you'll still kill her once I'm done. I know exactly how you operate. I've seen more than enough examples."

They walked in silence as Kien considered his words. Finally, the prince shrugged. "I will make one deal only. I keep the girl while you connect me into Earth's energy. Then I'll set her out of the way while you break the spell barring me from Moranaia."

Fen's heart thumped. "Why do you still want to poison the energy? Patrick and Victor are dead, and I don't want to rule anything. Not anymore."

"I was never doing it for you," Kien answered with a laugh. "You fools couldn't rule a nursery. The poison hurts my brother and sows dissent among the fae races. I'll need that leverage once I become king."

Shitshitshit. He was supposed to stop the energy poisoning, not worsen the situation. Fen looked at Maddy's innocent face. What choice did he have? If it saved the young healer from death, he would meet his fate with Vek without qualm. She would never be interested in him anyway. He was Unseelie, and he'd heard her call out for someone named Anna while she was dozing.

"Fine," Fen agreed. "I'll do it if I can. In theory, I'd need your blood and the blood of someone keyed to Moranaia's portal."

Kien wiggled the knife in his hand. "Slicing that scout's throat was for more than pleasure."

Fen wrinkled his nose, but he didn't argue. Blood tasted foul when it wasn't from the source. Just another bit of unpleasantness to add to the day. Then again, it would probably be a palate-cleanser after ingesting Kien's blood.

When they reached the narrow slice in the rock wall that held the portal, Kien halted. In a heartbeat's time, Fen connected with Earth's energy. And though his stomach lurched, he connected the thread to Kien's magic without any outward sign of his disgust.

He hoped.

A smile tightened Kien's lips as the connection snapped into place. Fen braced for betrayal, but the prince merely shifted to the

wall and set Maddy down against it. Then Kien entered the gap in the stone and gestured for Fen to follow.

As the prince disappeared from sight, Fen stooped over Maddy and brushed a hair off her face. Her eyes cracked open, and his blood chilled at the sight. But she didn't move. Smiling at her cleverness, he bent down and brushed a kiss on her forehead. Why not, if he was going to die?

Then he stepped into the crevice in the stone and prepared to help the dark prince break into the world he was determined to rule.

22

"Damn," Ralan cursed as they passed Fen's car on the shoulder of the road.

A truck had pulled up behind it, and a human male stood peering into the driver's side window. He hoped the guy didn't get himself killed, but he didn't have the time or energy to warn him away. Besides, if the human caught sight of Delbin holding Inona in the back seat, there would be trouble.

Bad enough that Cora slumped in the passenger seat. She'd slipped into a deep sleep as they drove, her energy reserves depleted. If he hadn't been able to sense through their bond that she was uninjured, he would have gone mad during the drive. His stomach roiled with worry as it was.

"Turn right into the next driveway," Delbin said. "We had to do this when we captured Kien. It's a bit more of a walk, though."

Ralan merely nodded and pulled into the driveway when it appeared. After a short way, the trees thinned to reveal the slope of a hill. At Delbin's direction, Ralan stopped the car and darted around

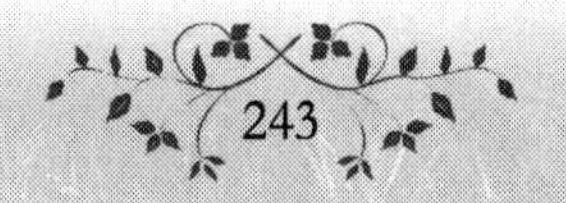

the front, gathering Cora in his arms while his apprentice struggled out with Inona.

They didn't speak as they hurried through the trees to the ridge on the far edge of the hill. Ralan gathered magical energy with each step, though his previous mental blast hadn't hurt Kien. He'd have to break through his brother's shield if they encountered him again. He couldn't carry Cora and wield a blade, and he'd never been very good at physical combat in any case.

But when they reached the gap in the rock wall that held the portal, they found Kai and Arlyn helping Maddy to her feet.

Ralan drew to a startled halt, Delbin just behind him. "What are you doing here?"

"You have your daughter to thank," Kai answered with a chuckle.

But Ralan wasn't amused. "What did she do?"

"Hijacked Lyr's mirror." A quick grin of appreciation crossed Kai's lips. "I wonder if she escaped before he made it to the study to see who triggered the spell. Guess we'll find out soon."

"I'm going to give her the longest lecture of her life," Ralan said. Then he noticed Maddy's dazed expression. "Are you hurt?"

She shook her head. "Fen bargained for me. I don't think either of them realized I was awake. Kien had Fen link him with the Earth in return for my life." Maddy blinked, and her tone filled with awe. "An Unseelie blood elf saving a Seelie Sidhe."

"Where did they go?" Ralan asked.

"Through the portal." She gestured toward the gap in the wall. "Something about using Kien's and Inona's blood to break a spell."

"Fuck," Ralan and Kai said at the same time.

Chances were good that Kien had reached Moranaia.

"Maddy," Ralan began. "I have Cora's keys. Can you make it around the ridge to her car? If Kien and Fen are in the portal, there should be no more danger out here. I would escort you myself, but we need to go."

The half-Sidhe hesitated for a moment but then nodded. "I'll do it. Won't that leave you stranded if you come back, though?"

"Give me your phone number," Ralan said, already tugging his cell from his pocket. "I'll call if we need help."

As soon as Maddy's number was programmed in, Ralan spun toward the portal. Lyr's safeguards on the gate might catch Kien—or they might not. Assassins had made it through before using a cloaking spell, so there was no telling what his brother would be able to do. Not only did Cora and Inona need healing, but Moranaia needed to be secured.

He would have to trust Maddy to fend for herself.

The mists of the Veil swirled around them as Fen drew Kien's blood from his wrist. Just a sip, but enough to make him want to vomit. As his stomach roiled, he used a touch of magic to seal the puncture wounds, out of habit more than consideration. Kien could bleed out for all he cared. Then again, it was probably best not to shed the prince's foul blood in the Veil.

Once Fen pulled away, Kien held out the knife. Fen hesitated, but delaying would ultimately do no good. His nose curled as he licked a drop of Inona's blood from the flat side of the blade. For a moment, his head spun as his body connected with the two new essences that had been introduced.

Then he dove into the curl of energy Kien had shown him, the one that led to Moranaia. As predicted, it fought against Kien's essence but allowed Inona's. Fen's brow creased with concentration as he struggled against the powerful spell. But finally, the resistance cracked with a force that rattled his teeth.

Kien would kill him on the other side, but Fen might have a chance to save himself. He didn't hesitate this time, shoving Kien away from him, toward the energy of Moranaia. Fen's heart pounded as the prince tossed a mocking grin over his shoulder. But Kien followed the momentum of the shove, not bothering to attack.

Laughter echoed. Then Fen was alone.

He peered around at the rolling mist and sighed. He barely understood the Veil, and a quick scan with his magic found no sign of Earth's energy signature. Fen took a few steps. Nothing. Was he going to be stuck in this place forever? His groan floated around him like the tendrils of fog.

Well, it was better than being dead.

Probably.

As soon as Kai pulled Ralan and the others through the portal, Ralan cast his strongest shield around Delbin. Just in time, too. His apprentice cried out, his eyes pinched closed in pain as the greater energy of Moranaia flooded his raw mind. He shuddered, but his arms stayed firm around Inona.

"Tamp down as I taught you," Ralan said.

Delbin's lips thinned. "Trying. That blast in the cave…"

"I assumed such."

Ralan examined the dark clearing, nothing but the shimmering light of the portal giving illumination. It was late here, probably nearing dawn based on the absence of both moons in the sky. But the portal was protected at all hours.

He turned to the guard to the left of the portal. "You. Has anyone passed through?"

The guard straightened. "Milord prince, I have not seen or detected anyone."

"Increase your vigilance," Ralan said. "There's a chance that an assassin has found a way through. Send out a call to the *Taysonal* to guard us closely on the way to the estate. I'm sure Lyr will have further instructions later."

"Ready," Delbin said, his voice strained.

Kai and Arlyn took the lead, Ralan and Delbin following. As they reached the trail on the other side of the clearing, two *Taysonal* dropped from the trees to guard their backs. Ralan cast his senses wide, but he detected no sign of Kien, only the scouts who watched their hurried steps along the trail.

Ralan sent a mental call to Lial. *"Where are you?"*

Even the healer's mind-voice was cranky. *"If you don't stop invading my mind uninvited—"*

"We have injured."

"My tower," Lial answered at once. *"How many and what type of injuries?"*

"Two. One collapsed after using her energy to heal the other." He grimaced as he sent an image of Inona's injury. *"She cauterized the wound, but we don't know how much damage there might still be."*

"Miaran, *she used fire? Never mind. Just come to the tower."*

"Lial is in his workroom," Ralan said aloud for the others.

Kai nodded, increasing his pace, and Arlyn frowned back at Inona. "I hope he can help."

At Delbin's swift intake of breath, Ralan lifted a brow at Arlyn. "I'm sure he can."

"Of course," she said quickly.

Arlyn likely wondered the same thing Ralan did—had Inona lost too much blood?

The trees flashed by as they rushed down the trail. Ralan stretched his senses across Braelyn, searching until he found Lyr's energy signature. He didn't have to force his way through this time. Lyr was awake, and as soon as Ralan found him, he made contact.

Anger slipped through with his words. *"Your daughter is in big trouble."*

"She's the least of our worries," Ralan said. *"Though she'll have her lecture as soon as I am able, even if she was right."*

"Eri ordered Kai on a mission," Lyr snapped. *"I can't imagine anything that would justify a child giving such a command to a member of my household, princess or not."*

Although Ralan understood his friend's anger, he didn't have time to stress over it. *"Then get a better imagination. We needed a guide and fast. Kien slashed Inona's throat and has probably broken through the spell blocking him from Moranaia. My bonded closed Inona's wound, but she's barely hanging on. I'll chide Eri, but it's difficult to be upset, considering."*

Silence. Then contrition mixed with concern slipped into Lyr's thoughts. *"You're heading for Lial?"*

"Yes." A gleam of light broke the darkness. *"We're close. Put the estate on high alert. Kien may already be here using one of those damn cloaks*

that slip through wards. I image he'll head toward the palace, but there's no guarantee."

"I'll take care of it. Keep me updated on Inona."

Ralan disconnected from Lyr as the trees thinned, revealing the clearing around Lial's tower. A mage light shone from a lantern beside the open door and illuminated the healer's face as he waited. Kai and Arlyn moved aside and let Ralan and Delbin rush past.

Lial ducked out of the way as Delbin strode through the doorway. Delbin barely glanced at the long workbench to the left, striding instead toward the small bed under the window on the right. Ralan hesitated for a moment before taking a seat in a chair over to the side. Carefully, he shifted Cora in his lap, settling her head against his chest.

She slept on, her breathing steady, but he was beginning to grow concerned. As Delbin lowered Inona to the bed, Ralan searched along his link with Cora. Her mind and energy were quiet, with no sign of turmoil or illness. He frowned. Her energy felt *too* still. Normally, Cora appeared calm on the surface, but inside she was all fire—not embers harshly banked.

His heart thundered as he waited. He wanted to insist that Lial check her, but Inona was in worse shape. Sick tension slithered through him, an anxiety that wouldn't be quieted until Cora's eyes smiled up at his.

Interminable.

Light glowed around Lial's hands as he lowered them to Inona's throat. He concentrated there for a moment before his hands shifted to her head and then along the rest of her body. When he returned to her throat again, he stayed there for an endless amount of time. The sound of Delbin's ragged breathing and the healer's occasional muttered curse filled the room.

The glow cut off, and Lial settled back on his heels. "What did she do?"

"Cora?" Ralan asked. "I'm not sure. The air heated, but there were no visible flames. Still, the wound cauterized."

"Will Inona live?" Delbin demanded.

"Would I be calmly kneeling here if my patient was still fighting death?" Lial scowled at him. "She'll have a scar, and she'll require a lot of rest to recover from the blood loss. I suspect she may need a mind-healer to help with the trauma of it. Gods know I would."

Ralan lifted a brow as Lial stood and approached. "You, admitting a weakness?"

"I know precisely what happens to the body when the throat is slit," Lial countered, for once not rising to the bait. "You have a good minute or two of terror at your inevitable death. And if the windpipe is also cut—"

"I get it," Ralan said quickly. "Just check on Cora."

As the light flashed in Lial's hand, Ralan closed his eyes. His skin tingled from the power as his cousin swept his magic over Cora, concentrating on her head. Only when the magic faded and the light stopped crashing against his closed eyelids did Ralan open his eyes.

"Well?"

"She drained herself, and she is not pulling in more energy. She'll stay like this until she can."

Ralan's breathing went shallow as the importance of that hit. "Why can't she connect to Moranaia?"

Lial shrugged. "It's part of her nature. Her body does not automatically draw from the world around her. There aren't even physical channels in her mind to do so."

"What…" His lips turned down as he recalled something she'd said. "She told me once that her people bond to places and to types of energy. What do you know about Galarens?"

"So she is from Galare. I suspected as much." Lial stared at him. Then he broke into laughter. "You found your soulbonded there? Maybe your father was onto something."

"Shut up, cousin." Ralan was not about to admit that Cora was the same princess he'd refused so many centuries ago. Lial didn't need more ammunition. "What can I do for her?"

Lial pursed her lips. "If she can't bond to the energy here? You'll have to take her back."

Damn. Ralan's arms tightened of their own volition. That was what he'd been afraid of.

The low murmur of voices trickled through Cora's mind, but none of the sounds solidified into words. She drifted, content to let the noise pass. Thoughts tried to form. Carelessly, she shoved them aside.

After a time, other sensations seeped in. Her hands were cold. A low rumble sounded beneath her ear. She shifted, and soft fabric brushed her cheek. She fought to open her eyes, but she didn't have the strength. When she tried to pull in power, she found nothing but void.

At least for a moment.

Just beyond her reach, she sensed a wealth of power. But she wasn't linked to that. Closer, though, there was one smaller source. The warmth her body was curled against. Blindly, she pulled a little. Only a little.

The murmurs solidified into words. "She will demand to go back anyway."

"Already running your bonded off, Ralan?"

"After what happened with Kien, she'll probably want the bond to be broken." A pause in the rumble beneath her ear. "I don't blame her."

She heard a soft snort. "Because your brother is insane? Surely she wouldn't do something irrevocable over that."

"After what she learned…" His breath ruffled her hair. "Trust me."

"Looks like you'll be causing another scandal, then. Prophecy or not, I can't see you remaining the heir if your own bonded refuses you."

"I'll deal with that when it comes."

Pain swirled through her as she fought to make sense of the conversation. What was wrong with Ralan? His worry and agony slammed into her chest, and she struggled to lift a hand against the ache. What was going on? Restlessly, she pulled in more energy.

"Lial, I feel…"

Cora's eyes snapped open, and she tried to focus her blurry vision enough to see Ralan. He held a hand to his forehead. Why was he pale? She squeezed her eyes closed again as blue flashed around them.

The other voice. "*Miaran,* she's pulling from you. I guess it's a similar link. But she'd better not pull too much or she'll sap you before you can regenerate yourself."

In that moment, she wanted nothing more than to snuggle against him and let herself be. To bask in the warmth of their

connection. But his words nudged at some memory just beyond reach. She couldn't relax until she understood.

"Slowly, Cora," Ralan whispered, bending down until his lips could almost brush hers. "I'll give you energy, but you have to let me do it slowly. Close your eyes and rest."

She tried, but that sense of uneasiness wouldn't let her. As power trickled in, drop by drop, Cora stared into his eyes. Grief. She'd seen his gaze full of confidence, arrogance, worry, passion—even fear. But this heavy sadness was new. Her hand drifted up to his cheek, and her fingers brushed his skin.

It did nothing to ease the pain she saw.

Strength began to return to her limbs, but memories flickered through her mind, too. Cora's breath hitched as she remembered the search for Maddy. The climb up the mountain. The tense confrontation in the cavern. Healing Inona. Stumbling from the cave and down the mountain before passing out in the car. She must have burned herself out.

Then what she'd learned about Ralan clicked with the words she'd just overheard. They were bonded, but he'd betrayed her before they ever met. He'd rejected her, sight unseen. Because of his refusal, her father had lost the throne, and she had fled her very home. She'd bonded with the very source of her life's greatest pain.

Her hand fell away from his face.

Ralan's eyelids lowered, shuttering his gaze, and he straightened. But although he surely sensed her anger and her turmoil, he continued to send her energy. Her chest constricted with the pain of it all. He expected her to sever their bond, but he was taking care of her. Could she do it? Divine, she should. He'd ruined her life. And based on his reaction in the cave, he was in love with a dead woman.

"Enough, Ralan," that other voice snapped.

Cora turned her head enough to see the source. A scowling male elf stood a few paces away. His auburn hair clashed oddly against his rust-colored tunic, the contrast far from soothing to her dazed eyes. She blinked and peered at him again. He looked vaguely familiar, but she didn't think they'd met.

"Who are you?" she whispered.

"The healer. Lial."

His expression was angrier than any healer she'd ever seen, but she nodded. "Okay."

"Make him stop before he drains himself dry."

She tipped her face back to Ralan. "Stop."

His wry smile didn't reach his eyes. "I can do more. I used to channel energy to Eri when we lived on Earth. Because of the energy poisoning."

Cora shoved against him as more power poured through. She knew exactly why he was doing this. Guilt. But even as she struggled to get out of his lap, he continued. His pale, closed face told her well enough of his resolve. Gathering her strength, she pushed herself to her feet.

"See? It's enough for now."

"It will never be—"

"Ralan!" Lial shouted, stepping close to the prince. "I will render you unconscious where you sit if you do not stop this now."

Ralan's eyes narrowed. "You may try to breach my shields, cousin, but you will not succeed."

Cora pushed her shoulders back and prepared to bluff. She hadn't decided what to do, but he didn't have to know that. "Stop sending energy, or I will have to sever our bond."

Not that she could, as far as she knew. When her magic was bound to a place, it was irrevocable. A person? She had no idea. He clearly didn't either.

The stream of energy cut off at once.

23

A thousand icy needles danced through Ralan's blood at Cora's threat. Her magic had created their bond. Could she end it herself without the aid of a priest? He stopped the flow of energy, though the emotions that streamed from her were tinged with uncertainty. She could prevaricate with her words, but her soul hinted at another truth.

He would wait until they were alone to call her on it.

"I owe you far more than a bit of energy, Cora," he said instead.

Her mouth firmed. "There's a lot to do, isn't there? Unless you killed your brother and saved Maddy while I was unconscious."

"We found Maddy unharmed outside the portal." Ralan paused to let her process that bit of good news first. Then he sighed. "But Kien escaped. He's probably found a way to Moranaia by now. The guards hadn't seen him when we came through the portal, but that's not necessarily a good sign."

As her forehead creased, her gaze skipped around the room. "The portal?"

"We're on my home world," he answered gently. "Moranaia."

Cora peered at the stone walls of Lial's work tower. Then her attention landed on Inona, stretched out on the bed with Delbin at her side. With slow steps, Cora eased her way over. She nibbled on her lower lip as she scanned Inona.

"Is she going to be okay?"

"Yes," Lial answered. "And when you have time, I would love to discuss the method you used. It's difficult to close an arterial wound so quickly."

"But she'll be scarred," Cora whispered. She stretched out her hand, forefinger extended, but let it drop before she made contact with the now-pale line on Inona's neck. "Elves almost never scar, especially with proper healing. My method is a clumsy imitation of a true healer's work."

"Many *true* healers would have failed to save her," Lial said, no hint of sympathy in his tone. "Or her brain would have been severely damaged by blood loss as they worked to close the artery. Fire, at least, is fast. I'm sure she'd rather have a scar than be dead."

Cora didn't answer, but Ralan could tell through their bond that she wasn't fully convinced. He had a feeling she wouldn't be reassured by anyone but Inona, and possibly not even then. He frowned. It wasn't insecurity he sensed from her. Regret? He wanted to ask her what was wrong, but he knew she wouldn't welcome the question from him.

Arlyn ducked her head through the open door and waved to catch Ralan's attention. "*Onaial* wants to know how things are going. He's been waiting to hear word about Inona. Should I tell him she'll live?"

Ralan smiled as Arlyn used Eri's word for father. But before he could answer, his cousin spoke.

"I will give Lyr a detailed update on her condition," Lial said, turning a frown on Arlyn. "You should go to bed, Ayala."

Arlyn's brows rose. "You aren't my grandmother, you know."

Lial winced, a rare sign of weakness, before his expression hardened. "I am aware."

"Sorry," she answered. A hint of regret lined her face. "I didn't think that through. I'll just be out here feeling like a jerk."

As Arlyn disappeared from the doorway, Ralan studied his cousin. What had happened to cause that odd interaction? He already knew about Lial's feelings for Lynia, Lyr's mother. Had Lynia rejected him? Had there been an awkward argument?

Ralan had too many of his own problems to find out.

Suddenly, Cora teetered on her feet, and her hand shot out to brace herself against the wall. Ralan stood, but she glared at him over her shoulder. "Don't. You can't spare more energy at the moment."

She was right. He knew she was right. But he didn't have to like it. "How can I help you?"

"I'm going to have to go home."

"Cora…"

"Not to Galare," she rushed to say. "My house in Chattanooga. It's near a portal to my home world. I can draw from there."

Lial's eyes narrowed on her face. "You didn't bind to Earth?"

"None of your business," Cora snapped.

Despite the situation, Ralan couldn't help but grin as Lial got a taste of his own surliness. But that brief moment of amusement was quickly gone. Once again, Cora was correct. Since she had no

interest in bonding to Moranaia, she would have to return to Earth to regain her strength. He would have to let her go without him.

"Let me settle things with Lyr. Then Kai and I will take you back."

Her solemn gaze met his. "We should speak about this in private."

Ah, damn. This was it. Pain seared him even as he nodded. He'd already guessed that she would want to sever their bond. At least she had the kindness to tell him privately. After he'd messed up her life, it was more than he deserved.

"Fine." He held out his hand. "Walk with me. We'll find a spot outside to talk."

Even Lial found something else to look at as Cora limped across the room. She rested her hand on Ralan's arm, but the tremble in her fingers told him it was support and nothing more. None of the casual affection that had begun to form between them. His gut twisted, but he held his arm steady, taking some of her weight as they walked out the door and past Kai and Arlyn.

Ralan blinked at the shift from mage light to darkness, abrupt enough that he didn't notice the dark blue tint to the sky at first. Blue, not black, and he couldn't see many stars between the branches swaying overhead. Dawn approached.

"The sun must be near to breaking over the horizon," he said. "Let's head toward the ridge where we can be alone."

The forest blocked true sunrise in many places, but there was a spot at the edge of Lyr's estate, a small ridge before a valley plunged down to the east, where they could get a clear view. The trees thinned enough there that he would be able to see approaching danger without the scouts perched in the forest overhearing their words.

Cora's steps were so slow that the sky had lightened considerably by the time they reached the spot. Ralan stopped on the smooth rock shelf and cast a small mage light above them. The harsh yellow painted her face in stark contrasts, and he swallowed against a lump of nerves at her unreadable expression. Even her energy felt muted.

"Careful," he said. "This drops off at the end of the shelf. Do you want to sit?"

She shook her head. "This won't take long."

Could she throw away their bond so quickly, then? His heart gave a hard thump. "Is this so easy for you?"

"Easy?" Within a breath, her anger flared between them, so furious and strong he couldn't believe he'd thought her energy calm. Banked, perhaps, but not still. "Not a damn thing in my life has been easy, in no small part thanks to you."

"I'm sorry," Ralan answered. He shifted his arm from under hers and took her hand. "Even then, I would not have wanted to hurt you. I don't make a habit of causing others trouble."

Cora snorted. "Don't you? You're the type who sees what you want, with your foresight or not, and then makes it happen. An arrogant prince through and through. I'll wager you've caused a fair amount of problems for others without ever even noticing."

"Of course I don't," he insisted.

But memories trickled through to mock his words. Lyr's face after he'd discovered that Ralan's faulty vision had placed Kai and Arlyn into peril. *You said there was no danger. I trusted you.* Ralan had helped to save them, but the error had almost cost them their lives.

And Kai himself after the latest meeting with Naomh. Before he'd stormed out, there had been no mistaking his frustration and

disgust. And maybe a hint of hatred. *I'm tired of you fucking up our lives with a smile on your face. Keep your prophecies to yourself if they concern me.*

Gods.

"I shouldn't have said that," Cora said softly.

"No, you're right." Ralan tugged his hand from hers. "All my life, I've thought I was in control. Should be in control. The future was mine to see and to guide, I thought, and even when I didn't use my Sight, I believed I knew best. But none of it mattered. I couldn't save Kenaren. And I didn't…at the time, I didn't even Look to see what could happen to you."

Cora paled at that. "You mean you could've seen those strands but didn't try? You didn't examine the possibility of marrying me?"

"*You* wanted to marry a stranger?" Frustration, pain, rage—all twisted within him like a tempest. "I was an arrogant bastard, okay? I assumed my father's plan was an idle threat because he didn't like Kenaren. I gave it no other consideration than that."

"Well, *my* father believed your family was serious about the alliance." Her lips pinched until they whitened. "He staked his entire future on it. Even now, they won't tell me how they are faring under Orn's rule. But I suppose you wouldn't have cared if Orn had managed to force me into marriage. To take my body against my will, night after night, while you lived your life without a bother."

Each word seared his heart with its truth. "Cora—"

"Have Kai take me home, Ralan." Cora swiped a tear from her cheek. "I'll do you the favor of not breaking our bond while you hunt down your brother. Once that is done, come find me. We'll have it severed then."

Had he thought losing Kenaren had hurt? Every past rejection, loss, betrayal, failure—none of them had brought the same agony as Cora's words. His breath heaved out, and he shoved his closed fist to his chest. His heart felt like it was folding in on itself.

Ralan opened his mouth, but the words to beg her to stay wouldn't emerge. What could he say? She was right. His selfishness had cost so many people. He hadn't seen Kien's hatred. He hadn't noticed Kenaren's worry or her growing distance, and she'd died for it. She and their child. Then he'd left his father without a seer for three centuries so he could nurse his hurt feelings.

On his return? He'd failed to save Lyr's mother from her near-fatal fall. He'd sent Kai and Arlyn into danger with a faulty vision. He'd let Maddy stay in Kien's grip for days because he had been too afraid to perform the blood magic spell.

No, he couldn't ask Cora to forgive him. He didn't deserve it. But perhaps if he could accept his fate, he could atone for it all. He would have Kai take Cora to safety. Then Ralan would hunt down his brother.

And face his own death.

How could he just stand there, staring at her with those haunted eyes?

His pain lashed her, a whip that only increased her own upset. But still he said nothing. Cora brushed her hair out of her face with a trembling hand. What else could she do but leave? Her heart twisted as his resignation crossed along their bond. It was perverse, but she had expected him to fight her rejection. At least offer a counter.

Her decision had been pure logic. Cora scoffed at herself. No, she couldn't say that. Hurt goaded her just as surely. He hadn't even Looked for her. He might have learned of their bond centuries ago and saved so many a great deal of grief. Orn would not have challenged an alliance with a country as strong as Moranaia. But Kien's words drifted back to her. Yes, Ralan would've had to choose between her and Kenaren, the mother of his child.

Cora wouldn't have stood a chance even if he had Looked.

She dropped her restless fingers from her hair and took a trembling step back toward the path. "Goodbye, Ralan."

"Let me help you," he said, rushing forward to grip her arm.

Cora jerked herself free of his hold. "No. I can walk by myself. You need to find your asshole brother. And when you do? Make him pay."

Ralan nodded, his sorrowful gaze studying her face. But again, he didn't speak. As she turned away and started walking, another tendril of energy spilled into her from him. Her trembling body steadied, her steps firmer, but she didn't offer thanks. Her throat constricted around the words she wanted to say.

Was the pain strangling her chest his or hers?

Maybe with distance, she would know.

The forest began to lighten around her, but Cora barely took note of the huge trees, their leaves blushed in bright colors. She stared at the dirt path, her concentration focused on each labored step. Only when she neared the stone tower did she look up. Thankfully, the two elves who had led them through the portal were still there.

Cora stopped in front of the male, the one Ralan had called Kai. "I'm told you can guide me back."

He shifted on his feet. "I'll have to verify that I can. Sorry. There's a lot going on."

"Figures," Cora said.

Ralan's voice sounded behind her. "Do it. I don't care if Lyr yells at me again. Or you, for that matter. At least I'm not smiling this time, hmm?"

An undercurrent of tension passed between the two, but Cora was too tired to wonder about it. She needed to get to her home portal while she still had the strength to walk. Thankfully, Kai gave a sharp nod. Then he turned to the other woman with a frown.

"Do you want to stay or go with me?"

"I'll stay," the woman answered. "I should probably be here as my father's heir. Not that I'm very useful in the role, but whatever."

The last was said with a quick grin that Kai returned. Another interplay that Cora didn't understand. Where was the female elf from? She sounded more like the people Cora knew on Earth than anyone here. Maybe if she'd stayed with Ralan, she would have found out the answer to the puzzle.

Not now.

"Cora."

Her heart gave a sad little leap of hope at Ralan's voice, but she stifled it. "Yes?"

"I left your pack in your car." His shoulders hunched as he looked away. "If your phone is still in your pocket, call Maddy to pick you up. She took the car."

"Thanks," she managed to say around the lump in her throat. "I've got it."

Then she spun away and followed Kai down another trail.

24

Though Ralan said nothing to Arlyn, she rushed forward when he started toward the estate. Her soft footfalls kept pace with his heavy ones as they slipped between the trees, but for a while, she didn't speak. A small mercy, since he knew he would struggle with civility. A mercy that didn't last.

"I can't believe you did that," she finally said.

He glared a warning. "This is bad enough without your critique."

"Only because you're an idiot," she said, unfazed by his anger. "I haven't known you for nearly as long as the others, but even I can't believe you would send your soulbonded away without a fight. *With* instructions on how to get home, no less."

Heat stole up his neck and into his cheeks. "You weren't privy to our earlier conversation."

"I never thought of you as a quitter."

His vision went as red as his face, and Ralan halted. Arlyn's eyes widened when he spun to face her. "She lost everything because of me. Her entire world. And I didn't know because I'm too damn

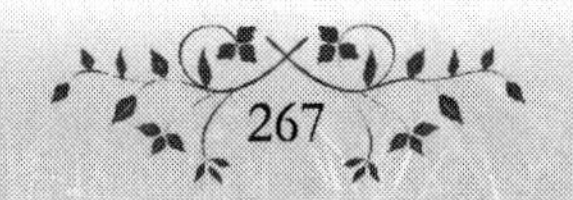

selfish to pay attention. I fuck up everyone's lives, just as your own bonded said."

Her brows drew together. "Kai told me about that. He didn't mean it."

"Of course he meant it. It's what seers do, isn't it? Hell, I almost got you both killed."

She scoffed. "Sure, Ralan. Because seeing possibilities is totally the same as creating them."

He ground his teeth. "If I had Seen the threat, you would not—"

"We probably wouldn't have gone," Arlyn interrupted. She lifted a brow. "My father would've argued to his last breath against it. Kien's spell would have been completed, causing gods know what kind of damage. Kai wouldn't have found his real father. I mean, being held inside a stone wall doesn't really make my top ten list of life experiences, but it turned out okay. Maybe there's a reason you can't yet See."

Unease slithered through him. There was truth to her words, and if she was right about that, had he been foolish where Cora was concerned? He thought back to Cora's closed, angry expression when she'd told him to return to her to have their bond broken. Maybe not. It would be easier this way in any case.

If she hated him, she wouldn't be devastated when he died fighting Kien.

"She insisted we have the bond severed once my brother is defeated," he merely stated. Arlyn didn't need to know the rest.

"I'm sorry," Arlyn said.

"Me, too."

Ralan propelled himself forward by force of will. He didn't want to see the pitying expression no doubt pinching Arlyn's face. Her relationship with Kai had started off rocky, but they'd resolved things. There would be no resolution for him and Cora save death.

The guard at the door to Lyr's study stepped aside without a word. Ralan slipped into the narrow passage that connected the study to the rest of the house and blinked as his eyes adjusted to the light. Then he strode into the room, his gaze going immediately to his daughter.

Eri sat in one of the chairs beneath the skylights. Her fingers twisted knots in her nightgown, and her dangling feet swung back and forth. When she glanced up and saw him, her eyes widened. Tears welled, and he steeled himself against them. His heart wasn't in the lecture he needed to give, but such was parenting.

He looked toward Lyr, who leaned against his desk, his arms crossed and his face twisted into a scowl. "Any sign of Kien?" Ralan asked.

"Nothing," Lyr said. "There hasn't been the slightest ripple in the wards. But we both know that means little."

Arlyn, who had followed him, walked over to her father. "Should I wake Selia? She might have insight after working with that assassin's cloak."

Lyr nodded, and his expression softened. "Good idea. Thank you, love."

She leaned forward and gave her father a quick peck on the cheek before rushing away. Despite everything, Ralan's heart warmed at the sight. A couple of months before, the two hadn't even met. Lyr still

privately expressed guilt at not knowing of Arlyn's existence sooner, but they were forming a solid bond now.

The swishing of Eri's feet caught Ralan's attention, and he spun to face his own daughter. Then his brows rose at the anger in her eyes. "Don't give me that look."

"You sent my new mother away," Eri said, her voice warbling. "Of all the strands, you picked that one."

His blood chilled at her words. "She asked to leave, Eri. It was what she wanted."

"I thought once Kai brought you both here, everything would be fine."

"That's why you broke the rules by meddling in grown-up magic?" Ralan demanded.

She lifted her chin. "You didn't say I couldn't use the mirror."

"Erinalia!" he snapped. "We both know I don't have to forbid every item on this estate by name. We do not use other people's magical objects, nor do we mess with their spells. It is common courtesy in Moranaia, as we have discussed already."

Her shoulders slumped, and she looked down at her lap. "I'm sorry. Lady Megelien told me it was important for Kai to go get you. She showed me what to do."

Ralan froze at that. "The goddess guided you?"

"Yes," Eri said. She looked at Lyr. "I really am sorry for using your mirror. I know I should've come and got you, but the Lady said it would be fine."

Lyr opened his mouth and then closed it, his expression stunned. Finally, he shook his head. "It's okay, Eri. But ask next time. I'm getting used to doing strange things for seers."

I trusted you.

Ralan's jaw clenched as the memory of Lyr's words shoved into his brain. Gods, he wished Eri hadn't been cursed with this same gift. Would she struggle to avoid hurting her friends someday? Be forced to guide them through the uncertain futures?

"Time for bed," Ralan said. "It's dawn, and I'm sure you haven't slept. I'm too tired to deliver the rest of my lecture, anyway."

Her usual grin lit up her face. "That's okay. I heard it all in a different strand."

A startled laugh slipped free, and he heard Lyr smother a chuckle. "Bed, Eri."

She stood, and her expression turned serious again. "You're going to have to work a lot harder with Cora gone. But we can talk about that later."

Ralan stared at his daughter as she darted out the door. He was too stunned to call her back, and he wasn't sure he wanted an explanation in any case. Not now. But he knew Eri.

There would be a later.

Maddy sat in her driveway, the car growing warmer by the moment as she stared at the light glowing in the living room window. It had taken her a good bit of time to stumble her way around the ridge to find Cora's car. Then she'd sat inside with the doors locked for a solid ten minutes as she'd waited for her phone to charge so she could use the GPS. She'd called her father and Anna to tell them she was fine before heading home.

Now she was oddly hesitant to go inside.

Inside their small condo, Anna waited. She was the best thing that had ever happened to Maddy. They'd been together for over a year and had lived together for three months. As soon as she walked in that door, Anna would envelop Maddy in her soft, loving arms. She would make a cup of tea and tuck Maddy onto the couch with a soft throw.

Maybe.

Dread tightened her insides. Anna was human. She'd learned of Maddy's heritage before they'd moved in together and had said it didn't bother her. But how could Maddy talk to her about all that had happened? Blood magic, energy poisoning, elves from other worlds—that was a lot of strange to accept.

Then there was Fen. Maddy dropped her head to the steering wheel and closed her eyes. That brush of his lips against her forehead had brought more than comfort. If she were honest, she'd felt inexplicably drawn to him from the moment he'd entered the cavern. It had been fear of his Unseelie magic, hadn't it? She refused to dwell on that brief tingle brought on by a man who'd helped keep her captive. Nope.

A knock against the glass had Maddy jerking upright, a scream slipping from her lips. Had Kien found her? She shoved a hand against her pounding heart, and she braced herself for danger. But instead of the dark prince she'd half-feared, Anna stood on the other side of the window, brows drawn in worry.

What had she been thinking? Kien wouldn't have freaking knocked.

Some of her tension unwound at the sight of Anna's heart-shaped face. The wind whipped her chin-length, blond hair into her eyes, and she pushed it back with her usual, sharp motions. Maddy

found herself smiling. She grabbed her phone from the passenger seat and opened the door, slowly so that Anna could shift back.

They stared at one another for a moment. Then Anna launched into her arms and smothered her face with kisses. "I almost called the police a million times."

"I know, love," Maddy whispered. She lowered her forehead to Anna's. "I'm sorry. All of this is so weird. I was just sitting here trying to figure out how to talk about it."

"You will when you're ready." Anna grabbed her hand and tugged. "Let's go in. You can take a shower and change, and then I'll make you some tea."

Maddy's smile widened.

Everything was going to be okay.

Ralan slumped into the chair Eri had vacated and let his head drop against the back. Outside the window, the sun peeked over the edge of the mountain, spilling light into the valley that stretched to the east of the estate. Rose-gold tipped the wispy clouds drifting across the bits of sky he could see through the break in the trees.

He might find it beautiful if his life hadn't gone to shit.

The steady drip of the water clock was the only sound as Lyr stared from across the room. Ralan counted thirty-seven drops before his friend finally spoke. "By all the gods of Arneen, Ralan, what happened?"

He forced himself to straighten so he could meet Lyr's eyes. As Ralan recounted the events of the past few days, his muscles tightened. His friend's expression remained impassive, yet thoughtful,

but the judgment was surely coming. He'd been affected by one of Ralan's faulty visions before this giant muck up, after all. Now all of Moranaia would suffer for it.

"If I'd Seen even a fraction of all this…" Ralan rubbed his hand across his face. "I should have been able to stop him in that cave. I could have ordered Inona out of the way before he caught her or found a way around his shielding. Something."

Lyr's brows pinched, and his arms tightened across his chest. "Has it occurred to you that Kien was supposed to return?"

Ralan stared at his friend in stunned silence. Then he shook his head. "What?"

"I've long had the feeling there was something greater at play here," Lyr said. "At first, I thought I was merely annoyed by your interference. But… *Clechtan,* Ralan. If the goddess Megelien has blocked your Sight but is giving your six-year-old orders? Something major is happening. Perhaps She wanted Kien back here."

"Maybe," Ralan murmured.

Echoes of other visions slipped into his thoughts. The island rising through the waves, a spell that would require Kai and Eri at the least. Eri would be queen of that place, but Ralan hadn't yet found the strand that led to its creation. Did Kien have anything to do with it? Improbable, but there was no way for him to know. Not until his Sight cleared.

Frowning, Ralan glanced back at Lyr. "I've foreseen a time when the elves might have to return to Earth. It's murky. A puzzle that has been bothering me for weeks."

Lyr's eyebrows drew up. "You think it's related?"

"I don't know." Ralan let out a slow breath in annoyance. "The vision is a fragment with no context. But if there's any possibility of

it coming true, I'd say you're right about something major brewing. The only clear thing I know is that Kai has to master his power over earth. If I can tell you more, I will."

Lyr peered at him for a moment. "I'm surprised you told me that."

"Me, too." Ralan shrugged. "But I'm weary. The burden of this gift… In a way, it was unfair of me to give you a taste of it. That fragment may be a future unrealized. Who knows?"

"There's a reason I've insisted on my people learning human languages." Lyr straightened, his arms dropping to his sides. "I've long thought our return inevitable. With advances in technology, humans are going to discover the magical races. I'd like to be prepared in case we need to send some of our people through to help."

The door opened, and Arlyn slipped inside. "Selia should be down soon. Iren was complaining about getting out of bed so early since he can't go watch the warriors train anymore."

Heaving a sigh, Ralan shoved to his feet. Once Arlyn's magic teacher got her son settled, she would come downstairs to plan. He would have to leave that in Lyr's hands. "It's time for me to return to the palace."

Lyr frowned. "With Kien nearby?"

"Now that he has found a way through, he doesn't need to kill you to try to break the spell binding him." Ralan rubbed his hand across his stomach at the odd tug within. An instinct, almost like a vision, goaded him, but he could find no clear strand. "He wants to be king. If he's heading anywhere, it's the palace. I just don't know how or when."

"What about Eri?" Lyr asked.

"She will be safer here. I'll kiss her goodbye before I leave." He hesitated. "You are still willing to care for her if…?"

Though a hint of uncertainty entered his friend's gaze, he nodded. "We will."

"Then I'll bid you farewell."

As Ralan strode through the door, he couldn't help but wonder if he would see Lyr again. If the kiss he gave Eri would be his last. He reached for the future strands for some hint, but they danced out of reach. As usual of late.

He headed out the back exit and started down the garden path. Morning birds called their songs, and the burble of water flowing over rock sounded through the empty trails. Light built around him, dancing between the branches along with the first falling leaves of early autumn. He breathed in the crisp air. Too bad he wouldn't be here for the Equinox Festival. The season of Morne was his favorite—he'd even used the word as his last name on Earth—and he would've loved to experience it here again. Yet another regret.

Ralan turned down the back trail. Only a few paces from the guest tower, the vision hit.

Cora stretched out a trembling hand, and a shimmer of blue leaped to life. Her head fell back, and her eyes slipped closed. For endless time, she stood there, her posture growing straighter and her hand steadier.

The portal to Galare?

He tried to focus the vision, but he stopped when it hazed. "*Watch,*" Megelien whispered.

The blue glow shifted, the wavering light becoming tinged with hints of black. Then a dark form materialized. As a man slipped out of the portal, Ralan tried to call out. But of course he couldn't. Cora's eyes snapped open as

the man's hand wrapped around her arm. He jerked her off balance, and she stumbled.

The stranger tugged her toward the portal with an angry scowl. "You will pay, Cora."

Ralan's vision went black before the world returned to painful focus. His heart pounding, he searched for his link to Cora. Although it was there, as solid as ever, her thoughts were sealed from him. Was it the distance, or had she blocked him on purpose?

He took off down the trail, darting around the guest tower on his way to the portal. There was so much he had to do, but none of it mattered. The kingdom had lasted millennia, and the palace was well-guarded. He would have Lyr warn Teyark to protect their father.

Selfish or not, he was going after Cora.

25

Cora shot Kai an annoyed glare as he walked with her along the ridgeline. Returning to the full dark of night was disorienting after seeing the dawn on Moranaia, but she could manage. She wasn't entirely helpless. "You don't have to stay with me until Maddy gets here."

With a quick grin, he lifted a shoulder. "You're unarmed, it's late, and Kien could be anywhere. You'll just have to deal with me tagging along."

"Then hand me a knife and go."

"Have I caused you some offense?" Kai asked.

Cora huffed. "No."

"Then what's the problem?"

"I want to be alone," she said. She stomped through the thickening forest as the ridge began to level out. "I don't want to think about any Moranaians right now."

"Ah," Kai said with a sharp nod. "You're ticked at Ralan. Easy to get that way, really."

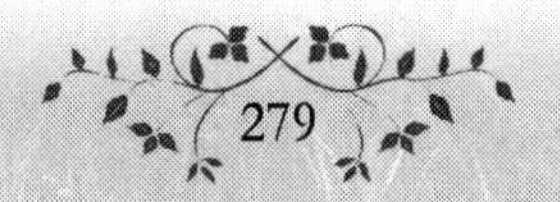

"I left your pack in your car," Cora muttered. "I'm surprised he didn't thank me for the good time while he was at it."

Kai made a choked sound. At her narrowed gaze, he made a valiant effort to smother the laugh. "Sorry. Not what I expected to hear from a princess."

She chilled at his words. He might have overheard that she was from Galare, but no one had mentioned her rank. "Princess?" she asked, careful to keep her tone even.

"You're bonded to Ralan, right?" Kai's eyebrow quirked. "That's the same as being married among my people. You'd be the same rank as him."

"Well, we're not on Moranaia." When they reached the driveway where Maddy was supposed to meet her, Cora nearly groaned. Her friend wasn't there yet. Frustration had her hands clenching as she rounded on Kai. "Look, you seem nice enough. But I really would like to be alone."

But the elf's easy humor had disappeared, his expression completely serious. "I owe Ralan."

She stifled the urge to punch him. "I don't care."

"I do." His lips firmed. "I was an asshole to him a few days ago when he was only trying to help. He messes up sometimes, but he's a good friend. He didn't deserve the brunt of my anger."

Cora scowled. "What does that have to do with me?"

A faint smile crossed Kai's lips. "It'll tick you off more, but…I'm not going to let Ralan's bonded hang out here unprotected. Not with Kien on the loose. And before you say it, it's not because you're female. You're weak from lack of energy. Believe me when I tell you that tromping through the woods at night with low energy is never a good idea."

Something in the tone of his voice told her he'd had a bad experience in just such a situation, but she didn't ask about it. Kai had a good point, as much as she hated to admit it. Ralan had given her enough energy to walk without toppling over, but that was it. If she had to use her magic in self-defense, she would probably collapse.

"Fine," Cora said. "But can we talk about something besides Ralan? Who was the woman who came with you?"

"Arlyn." Kai's expression softened. "My soulbonded. The estate we just left? She's the half-blood daughter of the lord in charge, Lyr. She arrived from Earth a couple of months ago. Ralan and Eri came back not long after she met us, actually." Kai winced. "Shit. Sorry."

She bit back a sigh. "Let's forget talking."

Two beams of light glowed through the trees, bouncing as the approaching car crept over the ruts in the dirt driveway. Cora stiffened, and beside her, Kai's hand rested on the hilt of his sword. Grimacing, she gestured at the forest.

"Maybe you should hide behind a tree. That might not be Maddy." She pointed at his weapon. "A guy standing around with a sword would definitely cause a problem."

With a grin, he cast a glamour around himself. "There. Problem solved."

Cora shook her head at him and turned her attention to the approaching vehicle. But she couldn't help the small smile that tipped her lips. If she lived on Moranaia, she had a feeling she would be friends with Kai. Then tears clogged her throat and erased her smile. Too bad she would likely never see his land again.

The car drew to a halt, and Cora peered inside. Maddy's worried gaze met hers, making Cora wince. She had to look terrible, and not just because of her mud-and-blood-stained clothes. She shoved a tangled hair off of her face. Would her friend notice the pain simmering under Cora's skin, waiting to erupt? She stiffened her spine and tried to blink back the tears threatening to break free.

As soon as she heard the click of the locks releasing, Cora jerked the passenger door open. Then she paused, her hand clenching the top of the door, and glanced back at Kai. "Thanks."

He gave a short nod and lifted a hand. "Anytime."

Cora didn't wait to see how long he lingered. Instead, she dropped into the seat and slammed the door. She pinched her eyes closed as Maddy turned the car around and started down the driveway. Her fingers curled into the coin holder on the door. She wanted to leap right back out of the car and chase after Kai.

No, she wanted to chase after Ralan.

Her bonded.

What had she done?

"Are you okay?" Maddy asked, her quiet voice full of concern. "Who was that?"

"One of Ralan's people," Cora whispered.

She'd stifled the ache all the way through the forest and during the Veil crossing. She'd shoved it beneath her aggravation at Kai's endless chatter. But in the presence of her friend's worry, the pain tipped free of its container, pouring through her blood until it burned.

Cora reinforced the wall she'd built between her mind and Ralan's before her distress leaked along their bond. But she still felt

the touch of his spirit where it linked with hers. She shoved her fist against her mouth and forced back a sob. Why had she let her anger take control of her heart?

Why hadn't he fought for her?

Maddy's hand touched her shoulder. "You're worrying me."

Cora forced her eyes open. Maddy had stopped at the end of the driveway, and her stern expression said she wasn't driving until Cora started talking. "I left Ralan. While you take me home, I'll tell you about it."

"Okay." Maddy returned her hand to the steering wheel even as she gave Cora a warning scowl. "But if you stop, I will, too."

Cora's tugged her aching fingers away from their grip on the door, only to tangle her hands together in her lap. "In the cavern, I found out who he was. Is. The prince of Moranaia."

"Is that a problem?"

In all of her years on Earth, Cora had never shared her history with another person, human or fae, except for Ralan. But she found the whole story spilling out. With each word, the burden grew lighter. Not the pain of loss but the remnants of the past.

"My father was so proud of the alliance he was forming with Moranaia." Cora sighed. "I admit I wasn't fond of an arranged marriage, but Orn was too terrible to contemplate. Then we received word that the prince would not honor the contract. Orn demanded we wed, so I ran."

"I'm so sorry, Cora," Maddy said softly. "I'm guessing Ralan was the one who broke the engagement?"

"According to him, he'd never consented. He thought it was an idle idea of his father's."

"Wait a second," Maddy said, her brows furrowing. "He never agreed?"

"No." Cora squeezed her hands together. "He was in love with someone else. He's a seer, but he didn't even bother to check if there could be a future between us."

Maddy's fingers drummed a rapid beat along the steering wheel as she frowned at the road. "Cora," she finally said. "I get that what happened really sucked. I'd probably be mad about it, too. But the way the guy looks at you… Damn. And the way he held you as he carried you to the portal? Dude looked like his whole world would end if your hair snagged on a branch."

Cora's heart thumped. "He didn't argue when I left. Not a word. Well, except to give me directions home."

"He's probably feeling guilty as hell," Maddy said. "You said it was how long? Three hundred years?"

"Three hundred and forty-two."

"I know you didn't exactly ask my advice." Maddy grimaced. "But you're going to get it anyway. Nurse your mad if you have to and then go work things out. Three centuries is a long time, and people change. Anyway, think of all the awesome things you would've missed if you'd gone straight into a marriage with him. Earth can be a fun place."

"That's true." Cora nibbled on her lower lip as memories flitted through her mind. She'd seen and experienced so many changes, and she'd made wonderful friends. She wouldn't have experienced any of that on Moranaia. "I'll think about it, Maddy. Thanks for listening."

"Of course."

Cora studied her friend, and guilt swamped her at the sight of the dark circles beneath Maddy's eyes. "Crap. I can't believe you're comforting me right now. How are *you?* You're the one who was kidnapped and held in a cave."

To think she'd called Ralan self-centered.

"I'm pretty shaken up," Maddy admitted quietly. "But they didn't hurt me. The Victor guy wanted to, but Kien warned him against it. They were worried about the damage a healer could do. If only they knew."

Cora winced at the dry tone of her friend's voice. "You'll get your magic worked out. It just takes time."

"I think I'm going to have to find a Master Healer, which means relocating." Maddy sighed. "I can scan people's bodies for injury, but that's about the only reliable thing I've managed. Well, I knocked Patrick unconscious. Go, me."

"Won't any of the Sidhe healers help?"

Maddy's mouth twisted. "We haven't found one who will train a half-blood from a nobody family living on Earth."

Unbidden, the image of the healer on Moranaia popped into Cora's mind. He was grumpy, but he'd been eager to speak with her about the method she'd used on Inona. If he'd been bothered that Cora wasn't a Moranaian elf, he'd given no indication. Would he help a half-Sidhe?

But if she didn't work things out with Ralan, she had no clue if she would return to his world. Best not to mention the possibility to Maddy. Instead, Cora filed the thought away for the future. She would barter her knowledge of fire-healing if she had to. Maddy deserved help.

After a quick glance around, Kai stepped into the small portal to the Veil. The energy embraced him, the rolling mist and swirls of color embracing him like a mother's arms. He settled into the power and met it with his own before searching for the thread that led to Moranaia. Crossing had been easier since Kien's energy poisoning spell had been disrupted, so it didn't take long to find it.

But just as he snagged it, a hint of disturbance rippled along his skin.

Frowning, Kai cast his energy in a sweep. Was Kien still working his way through the Veil? He reinforced his shielding as his magic brushed against a strange presence. Pulling a knife from his belt, he crept into the fog.

A form took shape, but Kai realized at once that it wasn't Kien. This male had short blond hair, unlike Kien's black, and when he turned, his face was unfamiliar. A lost traveler? It wasn't unheard of for the unskilled to go adrift in the strange mists of the Veil, especially if they lacked the talent to find the strands between dimensions.

"Identify yourself," Kai said, his voice ringing hollowly around him.

"I'm Fen," the fae answered. "I don't suppose you know the way out of this place?"

That name sounded familiar. His brow wrinkled for a moment before it hit him. Ah, fuck. The guy who'd helped Kien. "Death would be an easy way out."

Fen scoffed. "Nice line. Bet you had to hunt hard for something that cliché."

Kai found his mouth tipping up in a reluctant grin. "Got me there."

"Can we skip to the part where you tell me why you'd like to kill me? I usually remember the people I offend."

"The last time I heard the name Fen, it was in connection to Kien," Kai said, studying the other for his reaction. Would he deny it?

But the fae's shoulders slumped. "Figures. Look, I was trying to correct my mistake in working with the guy. I would've killed him if he hadn't kidnapped Maddy. She's too good to have her life ruined by this mess."

Kai's thoughts returned to the young Sidhe they'd found by the portal. She'd told them that Fen had bargained for her life, so it seemed he spoke the truth. But that didn't make him a friend.

"Where's Kien?"

"I shoved his ass through to Moranaia before he could kill me," Fen answered, lifting his shoulder in a quick shrug. "But I'm beginning to think I didn't do myself a favor. Just leave me if you want. I'll starve in here, so you can be assured I'll have a nice slow death."

Kai lifted a brow. "No supplies?"

"No blood." Fen smiled and revealed a set of sharp fangs. "I pull in energy through blood, not from the world around me. I need blood more than food considering how much magic I've used lately."

Normally, Kai would be fascinated. He'd heard of blood elves but hadn't met one. Now he just wanted to get home. "I'll guide you from the Veil if you'll allow yourself to be bound."

"Kinky," Fen said with a smirk.

Kai sheathed his knife and tugged a small coil of rope from the pouch on his belt. It was thin but strong, and it had been spelled to restrain magic. "I'm both straight and soulbonded. You're out of luck there."

Fen turned his back to Kai and held his hands behind him. "No chance of a triad?"

"Nope." Kai let out a soft chuckle as he wrapped the rope around the fae's wrists. He had to give the guy credit for being snarky under pressure. "Better luck on your next capture."

"Eh, you're not my type, anyway."

Kai drew his knife again. "This isn't going to improve the sentiment."

He shoved the blade against Fen's side and propelled him forward. As Fen began to walk, Kai grasped for the thread to Moranaia. The way had grown more turbulent as they'd talked, but it still shouldn't take long. With a heave of power, he tugged them toward home.

26

Ralan paced the clearing in front of the portal and tried not to lose his mind. He'd spoken to Lyr as he'd darted along the trail, and his friend had reassured him that the king would be warned. Then he'd connected with Eri, not wanting to leave without letting her know. She, of course, had already Seen the possibility and had sent a sleepy but understanding reply. He'd even contacted Delbin to check on Inona. She hadn't woken yet but was doing well.

What was taking Kai so long to return?

With a resigned sigh, Ralan plopped down on a nearby bench. Again. His fingers dug into the rough underside as he struggled for calm. He would be in time to help Cora. Megelien wouldn't have shown him the vision otherwise. Would She?

He closed his eyes and bowed his head. After a brief hesitation, he reached out for the goddess, a link once as familiar as breath. *"I have not intended to neglect your temple,"* he sent.

"AND YET YOU HAVE."

"You're right," Ralan agreed at once. *"As Cora so recently said, I have been more than careless. I can offer nothing but my profoundest apologies."*

Silence. *"HAVE YOU PREPARED YOURSELF FOR THE TRUTH YOUR DREAMS BRING?"*

Ralan sucked in a ragged breath. Was he prepared? In all honesty, he didn't want to die. Life was not for giving up or giving in. Life was for fighting. Still, not even the long-lived elves were guaranteed forever. If he had to sacrifice himself to the fire to save his people, he would.

"As much as I can be," he answered. *"But I confess I'm not looking forward to it."*

Her amusement and affection filled him. *"TELL ME WHAT BROUGHT YOU TO SPEAK WITH ME THIS DAY."*

She knew, of course, but She had always given him the respect of not saying so. *"Can I save Cora and still stop my brother?"*

"YOU ARE BOUND BY BLOOD TO YOUR BROTHER." Her soft laughter filled his mind. *"YOU DO NOT NEED MY HELP WITH THAT PART. I SHOWED YOU WHAT YOU MOST NEEDED. PERHAPS FOR YOUR HONESTY, I WILL SHOW YOU MORE."*

The blood spell. Ralan might have smacked his palm against his forehead if a burst of pain hadn't bloomed between his temples. Instead, he shoved his fingers against his eyes, a hiss slipping from his lips. His heart began to pound as visions flitted through his mind, faster than he could grasp.

"YOU WILL KNOW WHAT YOU NEED."

Then Megelien was gone—and so was the pain.

Ralan blinked against the light trickling through the leaves. For a moment, he stared at the broad trunk of a tree as he struggled to

process what had happened. Hesitantly, he reached for the future strands. His heart pounded hard when he immediately found the one leading to Cora.

Some were still muddled. He could tell with certainty that he would have several days, maybe a week, before Kien reached the palace, but the confrontation itself remained hazy. He couldn't track Cora's future beyond a few days, and his friends' lives were blurred as well. But he didn't care.

For the moment, at least, he knew what to do.

Remembering Lady Megelien's words, he searched along the link he'd formed with his brother. Close but not immediately so. And he thought...yes, Kien's energy was to the northwest, heading away from Braelyn. Ralan sent a quick message to Lyr with the information and then stood. Kai would emerge in a moment.

The guards on each side of the portal stared at Ralan as he approached. He merely smiled. No doubt he'd looked like a madman pacing the clearing and then speaking with Megelien. He didn't care. The guard on the right would laugh about it with his wife, and their good humor had a decent chance of leading to a child if they maintained that mood until later. A likely strand.

Gods, he loved having his Sight back at full strength. Mostly.

The portal shimmered, and Kai shoved Fen through. The blood elf's hands had been bound, but his expression appeared more relieved than concerned. Getting lost in the Veil tended to do that to a person.

Kai jerked to a halt at the sight of Ralan. "Let me guess. A vision?"

"I am asking for your help this time, not ordering it," Ralan said.

"*Clechtan*, Ralan," Kai said with a groan. "I wasn't really mad at you. I knew I had to go, but I didn't want to. I took it out on you."

Ralan shrugged. "Apology accepted."

"I didn't actually—"

"You were about to." Ralan couldn't stifle the quick grin. "Close enough. I had a vision about Cora in danger. Will you guide me through? We can take Fen back to Earth."

"Shouldn't we imprison him for helping Kien?"

"I ordered him to try to save Maddy," Ralan said. "So it's technically my fault."

"I would've done it anyway," Fen said.

Ralan waved a hand. "Whatever. I've talked to Lyr. If you're willing, we can go."

Kai frowned, his gaze going distant for a moment, before he nodded. "Arlyn is resting, and my energy reserves are decent. But once you arrive on Earth, you're on your own. I need to get back."

Nodding, Ralan strode the remaining steps to the portal. It should only take them a few minutes for Kai to return them to Earth. Then Fen was going to drive him to Cora.

"Are you sure you're going to be okay?" Maddy asked.

Cora lifted her backpack out of the trunk and slammed it closed before forcing a smile to her lips. "I'll be fine. Hey, at least the shop is closed tomorrow, right?"

Maddy leaned against her open car door. "I suppose."

"Just go home and rest." Cora headed up the sidewalk with a wave. "I'll call you in the morning."

Cora ducked inside the house before Maddy could argue. After she closed the door, she slumped against it, the heavy weight of her backpack digging into her leg. Only after she heard Maddy's car rolling out of the driveway did she start toward the kitchen.

Her heart twisted at the sight of the mess she'd left in the sink. The last meal she'd eat with Ralan. Even if Maddy was right that he had let her go out of guilt, so many obstacles stood between them. She had to do something about Orn, for one thing. If he found out that Cora had completed the alliance with Moranaia, he would surely try to sever it before their people found out. Even after all this time, her bonding to Ralan would give her father renewed political importance. Orn wouldn't be able to tolerate that.

Then there was Ralan's search for his brother. After encountering Kien in the cavern, Cora understood exactly why Ralan thought he would die while attempting to defeat him. It wasn't that Kien was some great, powerful, unbeatable mage. It was his utter, careless cruelty and his cleverness. He would try anything regardless of the cost.

That lack of caring was the most dangerous of all.

She had always known Orn to be a terrible man, but in Kien, she had witnessed true evil. She'd watched Ralan's mad brother murder in cold blood and then lick his knife clean. And Inona… Cora shuddered as the scene in the cave replayed in her mind. Orn was bad, but for the first time in her life, she had seen much worse.

Cora settled her backpack on the table. A dull thud caught her attention, and frowning, she slid the zipper open and peeked inside. She shoved aside the rolls of extra clothing, a bundle of rope, and a packet of dried food. Then she noticed a velvety black fabric pouch near the bottom.

With trembling fingers, she pulled it free. She stared at it for a moment, knowing what it was without even opening it. But she had to be sure. Her spine stiffened as she reached inside, and she shivered as her skin made contact with cool metal and smooth glass. After taking a deep breath, she pulled it free.

The mirror.

Cora stared at her own face, her lips pinched tight and her eyes lined with pain. He'd tucked the communication mirror in her backpack. But when? She dropped into a seat and leaned her elbow on the table, still staring at herself. He had to have done it after carrying her out of the cavern. Had he guessed that she would leave him?

I left your pack in your car.

She might have forgotten it if he hadn't reminded her. He must have wanted her to find the mirror sooner rather than later and realize that he'd thought of her. That he'd given her a way to call for him if she changed her mind. Maybe. She could guess all day, but she wouldn't know until she spoke with him again.

Her fingers tightened on the metal frame. Unfortunately, she didn't know how to use it. If she decided to. Though it was a risk with her energy so low, Cora allowed a small tendril of magic loose into the edge to see if she could find a clue. She found no hint of a spell she would need to latch on to. Too bad it wasn't as simple as picturing Moranaia or the man Ralan had spoken to before.

Or was it?

Light flared, tugging her energy from her as she inadvertently activated the spell. The room spun, and she blinked against the wave of dizziness as the mirror's glow settled. When it did, she found herself staring at Ralan's friend, his expression colder than a mountaintop in winter.

"Name yourself at once," he said.

The red-haired woman from earlier stepped into the image. "That's Cora."

The man's expression didn't change. "How do you have that mirror?"

"Ralan left it in my backpack," Cora said quickly. "I didn't mean to activate it."

"*Onaial*," the woman—Arlyn?—said. "Cora is Ralan's bonded. Remember? I guess he wasn't as clueless as I thought."

"So he has reached you?" he asked.

Cora's brow wrinkled. "What are you talking about?"

"He left to warn you about some vision he had," Arlyn answered. "I'm surprised he hasn't contacted you telepathically."

Heat rushed into Cora's cheeks at those words. It was possible he had tried, but she'd done her best to put up a shield between them. She wasn't about to explain that to a stranger, though. "I'll see if I can reach him."

"Forgive me for my rude greeting, Cora," the male said. "I am Lyr, the lord in charge of Braelyn. With so much danger of late, I feared the worst when I realized it wasn't Ralan calling."

"Understandable." Cora gave a wry smile. "I don't suppose you can cut this link? I'm not entirely sure how I activated it."

Lyr gave a slight bow. "Certainly. I bid you good day."

"Good day."

As soon as the magic winked out, leaving her reflection once more, Cora tucked the mirror into the pouch. She set it on the table and nibbled at her lip. What could Ralan have seen that would lead him back to Earth? It was possible his brother hadn't returned to Moranaia after all. Or there was Orn.

Only one way to find out.

Cora lowered the wall she'd built between herself and Ralan. At once, the emotion that had remained just out of reach rushed through her. Pain, worry, panic, regret. Gasping, she folded over from the force of it. Her hands dug into her knees as she fought to cope with all that flowed through their bond.

She extended a shaky mental hand, searching. *"Ralan?"*

"CORA!"

She let out a cry. *"Too. Loud."*

"Forgive me," he answered, softly this time. *"You're on Earth? I'm not too late?"*

On Earth? Cora pushed herself upright as the pain began to level out. *"I'm sitting in my kitchen. I accidentally used the mirror you left, and Lyr said you were coming back. What's wrong?"*

"I had a vision." Though his worry pinched her own heart, he sent her a mental caress. A gentle brush of reassurance that sent a shiver through her. *"You were by the portal to Galare, and someone came out. A man. He grabbed you."*

The hair on her arms rose. *"What did he look like?"*

"Tall. Long red hair. Aristocratic features. He wore a purple silk robe."

"Orn," she whispered into Ralan's mind. Her eyes darted to the back window where the sky had begun to lighten with dawn. *"When?"*

He hesitated. *"There are many options. You can wait for me, and we will defeat him together. If you go to the portal alone, there is a chance you can beat him. But there's also the possibility that he'll take you back with him. I can't see many variables past that. There are approximately twenty-two strands branching from this moment."*

Her brows lifted. Though he'd shared the information with ease, she had the feeling it wasn't common for him to give so much detail. It was more than he'd… *"You regained your Sight?"*

"The goddess restored some of it," Ralan answered. *"Enough to see this for certain. Wait for me. Fen is driving me over."*

"What if Orn comes through early?"

Another wave of reassurance brushed through her. *"He will not,* mialn. *This I promise."*

Despite everything, heat sparked low in her belly at the smooth confidence of his tone. She gritted her teeth against the sudden urge to flirt. *"I'm still angry at you."*

"I know." Worry and amusement rang through his mental voice. *"You may tell me just how much once you are safe."*

"Well, don't delay. I need more energy soon."

Warmth curled through her, and a hint of her strength returned. *"Rest. I'll see you soon."*

As he ended the mental link, her stunned gaze landed on the pouch she'd set on the table. Whatever accident had led her to activate the mirror had been a fortuitous one. She never would have expected Orn's arrival. He hated leaving the comfort of his home, and he considered Earth to be a wild place with no purpose. Even if he'd changed his mind about Earth, her father had told her that Orn had wed. What could he still want with her? If it wasn't marriage, it had to be her death.

Although Ralan had told her to rest, Cora couldn't sit still. Not after finding out that her greatest enemy would be stepping out of the portal to grab her. Instead, she headed to the sink and began to wash the dishes. Her nose wrinkled at the dried-on leftovers. She

could take out her frustrations on the grime while she considered the best way to handle Orn.

And handle him she would. She'd seen true evil, and Orn's shallow cruelty didn't compare. She would face the demon who had taunted her for so long. Then she would help Ralan conquer a real threat.

27

As soon as Fen put the car in park, Ralan unsnapped his seatbelt and grabbed for the door handle. "Tell your uncle to come find me before he kills you."

Fen let out a scoffing noise. "Yeah, that'll work."

"The Unseelie king courts war with Moranaia if it doesn't." Ralan smirked. "That should get his attention."

"I doubt he'll believe me."

"Then you'd better work hard at being convincing. I don't have time to track him down." Ralan did a quick check of the strands. "There's a good chance you'll be fine."

"A good—"

"Stay out of trouble, Fen," Ralan said as he opened the door. "You'll be useful if you stop being an idiot."

He shoved himself out of the car and slammed the door before Fen could retort. Ralan didn't have time to debate the blood elf's future. Instead, he strode up the sidewalk and straight through Cora's front door. Considering all they'd shared, knocking felt stranger than the alternative.

Ralan followed her energy signature and the clink of silverware against dishes. When he reached the narrow archway leading into the kitchen, he leaned against the frame and watched her as she lifted a plate out of a sink full of soapy water. Warm contentment filled him just at the sight of her.

Even if she had started scrubbing a plate as though it was an enemy in need of banishing.

"Cora."

She yelped, and the plate slipped from her hand with a plop and a clatter. She spun, water dripping down her shirt as she glared at him. "I didn't hear you come in."

He shrugged. "Our souls are connected. Knocking seemed a bit quaint."

"You could've made some noise." Her lips twisted as she reached for a towel to dry her hands. "How long have you been staring at me?"

"Not long enough. Never long enough."

Her throat worked as she swallowed. "You didn't seem to feel a great deal of attachment earlier."

"You deserve better than me." Ralan's chest squeezed at her hurt blended with his own. "And I thought it might make my death easier on you if you hated me."

Cora's eyes filled with hope. "Have you Seen more clearly?"

"No," Ralan answered, grimacing. "But the goddess asked if I was ready to accept the truth of my dream. That's answer enough, isn't it?"

The lurching of her stomach hit him in the gut. "This is bullshit."

"I'd have to agree," Ralan answered. One corner of his mouth tipped up.

Cora dropped the towel to the counter and strode over. She bit her lip. Then she lifted her hand to his cheek. "I've mostly enjoyed my time on Earth."

Ralan opened his mouth, then snapped it closed. Where was she going with this? "And?"

"My pride has been bruised over your rejection for centuries," she said. "But it was just that—pride. We would have missed a great deal of our lives if we'd gone through with the marriage three hundred years ago. You wouldn't have your daughter. I wouldn't have found my art, at least not in the same way."

He lifted his hand to cover hers. "Then you forgive me?"

"Maybe I shouldn't, but yes." Her soft sigh brushed across his lips as she moved closer. "But I'm still mad at you for sending me off *with directions*."

"I wanted you to find the mirror," he muttered.

A true smile curved her mouth. "I'd wondered."

"Come home with me," Ralan whispered, his heart pounding. "Once we stop Orn."

"I…" Uncertainty slipped into her eyes. "I'm not sure I'm ready to link my energy to Moranaia. If there were a portal to Galare to renew myself, the decision would be easier."

Ralan frowned as he considered the problem. "My father might know of one. I'm not sure how he contacted your father. If there's not, I'll feed you energy while you decide."

"That's risky."

"Give it a week." He lowered his hands to her hips to draw her closer. "We both know I'm likely to die. I'd like to spend my remaining time with you."

Cora winced. "I'm not sure if that's romantic or terrible."

"I guess it's both," Ralan answered wryly. His hands tightened as she swayed a little. "In any case, Eri might never forgive me if I come back without you. Apparently, there was a strand where I didn't let you go, and she was not pleased that I didn't take it."

Cora's breath hitched on a laugh. "She's six?"

"Supposedly." Ralan grinned. "I'm not looking forward to adolescence."

"Who does?"

Though humor filled Cora's eyes, Ralan's heart squeezed as she swayed against him again. "We need to get you to the Galaren portal. It's tougher for me to channel energy here."

Cora nodded, but she lowered her hand to his shoulder and squeezed. "I don't want you to kill Orn. Leave him to me."

"He will be overthrown rightfully," Ralan said. "But I can—"

"No." Cora's expression hardened. "You'd better find the strand where I solve this problem myself because I refuse to have someone else do it for me. I've been running from this for too long."

"If I can tell you the optimal—"

Cora's finger pressed across his lips. "I don't care if you're a seer. You aren't going to guide me. If you want a relationship with me, it will be as equals. I am not a project, a quest, or a divine mission."

Frustration simmered in his blood at her words. He could guide her so easily to the best path. The safest. Why wouldn't she let him tell her what he'd Seen? It would be fastest if he simply took control of Orn and wiped his memory of Cora. She wouldn't be disturbed again if they took that strand.

Then again…he frowned as he let his mind expand farther from that point. Orn wouldn't be deposed as quickly, and the people of Galare would suffer for it. Ralan started to shuffle back through the earlier strands, trying to determine which would be best overall, but Cora's finger tapped against his lips, breaking his concentration.

"What kind of partnership would we have if I did nothing but follow your lead?"

Ralan took her hand in his, freeing his mouth. "If I see disaster, shouldn't I say so?"

"Sure." Cora canted her head, and her smile took on a wicked tilt. "Then I can decide if I'm in the mood for disaster. In this case, I know Galare better than you do. I'll handle Orn. Just guard my back."

Ralan stared at her, stuck somewhere between admiration and annoyance. He'd been cursed, yelled at, blamed, doubted, and scorned for the orders he'd given because of his Sight. But this was the first time in his life he'd been ignored. With a shake of his head, he pushed a stray hair from Cora's face.

And relented. "Fine. Lead the way, my love."

Cora did her level best not to let Ralan see how shaky she was, but it was impossible to hide it completely considering their connection. Sighing, she closed the back door and settled her hand on his offered arm. She might not be leading, but she sure wasn't yielding.

I still can't believe I got away with bossing him around, she thought, satisfaction pooling in her gut. They hadn't been together long, but she'd had plenty of opportunity to see how others gave in to Ralan's commands. Even Delbin, though he delivered a fair amount of

pushback. No matter where Ralan went, his bidding ended up being done.

Well, he might be a prince, but she wasn't one of his subjects.

The sky was turning gray with the dawn, the half-light haze giving her backyard a soft glow. A strange sense of déjà vu hit her. Only a couple of hours earlier, she'd walked with him near another dawn on another world. At that time, she'd had every intention of leaving him and never looking back. One side of her mouth lifted. So much for that.

When the small stand of trees closed around them, Cora searched the area. No sign that Orn had broken through. How had he realized this portal led to her? Blood relatives could speak through the portal along their shared bond with the land. That connection was how her parents knew when she tapped into Galare's energy, but anyone else on Galare would have to monitor the gate with magic to detect a person speaking from the other side.

After Cora's first few decades on Earth, she'd learned to shield her presence at the portal from all but her family. It had been easy for Orn's minions to track her when she drew in power, and she'd almost been caught several times. Once she'd built the shield, she'd only had to stay wary on the off-chance she was in visual range of the portal when someone traveled through. Once they had stopped detecting her, all had assumed that she'd bonded to Earth's energy and didn't need to renew herself at the gate anymore.

Cora paused before she and Ralan reached the shallow indention in the hill that hid the portal. She pulled her hand from his arm and met his eyes. "Find a place to hide."

Ralan lifted a brow. "Hide?"

"You're supposed to have my back, remember?"

He grumbled a few choice words, but she only tapped her foot impatiently until he spun away. Ralan chose a tree to the left of the portal, out of the direct line of sight of anyone exiting, and did his best to duck behind it. Cora chuckled at the sight of his shoulder sticking past the edge.

The trees here were fairly small, so it would have to do.

Cora stepped closer to the portal and stretched out her hand. The blue glow leaped to life, and a shiver went through her entire body. Power poured through her in a torrent, filling all the hollow spaces that had left her weak. She struggled against the urge to close her eyes. She couldn't lose herself in the sensation, not with the threat she was under.

When Orn stepped through the portal, she was ready. She hoped.

His dark eyes fastened on her at once, and he strode toward her. "Enough of your defiance, Cora."

She lowered her hand to her side. "How did you know I was here?"

"Your dear father let it slip that you'd bonded with some new source." Orn sneered. "Didn't you realize that your energy shifted? Whatever you used to hide yourself no longer works. Simple enough to track the portals once I knew to look."

"Why would my father speak to you?" Cora demanded.

Orn waved a hand. "He is wise enough to know not to anger the king."

Cora pulled heat into her palm, though she was careful to allow no visible flame. "If you have harmed my parents, you will pay."

"Now, Cora. Is that any way to speak to your future husband?"

She was so startled she almost lost control of her fire. "What? Father said you'd married."

"I've no doubt she'll die in childbirth in a few months. Or something." He shrugged. "It takes time to plan a royal wedding, too. You'll have plenty of time to resign yourself. Unless you'd rather I kill you?"

Ralan's anger seeped into hers until Cora thought she would explode with it. "Considering I'm already married, I suppose you'll have to try for the latter."

That caused his composure to slip. First shock and then anger clouded Orn's eyes. His nostrils flared as he took a step closer. "You're lying."

"I didn't bond to a place," Cora said. "I bonded to a person. I am out of your reach. Why don't you just go home? I have no interest in Galare's throne."

"You must come with me," Orn said, his hand darting out. She let his fingers wrap around her arm as he glared at her. "My marriage has not…"

As his mouth snapped closed, Cora smiled. "Hasn't made up for your terrible leadership? I suppose that explains why you finally came here yourself. Have your spies bailed on you?"

Orn's face reddened, and his fingers tightened, biting painfully into her skin. She must have scored a hit. Cora ignored the pain as she stared into the harsh planes of his face. Had she really let fear of this man control her for three centuries? She'd been a coward, running away from Galare instead of standing up for herself, and he'd made her a slave to her own terror.

Well, she'd found her power on Earth. And she refused to give that up.

"When I bend your body to my will—"

She shoved her hand to his throat, the force cutting off his words with a sputter, and let her fire rage free. But unlike with Inona, she had no intention of healing. Orn let out a choked scream, and his hands jerked to her wrist. Only to drop them as her fire scalded his palms. She held firm as flames whipped around him. She wouldn't kill the lawful king of Galare without imminent threat, but she would make him regret every moment of fear he had caused.

The acrid smell of burned flesh wafted around them, and Cora gagged. But only when Orn's scream faded to whimpers did she let him fall at her feet, the tendrils of fire winking out. His ragged breaths blended with his soft moan as he lifted his fingers to his welting throat. Hatred and fear pinched his eyes when he glanced up at her.

"You will pay," Orn rasped.

"Sorry," Ralan said as he slipped up beside her. "The future says no on that one."

Cora tossed Ralan an annoyed look, but she couldn't stay too aggravated with him. He'd done an admirable job staying out of it so far. "He's a seer, so he'd know," she said.

Orn tried to clench his hands and cried out in pain. "Seer or no—"

"Go back to Galare," Cora bit out. "I won't try to interfere so long as you leave my parents alone. Or would you like me to announce to your kingdom how you came by the burns you bear? Not even our king is allowed to kidnap and threaten."

Ralan nudged her shoulder with his. "That would not be the better choice for him, love. Let's do it."

Cora stifled a laugh. She knew very well that Ralan didn't want to go to Galare with Kien still on the loose. But Orn must have believed his words. Skin going pale, the king shoved himself to his feet. He wavered for a moment before stumbling toward the shimmering portal.

Orn scowled over his shoulder. "Pray you do not cross paths with me again."

Then he was gone.

Cora stared at the soft blue glow, her mouth going slack in disbelief. Half expecting Orn to return, she waited. But the portal's light winked out when the gateway cut off from the other end. The chirping of early morning birds filled the silence as she blinked at the dark indentation in the side of the hill.

How could it be finished, just like that? Her knees weakened as relief washed through her. Freedom. She struggled to grasp the word. Claim it. The thought of living without looking over her shoulder was almost beyond belief.

It had taken her too long to realize that Orn's cruelty was a mask for his cowardice. He did everything he could to solidify his power except for the one thing that would really work—lead with compassion and strength. If his allies had deserted him and his marriage hadn't worked out in his favor, then his reign would soon be at an end.

And if he came for her again, she knew without a doubt that she could defeat him.

Now it was time to take out Kien.

As soon as the kitchen door clicked shut behind Cora, Ralan tugged her close. He wrapped his arms around her waist, settled her body against his, and buried his face in her hair. He'd stood aside while she faced her worst enemy. He'd waited patiently while she'd sent a warning to her parents through the portal. Now he needed to hold her.

Cora pulled back slightly, slipping her arms around his neck and staring into his eyes. "Are you okay?"

"You would have to pick the riskiest strand," Ralan grumbled.

She chuckled. "Yeah, I'm such a risk taker."

Visions of strands not taken flitted through his mind. The danger she'd been in…

Ralan's control snapped, and he took her mouth with his. All of his fear and frustration poured out as he plundered her lips, his tongue diving deep until her taste was branded with his. Blended, as he hoped they'd always be.

Her fingers threaded through his hair and gripped tight as she moaned. A new flame leaped between them, but this one was of passion. Ralan basked in her fire as it sang through his soul. He let it consume him.

When he gripped her thighs and lifted, she wrapped her legs around his waist. Mindless, Ralan backed her toward the wall. Her ragged breathing filled his ears as he ran his mouth down her neck.

"Don't s'pose you can magic away clothes?" Cora gasped.

A chuckle rasped from his lips. "Not a power of mine."

"Damn," she gasped as he closed his mouth around her nipple despite the fabric in the way.

Her hands went to the hem of his shirt, and he balanced her weight against the wall so she could tug it free. "Bedroom?"

She pulled off her own shirt, and her gaze burned into his as she unhooked her bra and tossed it. "Why bother?"

What little brain power he had left evaporated as his body hardened further. Ralan dropped her legs only long enough for them to shuck their pants. Then he pressed her back against the wall and entered her in one stroke. His forehead lowered to hers and their harsh breaths blended as joy flowed between them.

Then they let the fire rage.

28

"At least I got some sleep this time," Kai said as they stood before the portal to the Veil.

Ralan only laughed, but Cora nudged him with her elbow and gave Kai an apologetic smile. "It's my fault you had to guide us across so many times. Sorry."

Kai shrugged. "I'm happy to see you looking so renewed. Galaren energy must be powerful stuff."

Heat rushed into her cheeks, and Ralan let out a snort. "Yeah."

"Ah." Kai rubbed his hand across the back of his neck and grinned. "Let's get going."

Cora and Ralan followed Kai into the portal, and the mists of the Veil wrapped around them. But not for long. Her stomach lurched as Kai pulled them through with a soft pop of energy. Her head spun, and when they emerged into the light, she stumbled against Ralan. He wrapped his arm around her waist to brace her.

Ralan frowned down at her as she blinked his face into focus. "What's wrong?"

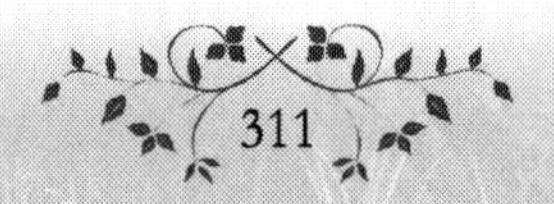

"That was…sudden."

Kai leaned over, his brow creasing as he studied her. "I didn't go any faster than last time."

As the world finished steadying around her, Cora brushed off their concern. She'd been so tired when Kai had guided her back to Earth that she probably hadn't noticed the jolting shift in energy. "I'm just not used to crossing like that. The portal to Galare is practically instant since it doesn't pass through the Veil the same way."

"I should take you to Lial."

"The healer?" Cora chuckled and stepped out of his hold. "I'm fine. Let's go."

They stared at her until she made a sharp gesture and spun away, heading for the trail they'd taken earlier. The path was dirt, not paved, but it was well-defined. Cora felt confident that she could make it to the estate. Probably.

It only took a moment for their footsteps to ring behind her.

"Turn right up ahead," Ralan said as his hand slipped around hers.

The soft sounds of the forest sighed around them, and Cora let the peace of it soak in as they walked. Now that she wasn't weak and hurt, she found herself studying the forest in fascination. Though huge, the trees here weren't like the redwoods of Earth. These were deciduous. If the trees around Chattanooga grew to several times their size, then they might be close. She noticed a leaf skittering across the trail. A totally different shape than any leaf she'd seen before.

Would she return to Earth once the battle with Kien was over, or would they find a way to save Ralan? It would be a major step to

relocate to Moranaia to be with him. Then again, she was used to moving. She'd been considering selling the business to Maddy and Jase in a year or two anyway. This world could be her next new start.

Except here, she could be herself.

Cora had left her options open on Earth. Before they'd called for Kai, she had dropped off the single outfit she'd managed to design for Vek and left Maddy instructions for completing her business with the prince. Maddy would be able to handle the money exchange and other clothes. Cora had also left a letter asking her friends to consider taking over the shop if she decided not to return. Either way, it would be okay.

"You're quiet," Ralan said.

She glanced at his curious face. "Just thinking about the future. I hope Maddy and Jase decide to take over The Magic Touch if things work out here."

"I called my lawyer and had her transfer my clothing line to my assistant," he said quietly. "If I don't return within a month, my other business interests will be closed out and left in trust for Eri."

"Oh."

Cora didn't know what to say to that, not with Kai so near. How much had Ralan told the others about his visions of the future? *"Who else knows?"* she sent.

"Only you, though Lyr suspects. And possibly Eri." His solemn gaze met hers. *"Lyr and Meli have agreed to raise Eri, but with us being bonded, there is much to consider."*

Her mouth fell open, and her grip on his hand tightened. *"I…"*

A sad smile crossed his lips. *"You haven't met her yet, and you aren't certain you want to stay. I know."*

"And I'm not part of your culture." Cora's shoulders slumped. *"Dammit, this is too much. Why in the Divine we've been brought together like this only to—"*

"Are you two okay?" Kai asked, peering over his shoulder at them.

Cora forced a smile. "Sure. Except for Ralan's crazy brother on the loose. You know, normal."

Although Kai chuckled, he studied her with a shrewd expression that said he wasn't fooled. Fortunately, they stepped onto a paved path, and her attention was captured by the garden they entered. She shoved her worry aside and let her wonder for the carefully arranged flowers show on her face. Better to contemplate how the elves had managed to make a garden look like an elaborate section of forest than to think of the future.

Ralan tugged her to a stop next to a stone tower tucked between two huge trees. Kai gave a quick goodbye and darted for the main estate, clearly eager to get more rest. As Ralan led her through the door and up a staircase that curled around the side, Cora's heart began to pound. She wiped her sweaty hand against her pants and followed him up.

His daughter was up there. His world.

"Nervous?" Ralan asked over his shoulder.

Cora grimaced. "More than a little."

"I sent a call ahead to make sure she was awake." His expression softened into a blend of love and exasperation. "She knew we were coming, of course. She's excited."

Somehow, that didn't make it better.

Cora's stomach had climbed into her throat by the time Ralan pushed open the door to his rooms. She glanced around the cluttered

sitting area, and she couldn't help but smile at the group of dolls strewn across the center of the floor. A hint of red colored Ralan's face as he bent to pick up a discarded dress.

"I see she's had fun beyond ordering Kai around," Ralan said.

A squeal rent the air, and a miniature female Ralan launched herself across the room from a nearby door. Cora shoved her hands in her pockets as the dark-haired child jumped into her father's arms. As he hugged Eri close, Cora's mouth went dry.

After a moment, Ralan lowered the child to her feet. Eri tilted her head, her golden eyes fastened on Cora. Then the little girl raced forward. Cora let out a soft *oomph* as Eri crashed into her, wrapping her arms around her waist and squeezing tight.

"You're finally here," Eri said. "I can't believe it!"

Cora blinked down at the child. "I…"

"Yeah, I know, you can't see the future so you don't know me," Eri said in a rush. "Don't worry. You're a great mom. We'll be friends."

The last week had been beyond crazy. Cora had found a bonded, searched for her friend, faced a madman in a cave, healed Inona, and defeated Orn. But out of everything, it was Eri who left her speechless.

"Eri," Ralan began, exasperation creeping into his voice. "You're going to scare her away. Behave."

"But the futures—"

"The only future you should concern yourself with right now is the one where you clean up this mess."

When Eri scrunched up her nose, Cora found herself laughing. It was such a *dad* kind of line. She tried to stifle her humor as Ralan

frowned at her, but the *stop being a bad influence* glare made her laugh harder. She hadn't had a chance to see this side of him before.

And it was adorable.

Ralan sidled up beside her as Eri began to grab her dolls from the floor. He leaned close. "You're not going to gang up on me, are you?"

Cora bumped her shoulder against his. "Only when you deserve it."

"That doesn't sound promising," he said with a chuckle.

For that one moment, everything was perfect. Lightness filled Cora, a happy, buoyant feeling that made her itch for canvas and paint so she could capture it forever. Despite the inevitable difficulties, they could make a good family. A solid family. For those few precious minutes, she shoved aside all else and let that reality be.

Then Eri paused on her way across the room, dolls bundled in her arms, and looked over her shoulder. "Inona will wake up soon. You should leave now to see her."

The words were delivered so naturally that it took Cora a second to recognize the power behind them. She stared after the child dancing from the room with her toys. Inona *will* wake up soon, Eri had said. Not *might* or *could*. Cora shook her head. Ralan might be bossy and imperious, but his daughter was frighteningly casual.

She glanced over to see Ralan rubbing his hand across his face. "I've lost count of how many times I've told her not to do that."

"Sounds like you need a more effective punishment."

Ralan sighed. "It hasn't been that long since her gift manifested. Let's just say it's a work in progress."

"I bet," Cora said. Then she shrugged and started for the door. "I really do want to see how Inona is doing, though. No use wasting the advice."

"This had better be clean when we get back," Ralan called out as he followed.

Eri's muffled voice sounded from the other room. "Okay!"

As soon as they made it to the bottom of the tower, Ralan took Cora's hand and guided her along one of the meandering trails. To their left, the main estate took shape, and she gaped in appreciation. The tan stone structure curved around the trunks of trees, and windows glinted in the mid-morning sunshine. She narrowed her eyes to try to make out the carvings on the walls, but the trail didn't get quite close enough. She'd have to check it out later.

Finally, they reached the healer's tower. The door was closed this time, so they paused for Ralan to give a sharp knock. Lial himself jerked the door open a crack and stuck his head out to glare. Cora tensed, prepared to leave, but Ralan gave no sign of budging.

"My patient is resting," the healer snapped. "You should have sent a call ahead."

Her bonded's calm expression didn't change. "Inona is about to wake. Cora wants to see how she's doing."

"Cora?" Lial's eyes widened as he noticed her presence. "Arlyn said you'd gone."

"I came back," Cora said softly.

The healer peered at her until she wondered if he'd slam the door on them without another word. But he surprised her by opening the wooden slab wide and gesturing for them to enter. "Stay quiet. Delbin is enough of a bother."

The former exile sat in a chair beside Inona's bed. His foot tapped incessantly, shaking his whole leg, and he dragged his hand through his hair as he stared at Inona's motionless form. Delbin gave an absent wave as they entered, but not even Ralan, his teacher, merited much attention. She couldn't say she blamed him.

Lial stopped Cora with a hand against her shoulder. "You should come upstairs so I can check you for any lingering problems."

Ralan frowned at the healer. "Her energy was restored."

"Which is the optimal time to find out if she had damage from the energy drain," Lial said, his tone implacable.

"There's a chair right—"

"Good gods, Ralan," Lial muttered, so low she almost had to strain to hear. "I'm not going to assault your bonded in my chambers. She's far from the first I've treated up there when the bed was occupied. I would rather Inona wake naturally and not because of our talking."

Scowling, Cora shoved at Ralan's shoulder. *"What's your problem?"*

"I don't want to be apart from you," he answered. *"And my cousin can be difficult."*

His words did nothing to soften her annoyance. *"Well, chill out. If you're going to be so protective that I can't see a healer without you, this isn't going to work."*

"It's not just any healer. It's Lial." Ralan's lips turned down. *"I'd trust him with my life, but that doesn't mean I want him telling you stories of my youth. It's…embarrassing."*

A smile broke across her face, and she patted his cheek. *"Deal with it."*

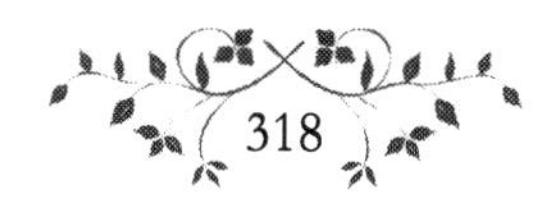

Cora nodded at Lial and followed him to the circular staircase near the back. She gave Ralan a wave as she climbed up and almost laughed at his worried scowl. What was he so afraid of her hearing? When she had more time, she would have to find out. Those stories were probably awesome.

They entered a sparsely furnished but cozy room. A large bed settled against the left wall, a wardrobe beside it. Beneath the window on the right, two overstuffed chairs had been placed beside a table, and bookcases spanned another wall. Though mostly tidy, the room was comfortably lived-in. She smiled to see the rumpled covers on the bed and the book left opened on the side table.

Lial motioned toward one of the chairs and waited patiently as she sank into it. Then he knelt beside her. "My scan shouldn't take long. If you are ready."

She took a deep breath, searching his face for any sign of ill-intent. Despite her annoyance at Ralan's bossiness, she was nervous. She didn't know this man, though he'd already tried to heal her before. She'd been unconscious then. Would it hurt or be uncomfortable when Lial used his magic?

"Should I be bracing myself?"

Lial's brows drew together, and he shoved a long, auburn hair from his eyes with a sharp flick. "For what?"

"Healing isn't painful at home," Cora explained. "But I have no idea how things work here."

"I see." His harsh expression eased, and she caught a hint of humor beneath his gruffness. "And my cousin's reaction probably didn't help. When my magic sweeps through, it should give a peaceful feeling. I give my word that it doesn't hurt."

Cora sucked in another breath and then nodded. "Fine. I'm ready."

Though his lips took on a wry slant, Lial stretched his hand out, and blue flared to life. She closed her eyes and tried to relax as his hand drew near. But as soon as the soft light settled into her body, her muscles loosened with relief. Her breathing slowed, and her thoughts began to drift aimlessly.

When his power faded and the world returned to sharp focus, Cora had to bite her tongue against requesting another scan. *Peaceful* was definitely an understatement. She blinked her eyes open to see Lial staring at her, and her skin heated in a flush.

"Do people injure themselves so you'll use your magic on them?"

He surprised her by letting out a soft laugh. "My personality works well enough as a deterrent. In any case, not all react as strongly as you did."

She thought back to his surliness during their first meeting. Definitely enough to scare off repeat offenders. Cora studied his face, wondering how much of his attitude was self-defense. Or show. Maybe if she stuck around long enough, she'd figure him out.

"Did you find anything wrong?" she asked.

Lial's expression turned inscrutable. "Not exactly."

Cora stiffened at that, undoing the relaxation his magic had brought. "What do you mean?"

"I thought I caught a hint earlier, but I was rushed. I was quite annoyed to find that you'd left before I could speak with you." He paused, and her heart gave a harsh thump. "Truthfully, I could have done this below. But I wanted to speak with you privately if my suspicions were correct."

Cora clenched her hands against the urge to shake him. "Just tell me what's wrong."

"You're fine. Perfectly healthy." Her relief was short-lived as he pinned her with a pointed look. "Both of you. You're pregnant."

What? Cora stared at him, uncomprehending, as she struggled to make sense of his words. Her fingernails dug into her palms, and she shook her head. "Not possible. We were only together…two or three days ago?" She tried to count back, but her muddled brain wouldn't cooperate. "That's too soon to tell."

"Not for me," Lial said. Annoyance and compassion warred in his gaze as he knelt beside her. "I wouldn't lie about this, Cora. I realize we are strangers, but I take my calling as a healer very seriously."

"I didn't think you would…" She squeezed her eyes closed. "My energy is different. Maybe you're mistaken?"

Exasperation rang in his tone when he spoke. "I trained for hundreds of years honing my gift and have worked as a healer for hundreds more. I have plenty of experience with pregnancies, even with women of mixed blood. I am *not* mistaken."

Cora forced her fingers to uncurl before she bruised her palm. Her heart raced at a rapid pace, and she struggled keep her panic from reaching Ralan across their bond. He couldn't know. Great Divine. He was heading to likely death, a fate all but promised by his goddess. What would it do to him to find out this news? If there was even the slightest chance of his survival, he couldn't be distracted. This was beyond a distraction.

"It is uncommon here, where children are treasured," Lial began, "But there are things that can be done at this early stage if you do not—"

"No," Cora said, her eyes snapping open. Her hands shifted to her stomach as a fierce protectiveness swept through her. "Don't even suggest such a thing."

Was it her imagination, or was that relief crossing his face? If so, he gave no comment, merely nodding and pushing to his feet. "I realize that things are tense between you and Ralan, and I don't need to know why. His *drec* of a brother is reason enough for trouble. I will leave it to you to deliver this news as you see fit. That's why I insisted on examining you up here."

"Thank you," Cora whispered.

Lial turned slightly, his face tilting toward the window as he gave her a moment to process. She glanced down to where her hands pressed against her belly. Galarens weren't particularly fertile, a problem shared by many of the fae races, so pregnancy hadn't been of much concern over the centuries. Her breath hissed out. It definitely should have been.

She sent her energy deep, searching for that hint of life. Her hands went clammy when she found it. The tiniest spark, so small she wouldn't have seen it if she hadn't been looking. What was she going to do? She didn't want to stay on Moranaia without Ralan, but this child was a royal heir. She wouldn't have much time to decide. As part Galaren, her unborn child would need to remain immersed in the energy where they'd be born. That first syncing was the strongest and most important bond.

Why, why, why did this happen now?

Ralan's mind brushed against hers, and his worry trickled through. Cora needed to connect, to offer some reassurance, but she had no idea how she was going to talk to him without sharing the news. She straightened in her seat and tried to shove her panic deep.

But before she could connect, a cry sounded from below. Lial spun, striding for the stairs, as Inona's scream echoed up to them. Cora jerked to her feet. Her own worries slipped from her thoughts as she followed him down.

29

Ralan pressed a finger to Inona's forehead, a focus for his power as he took control of her mind. Not fully, but enough to help ease her blind terror. Though her scream cut off, her fingers remained pressed to her throat. Her wide, panicked eyes flicked around the room, and her chest heaved with her frenzied breaths.

Footsteps clattered down the steps behind him and pounded across the floor. Lial knelt beside Inona, casting Ralan a grateful glance as he took control. The healer's magic lit the shadowed alcove, and he pressed his hand to Inona's forehead over Ralan's finger. As the tingle swept up Ralan's arm, he stepped back and let his cousin do his work.

Thankfully, Inona didn't scream again when Ralan released her mind. She slumped against Delbin, who had tried to comfort her when she woke. But his poor apprentice hadn't been able to break through her blind panic. After all, the last thing she remembered was having her throat sliced open.

Cora sidled up behind Ralan, and the soft weight of her hand settled on his shoulder. Still watching Inona's face for signs of panic,

his reached up and twined his fingers with Cora's. Then a hint of his bonded's fear slipped through, and he frowned over his shoulder as he took in her pinched expression.

Had something happened upstairs, or was she worried about Inona? He'd sensed an odd swirl of emotion from Cora, quickly stifled, just before Inona woke. He wanted to ask his bonded what had happened, but now she stared at the other woman. Perhaps Cora was concerned about the scout's reaction to her injury and Cora's part in the initial healing?

The healer's magic winked out, drawing Ralan's attention. He shoved aside his unease and peered at Inona. Thankfully, the blind terror had faded to mere fear, and there was awareness in Inona's eyes once more. Her fingers brushed back and forth across the raised scar on her neck.

"How am I alive?" she croaked.

Cora's fingers tightened against his. Ralan sent Lial a questioning look. "Her voice—"

"Is undamaged," Lial said, his expression tightening. "Though perhaps a touch strained by the screaming."

"I'm sorry," Inona whispered.

Delbin tucked her against his chest and glared at the room in general. "You have no reason to apologize."

"My timing was poor." Inona slumped against Delbin. "I thought I could escape his grip, but I was wrong. I shouldn't have been that close to him in the first place."

"Gods, Inona." Delbin's arm tightened around her waist. "The whole thing was a clusterfuck. You aren't any more to blame than the rest of us. And out of all of us, you're the one who almost died."

Inona's gaze lifted to Cora, and a slight smile lifted her lips. "Thank you for saving me."

"But I…" Cora tugged her hand free and took a step forward. Ralan ached to hold her as her upset slithered through him, but he knew she would rather face this on her own. "I'm not much of a fire healer. You'll be scarred because of me."

Inona slid away from Delbin. As she shifted toward the edge of the bed, peered at Cora. "I do not care."

"But elves rarely—"

"I will do you the favor of not describing that moment after the knife sliced. Once you've faced death like that, a scar is nothing." Inona reached out a trembling hand and took hold of Cora's wrist. "And I'll tell any who ask all about the woman brave enough to sear my wound closed before I bled out on a cavern floor while chaos reigned around us."

The tension eased from Cora's shoulders, and her soft sigh filled the silence. Finally, she nodded. "I'm glad I was able to help. And thank you for trying to get to Maddy. You wouldn't have been caught by Kien otherwise."

Frowning, Inona glanced around the room. "Did you save her? What happened? Please tell me Kien is dead."

Ralan's hand settled on Cora's lower back as he stepped closer. "Maddy is safe on Earth, but Kien got away."

"*Miaran,*" Inona cursed. With a soft groan, she settled back against Delbin. "How long until we leave again to hunt him down?"

A dark scowl built on Delbin's face, but Lial spoke first. "*You* won't be."

Inona stiffened. "I am healed. I'll be ready after a little more rest."

"You lost a great deal of blood," Lial said. "And you'll be going to a mind healer."

"I can handle—"

"You cannot." Inona opened her mouth to argue, but Lial's glare cut her off. "You're trembling where you sit from the memories you're trying to repress. Until you can manage your panic, you will be no good in battle. I will not release you to resume your duties until I am certain you are fully healed."

Ralan did a quick scan of the strands and nodded at his cousin's assessment. "I'm sorry, Inona. I do not foresee you coming with us when we leave to fight Kien."

Her brow furrowed and her eyes flashed, but Inona's spirit was stronger than her body. She slumped into Delbin's side as weariness overtook her anger. "Fine," she relented. "Though I would love to have my revenge for what he did."

Ralan shoved his hand through his hair as his own exhaustion hit. "You and so many others."

Inona grimaced. "I suppose you're the first in line."

He thought back to the words his brother had spoken in the cavern. The way Kien had warped Kenaren was enough, but her torture and death…their child… Ralan swallowed hard and forced those memories away. They would do him no good now.

"Take your time healing, Inona," he merely said. "Kien will be defeated if it's the last thing I do."

And it probably would be.

Cora fell quiet as they returned to the guest tower. Though Ralan glanced her way more than once, her closed expression kept him from asking all the things he wanted to know. Was she still upset about Inona, or was something else wrong? The worry gnawed at his gut with jagged teeth, but he didn't want to pressure her.

Ralan took her hand as they strolled along the garden path. His insides gave another twist as her damp palm met his. It could be the heat causing her to sweat—or it could be nerves. He reached out to her along their bond, but her feelings were muffled behind a mental wall he wasn't certain he should, or could, penetrate.

Finally, he broke. "Did Lial give you bad news? Is something wrong?"

"No," she said. "He said I'm healthy. There's nothing wrong."

He narrowed his eyes at the oddly cheerful tone of her voice. "I sensed your distress, Cora. Before Inona woke."

"I was worried about her," Cora answered.

He frowned. Her voice sounded more normal, but she'd looked away. "You're hiding something from me."

"Ralan—"

"The wall you've tried to put between us says more than any words."

Cora pulled him to a stop beside a cheerful stand of flowers. "I don't want to burden you. Not now. There's too much at stake."

His jaw clenched with frustration. "You don't think it's a distraction to know you're keeping secrets? I *feel* your upset as my own, no matter how much you try to distance me from it."

"Fine," she snapped. "I'm worried about the future. How could I not be? In a few days, you could be…" Her throat worked. "I don't know if I want to bond to the energy here, and I need to decide

soon. But without you, a link to Moranaia will bring only pain, a reminder of your loss. There's Eri, who was attached to me before we ever met. And there's…there's so much to think about. It keeps circling in my head."

Ralan gathered her close. "I'm sorry I can't See for you. Perhaps if I ask Megelien, she will offer some reassurance."

Cora nuzzled her face against his neck. "Don't. I'd rather decide on my own."

"Okay," he answered.

He held her for a moment, just held her, as the wall she'd built crumbled. Her concern swirled through him, but at least now, it had a name. Ralan bent and placed a soft kiss on her temple. When she pulled back, he smiled and smoothed the worry line from her brow with a gentle finger.

"Let's go get some sleep," he said. "We'll need to prepare to head to the palace tomorrow or the day after."

Her lips pursed. "Prepare? That sounds somehow ominous."

"For one thing, I want to design a court dress for you." Ralan ran his gaze down her body. "As nice as you look in jeans and a T-shirt, I'm guessing you'll feel far more comfortable in our style of clothing when you meet my father."

"A custom Roland Morne?" A grin broke across her face. "To think all I had to do was bond with him to get one. I hope that hasn't been a requirement for other clients."

He found himself chuckling. "Absolutely not."

"I guess that's acceptable, then."

As they made their way through the garden, holding hands, Ralan tried to stifle the sense of worry that wouldn't depart. Some

of it was hers, now that she'd stopped trying to hide her turmoil, but there was something else. Some niggling sense that refused to grow clearer in his mind.

Something was still wrong—and he was going to figure out what.

Though Cora's limbs had grown heavy with exhaustion as she curled around Ralan, she couldn't settle into sleep the way he had. She'd lied to him. Oh, not directly. She *was* worried about the future, and she *did* need to decide if she wanted to bond to Moranaia's energy. But she couldn't lie to herself about the biggest part of her concerns.

One tiny little life.

What's your favorite thing in the world? she'd once asked him.

His answer? *Being a father.*

She buried her face in his shirt as guilt swamped her. Ralan would be beyond elated to learn of their child—under normal circumstances. But what would he do if he found out in the midst of this crisis? He was barely resigned to leaving Eri. The thought of leaving two children might be too much.

His own goddess had guided him down a path of death to stop Kien. Would he obey Megelien if she told him?

Cora bit back a groan at the temptation of that thought. Maybe she should tell him. Then he wouldn't sacrifice himself to this cause. But what would that do? It might change the future in some dire way she didn't understand. Too bad she couldn't talk to this goddess herself.

Could she?

Slowly, Cora untangled herself from Ralan's sleeping form. She kept her gaze on him as she eased out of the bed and headed toward the door. Eri had been playing in the main room when they'd entered, and the girl might be there still. Perhaps she'd have a way for Cora to speak with the goddess Megelien.

Sure enough, Eri had settled on a low couch with a couple of her dolls. She smiled as soon as Cora closed the door behind her. "Hello!"

Cora hesitated, unsure of the wisdom of this course of action. Eri was a seer, but Cora did not want to grill a child on the future. No matter her fear, Cora would not stoop so low as that. But a seer would know how to contact her goddess, right?

"Sit down," Eri said cheerfully. "I'll tell you what you need to know so you can get some sleep. You need rest."

Cora nibbled her lower lip as she approached the couch. Did Eri know about the pregnancy, or had that statement been an innocent one? Even though Cora had restored her energy at the portal to Galare, she hadn't had any true sleep in quite a while. And the new life within was already pulling on her, physically and magically. She had no doubt she looked exhausted.

With a sigh, she settled on the couch next to Eri. The girl's sweet face had gone bright with happiness, but there was a knowing glint in her golden eyes. Good grief, she was so much like Ralan. Not just the similar cast to their features, either. It was the unerring confidence that shone from them like a light.

"I'd like to learn how to speak with your goddess," Cora said, careful to keep her voice low.

"That's not what you need." Eri set her dolls carefully between them and leaned closer. "My *onaial* thinks he has all the answers, too, but he doesn't. And I have way too many."

Sadness pinched Eri's eyes. She knew, Cora realized. She knew all of it. Unthinking, Cora reached out to give the child's hand a squeeze. "If there's a way…"

"I know." Eri's shoulders slumped. "And there's not a lot I can say about it. You're doing the right thing, even though it bothers you. When the time is right to tell him about my sister, you'll recognize it."

"Sister?" Cora lowered a shaking hand to her stomach as she stared at Eri's solemn face. "You really do See too much."

The girl picked at the smooth fabric of her dress. "Yeah. I guess this is the kind of stuff seers say a lot, but you really will know the right time. It'll drive him crazy wondering, but it'll be okay."

"I did *not* want to ask you about the future," Cora said. "You don't have to tell me these things."

Mischief replaced the sad gleam in Eri's eyes. "Of course I do."

Cora sighed. "Right."

"While you sleep, can I go play with Iren?" Eri jumped to her feet, dancing around in excitement. Once again, she was only a child. "I promise we won't leave the garden. There are guards up in the trees to make sure we're safe."

"Oh." Cora rubbed her hand across the leg of her pants as she considered the question. She was technically Eri's stepmother, but it still seemed strange. Would Ralan be upset if she gave his daughter permission to leave? "I don't know."

"He won't be mad," Eri said.

Cora stifled a smile at the girl's words. The blind confidence of a child or the words of a seer? It didn't matter either way, though, did it? The gardens should be safe enough, and maybe it would be good practice for her new role.

"Okay, go ahead." Cora tried to think of what Ralan might say. "And no using your Sight carelessly."

"That's easy." Eri's smirk was all Ralan. "I'm never careless."

Cora stared after the little girl as she darted out the door. Great Divine. She'd joked about adolescence being difficult for everyone, but Ralan's fear now settled into her own heart. Eri was only six. How in the world would they handle her when she got older?

Then a new thought chilled her blood. What if the child she carried also shared his gift? Cora straightened, resolve strengthening her muscles. She'd better find a way for Ralan to live because there was no way she could handle two child-seers on her own. As she stood, she sent up a silent prayer to the goddess she didn't know how to contact.

Please.

30

Ralan tapped his finger against his lips as he scrutinized Cora once more. He'd borrowed one of the seamstress's assistants, an affable man who chatted about his wife as he used a cutting spell to trim away a stray piece of fabric, and they'd started work on the dress several hours before. Now, the first part was almost done.

Layers of thin, teal fabric danced down her body, flowing like water as she shifted impatiently on her feet. Like many summer dresses on Moranaia, the fabric itself was thin enough to see through but layered and embroidered until the dress was opaque. He grinned as Cora glanced down, her lower lip caught between her teeth. She'd already complained twice about feeling naked.

If only.

He shifted back to the overrobe draped across a chair before he went hard. Again. He typically used dress forms to design, not real people, and he sure as hell hadn't created a dress on his own bonded before. This was an entirely different experience. If they

were alone, well… His brain wouldn't have been able to formulate a single design. She wouldn't have been too happy to arrive at the palace naked.

Eri skipped into the room, further eradicating his arousal. Thank goodness. They had to leave in the morning, and Cora really did need something to wear. He would commission more for her when they arrived at the palace. From someone hopefully not so easily distracted.

"That's pretty," Eri said.

Ralan peered at the heavily embroidered overrobe and nodded. "I was lucky that I could find something that could be adapted on such short notice."

The robes, floor-length, sleeveless vests worn open over a dress or tunic and pants, were typically the most elaborate part of Moranaian formal wear. But they were also expensive and time-consuming to create, many kept as heirlooms and passed down over generations. Fortunately, the seamstress had one on hand from a customer who hadn't liked the design. It needed few alterations.

He lifted the overrobe, scanning the whirls of bronze, copper, and coral falling like abstract flowers down the back. He'd designed the teal dress to match. Now to see if his vision had been a good one. He smiled at Cora as he carried it over, revealing the design to her with a flourish.

"Wow," she said. "I know you didn't have time for that piece. Surely."

His laughter rumbled around them. "No, not even I am that talented. Let's see how it fits."

Cora held out one arm and then the other as he settled the overrobe into place. Ralan tilted his head, studying the fit. He pursed his lips and glanced over at Farac, his assistant. "Can you take in the shoulders without ruining the embroidery?"

Farac nodded. "Certainly."

Ralan watched as the assistant leaned forward to alter the garment with a touch of his magic. That was a talent Ralan didn't have—he'd created his designs the same way humans did, with needle, thread, and scissors. Without the help of Farac's magic, he never would've had something ready for Cora so quickly.

"Those colors look great together," Eri said.

Ralan smiled as Farac stepped back and the full outfit was finally revealed. As he'd hoped, the overrobe looked like fall flowers dancing over the clear mountain lake near the palace. He'd played for hours near that lake as a boy, but Cora's beauty brought far from childish thoughts to mind.

"You're gorgeous," Ralan said softly.

A blush stole into her cheeks. "Thanks. I don't suppose you'll let me see?"

He removed the cloth from the mirror on the wall. Then he stepped away, satisfaction filling him at her gasp. Cora stared at her reflection with wide eyes, her fingers sliding carefully over the soft teal fabric of her dress.

"I thought for sure this would be more revealing," she admitted.

"The design is handy for our summer heat." His tension eased at the awe in her reflection. "You like it?"

A quick grin crossed her lips. "I guess it was worth bonding with you to get one of your designs."

Farac let out a sound somewhere between a laugh and a cough. Chuckling, Ralan crossed to her side and lifted her hand. "I got the better end of the deal. I got you."

As Cora's eyes softened, he heard Eri groan behind him. "If you're going to kiss, I'm out of here."

Ralan grinned over his shoulder. "Fathers do tend to kiss mothers."

"Yeah, yeah," Eri answered, but he could tell by the gleam in her eyes that her annoyed tone was mostly for show. "I'm going to go play in my room. Would you open the door for Lady Lynia so Lial has less time to fuss at her?"

His humor fled instantly. "Eri, you are not supposed to—"

"Her back is hurting," his daughter said with an unrepentant shrug. "You know how Lial is when he fusses."

She darted into her bedroom before he could chide her further. Dammit. Ralan rubbed his hand across the back of his neck. It didn't matter how many times he told her not to—Eri refused to let even him guide how she used her talents. A great quality. When she was older.

Cora caught his eye when he turned back to her. "Well. Are you going to do it?"

With a wry shake of his head, Ralan strode across the room and pulled the door open. Almost at once, Lial's voice echoed up the stairs. "You could have called for Ralan to meet you in the library."

"Feel fortunate that I allowed you to carry my book," Lynia answered, annoyance echoing in her tone. "Otherwise, I would hit you with it."

Stifling a laugh, Ralan eased away from the door. He caught Farac's gaze. "I appreciate your help today. I would not have been successful without it."

"It was my pleasure," Farac answered, catching the hint at once. "If you are satisfied, I will head home."

Ralan nodded. "Certainly. May you have a pleasant evening."

And Farac would, Ralan knew. But he wasn't going to tell the assistant that. Confidence in a future outcome was a sure way to ruin said outcome. Instead, he watched as Farac crossed paths with Lynia and Lial at the top of the stairs before heading down.

Ralan focused on the newcomers.

"Welcome," he said. "Please come in."

The pair made it to the landing, and Ralan held out a hand a moment before Lynia stumbled, providing something for her to grab. She cast him a shocked glance after she righted herself, but she didn't comment. Instead, she continued through the door and into the room, pausing a few steps in at the sight of Cora.

"Forgive my interruption," Lynia said. "I didn't know you had a visitor."

He lifted his brows. "No one has told you of recent events?"

"I'm afraid not." Lynia's eyes narrowed on Lial. "Some are too busy lecturing me like a child to otherwise be of use."

The healer's jaw set as he scowled at the room in general. "You were supposed to come by so I could check your back."

"Later," she said sharply. Then her face softened into a smile as she turned her attention to Cora. "We are being unforgivably rude. Perhaps Ralan could introduce me to his guest."

Ralan turned to his bemused bonded. "Cora, allow me to present Callian Myernere i Lynia Dianore nai Braelyn. You've already met her companion, Callian iy'dianore sebarah i Lial Caran nai Braelyn."

At her nod, he continued. "Lynia and Lial, this is Moranai Elateror i Cora Moreln se Ralantayan nai Moranaia."

Cora startled a bit at her formal title, decoding the meaning at the same time as the others, but Lynia was too busy giving Lial a quick glare to notice. "Elateror? I hadn't heard that you found your soulbonded, Ralan. Congratulations," Lynia said once she'd spun away from the healer. "It is a pleasure to meet you, Princess Cora."

"Likewise, Lady Lynia. And it's just Cora, please," his bonded answered. Ralan peered at her, concerned by her sudden pallor, but her voice was calm as she spoke. "If you will excuse me, I believe I will go change from my formal clothing. I have a feeling you have important business to discuss."

"You should be included, too," Ralan said with a frown.

Cora paused to pat his cheek on her way to their bedroom. "I will be. I just want to get off my feet without wrinkling my formal clothes."

He stared after her until the door closed behind her. Then he advanced on his cousin. "What's wrong with her? She said you told her she's healthy, but she has not been the same since speaking with you."

Lial's nostrils flared, his grip tightening on the large tome he held. "I will not share information on my patients to anyone except the lord or lady who outranks them, and then only as it pertains to the safety of the realm. But you know I would not have released her from my care if she were unwell."

"I am a prince. You may tell me—"

"And she is your equal." Lial tilted his head, his lips twisting. "I suppose I could share any information I might have with the king. If you'd like to get him involved?"

Ralan's teeth ground together. Gods, he wanted to smash his fist into his cousin's face. "So there *is* something."

"Enough." The anger in Lynia's voice silenced both men. "My back hurts, and I didn't come all this way to stand here while you two argue. Ralan, I can assure you firsthand that Lial will not leave someone alone if he believes they need his aid."

His cousin's attention shifted immediately to Lynia. "Your back? I told you not to do this."

"Shut up, Lial." Her lips thinned into a white line, and she held up a hand when the healer sidled nearer. "If I might sit?"

Ralan gestured for them to take the couch and pulled over two more chairs for himself and Cora. Lynia settled to the left, her posture stiffening despite the pain it must have caused. When Lial tried to scoot closer, hand outstretched, she gave him fierce glare. One that gave even the healer pause.

"Let me remove your pain," Lial murmured.

A flush rose in Lynia's cheeks. "Not now."

Comprehension hit as Ralan took in her tight expression. It wasn't that she was angry with his cousin. She was embarrassed. Why couldn't Lial see that? The man was an excellent healer, one of the best, but sometimes he had no clue about people. And this particular lady did not enjoy showing weakness.

The bedroom door clicked open, and Cora emerged, her face still pale. Although she smiled when she sat in the chair beside him, the motion didn't quite reach her eyes. Ralan's hands tightened on the armrests as he resisted the urge to question her. How could he mock Lial's lack of knowledge when he couldn't figure out what was wrong with his own soulbonded?

"Please hand me the book," Lynia said softly, though the scowl she gave Lial brooked no argument. "And if you try to tell me you'll hold it for me, you'll need to find a healer for yourself."

Ralan's lips twitched. There was no way in hell he was stepping into that argument. Lial passed the heavy tome over without a word. It was about time his cousin found someone who wouldn't take his shit. Who would've thought that person would be Lyr's mother?

The soft skitter of turning pages filled the room as Lynia flipped to the section she sought. A victorious gleam filled her eyes as she glanced up, her finger poking against a line of text. "It took a while, but I found it. Kien's downfall."

Heart pounding, Ralan leaned forward, elbows on knees. "What do you mean?"

"If he managed to latch himself into Earth's energy, he could cause a great deal of damage to that energy when he dies. Even if he dies on Moranaia." Lynia tapped the page beneath her hand. "Things didn't get that far the last time the energy poisoning spell was used, but there was a fair amount of theorizing on the matter. When you kill Kien, you'll have to cut off his magic instantly."

Beside him, Cora shifted in her seat. "Why? My people bond with a place's energy, but that place is unharmed upon our deaths."

"I imagine you don't send the full force of your power into a spell designed to kill," Lynia retorted. "He could use this connection as leverage to save himself. Tell me, is he allergic to iron?"

Ralan thought back to his childhood. Had his brother reacted to the metal? "I believe so. More than I am, if I recall correctly."

"Sensitive enough to have his energy drained by steel?"

"I can't be certain of that," Ralan answered. "But I could ask Teyark. He's older, so he might know."

"If he is…" Lynia paused, her shoulders stiff and her expression hard. "I want you to kill him with the sword they used on my Telien. I may not be a warrior, but I can do my best to see my love avenged."

Silence fell after the terse pain of her statement. The color leeched from Lial's face as he averted his gaze. Lynia's hands clenched together over the open book. She didn't seem to notice the hurt simmering around the healer, but Ralan did. He doubted his cousin begrudged Lynia her grief, but that didn't mean her words had been easy to hear.

"I'm not the greatest swordsman," Ralan finally said. "But I will do my best."

If he had to use a blade to defeat his brother, well… It was no wonder he was destined to die.

31

Chest heaving, Ralan jerked upright. He blinked his eyes clear of the vision that had haunted his dreams. Blood. A blond version of Kai slumped in the middle of a stone floor, red seeping in a pool beneath him. Ralan shoved his hair out of his face and struggled to get his breathing under control.

A soft sound from Cora drew his attention. She sat up, a disgruntled frown pinching her forehead. She'd been sleeping against his chest when he'd woken. Lost in the grip of the dream, he had barely noted her soft form sliding off of him.

"Sorry, love," he said, his voice rough with sleep. "Did I hurt you?"

She leaned her head against his shoulder. "No. What's wrong?"

"We have a slight change in plans." Ralan turned to press a kiss to her silky hair. "We have to get to the palace. Now."

Cora leaned back with a frown. "What?"

"Kien made himself a new strand," Ralan said. "I need to contact Lyr."

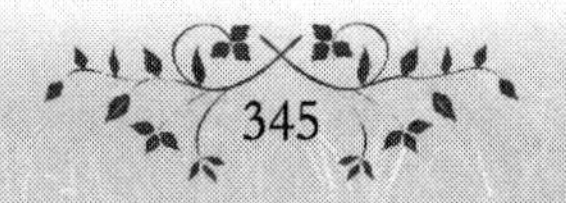

"I'll get dressed."

As Cora slid off the bed, Ralan sent his mind out. He found Lyr at once, but it took a moment for his friend to wake enough to make the connection. *"Ralan?"*

"Kai has a brother, doesn't he?"

"A... Yes. What?" Confusion and annoyance crackled along their mental link. *"It's two marks until dawn, and you want to know about Kai's brother Moren?"*

"I just had a vision of a blond male who looks like Kai lying in a puddle of blood in a large stone room. Like a Great Hall from a medieval castle." Ralan slipped out of bed, striding toward the dressing room as they spoke. *"Sound familiar?"*

"Moren is checking on one of the small holdings to the west," Lyr answered. *"He isn't at his estate, Oria."*

Ralan tugged on the tunic he'd left out for their morning departure. *"Something must have changed. This strand didn't fucking exist yesterday. If Kien hasn't found him yet, he's about to. He'll use the gate there to make it to the palace faster. Cora and I are preparing to go now."*

"I'll wake Kai and send guards through."

"Lyr." Ralan stilled, hands lowering to his sides. *"Now is the time for honesty. I've hinted as much but... I am unlikely to return this time. I don't know how Cora will feel about raising Eri on her own. We've barely been together, bond or no."*

"Miaran." Lyr's mental voice went gruff. *"As I have promised, Eri will be cared for. You have my word. If Cora wishes to stay, she will be welcome. But Ralan? Prove that particular vision wrong."*

"Believe me, I will try."

Once he'd disconnected with Lyr, Ralan finished getting dressed. Then he buckled on the sword Lynia had delivered just before bed. He hadn't asked why she had it, though he would have assumed that Lyr would keep the dangerous weapon well-secured. It didn't matter anyway. If Ralan could help her avenge her bonded, then he would.

He glanced up at a flicker of bronze and teal to find Cora standing before him in her formal clothing. "I wasn't sure what I should wear."

"That's as good as anything at this time of night." A corner of his mouth lifted. "Though you might want to brush your hair. I'm going to go say goodbye to Eri."

Her brows lowered, and her hands twisted together. "Okay."

A lump formed in Ralan's throat as he turned away. Cora knew as well as he did that he hadn't been talking about a temporary goodbye. By all the gods, how was he supposed to bid farewell to his only child, and in a few moments' time? It was intolerable.

Only one small reason that Kien deserved to die.

When Ralan pushed open Eri's door, he had to blink against the soft glow of mage light. His daughter sat cross-legged in the middle of her rumpled bed, clearly waiting for him. She tipped her head back as he approached. The gleam of her wet cheeks arrowed into his heart, searing like fire.

"*Onaial*," she whispered.

The bed dipped as he lowered himself to the side, careful to shift the sword out of the way. His own eyes grew damp as Eri launched herself into his lap, her small arms circling his neck. She buried her face against the hollow of his shoulder, and her tears soaked through the fabric of his tunic as she sobbed.

Ralan wrapped his arms around her back, squeezing her small form close. The berry scent of her black hair drifted up, and he closed his eyes to savor it. To take it into himself for all time. His life had been smoke and shadows before Eri had filled it with her light. He wanted to give her the world, but instead, he was giving her pain.

"I don't want you to go," Eri wailed.

His arms tightened. "Nor do I wish to leave. I love you. Always."

Her breath came in hiccups between her soft sobs. "I can't tell you what I See."

"I know what you See," he whispered.

"You *don't*." Eri pushed back against his arms until she could look into his eyes. "You've given up. I can't…"

The thudding of his heart startled through him. "Are you saying there's hope?"

Eyes wide with fear, Eri shook her head. "I don't know. I've never seen so many strands. I can't track them on my own. Lady Megelien says I can't say anything. *Onaial*, I don't know what to do. I don't *know*."

"Oh, Eri." Ralan gathered her close, rocking her gently as she cried against his shoulder. "Sometimes, even we aren't meant to know. It's better that way."

"This isn't better."

He ran his hand down her hair. "I know. But it's all we have."

"I love you more than anything." Her sniffles rang in his ear, and his aching throat convulsed around the words of reassurance he wished he could offer. "I want to live here with you, and Cora, and my sister, and maybe a brother. I don't want you to leave."

A sudden sense of urgency tugged through him, turning his stomach, but he made no move to release Eri. "No matter where my body may be, my spirit is with you. Always."

"I know." Her arms tightened for a moment before she pulled back. "You need to go."

Ralan stood, settling Eri against his hip. "I'm taking you to Lyr and Meli. I don't want you alone tonight."

"I'll be okay," she said.

Her soft, small voice twisted his insides. "No arguments, Eri. This is hard enough."

He forced his leaden feet to propel him to her door and out into the sitting room. Cora waited beneath the only glowing mage light, her beautiful face pinched with worry and pain. Her gaze landed on Eri's tearstained face and then darted away as she swallowed, her eyes glinting.

Ralan's throat burned with his own repressed tears. But he couldn't break down, not now. Maybe not ever. As he started down the tower stairs, Eri's words floated through his mind. *You've given up.* And she was right—he had. Megelien's words had cemented the vision of his death in his mind.

Could there be another way? Could the Goddess of Time Herself be wrong?

He sent a silent prayer Her way, but She remained silent. She'd told him that he'd have everything he needed to know after their last conversation, and it seemed She'd meant it. Was he missing something? With each step through the gardens, he searched the strands. They would reach the palace, that was clear. He'd confront his father and Teyark about the information they'd kept from him. Kien would arrive.

Then a blur.

Frustration clawed at him as he led Cora into the main part of the house. His bonded's eyes darted around the winding hallways, taking in the walls carved with various patterns or scenes. Dimly lit globes hung from sconces that resembled tree branches. Here and there, the walls curved around actual tree trunks. Too bad he couldn't find the answers he sought within the whorls of wood.

When they reached the main entrance, Lyr and Meli already waited. Ralan strode past the staircase curling around a broad trunk and past the double front doors. Ahead and to the left, his friends stood beside a carved stone arch, the focal point for the gate that allowed transportation between any linked portal. Beyond that, the huge trunk of Eradisel, one of the nine sacred trees, filled the space.

As Ralan halted beside Lyr, he gave brief consideration to consulting her. But Eradisel was the tree of Dorenal, Goddess of Portals and the Veil. She might offer comfort, but she was unlikely to know the future any better than he did.

Lyr noticed the sword at Ralan's waist and paled. "How did you get that?"

"Your mother brought it to me."

"She—" Lyr's mouth snapped closed, and his jaw clenched.

"Steel may be needed to defeat Kien," Ralan explained. "She wanted me to use the same blade that felled your father. Fitting, since his murder was part of Kien's plot."

Lyr gave a sharp nod. "Indeed."

"Have you received word about Kai's brother?"

"You were right about the attack. It had just occurred a few moments before my guards' arrival," Lyr answered. "Their healer is tending to him now, and he seems likely to recover."

"Good."

Ralan's hands tightened ever so slightly on Eri, and for a heartbeat, he allowed himself to hold her close. She burrowed her face against his shirt and sniffled. Then she pushed at him until he lowered her to her feet. She stared up at him with her bright eyes, so full of love and fear. He bent down and placed a kiss on her forehead.

With a soft cry, Eri spun away. She ran to Meli, tucking herself against the lady's side as tears ran down her face. "I love you," she whispered.

"I love you forever," he answered at once.

The spell linking Braelyn to the palace flared to life. As the light settled into an image of the portal room, Cora placed her arm on his. He kept his gaze on Eri with each step they took. His last sight before they crossed through the gate was his daughter's brave, tearstained face.

Cora's hand clenched around Ralan's arm as they emerged from the portal—directly into a room filled with warriors. She'd seen a few of them before they had stepped through, but in that breath of time, the number seemed to have doubled. Fortunately, the hands that had gone to sword hilts fell away as Ralan swept a glare around the room.

"A fine way to greet your prince and his new bonded," Ralan said.

"Forgive us, Elaiteriorn," the female directly across from them said as she tapped fist to chest and bowed. "Lord Lyrnis sent warning that your brother might arrive at any moment. We feared that you wouldn't step through alone."

Cora had never seen Ralan's profile so stony, but he nodded at the guard. "Leave us for a moment."

"My prince," the warrior began. "We've been ordered to stay by your side."

"I need a moment with my bonded." Ralan's expression chilled further. "Unless the spell barring my brother from this gate has been shattered, I should be safe enough. Obey my command or be reassigned."

The guard's mouth pinched, but she inclined her head and made a sharp gesture at the others. Bemused, Cora stared after them as they filed out the door and closed it behind them. Then she glanced up at Ralan.

"What is it?"

"I forgot something."

He reached up and pulled a chain from his neck. His pendant dangled between them as he held it up, and her breath caught as the light flickered against the symbols carved on its surface. She'd felt the medallion pressed against her flesh in the heat of passion, but she'd never had a chance to examine it.

With a small sad smile, Ralan lowered the chain over her neck. Cora looked down to the heavy silver disk as it settled between her breasts. She lifted it, still warm from his body, in the palm of her hand and stared down at the design engraved in the center. Small letters spelling his rank and name circled a stylized tree. A royal crest? Her thumb traced over the indentions, and she shivered.

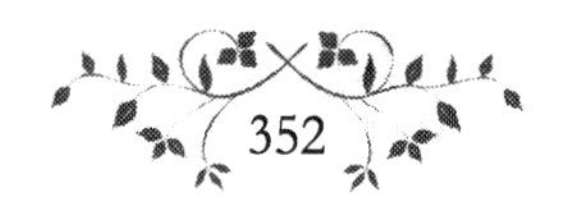

"You sent the guards out just to give me your necklace?"

His lips firmed. "Any who see us will know that you are mine."

Cora lifted a brow. "Yours?"

"As I am part of you." His expression softened. "I meant to give you the necklace sooner. Wearing it now will announce that we are soulbonded to any we may pass. It might save you some grief from overzealous warriors or spiteful courtiers."

She almost made a quip about jilted lovers but remembered his past beloved just in time. The last thing he needed was more pain. "Thank you. I will treasure it."

"I…" His throat worked as his voice trailed off. "I don't want to give up on surviving this. Not just for myself. The agony of a broken soulbond is said to be intense. I wouldn't have…"

Cora cupped her hand around his cheek. "I bonded us. Of all the pain you carry, don't let the bond be a source of regret."

"It never could be."

Swallowing back tears, Cora forced a tremulous smile. "Let's go see if we can find a way to change fate."

His fingers brushed her chin, tilting her head up for a soft kiss. Then he nodded and offered his arm again. "Let's do it."

32

Tension coiled through Ralan until he thought he'd either snap or turn to stone. He barely noted the handful of drowsy but well-dressed courtiers they passed on their way across the formal entry. Useless lot. No doubt they'd been dragged from their beds by their assistants as soon as the king had left his chambers. No matter what world he was on, there was always someone waiting to pounce on the latest drama. Thankfully, none dared approach. He no doubt would have snapped at any who'd tried.

Cora leaned closer. "I think you're the one who ended up underdressed."

Blinking in surprise, Ralan looked down, realizing that he'd forgotten to don his formal overrobe. He'd meant to fetch it after saying goodbye to Eri. Well, nothing for it now. At least the thin Heir's Crown weighted his brow.

"Maybe I'll start a new, simpler style," he said.

Despite everything, Cora chuckled. "Trendsetter."

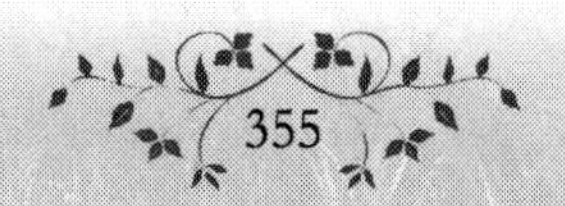

They mounted the small set of stairs at the far end of the entryway and passed through the huge double doors leading into the Great Hall. This room was blessedly empty and would remain so until the king sat in the throne on the far dais to receive morning petitions. Ralan scanned the area but saw only the green and blue striped pennants and elaborate tapestries that had graced these walls for thousands of years.

As he turned unerringly toward a door in the far-right corner, Ralan sensed not only his father's presence but also Teyark. Good. There were things he needed to say to his father and brother before Kien arrived. Key among them? Why they had neglected to tell him of Kenaren's torture and death. It was possible that Kien had lied, but Ralan had a sick feeling that he hadn't.

Their footsteps echoed hollowly through the huge room, an eerie sound in a place that was usually teeming with people. As they crossed the expanse, the sound increased, and he looked over his shoulder to see six of the *loreln*, the royal bodyguards, trailing behind them. He'd been accustomed to having them around before he'd left for Earth, but after so many centuries away, the sensation was a strange one. Too bad he couldn't send them away for more than a few moments in his father's domain the same way he could at Lyr's estate.

At least they wouldn't follow into the king's private study.

Ralan cast Cora a reassuring glance as he opened the door and gestured for her to precede him. But if she was concerned, her expression didn't show it. She might have lived on Earth for centuries, but in that moment, she was every inch the royal princess she'd been born to be. Were he to live, she would make a queen beyond compare.

The door closed behind them, and Ralan shifted to Cora's side. Two pairs of eyes widened on his bonded as her hand returned to his arm. Hadn't they expected him to bring her? Perhaps not. Teyark shoved to his feet, his chair scraping with the movement. But Alianar, his father, stared for a bit longer before standing from his seat behind his desk.

Then the king's gaze shifted to Ralan's other side, and a scowl pinched his face. "You didn't bring her."

Ralan's brows rose. "Eri? Of course I didn't."

"I thought we moved beyond this on your last visit," his father said. "I swore I would not ask her, or you, for knowledge of the future."

Ralan waved a hand. "Her absence has nothing to do with you. I would not bring her into Kien's grasp. Did you truly expect me to bring my child into certain danger?"

The king glanced at the medallion on Cora's neck before returning to Ralan's face. "You brought your soulbonded. One that none of us knew about. I would have offered congratulations sooner had you bothered to send word."

"We are newly bonded." His teeth ground together as he struggled to hold back his temper. "I was too busy trying to handle Kien to send you a personal message on the event. Perhaps if you had taken care of him sooner, that wouldn't have been a problem."

Teyark took a step forward. "Ralan—"

"I don't want to hear it." Just like that, his control snapped. "Not from you, Teyark. You greeted me happily upon my return, which I was glad of. But in all the time we spent together since, you never bothered to tell me that you found Kien torturing Kenaren after I'd

left. He cut my child from her womb. He murdered my beloved. And you didn't think you should tell me?"

Though his hands clenched, Teyark's face went pale. "I wanted to, but Father ordered my silence. It…seemed the correct action. You'd moved on."

"You thought my absence for three centuries was a sign of moving on?" Lost in his anger, Ralan didn't notice when Cora's hand dropped from his arm. He strode forward, shoving past Teyark to stand in front of his father's desk. "You could've told me, too. All of this is on you. Dammit, Kien tortured her. And you merely exiled him? He deserved death."

Alianar dropped heavily into his seat. "Do you think I do not know this? It is my weakness. *Miaran*, Ralan. He's my son. Could you order your own child's death so easily?"

Ralan's stomach lurched at the very thought. He spun away from his father as the truth of it hit him. No, he probably couldn't. Gods forbid that Eri ever go bad, for he couldn't imagine ordering her death. Ever. He shoved his hand through his hair. His father really had been dealt an impossible choice, even for a king.

His eyes lit on Cora, waiting still and wan in the center of the room. Ralan took a deep breath, for the first time realizing that some of the pain curling through him wasn't his own. The words he'd said to his family played through his mind, and he wanted to groan. Did she think he didn't care for her? His love for her had grown within him, taking root in his very soul, but he couldn't express it. Not until he'd put the past to rest. He needed to tell her that.

"Kien never should have escaped his exile," his father continued. "I still do not understand how he managed it. I swear that I would have killed him myself if I'd realized the trouble he would cause."

The king's words barely registered as Ralan stared at Cora. She swayed on her feet, and her face had taken on a greenish cast. He rushed forward, his hand going to her waist as she swayed again. Had he upset her so gravely? His heartbeat pounded in his ears as he led her to a vacant chair.

"Cora?" He knelt beside her, taking her hands in his and rubbing her knuckles. "Are you unwell? I knew Lial was hiding something."

She took a deep breath and tried to smile. A dismal failure. "I'm sorry. I'm fine, really."

"You're not." Ralan stared into her pained gaze. "I'm not holding a flame for Kenaren, my love. All I have left for her is hurt and regret."

Her sigh ruffled his hair. "I can feel that for myself. Please don't worry about me. I didn't eat much last night, and I'm tired from the battle with Kien. Speak with your father. I'll be okay."

He peered at her as she averted her eyes. Her body should have recovered after all the sleep they'd had. He couldn't fathom Lial releasing a patient who was ill, but it seemed he had. "I'll take you to the palace healer."

"I don't need a healer," she ground out. "There's more important stuff to worry about right now."

Frustration pooled in his gut. She clearly wasn't fine. He hadn't seen her so pale since the portal crossing had made her ill. But… Ralan stiffened as it all clicked into place. *I want to live here with you, and Cora, and my sister, and maybe a brother,* Eri had said. But not maybe a sister. Oh, Gods. His blood went cold. It was impossible, wasn't it? It was far too soon for her to be pregnant. Fate would not be so cruel.

"Cora—" A sharp knock sounded on the door, interrupting his words. "Send them away," he snapped.

"He's here," the king said softly.

Ralan turned a scowl on his father. "What?"

"Kien." Alianar stood, his expression going hard even as pain pinched his eyes. "I ordered the *loreln* to escort him to the Great Hall as soon as he arrived."

"What?" Teyark cried. "Why would you do such a thing?"

"It is time we deal with this." The king rounded his desk, striding for the door. "My son is gone. I will not hide from the monster he has become."

Ralan jerked to his feet. "You cannot."

Alianar spun, his hand on the doorknob. "The responsibility is mine."

"My Sight is cloudy, but through everything, one thing remains true. You must not confront Kien yourself." Ralan's mouth went dry. "Let me go first."

"You will not die for my failure."

Teyark rushed forward. "Let me go. I should have killed him when I found him with Kenaren. It is my failure, too."

"It must be me. It is foreseen," Ralan insisted. "Stay here and guard Cora."

At that, his bonded shoved herself to her feet, her narrow-eyed glare trained on his face. "If you think I'm going to stay behind, you're an idiot."

His chest squeezed tight. "There is too much danger. You're…"

"I know exactly what I am." As she tipped her chin up in defiance, she shrugged the heavy overrobe from her shoulders and let it fall. "Did you forget what I did to Orn? I am not helpless."

"For the gods' sake, Cora—"

"We do not have time for you to argue," his father said, turning the knob. "If the futures call for you to go, then do it now."

Ralan gave Cora a helpless, questioning look, but she only shook her head. If she was pregnant, she clearly wasn't going to admit it.

Fuck.

He'd guessed.

Cora fought against the urge to confirm what he so obviously suspected. But the words froze in her throat. Eri had told her that she would know the right time to tell him, and now wasn't it. Was it? Her heart seized as his father started opening the door. Ralan was about to go out there, straight into danger. Shouldn't he know first?

She opened her mouth to speak, but he'd already spun away with a sharp curse. There had to be a reason that Eri had told her to wait. A shiver trickled down Cora's spine as she strode after Ralan toward the door. If she'd guessed wrong, she would never forgive herself.

His brother, Teyark, stood silently as they neared. His mouth pinched into a thin grimace, and the eyes that met hers bore their own measure of pain. He looked a great deal like her bonded, despite the heavy muscles of a warrior, but there was a weight to his gaze that suggested he was much older.

Ralan paused, and his voice lowered when he spoke. "Is Kien susceptible to steel?"

"Yes," Teyark answered. "Why?"

"If I fall, kill him with steel or iron. It is vital."

As soon as Teyark nodded, Ralan strode past him and out the door.

Bile rose in Cora's throat as she followed him into the huge main room. But this time, it wasn't empty. In the center, Kien stood, ten warriors ringing him with swords drawn. More guards lined the walls, but the prince didn't appear concerned. A smirk tilted his lips as he watched them cross the expanse of floor.

The door snicked closed behind them, and Cora looked back to see Teyark and the king following. She fought a wave of dizziness as she returned her attention to the dark prince. Now was not the time to be sick. If there was any way she could save Ralan, she would do it. She would blast a smoldering hole through Kien herself, regardless of where his energy was bound.

Ralan's mind brushed hers. *"Talk to me."*

"Not the time," she whispered back.

"I'd say we're running rather short of that commodity."

"I'm following your daughter's advice." Cora sucked in a breath. *"Maybe you should, too."*

He fell silent at that. Did he know what she meant? Though she hadn't intended to eavesdrop, Cora had heard some of Eri's words to him when he'd said goodbye. *You've given up,* she'd cried. Well, if that distressed the child, there was a reason. No matter what Ralan believed, there was something to fight for.

When Ralan halted a few paces from the line of guards, Cora stepped up beside him. Her palm itched against the desire to place her hand over her belly, but she straightened her spine instead. Kien would not miss such a gesture, and she refused to give the bastard something else to use against them.

"Quite the welcome home," Kien said smoothly. "Only Mother is missing."

The king halted beside Cora. "She is out of your reach."

Kien lifted an eyebrow. "I suppose you neglected to tell her about your invitation to me? I'm surprised you knew I would be at Pereth's estate. I thought our friendship had gone unremarked."

"I hear you left your *friend* near death."

"Alas, he was not eager to renew our acquaintance." A dark glint entered Kien's eyes. "But his blood was of great benefit, so perhaps I will forgive the slight."

Cora buried her trembling hands in the folds of her dress to hide their shaking. The motion caught Kien's attention, but Ralan took a step forward, drawing his brother's gaze back. "This game will be finished today."

"What a useless, cliched line." Kien lifted a hand, and an orb of energy sprang to life in his palm. Dull gray swirled sickly around lines of white. "Do you see this? Attack me, and I'll cast this little spell straight into my connection with Earth's energy. Perhaps you should let me. After all, it might kill me. But there's no telling what it'll do to all the fae living there."

Resolve flowed along their bond as Ralan's hand landed on the hilt of his sword. "You're too weak to fight one of us?"

Kien laughed. "*You* want to challenge me to a swordfight? Not Teyark?"

"You've spent years trying to kill me," Ralan said. "So I'll give you one fair chance."

33

Deadly calm layered like ice over the worry and fear in Ralan's heart. He waited as his brother's eyes narrowed on his face. Everyone in the room, save possibly Cora, knew the offer was foolish. Although Ralan had been trained the same as his brothers, he'd never been more than adequate with a sword. His Sight was as much hindrance as help, the strands of possibilities difficult to examine in the heat of battle. Teyark was the warrior in the family.

"You're up to something," Kien said.

"Of course," Ralan answered. "As are you. Really, brother, what is your grand plan? Your spell might save you from being attacked by the *loreln* before your hand reaches your sword hilt, but you know well enough that we won't hand over the throne to save Earth."

"I see even your nobility has a limit." Kien's smile turned mocking. "And here I came to challenge Father quite honorably for the throne."

"Then—" the king began.

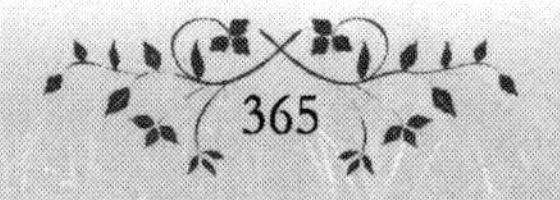

"You'd still have to face me and Teyark to ascend," Ralan said, smoothly interrupting his father before he could accept the challenge. "Your hatred for me is strongest. Defeat me first."

Kien's low laughter echoed through the room. "So eager to meet Kenaren? Your new bonded must be thrilled."

Ralan's heart pinched at the hurt those words must have caused Cora, but he refused to let the ache show. He kept his eyes trained on Kien. "I'm weary of you. I'd like to have done with you and move on with my life."

"Your confidence is admirable but, as always, misplaced." With a shrug, Kien wrapped his hand around the hilt of his sword. "Very well. I will accept your challenge first. Let the people of Moranaia see my benevolence."

Ralan snorted. His brother's idea of benevolence had always been perverse at best. "May all in witness acknowledge our rightful duel." He gestured toward the guards surrounding his brother. "Take your places at the perimeter to ensure that honor is met."

The *loreln* hesitated for a moment, clearly unhappy with this turn of events, before repositioning themselves. Ralan couldn't blame them. Of all the ways he'd envisioned confronting his brother, this farce of a duel hadn't been one of them. He reached for the strands, hoping he could confirm the rightness of his choice now that he was in the heat of the moment, but his Sight had gone so muddled that he couldn't even see the futures of those not affected by the battle.

He turned to his family. Cora's eyes glistened, but her posture was. *"Create a new future,"* she sent.

A sad smile crossed his lips. *"I will try."*

Teyark stared at him, shock and concern lining his face. "Why didn't you let me go first?"

Ralan lifted a shoulder. "I don't know."

"You said this was foreseen," the king said, stepping closer. Anger furrowed his brow and sparked from his eyes. "Gods help me, Ralan, if you lied, there will be consequences."

Ralan's nostrils flared. "I did not. But only a few strands have been clear."

"And this," Kien interrupted, his tone almost pleasant, "Is why a seer should never be king. Unreliable, tricky lot. We all know it, yet you made him your heir. Why do you think I've fought for so long? It is all to save Moranaia from that folly."

"Yes, brother. A butcher who uses dark magic is clearly a better choice," Ralan drawled.

"I suppose the point will be moot once I defeat you."

"We shall see." Ralan scanned his family's faces one last time, lingering on Cora before returning to his father. "You should remove yourselves to the dais. Teyark knows what to do if I fall."

For a moment, the king looked like he was going to argue. His face reddened and his hands clenched. But Teyark interceded. "The duel has been called, Father. Honor demands its completion."

Ralan stared at King Alianar, taking in the lines that had deepened in his father's face. His hair appeared even grayer than a few months before, and his shoulders bowed with the weight of almost three thousand years of rule. Grief shadowed his eyes as he nodded. So much was unresolved between them, and now it might never be. Not if Ralan maintained his stubborn pride.

"I forgive you," Ralan said softly. "For all of it. Now go."

He flicked his eyes toward Cora and lifted his brows, not wanting to deliver his other message in Kien's hearing. *Protect my bonded.* Not because she was weak. If Ralan died, the pain would overcome her. He would not have his brother kill her in that vulnerable moment, a feat that would be all too easy.

His father paled, but both he and Teyark nodded. Message received. As they gestured for Cora to follow them to the dais, she darted forward, pressing her trembling lips to his in a quick kiss before she rushed to stand with the other two in front of the king's throne.

Ralan spun to face Kien as he tried to forget his bonded's fear and grief. "Draw your blade."

"Took you long enough." Metal rang as they both pulled swords free. The corner of Kien's mouth lifted. "You seem less than confident about the outcome, brother. Perhaps your cursed Sight has finally led you astray."

"We all know the future is never set."

Ralan strode forward, lifting his blade to parry Kien's oncoming thrust. The strands remained murky and useless, but he'd trained enough over the centuries that muscle memory kicked in. The clang of metal rang through the room as they danced back and forth across the floor, swords clashing. Through it all, his brother's smirk never slipped.

They both knew Kien was the superior swordsman.

From outside the closed double doors, a few shouts sounded. Then a muffled scream. Ralan tried to focus on his brother. Kien was a mage, and magic wasn't strictly forbidden during this type of duel. Why hadn't he used it? No illusions or flickering lights. No spells designed to stun.

Ralan sent his own power outward, searching for some crack in his brother's shielding. The mental blast had bounced off in the cavern, so that would be useless to try again. At least until he found a weakness to exploit. But Kien had clearly spent a great deal of time preparing to deal with a telepath. Ralan's magic slipped along his brother's shield like water over a glass sphere. He needed to shatter it, but it was all he could do to counter Kien's blows.

"You aren't as terrible as I expected," Kien said.

Ralan grunted with effort as he parried and feinted. "I'm older."

"Not wiser."

Kien dodged left and then ducked, his sword slipping under Ralan's guard. Ralan hissed as the blade slashed along the side of his abdomen, cutting a deep gash into his skin. He bit back a shout as the pain of it hit, but Cora's soft cry echoed across the room. At once, he shielded as much of the agony from her as he could. And prayed it was enough.

Ralan danced back, trying to breathe through the pain. His hand convulsed around the hilt of his sword until he firmed his grip. Then he shoved it all aside and charged his brother. Dammit, he couldn't go out like this. Kien could be defeated. He had to be.

"You may thank Lyr's bonded for that blow," Kien gritted out. "It was in her honor."

Smiling at the memory of Meli, quiet Meli, stabbing his brother in the side, Ralan parried the next thrust. "She did more damage."

Kien's smirk dropped. "Fuck this."

The blows came frenzied, then, and Ralan knew he wouldn't be able to keep up for long. Even without the injury, his body was weakening. The sword grew heavier in his hand, his parries a hair

slower each time. Strength dripped from him with the blood that poured from his side.

When he saw the opening, he didn't hesitate. Ralan slipped his sword through, aiming for his brother's black heart. But Kien caught the movement, feinting just enough to change the course of the blow. The steel blade slipped through his brother's gut instead.

Kien's eyes went wide, and the sword dropped from his hand. Then he smiled. "Not a killing blow."

Fury roared through Ralan at his brother's mocking words. They both knew such a strike would cause a painful death without the intervention of a skilled healer, and quickly. But it *could* be healed. His hand trembled as he tried to gather enough energy to twist the blade and push it deeper, but Kien shoved himself free of the sword with a heave.

Kien stumbled, then dropped to his knees. Still. Fucking. Smiling. "Big mistake, brother," Kien taunted.

A flash of light. Dark magic darting free, winging toward the dais.

The vision gave him mere moments to act. Suddenly, Ralan knew how he would die. He spared the quickest glance for Cora, sending his love along their bond, before he propelled himself forward. Directly in the path of the spell his brother had just cast.

The agony was instant. Searing. Ralan did scream, then, as the death spell overcame him. He hit the ground hard, but the impact was nothing compared to the magic roaring through his body. Kien had been saving his power for a reason. A final blow for the king.

As darkness dulled his wavering vision, regret and relief twined within him. He'd saved his family. No other strands were meant to be.

Cora's knees buckled as the pain swept through her, unrelenting. Teyark's arm curved around her, supporting her as the world hazed around her. No. Great Divine, no. Whatever spell Kien had cast, it was killing Ralan. She felt him weakening with every heartbeat. But he'd stabbed his brother with steel. Kien should have been drained of power.

Her chest heaved as she fought against the pain. Her vision cleared enough to focus on Ralan's slumped form, and she let out a cry. Shoving free of Teyark, Cora stumbled across the floor toward her bonded. She barely noted Kien, already surrounded by several guards.

"Leave him to me," King Alianar called out.

"Use Ralan's sword," she heard Teyark urge.

She didn't care.

As soon as she reached Ralan, she dropped down beside him. Blood from the gash in his side squished into her knees, but she didn't care about that, either. Her hands went to his face, and her heart skipped a beat at the hazy, vacant look to his eyes. Almost gone.

No.

Agony surged through her, pounding through her blood, as she latched onto their bond and kept it strong when he'd wanted to shield her. Like there was any way to shield this. Her own vision grayed as she pulled upon her power, and the air around them began to heat. Then she shoved herself into him, seeking the source of the damage.

She sealed the gash first. His body lifted and slammed down as she seared the wound closed with her flame. But still, he slipped away. A cry tumbled through her dry lips as she poured more power in.

It wouldn't be enough. She didn't have enough.

Not here.

As Ralan's heartbeat slowed beneath her hand, Cora reached for the wealth of energy that eddied around her. She'd already decided to stay on Moranaia if he lived. Now it was up to her to ensure that he did.

Without hesitation, she cracked open the wall that separated her from his world. The power flooded in, binding to her spirit in a pale imitation of the soulbond. A shiver tracked through her entire body, and her hands shook where they rested against Ralan as the full measure of Moranaia's vast power scored through her.

But when her vision cleared, Ralan's chest had already gone still.

Fire.

His brother's spell. Cora's power. Like his dream, he thought it would never end. But just as in his dream, it did.

Physical sensation faded, and his mind began to drift. He hoped Teyark remembered to use the steel sword to finish off Kien. He hoped Cora decided to stay with Eri. She'd need help with their child if his suspicions were correct.

Their child.

He waited for the surge of pain and regret, but it didn't come. It was too cold for emotion here. Everything was cold. But that couldn't be right. Not with Cora's heat.

A soft glow filled the darkness where he drifted. This was it.

"No."

Cora's voice rang through his mind, startling through the chill. "Too late."

"My fire consumed the spell. Come back."

The glow grew brighter as he struggled to comprehend. "Can't be."

"Ralantayan Moreln, you will not leave me." As her voice grew stronger, the light dimmed. "Your soul is bound to mine, and I am not letting go."

"Dark. Cold."

"Fight it." Her pain reached him, piercing the stillness that bound him. "I need you. Eri needs you. Our other child needs you."

"Cora."

"You were right. I'm pregnant." Her words rang through his head, and a hint of her desperation cracked into his heart. "And if you don't get your ass back to your body, I might cause her damage with all this magic use."

The impassive calm that had held him shattered. She was using her power up on him. And with Galare so far away. The physical pain of his body itched at his consciousness, but he no longer fought against it. Without hesitation, he latched onto Cora and let her pull him through.

34

Cora had never seen anything as wonderful as Ralan's golden eyes. But she didn't get to see them for long. Almost as soon as his eyelids flicked open, he slammed them shut again. A moan rattled through his throat, and his body quaked beneath her hands. She wanted to collapse across his chest and hold him, but instead she sent her magic back through him, trying to find out if there was another reason for his pain.

Unfortunately, her healing skills were more of a blunt instrument than a fine tool.

"Were you hurt elsewhere?" she whispered.

"Heat. Too much."

"Oh!" Cora pulled her hands away and winced at the raw red marks welting on his chest. Even his shirt had been burned away where she'd touched him. "Oh, no. I can't heal that. I don't think more fire will help."

"Kien?"

Her heart clenched at the rough, pained sound of Ralan's voice, but she glanced up to see what had happened to his brother. The

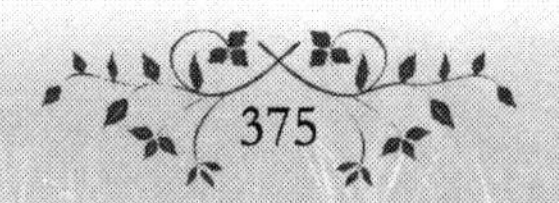

king stood above Kien's prone body and fastened his gaze on his son. Ralan's sword was clutched in his father's hand, but she couldn't tell if he'd stabbed Kien or not. Cora gave Kien a closer look. His chest still rose and fell, and his eyes were open.

"Not dead yet," she whispered. "But I'd guess soon."

Ralan shifted, pressing his palms against the floor as though he intended to get up. Frowning, Cora pinned him with a hand to his chest. "Stop. You're in no condition for this. He's being dealt with."

"Prop me up," Ralan said. "Please."

A wealth of emotion poured into that single word. Cora slipped around behind him and helping him ease his chest into her lap, his head propped up on her belly. After all the grief his brother had put him through, Ralan deserved this moment of resolution. She only prayed the king had the resolve to complete the task.

Fireballs were still not off the table.

"You have proved yourself an enemy of Moranaia," the king said, no sign of hesitation in his voice. "I gave you a chance at redemption, an opportunity that should never have been offered. I, Moranai Lor i Alianar Moreln nai Moranaia, sentence you to death for your crimes against your House, your people, and more races of fae than I care to count."

Unease slithered up Cora's spine as the king raised the blade. Why had he paused to deliver an edict? Lynia had advised them to kill Kien quickly. Ralan shifted against her, and his own worry crossed through their bond. *Do it!* she wanted to shout. But that kind of distraction wouldn't help.

Kien's lips twisted up even as the sword descended. Cora tensed, but he made no move to fight back. Light flashed. She squeezed her eyes closed against the sudden, bright glow as the ringing sound of sword striking stone filled the room. Crap. Surely, he hadn't found a way to escape, had he?

The light cut off, and metal clattered on stone. Her heartbeat pounded in her ears as Cora forced her eyes open. The bloodstained sword rested near Kien's unmoving body, and she slumped in relief. Thank the Divine he hadn't discovered a spell to transport himself away. But then she saw his head lolling a few feet away from the rest of him, and her stomach heaved.

Shoving the bile down with all her might, Cora turned away. Whatever that light had been, Kien was well and truly dead.

Ralan's body went lax in her arms. His eyes were open, just a slit, and something like peace had eased the harshness that had always hovered beneath the surface of his resolve. His hand lifted slowly until it settled over hers atop his chest.

"Let her in."

The king's stony voice caught Cora's attention. He stood over his son's body, but his attention was on the large double doors. She didn't need a connection to Ralan's father to feel the pain that throbbed through the room like a heartbeat as he waited for the guards to unbar the doors. But he stood tall, his head held high and his expression impassive despite his obvious turmoil.

As soon as the portal swung open, a woman shoved her way through. Ralan's breath hissed out, and for one terrible moment, Cora feared that he'd had another love he'd been pining for. He squeezed her hand as though he sensed her worry and tipped his head back to meet her eyes.

"My mother," he whispered.

Cora saw the resemblance, then, although all three of the brothers looked a great deal like their father. "Oh."

The lady let out a sharp cry as she saw Kien's body slumped across the floor. Her hand flew to her mouth, and tears slid down her face as her gaze met the king's. "You?"

"He came to kill us all, Enielle," the king said softly.

Her broken voice crackled through the air. "I'm glad it was you. We should have…"

As she looked away, Enielle noticed Ralan, and her already pale face whitened further. "Oh, Gods."

"I live, Mother," Ralan said, his quiet voice filling the silence.

Enielle let out a harsh sob as she dashed across the room. She knelt beside her son, her shaky hand going to his cheek. "I sent for the healer. I'm sorry. I'm so sorry. This is all my fault. I begged your father to exile him when they found Kenaren. I already thought I'd never see you again, and I couldn't bear to lose two sons. Instead, I almost lost you all."

Cora could feel Ralan weakening, but he managed to give his mother a soft smile. "Ah, *Laiala*. Be at ease. Cora saved me."

The lady blinked, only then seeming to notice that her son rested against another. Her expression went blank with shock. Then she caught sight of the medallion around Cora's neck. "You've bonded?"

"Yes."

Enielle frowned. "But when?"

"Only a few days back, your majesty," Cora answered for him. "While we searched for Kien on Earth."

"You needn't call me majesty since I am not queen." Enielle's lips thinned, but she appeared more sad than angry. "But I am happy to hear of your bonding. Once…once we have recovered, perhaps we will have a celebration."

Heat rushed into Cora's cheeks. "Please forgive my lapse. I have only just arrived."

"It is no matter," the lady answered gently.

Cora had a feeling that it was a great matter, indeed, but now was far from the time to ask Ralan about it. There was much about his family she didn't know. Now that she'd linked with Moranaia's energy, she would have the rest of her life to find out. A bit over nine months, at the least, since it would cause their child harm to leave.

A terse exclamation sounded from the door. The crowd of gawking courtiers parted, and a slim, dark-haired woman strode through, two elves holding a stretcher close behind. The healer? The woman barely glanced at Kien's body, instead hurrying directly toward Cora and Ralan.

As she knelt beside them, her brows lifted. "Burns?"

Cora bit her lip. "I…"

"The price of my life," Ralan said softly.

"I see." The healer gave him a quick examination before nodding. "We'll carry you to my workroom."

He shook his head. "I will walk."

"What?" Cora scowled down at him. She more than any could tell how tired he was. "You must be joking."

"At least beyond the crowds." His jaw clenched. "Can you heal me enough for that dignity?"

The healer let out a long sigh, but she smiled. "Of course."

Unlike with Lial, there was very little light or color as the woman lifted her hands over Ralan. Fascinating. It worked well, though. In moments, he'd regained enough strength to sit up. A few more, and the healer and Cora were able to help him stand. He wavered on his feet, his muscles clenched tight, but he stood.

"Thanks to the strength of my son and heir, a traitor has been defeated this day," the king said, his low, hard voice cutting through the murmurs of the courtiers crowding the door. "Kien Moreln is no more. For his crimes against Moranaia and nature itself, he has earned a traitor's burial."

Gasps sounded from the crowd, and Cora heard Enielle stifle a sob. As if on cue, several of the guards lining the wall rushed forward to remove Kien's body. Their expressions never shifted from cold impassivity, but Cora winced in sympathy. She'd hate to be the poor soul who had to carry the bastard's head.

"My prince," the healer began.

"I'm ready," Ralan said. "Let's go. Slowly."

Cora kept her arm beneath his shoulder as they shuffled around the pool of blood and out the doors. The courtiers parted in a wave, their eyes wide on Ralan as they tapped fists to chests and bowed. Cora tipped her chin up and tried not to think about the picture they made. They might be covered in blood, but Kien was dead.

That was all that mattered.

Lyr stared at Kai's image in the communication mirror and struggled to focus on his words as he reported on his brother's

condition. They'd heard nothing from the palace. Eri had curled in Meli's lap in one of the study chairs, her small head nestled on his bonded's shoulder. If the young seer knew anything, she hadn't said. Quiet. It was far too quiet.

Kai waved a hand. "Lyr?"

"Forgive me." He ran his hand through his hair. "The wait is beyond difficult. Thank you for letting me know that Moren is healing well."

"I should be back in a few days' time at the most. Is Arlyn resting?"

"Yes." Had that been concern in Kai's voice? Lyr frowned. "Is she unwell?"

Kai shook his head, but his expression had gone oddly blank. "Of course not. She's fine."

"If that ceases to be the case, I trust you will tell me."

"I will. Or rather, she will."

A harsh, choked sound slipped from Eri, and Lyr bid Kai a hasty farewell, cutting off the link as the child's sobs filled the room. Lyr darted around his desk and over to the chair where Eri cried against Meli's shoulder. His bonded gave him a helpless look as she rubbed the child's back and whispered soft words of encouragement.

He dropped down beside the chair and placed his hand against her quaking shoulders. "What is it?"

"It's over," she wailed.

Lyr's heart lurched at those words. He had no idea of the scope of her Sight, but whatever she'd Seen didn't seem good. "I'm sorry, Eri. I—"

"No," Eri said, lifting her blotchy face to look at him. "He lived."

Shock and relief rolled through Lyr, stealing his words for a moment. Then his brow creased. "Why are you crying? I thought…"

"It was so close." Eri shuddered in Meli's arms. "So close."

With a soft smile, Meli tucked Eri's hair behind her ear and gathered her nearer. "Let it out. You need to."

Lyr stood, baffled but trusting his bonded's instincts, and headed toward the mirror. After Eri's cry, Kai no doubt paced the floor wondering what had gone wrong. Thank goodness that this time, Lyr had good news to deliver.

Ralan's bleary eyes focused on Cora as the healers bustled around his bed. A worry line creased her brows when she took his hand, and he tried to give her fingers a squeeze. Damn, but dying was exhausting. Even if he'd only died for a few drips of time. His vision hadn't been wrong, after all. But it hadn't been entirely correct, either.

She'd saved him. He still couldn't believe… Then the memory of her words slammed through him. She'd drained herself. His breath hitched at the thought. "Your energy. Gods. We need to find a way to Galare."

Her hand tightened over his. "Calm down. I linked to Moranaia."

"You…" He swallowed hard. "You hadn't made the decision to stay. I'm sorry."

"Stop," she said. "I'd already decided, you know. In my heart. I just needed a bit of a push. And our child deserves to be born here. Her first energy bond should be to this world."

His gaze dropped to her belly, and a sense of awe overcame him. "It's true, then?"

She huffed. "Of course. I wouldn't lie about that."

"It was an effective way to pull me back." Ralan smiled, his hand itching to rest over the life they'd created. But he was too damned tired to make his muscles cooperate. "I love you, Cora."

Her eyes widened. "You do? I love you, too, but I thought… Well, there was Kenaren."

"My love for her was a distant shadow of what I feel for you," he said. "Bound up in pride and stubbornness. She was a talisman, proof that I could live for myself instead of for my father. Perhaps she sensed it, and that's why she was drawn astray by Kien."

"I'm sorry."

For the first time in centuries, true peace settled through him. "The past is as it should be. But I had to work beyond it myself before I could tell you how I feel."

Cora leaned down and brushed a kiss across his lips. "I really do love you, too."

The healer halted beside the bed, a book in her hands, and he struggled to keep his eyelids open as she peered at him. "I've checked my reference on the type of spell he used. I'm not sure how you're still alive."

Ralan let out a soft laugh. "Megelien knows."

"I'll look for any remnants and heal your burns," she said. "Try to rest."

But he knew he wouldn't.

35

As soon as Kehda's healing magic winked out, Ralan shoved himself to his feet. She'd given him a bit of strength with the healing, but his feet still felt weighted as he started for the door. With a hiss of breath, Cora rushed after him. He didn't pause. If he stopped now, he'd collapse.

"What are you doing?" Cora demanded.

"I need to get back to Eri."

"Oh, Divine," Cora muttered beneath her breath. "Could we send for her? You need rest."

Ralan kept his eyes on the ground lest he stumble. "No. Not until I'm well enough to mind her properly. She will cause enough chaos in court when I'm at full strength."

Cora's footsteps kept pace with his. "Foreseen?"

"Yes." He chuckled. "But I didn't need to Look to know. You've seen how she is."

Her amused voice slid across the space between them. "Good point."

The distance to the Great Hall wasn't quite as eternal as his earlier trip, but it was close enough. Sweat beaded Ralan's brow, and his muscles trembled with the effort. Unfortunately, it was necessary. He had no doubt his parents would have appeared in the healer's room soon, demanding he stay in the palace indefinitely. His decision would bear more weight if he delivered it on his own feet before his father's throne.

They passed through the entryway, empty except for the guards standing at intervals along the walls. Outside the windows, the sun shone brightly against the mountains rising in the distance, though a few dark clouds lingered near the northern range. Difficult to believe they'd defeated Kien before it had even reached midday.

So much could change in the space of a morning.

A single guard stood in front of the double doors to the throne room. With a wordless bow, she opened one and gestured Ralan and Cora through. It closed behind them immediately, echoing in the silence as they paused just over the threshold. Ralan scanned the room and found it empty. All sign of Kien was gone, even the blood.

Steeling himself, Ralan walked with Cora to the spot where his brother had fallen. The freshly cleaned stone gleamed in the bright light, but he noticed on a dull spot. Carefully, he knelt, running his fingers along the dent gouged in the floor. The spot where the sword had struck during the beheading.

"Father said he would leave the mark as a sign of what happens to traitors."

Ralan glanced up at his brother's voice and found Teyark standing a few paces beyond the open door to his father's study. "Where is he?"

Teyark pointed a thumb over his own shoulder. "Finishing up the final decree notifying the kingdom of Kien's death. I'm certain your heroism will be lavishly described."

"Jealous?" Ralan asked lightly as he stood.

But his brother's expression remained grave. "No. I…I truly am sorry, Ralan. I wanted to tell you."

"Be at peace with it." After living through his own death, Ralan couldn't summon his earlier anger. Not even the elves were guaranteed their millennia, and he refused to waste time lingering on what had gone before. "Our family has had enough discord."

"Agreed," Teyark said. "Thank you."

Ralan twined his fingers with Cora's, and they started their slow way across the room. "And thank you for trusting me to fight Kien."

"I still don't understand why I couldn't have done it." Teyark's lips twisted. "No offense, but he'd have been dead much faster had it been me wielding the sword."

"In all honesty, I'm not certain, either," Ralan said, shrugging. "I was guided by Lady Megelien Herself. Perhaps you wouldn't have been fast enough to step in front of Kien's spell, or some other strand might have been started. I only knew that it had to be me. I assumed I'd die in the attempt."

Teyark lifted his hand as they neared. "You knew you would die?"

"One of the few things I'd clearly foreseen."

His brother stared in stunned silence. "*Miaran,*" he cursed.

"Agreed."

They walked together toward the study door, Teyark keeping pace with Ralan's sluggish steps. After a moment, Cora spoke. "Why didn't the steel affect him?"

Ralan tried to turn his hazy memories back to the moment when the spell had been cast, but he could draw up little beyond his panic. "Good question."

"I think it did," Teyark said. "He was more powerful than that spell he threw at Father, but he had nothing left to defend himself with after that. Except… Well, I'm not certain what to make of that flash of light. To the point, though, I suspect he built up a little resistance over the years."

"That makes sense," Ralan said absently.

His attention shifted to the futures, the strands unfolding once more. He would have to direct Lyr to contact his emissaries in the various fae realms. Kai and Arlyn would almost certainly have to return to Earth, at least once Kai had finished his training with Naomh, and they would need to search for more earth-healers to clean up the energy poisoning.

Yes, there would be a great deal to do.

Cora's fingers tightened on his, and Ralan blinked, bringing his surroundings back into focus. They'd stepped into the study. His father sat behind his desk, head bent as he scratched his pen furiously across paper. His mother slumped with eyes downcast in one of the reading chairs by a window. Corath, Teyark's bonded, paced along the other side of the room, clearly agitated by the day's events.

Teyark strode over, and his bonded drew him into his arms. Then Teyark pulled away and slipped his arm through Corath's. "Do you need us here?" he asked Ralan.

Ralan shook his head. "Go ahead. Although… Corath, I may have need of your ingenuity soon for some new weapons. May I contact you for aid when the time comes?"

A curious glint entered the elf's eyes. "Certainly. I admit I'm intrigued."

Enielle head snapped up, and she frowned. "What are you doing up, Ralan? You must go back to the healer's rooms at once."

"Later," Ralan said to Corath, who nodded and tugged Teyark toward the door. Though exhaustion beat at him, Ralan shifted closer to his mother. "I will not be staying right now."

"But you must!"

His father put down his pen at that. "She is correct. There is much turmoil, and you are ill."

"I must get back to Eri." Ralan lifted his free hand as the king's brow lowered. "That is no slight against you. I hinted as much before, but I tell you this plainly now. Her Sight is more powerful than mine. I'll need to be at full strength before I bring a child of her power into the royal court. Trust me."

Sadness filled Alianar's expression, but he nodded. "I do."

"Is the expanse of land south of Braelyn still largely unpopulated?" Ralan asked, although he knew the answer already.

A puzzled frown creased the king's brow. "Yes."

"I would like to construct a second palace there. Or perhaps an estate similar to Lyr's." Ralan smiled at Cora. "And not just because I would like privacy for my new family. Lyr is an excellent guardian for the portal, but we may need more guardians to the south, in the lands beyond the scope of his domain."

"Do I want to know why?" his father asked, weariness creeping into his voice.

"Not today," Ralan answered. "We have all had more than enough for today."

"Indeed." The king ran his hand across his face and sighed. "I will commission the proper artisans. I trust you will speak with Lord Lyrnis? I would not have him feel slighted by this new outpost."

Ralan nodded. "I will do so once I have rested."

"Then go on with you." A slight smile tipped his father's lips, though worry still pinched his eyes. "You look like you're about to collapse where you stand."

"You aren't far off, Father," Ralan said. "Not far at all."

Eri launched herself at him as soon as he and Cora stepped through the gate. With an *oomph,* he pulled his daughter close, almost stumbling back through the open portal until Cora steadied him. He wrapped his arms around Eri and lowered his face into her hair as she squeezed him tight.

"*Onaial,*" she cried, her tears dampening his shirt. "Thank the Gods. You chose the right path. Oh, thank goodness."

"Shh," he whispered. He swayed side to side, the same way he had when she was an infant. "It's okay."

"You don't know how close it was. You don't."

Ralan recalled the cold darkness where he'd drifted, and he shuddered. "I can guess."

"We thought you were dead when she started to sob," Lyr said.

"It was a close thing." Over Eri's shoulder, Ralan met his friend's gaze. "I actually did…well, let's just say Cora pulled me back."

Worry pinched Meli's face as she stared at his daughter. "She told us you were alive, but it was difficult to believe it with the way she cried."

Sniffling, Eri pushed against him until he lowered her to her feet. Although tears ran down her face, a radiant smile broke free. She danced over to Cora and hugged her around the waist. "You picked the right time."

Ralan frowned at that. Had Eri given Cora a hint of the future without his knowledge? She must have, for Cora laughed and nodded. "Looks like it."

A wave of weakness hit, and Ralan swayed until Cora's fingers wrapped around his arm. He glanced around the room, hoping for the healer, but only Lyr, Meli, a few guards, and his family stood in the entry room. He sighed. More walking it was, then.

"Is Lial in his workroom?"

Lyr's brows lowered. "I believe so. Can't you reach him?"

Even the thought of using his telepathy made Ralan want to curl up in the floor and nap. Not that he didn't want to do that anyway. "Too weak."

Lyr stared into the distance for a moment and then gave a sharp nod. "He'll be waiting."

"My thanks," Ralan said. "We will speak more later."

One of the guards held the front door open, and Cora slipped her arm beneath his shoulder as they exited and started down the trail. His heart lifted at the sight of Eri dancing along in front of them, her upset beginning to fade. But damn, the path was long. By the time they reached the healer's tower, Ralan thought for sure that the sun must be setting. But no. The length of the walk existed solely in his tired mind.

Lial stood framed in the doorway, much as he had when they'd carried Inona and Cora back from Earth. But this time, Cora

supported Ralan. He didn't mind. How could he? They would make a good team. He'd thought so before, when his Sight was muddled, but now he could See it.

"Eager to see me again so soon?" Lial asked with a wry twist of his lips.

Ralan laughed. "I'm not sure I should answer that."

"Probably not."

At the door, Ralan caught Eri's eye. "Stay out here, love. This shouldn't take long."

"I know," Eri said before skipping over to examine a small flower garden.

The bed was empty when they entered. Inona must have been well enough to return to her own room—or Delbin's. Ralan would have to see how his apprentice fared later. As Eri plopped into a nearby chair, Cora helped him sit on the side of the bed without falling on his face. He wrapped his fingers around her arm when she made to leave and tugged her down beside him.

"Check Cora first."

Lial studied them both. "Why?"

"I want to make sure our child wasn't hurt when she used her magic," Ralan said, staring at his cousin. "She healed me with her fire."

Lial knelt beside Cora and held his hand over her stomach. "Do you feel unwell?"

Cora shook her head. "Not at the moment. I've been getting dizzy off and on, but I don't know why. It should be too soon for me to have symptoms, shouldn't it?"

"Hmm." Lial's eyes glazed as his hand began to glow blue. After a handful of heartbeats, he settled back on his heels with a smile.

"Your exertion caused no harm. I'd say you are a several days beyond what you expect, thanks to having crossed the Veil three times. Even with a guide as skilled as Kai, the odd flow of time there can cause strange effects."

She shook her head. "I don't even want to think about that bit of oddness."

"In any case, your body doesn't seem to react well to the surge in hormones and the increased strain on your energy reserves. It is a bit early unless you're sensitive." Lial patted her hand. "Lucky you."

"Great," Cora muttered.

Ralan stared at his cousin. Lial had actually given her a comforting pat? He'd never seen the healer quite so gentle. "Can you help?"

"I'll give her a potion against nausea, but her body will have to adjust on its own." Lial pulled the remaining chair to Ralan's side and sat. "Now. What happened to you?"

As his cousin listened, Ralan described the battle, Kien's spell, and Cora's actions to save him. "Kehda helped some, but I left as soon as I could."

"*Clechtan,*" Lial grumbled. "Our cousin has always been too soft. I'd have knocked you out. A death spell? Good Gods."

"Cora's fire seared it out."

"We really must talk about your methods," the healer said. "Later."

Ralan settled back and let the healer's power sweep through him.

After the healing was complete, Lial produced a potion from his workbench for Cora's nausea. Then Ralan bid his cousin farewell and headed out the door. She started to follow but paused at the threshold, clutching the smooth vial in her hand as she peered at the healer.

"Lial?"

He glanced up from the other vials he was settling into place on a shelf. "Yes?"

"I'm really not sure how to ask this," she asked, then winced at his concerned frown. "That sounds serious. It isn't, not exactly."

"Now I'm curious," he said.

Cora took a deep breath and went for it. "I have a friend on Earth. She's half-Sidhe, and she has the healing gift. But she's having trouble with it."

Lial's lips pursed. "What kind of trouble?"

"She almost killed someone once. It slips out of her control sometimes and does the opposite of what it should."

"Are you asking for my advice?"

"Not exactly." Cora nibbled at her lower lip. "The Sidhe healers she contacted have refused to work with her because she's half-human. I'm not asking you to personally take her on, but do you think if she came here, she might be able to find someone to train her?"

The healer frowned. "It is possible. I will consider the matter and get back to you."

"Thank you," she said before ducking out the door.

Cora settled her hand against Ralan's elbow as Eri rejoined them, dancing ahead on the path to the guest tower. It hadn't been the answer she'd hoped for, but it was better than she'd feared. Truthfully, she wasn't even certain she would be able to convince

Maddy to come, not without Anna, and Cora needed to find out if humans were allowed. But no use trying if it wasn't a possibility.

"Do you think he will do it?" she asked.

Ralan nodded. "That's the likeliest strand."

"We'll have to send one of those mirrors over so I can speak to Maddy and Jase." Cora leaned her head against Ralan's shoulder. "They can handle the shop, but I hope one of them will buy it. If we can manage that right now. I'll need to stay here until the baby is born since our energy is bound. It could cause harm to leave now that she's attuned."

"Good thing Lyr won't mind us staying for a while longer."

"When did you speak to him?" Then she chuckled. "Never mind. I'm guessing you Saw it."

His own laugh rumbled close to her ear. "Yes."

Cora smiled. One thing was certain—being bonded to a seer would never be dull.

Ralan knelt before the altar and sparked the first of nine candles into life. Their rooms were quiet, nothing but the soft sound of Cora's steady breathing reaching his ears. His family slept, but one thing remained before he could seek his bed. Centering himself, he let his eyes slip closed as Megelien's candle lit at the touch of his magic.

"Thank you," he sent.

For several breaths, he thought she wouldn't answer. Then her presence surged into his mind. *"WELL DONE."*

A lump formed in his throat at the pride in her tone. *"None of it would have worked without your aid."*

"YOU HAVE NO IDEA HOW ACCURATE THOSE WORDS ARE."

"I can guess." Ralan hesitated. But there was no use in not asking. She would know. *"You told me to prepare for the truth of my vision."*

"SO I DID." Humor slid into her mental voice. *"THE VISION WASN'T WRONG, HMM? I SUPPOSE I DID NEGLECT TO SHARE SOME OF THE POSSIBLE STRANDS."*

Ralan bit back a chuckle lest he wake Cora. *"I am glad I didn't know."*

"YOU WOULD HAVE DIED HAD YOU KNOWN."

For a heartbeat's time, he considered asking more. This time, he didn't. *"Thank you for your aid."*

"ALWAYS," she said simply, making his brows lift in surprise. *"NOW GO REST. YOU MAY PAY ME OBEYANCE WHEN YOU AREN'T LIKELY TO COLLAPSE ON MY ALTAR."*

Before he could answer, Lady Megelien was gone. Smiling, Ralan extinguished the candles and crawled into bed. As his body numbed with exhaustion, he curled against Cora's back. His hand lowered to her stomach, and he smiled softly as his mind began to wander.

Joy suffused his drifting thoughts as he slipped into slumber.

Made in the USA
Las Vegas, NV
19 May 2023